A
Dangerous
DUET

Also by Karen Odden

A Lady in the Smoke

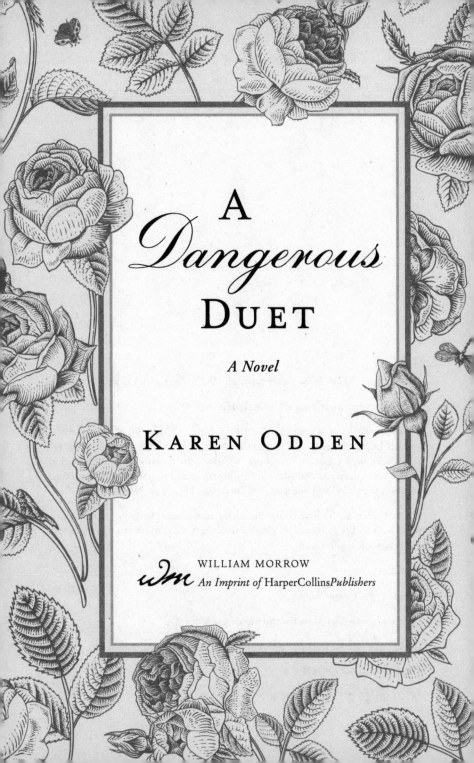

A Dangerous Duet

A Novel

KAREN ODDEN

WILLIAM MORROW
An Imprint of HarperCollinsPublishers

HarperCollins books may be purchased for educational, business, or sales promotional use. For information, please e-mail the Special Markets Department at SPsales@harpercollins.com.

FIRST EDITION

Designed by Diahann Sturge

Title page art © Olga Korneeva / Shutterstock, Inc.

Library of Congress Cataloging-in-Publication Data has been applied for.

ISBN 978-0-06-279696-7

18 19 20 21 22 LSC 10 9 8 7 6 5 4 3 2 1

For George, Julia, and Kyle, always

A
Dangerous
Duet

Chapter 1

London, 1875

*T*he back door of the Octavian Music Hall stood ajar, and a wedge of yellow light streamed out into the dark, crooked quadrangle of the yard. I picked my way toward it across the uneven ground, glad that I was in stout boots and trousers instead of my usual skirts. It had rained all day, and I tried not to think about what might be in the muck under my feet.

A tall, broad-shouldered figure stood silhouetted in the doorway: Jack Drummond, the owner's son, a stolid and taciturn young man who helped build scenery and props and fixed things when they broke. As he'd never said much more than "Good evening" to me, I knew very little else about him except that he let us performers in at the back and then went round to the front door to keep the pickpockets from sneaking in. I felt a secret sympathy for those ragged boys, desperately in need of a few pence for supper.

Once the curtain rose, the men in the audience, most of them well into their cups, would be staring agog at a Romany magician or a half-naked songstress or some flame-throwing jugglers. It would've been child's play to find their pockets, and chances are most of the men wouldn't have missed a coin or two.

Jack touched his cap briefly as I approached. "Mr. Nell."

"Evening," I muttered. My voice was naturally low, but to bolster my disguise I pitched it even lower and hoarser.

"Mr. Williams needs to see you before the show."

My heart leaped into my throat. I'd done my best to dodge the foul-tempered stage manager since he'd hired me weeks ago.

"Did he say why?"

"No. But don't worry. He didn't look mad." His dark eyes met mine, and he gave a faint, wry smile. "Leastwise, no madder than usual."

I snorted. "Good."

From the bell tower of St. Anne's in Dean Street came the chimes for three-quarters past seven. Fifteen minutes until curtain.

"He'll meet you at the piano," Jack said.

I hurried down the ramp that led to the corridor below the stage, feeling inside the brim of my hat to make sure that no stray hairs had escaped my phalanx of pins. Then I turned toward the flight of stairs that led up to stage right. The hall above, where the audience sat, had been elegantly renovated a few years ago when the Octavian opened, with crystal chandeliers and paint in tasteful hues of blue and gold. But the rabbit warren of passages and rooms underground was original to the hodgepodge of buildings that had stood here a hundred years ago, when the entertainment on a given night was likely to be bearbaiting and cockfighting, and the animals were brought up from below. The air stank of mold and rust; the plaster was crumbling off the brickwork; and the wooden steps had been worn down so far that the nailheads could catch a misplaced toe or boot heel and send one sprawling—as I knew from experience.

Slow footsteps thudded above me. Jack's father—whom everyone called by only his surname, Drummond—was coming down. He was a burly man, a full head taller than I, with the same unruly black hair that Jack had, thick black eyebrows, and a cruel mouth. I smelled the whiskey on him as he drew close, and I put my back against the wall to let him pass.

"Evening," I croaked, same as I'd said to Jack.

He didn't even glance at me. Motionless, I watched as he descended and vanished into the lower corridor; then I allowed myself a deep breath and continued on my way.

At the top of the stairs, I ducked through a set of curtains to enter the piano alcove where I'd spend the next two hours. My spot was in the corner of the hall near stage right, with a second pair of curtains to separate me from the audience until the show began. The stage, which I could see from my piano bench, was elevated off the hall's plank floor—wooden boards that had no doubt once been glossy, back before they'd absorbed hundreds of nights' worth of spilled gin and ale.

From the sound of it, members of the audience had already spilled a good deal of gin and ale down their throats, for they were more boisterous than usual for a Wednesday night. Curious to see why, I parted the curtains slightly and peered out, but nothing seemed out of the ordinary. Some of the men had found seats at the round tables; the rest were still gathered at the bar, where beer and wine and spirits were being distributed from hand to hand.

The room was large, with walls that curved at the back so it resembled a narrow U. According to Mrs. Wregge, the hall's cheerful purveyor of costumes and gossip, the builder believed that keeping everything in eights would protect against fire—hence the "Octavian." He was so persistent in this belief that he moved the walls inward by a yard, so that the seating area measured sixty-four feet at its longest point. Eight gas-lit chandeliers sent their glow flickering across the room; eight spiraling cast-iron pillars supported the balcony; and each pillar had twenty-four turns from bottom to top. Perhaps the spell of eights worked because during every performance, glowing ashes from the ends of cigars and French cigarettes dropped onto the floor, and still the building remained intact.

As I did every night, I said a quick prayer that the magic would hold. This job not only paid three pounds a week; it let me finish by just past ten, which meant I could arrive home before my brother, Matthew, returned from the Yard. The coins I earned were forming a satisfying, clinking pile in the drawer of my armoire, and combined with other money I'd saved, I now possessed over half of the Royal Academy tuition that would be due in the fall. Provided, of course, that I succeeded at the audition in a fortnight.

A flutter of apprehension stirred beneath my ribs at the thought, and I suppressed it, turning deliberately to the piano, lifting the wing, and fitting the prop stick into the notch.

It was a good instrument—surprisingly good for a second-rate hall—a thirty-year-old Pleyel, with a soft touch and an easier action than my English Broadwood at home. The problem was that the French piano didn't care for our climate; it fell out of tune easily, especially when it rained.

I untied the portfolio ribbons and laid out the music in the order of the acts. First came a man who called himself Gallius Kovác, the Romany Magician, and his assistant, the lovely Lady Van de Vere. He was no more a magician who'd learned his trade from his Romany grandfather than I was, and his accomplice's real name was Maggie Long. She was exactly my age— nineteen—and the natural daughter of a wealthy tea merchant and his mistress.

After their last trick, I would play a selection of interlude music while stagehands rolled the magician's paraphernalia off the stage. Then I'd accompany a singer who called herself Amalie Bordelieu. Her songs were French, but her accent offstage was pure Cockney, and her curses came straight off the London Docks. I'd heard them one night when she and Mr. Williams had a heated row in her dressing room. From the tone of it—caustic on her side, surly on his—it seemed to me that her anger derived from a long-standing resentment. Amalie was the only one of us who dared confront Mr. Williams; she had that luxury because she was too popular with the audiences to be turned out.

Gallius and Amalie were our only permanent performers; the next few acts of the program varied. To remain novel and exciting, most entertainers traveled among the hundreds of music halls in London, remaining in each for anywhere from a week to a few months before moving on. This week, Amalie had been followed by a group of jugglers, who rode strange little one-wheeled contraptions and threw flaming candlesticks; next came my friend

Marceline Tourneau and her brother Sebastian, with their trapeze act; and then, a one-act parody of marriage, complete with
a deaf mother-in-law and six unruly children. Over the past two
months, I'd also seen a ventriloquist, a group of six German knife
throwers, trained dogs, men on stilts, an absurd dialogue between two actors playing Gladstone and Disraeli, three women
singing a rollicking verse about the chaos they'd unleash if only
they had voting rights, and an adagio in which an enormous man
juggled two girls. The final act was always one of London's *lions
comiques*—groups of men who dressed as swells, in imposing fur
coats and rakish hats, twirling their walking sticks and singing
about gambling and whoring and drinking champagne. They
brought the crowd to their feet every time.

From backstage came the clang of bells, signaling that the
show would begin in ten minutes. Where was Mr. Williams, if
he needed to see me so badly? And what could he possibly want?
I searched my memory for anything I might have done wrong the
night before. The show had gone mostly as usual. He'd shouted
himself apoplectic because Mrs. Wregge's cat Felix had streaked
across his path backstage, twice. But he was always ranting about
something.

I sat down on the bench and lifted the fallboard. The ebony
keys had scrapes along their surfaces and the ivories had yellowed.
Still, they were keys to happiness, all eighty-eight of them.

I ran a quiet scale to warm my fingers. I hadn't played more
than a dozen notes when I realized that the E just below middle C
was newly flat. And what had happened to the B? I pushed the
key down again: nothing, and the silence made me groan aloud.
Not wanting to risk Mr. Williams's wrath, I'd bitten my tongue
as, with each passing week, I'd had to shift octaves and rework

chords to avoid the flat notes. But this was absurd. I would have to convince Mr. Williams to hire someone to fix it, despite his being a relentless pinchpenny.

I put my foot on the damper pedal, heard a clink, and felt a scrape on the top of my boot.

What was that?

Ducking my head underneath, I saw that a long screw had come loose from the brass plate, which now rested on top of the pedal, rendering it useless. With a sigh, I reached in my pocket and took out a farthing coin that had thinned around the edge; it had served as a makeshift tool before. I crawled underneath, pushed the plate into place, and used the coin to turn the screw until it bit into the wood. I ran my thumb over the head; it wasn't quite flush, but it would have to do for now.

"Ed! Ed Nell!" Mr. Williams barked. "Damn it all! Where the devil is he?"

I scrambled out from under the piano. "I'm right here."

"Oh!" Mr. Williams scowled down at me, his bald pink pate shining in the light from the two sconces. "There's a new act tonight. A fiddler. Found him yesterday, busking at Covent Garden."

Was that all?

"He's not expecting me to accompany him, is he?" I asked, as I stood and brushed myself off. It was no business of mine who Mr. Williams brought in, but most of the musicians who played near Covent Garden weren't much to speak of.

"Nah. He'll be after Amalie. Just give him a few chords."

I kept my surprise in check. Mr. Williams must think pretty highly of the man to insert him when people were still sober enough to be listening.

"What's he playing?" I asked.

"How would I know?" He waved a hand toward the audience. "Hope he can make himself heard over that."

"They're louder than usual tonight."

"It's because of Jem Ace."

"Who's—" I started to ask, but fell silent as the curtain parted and Jack appeared, a troubled expression on his face. His gaze brushed over me and fixed on the manager.

"The Tourneaus aren't here," he said.

"What do you mean, they're not here?" Mr. Williams demanded.

I felt surprised myself. Marceline would've told me if she and Sebastian were leaving for another hall. They had never missed a show before.

Jack shook his head. "That's all I know. And Amalie needs to see you. Her new costume is falling off, and Mrs. Wregge says there's no time to fix it."

The stage manager turned away, muttering under his breath.

"Mr. Williams—wait—please!" I said hastily. "Is there any way you could have the piano tuned? The keys are horribly flat. Listen." I played a rapid scale. "And the B isn't even working."

He waved a hand. "Jack'll look at it later."

Jack sketched a nod.

I bit my lip, not wanting to be rude, but also not wanting to damage the piano further. "Well, you see . . . it needs someone who's specially trained and—"

But he was already pushing aside the curtain. "Put up with it," he said over his shoulder. "Nobody but you's going to notice." He turned back, his expression sour. "And be ready to switch Amalie out of order—maybe after the fiddler—or she can take the Tourneaus' spot, if they don't arrive. Blasted tart and her costumes. More bloody trouble than she's worth." Then he and Jack were gone.

Somewhat exasperated, I tugged at the cords that drew back the curtains separating me from the audience. It was mostly working-class men, still jostling into their seats and shouting good-naturedly to the boys who hawked cigars and cheap roses from trays that hung around their necks. As I surveyed the crowd, I realized Mr. Williams was right: no one would notice a piano out of tune, much less a missing note. And why should I care if it sounded horrid, so long as the audience was satisfied?

You're not playing Beethoven at St. James's Hall, I reminded myself as I took my seat. *And what's more, you never will if Mr. Williams decides that you're more bloody trouble than you're worth. You're not irreplaceable the way Amalie is.*

At eight o'clock precisely, two men on the catwalk pulled the ropes to swoop the curtains in graceful waves toward the ceiling. The sapphire-colored velvet with its gold trim had been mended a dozen times by Mrs. Wregge—I'd seen her perched on a stool, her needle flying across the fabric gathered in her broad lap—but in the flickering light, the patched bits were invisible and the velvet looked rich and elegant.

I struck up the dramatic prelude as Gallius Kovác strode onto the stage, his black cape flapping, his tall black hat—rumor had it he'd stolen it from a police constable—shining under the lights, his mustache waxed to fine curled ends. He extended his hand to stage right, and Maggie pranced out in a costume that never failed to elicit whistles from the crowd—a green-and-gold dress cut low to reveal the curve of her breasts. Her black hair was curled into ringlets and pinned up with sparkly combs. Her lips were painted red and her lashes darkened, like the ladies on the postcards from Egypt that hung in the window of Selinger's Stationers.

Gallius's first feat was to pull two birds out of his hat. But nine men out of ten were looking at Maggie, not the birds. The feathered creatures flapped up to the rafters unnoticed, while Maggie preened and strutted and winked at the audience. At her feet landed a small storm of roses, sent flying toward her by men who probably thought she treasured the blooms. After her performance, she returned them to the rose boys to sell again, and they split the two-penny profits.

I knew Gallius's routine well enough to match the music with the tempo of his tricks. So when he pulled a rainbow of handkerchiefs out of his hat, I rolled the chord. When he made Maggie disappear, I made the piano notes deep and trembly. And the crescendo came when she reappeared out of a box that vanished in a cloud of smoke.

His final trick was to run a sword through Maggie's neck. I asked her once if he ever poked her by accident, and she gave her sly smile. "That sword bends right through the metal collar. I made him show me 'afore I let him get anywhere near me with it—or with any other part of him that pokes, neither." She laughed out loud, and I felt my cheeks grow warm.

"Well, ain't you the innocent," she teased me, winking.

"I'm not innocent," I muttered. But she was right: I'd flushed again the following night, when I came upon Maggie and Gallius in the murky gloom of the back hallway, him with his hands inside her skirts and her with her arms wrapped hard around his neck.

Gallius and Maggie left the stage, and I played some interlude music, a medley of popular tunes, all the while keeping my eye out for Amalie, or for whoever might appear next. It turned out to be the new violinist, entering from stage right, and I wound up hastily so he didn't have to stand there waiting to begin.

He was handsome as anything—tall and slender, with silvery blond hair combed back from his forehead, a well-cut mouth, and bones that showed fine yet strong under the stage lights. I put his age at a year or two over twenty. He was dressed in a tailored coat and pants that bore no sheen from wear at the knees or cuffs, which made me wonder what he was doing playing here—or busking in Covent Garden, for that matter.

There was an air about him that made even this audience give him something approximating real attention. He offered a small, formal bow to the crowd; then he set his bow on the strings and began.

It was a piece I'd never heard, beautiful and haunting—and he could *play*. His bow stroked smoothly and powerfully across the strings, bringing forth the instrument's sweetness with none of the shrillness produced by a mediocre violinist.

But it was the wrong piece for this audience. These men didn't want beautiful and haunting. They wanted fast and loud, bright and bawdy, or downright silly. I felt their indifference flare to irritation, even before the grumbling began, and I prayed they'd give him a chance to finish.

Something small and white—a dinner roll—flew past his ear. He looked out at the audience, and I could tell he was surprised. Clearly, he wasn't used to this sort of reception, but he played on until a turnip hit him square in the stomach. His bow popped off the strings, and across his face flashed a look of uncertainty, followed by a hot flush of shame and anger as the groans and hisses turned to catcalls and laughter.

The sounds made me flinch, and he turned to me, glaring, as if he expected I'd join in the abuse. Once, I would've sat there, feeling as helpless as he. But a few weeks ago, when one of the

dancing dogs had gone missing and I'd had to fill the time between acts, I'd played "Libiamo ne' lieti calici," the drinking
song from the first act of *La Traviata*. The popular opera by
Verdi had just returned to London, so the melody was on everyone's lips, and the audience had cheered lustily for a full minute
afterward.

I riffled through my portfolio quickly, hoping that he knew it.

I couldn't see his expression as I played the opening chords,
but by the fourth measure, he was with me, his bow flying across
the strings. The words in their English translation ran through
my head: *Let's drink for the ecstatic feeling / that love arouses . . . /
Let's drink, my love, and the love among the chalices / Will make the
kisses hotter . . .*

It was a fine piece of music for a violin, and I softened my playing so that his could be heard, falling completely silent as he drew
out the last brilliant chords.

Above the sound of stamping feet came cries of "Bravo! Bravo!"
The violinist pointed his bow toward me and inclined his head
toward the audience. They roared their approval, and he bowed
again and left the stage.

With a small feeling of triumph, I found myself smiling as I
played some interlude music to fill the time until the next act—

And then Amalie fluttered in from stage left, wearing a costume that seemed composed entirely of dyed feathers floating at
her bosom and around her waist and thighs.

It was outrageous, even for her.

Like every man in the theater, I caught my breath. My fingers
fumbled her introduction, even missed a few notes. But the audience couldn't have cared less. They went wild for her, cheering
and shouting. She sang four songs in French, and as usual, dozens

of men hurled roses at her, which she gathered up as she exited stage left, amid a rain of pink paper petals dropped from above.

THE SHOW FINISHED at a quarter past ten, and I put the music into my portfolio and started down the stairs, hoping it wasn't raining, as I'd left my umbrella at home.

Mrs. Wregge was on her way up. "I say, have you seen Felix?"

"No. Has he escaped again?"

"I had the door open for not half a second, and he dashed out!" She shook her head so vigorously that her chin wobbled. "If Mr. Williams sees him, he's going to wring his neck—and mine, too."

"I would think he'd be grateful that Felix catches the mice."

"And so he should!" she said in a stage whisper. "He has the benefit of a fine mouser, while I have all the worry of keeping the two of them apart."

I couldn't help but smile. "It's your own version of cat and mouse, isn't it?"

She chuckled ruefully and pointed up the stairs. "He's not up there, is he? Mr. Williams?"

"I haven't seen him."

With a huff, she moved to continue her climb, but I put a hand on her arm. "Do you know what happened to Marceline and Sebastian? They weren't here tonight."

"No." Her kindly brown eyes sobered. "And it isn't like them to miss a show."

"No, it's not," I agreed, my feeling of misgiving growing. "Well, good night."

Turning away, I hurried down the stairs—and caught my heel on one of the treacherous nails near the bottom. With a cry, I pitched forward, nearly tumbling to the ground.

"Are you all right?" came a male voice.

Startled, I peered into the dark corridor.

"I'm sorry. I didn't mean to frighten you. It's Stephen Gagnon. The violinist." He came out of the shadows, his pale hair gleaming in the dim light. "And you're Ed Nell, the pianist."

My heart began to fall back into its normal rhythm. I cleared my throat. "Yes, that's right."

Two stagehands approached carrying a load of bulky wooden planks, and Stephen and I squeezed back against the wall. "We should move," I said. "They have to bring all the properties through here."

He motioned for me to lead the way, so I walked toward the ramp that led out to the yard. This part of the corridor was hung with metal lanterns, and by their light I could see him clearly. He was taller than I; his face was clean-shaven, his eyes a rich hazel. He stood with an easy elegance that spoke of time spent in drawing rooms.

"Thank you for what you did," he said. "I'd have been turned into mincemeat out there."

"I'm just glad you knew the song," I said.

"You play very well. I must say I was surprised." He glanced around us and tapped a few fingers against the water-stained plaster. "This isn't exactly—"

"Yes, well, I'm here for the money."

He grimaced. "So am I."

There was a story there, evidently, but I could hardly ask directly. So instead, I said, "Mr. Williams mentioned that he found you in Covent Garden. Have you studied somewhere?"

"At the Royal Academy, here in London."

I felt a stab of envy. "You're lucky."

"Yes, I suppose I was." There was a slight emphasis on the last word. "Where do you study?"

"Just—just privately, until last year." The thought of Mr. Moehler's passing still pained me.

"Do you play here every night?"

I shook my head. "Mondays, Wednesdays, and every other Thursday. Carl Dwigen, the other pianist, plays the rest."

His eyes lit up. "Will you be here tomorrow, then?"

I nodded. "I take it Mr. Williams asked you back?"

"Thanks to you. Wednesdays, Thursdays, and Sundays for now." He shifted his violin case under his arm. "Say, I don't suppose you could help me pick a few other songs that the audience would like."

"Of course." As I looked at him, a thought occurred to me. "You don't happen to know how to tune a piano, do you?"

"No. I noticed some of the notes were off. Bad luck." He flashed a consoling smile.

"It gets worse every week. Jack Drummond is supposed to take a look at it, but—"

"Jack Drummond?" he interrupted. "Who's that?"

"He's the owner's son. He does all sorts of work around here. I'm sure you'll meet him at some point."

Stephen's face wore an odd expression.

"Do you know him?" I ventured.

"No, not at all. But I—well, Mr. Williams led me to believe the music hall was his."

"In a way, it is," I said with a shrug. "Mr. Drummond is the owner of the building, but he doesn't have anything to do with the performances. Mr. Williams manages all of us."

The back door opened, and a uniformed police constable hurried in, leaving the door ajar behind him. He passed us without a glance and headed down the corridor.

"Wonder what he's here for," Stephen said.

We leaned around the corner and watched as the constable entered Drummond's office without knocking.

No one ever did that, so far as I'd seen.

"Could you meet me here tomorrow, before the show?" Stephen asked. "At seven o'clock?"

"I'll try. I should go now, though."

"Well, good night, then." He held out his hand for mine.

I stared at it. Until now, I'd managed to avoid shaking hands in my disguise. But if I ignored his gesture, what would he think? My hands weren't small, and they were strong with practice, so I took his hand firmly, trying to perform the act as a man would. However, surprise flashed over his face, and he trapped my hand between both of his, turning it over so he could study my palm. My heart sank. I pulled away, sharply regretting that I'd stopped to talk to him.

His teasing grin faded. "What on earth's the matter? I'm hardly going to snitch on you, seeing as I need your help."

I recognized the truth of his words. "I'm sorry. It's just—they'd only pay me half as much if they knew."

"If they even kept you on," he added bluntly. "From what I know, there's a distinct prejudice against lady pianists. How long have you been here?"

"Nearly two months."

His expression became admiring. "Well, I hope I'm that lucky." He bent his head toward me. "What's your name? Your real name, I mean?"

I kept silent.

"Come on," he coaxed. "I can't call you 'Ed' now."

"It's Nell," I said reluctantly. Marceline was the only other person who knew the truth. But admitting it to her had been a relief, for we had commiserated over the ways young female performers were at a disadvantage. With Stephen, I only felt a new inequality, a disadvantage that existed on my side alone.

"Short for Ellen?" he guessed.

"Elinor." I paused. "I go by Ed Nell here."

"Ed Nell," he said, trying it out with a grin. "It's perfect. I could even call you Nelly in front of people, and no one would suspect."

I gave him a look that made him instantly turn penitent.

"I won't say a word," he promised. "I think you were clever to come here looking for a job." And then, sincerely, "*I'm* certainly glad you did."

He intended his words to reassure me, and I managed a smile.

"Well"—he shifted his violin case again—"I'm told I have to find the wardrobe mistress for a proper costume. I'll see you tomorrow?"

"Yes. Good night," I replied and started up the ramp.

The constable had left the back door cracked open, and as I crossed the yard, the church bells chiming three-quarters made me start.

How had it gotten so late? And what if this were the one night Matthew came home early?

I quickened my pace along Hawley Mews, trotting past the Crown and Thorn, where jangling piano music and masculine laughter spilled out the open windows. At the corner, a prostitute called out from below the awning of the chandler's shop. I had already passed her before I realized that her invitation was meant for me. I moved faster, dodging around a pile of refuse before halting at the corner of Grafton Lane.

Usually I went home by way of Wickley Street because it was lit by gas lamps. Grafton Lane was narrow and poorly lit, but a good bit shorter.

Dare I risk it?

A night-soil man, his cart pulled by a nag with heaving flanks, came out of the alley, and after he passed, I peered in. The passage was eerily empty of people, but the clouds from earlier in the evening had mostly dispersed, and the moon, nearly full, cast a generous silvery light. I thought again of Matthew coming home, checking my bedroom, and not finding me there—and I turned in. Following a series of narrow streets, I worked my way roughly westward until I reached quiet Brewer Street, where all the inhabitants' windows and doors were closed to the night air and its miasmas. With only another few hundred steps, I'd reach Regent Street. There, gritty Soho ended and fashionable Mayfair began, the boundary marked by Mr. Nash's famous pillars, the ones that looked like something out of ancient Greece but were only stucco painted to look like rare white marble.

I was almost there when a low cry, quavering and full of pain, sounded from a dark pocket between the buildings to my left. My steps slowed. Wary of lingering—I knew enough from Matthew about the tricks that cutpurses could play—I strained to see who had called out. It could be a prostitute, or a beggar, or some unfortunate drunken soul who had fallen on the way home from a pub.

But the next cry was pitched high, like that of a woman or even a child, and it held a note of fear as well as pain.

The moon had edged behind a cloud, but I could just make out a small still form huddled beside a drainpipe. "Who's there?" I said softly. "Are you all right?"

The only answer was a ragged breath.

I moved forward cautiously, and when the figure remained motionless, I bent down and reached out. My hand touched what felt like a shoulder, muscled but small. A moment later, the moon reemerged, and I could see that the shoulder belonged to a young woman who'd been beaten badly. Her eyes were closed, her face was dark with bruises and blood, and her thick black hair was a matted tangle. I recoiled in horror, pulling my hand back.

Simultaneously I realized who it was.

"Marceline!" I sank to my knees and groped for her wrist. Her skin was cold and her pulse weak, and as I drew my hand away I felt the stickiness of blood and noticed that her arm lay at an odd angle. "My God, what happened?" I whispered.

She didn't make a sound.

Fearful of hurting her, my hands hovered, not knowing where I might touch. What could I do? Though she was smaller than I, I didn't think I could carry her.

And where could I take her? How would I get her there? My thoughts leaped and scattered uselessly, and I took a deep breath to tamp down my panic. *Think,* I told myself sharply. *Hysteria isn't going to help either of you.*

Could I take her home? No, that was impossible. How could I explain her presence to Matthew and Peggy?

Marceline gave another low groan, as if she were in agonizing pain, both mental and physical. That decided me. I'd take her to Dr. Everett.

I had rested my hand lightly on her back to reassure her of my presence. She moved convulsively as I bent over and spoke in her ear. "Marceline, I'm going to get help."

I raced to Regent Street and raised my arm. Two cabs, occupied, clattered by, and I despaired of finding one that was free at this hour. But at last another appeared and slowed.

"My friend is hurt and needs to go to hospital," I called up to the driver. "She's just at the corner, but I need help fetching her."

He tilted his head back and looked at me suspiciously. "What'd'you mean, she's 'urt? I ain't takin' 'er if'n she's drunk, or just been roughed up by a customer—"

"She's not a prostitute!" I retorted, my mind quick to assemble a story that would bend his sympathies toward us. "It's her brute of a husband that's to blame, when he drinks up every bit of money she earns taking in washing! I'll give you an extra two shillings for the fare." Still he seemed undecided. "Please. If she stays out all night, she'll be dead by morning."

He grunted and began to climb down from his box. "Where is she?"

I pointed. "At the corner, just there. On the ground. But be careful—her arm may be broken."

His eyes narrowed, and I thought I saw a glimmer of curiosity, or perhaps disgust at the thought of a man who would do such a thing. "You stay 'ere with my 'orse."

I nodded and caught the reins he tossed me. The mare took not the slightest notice, and I stared at the entrance to the alley until my eyes burned.

Finally, he emerged, carrying Marceline, and together we put her inside the cab.

"Which 'ospital?" he asked.

"Charing Cross, please, in Agar Street, off the Strand."

We rolled forward, with me cradling Marceline close, trying to absorb the jolts of the ride. But as we drew up to the tall iron gates of the hospital, I realized my own predicament.

I knew there would be a guard to receive her, for as Dr. Everett often said, disease pays no heed to regular hours. But if I took Marceline inside, I'd have to answer questions, and I wouldn't be able to keep up my disguise around people who knew me. I had been here too many times to help the doctor with his books and play the piano for patients.

The cab halted, and I dismounted on the right side and remained in the shadows, close to the wheel.

"I don't want to be seen," I said to the cabdriver. "Can you tell the guard that you found her?"

He snorted and muttered something under his breath but went silent as I handed him the fare plus the extra I'd promised.

"The bell is just there." I pointed to the metal box and hurried away to the far side of the street. From the shadows between two buildings, I observed the guard, Mr. Oliven, emerge from the guardhouse. He and the driver exchanged a few words, and Marceline was shifted out of the cab and into his arms.

She was so limp and motionless that she might have been dead. A hard lump filled my throat as I watched him carrying her across the lit courtyard to the front door, and I remembered the night I'd met her.

It was my first performance at the Octavian. I'd only had a few minutes before the show to leaf through the music Mr. Williams had given me, and I hadn't noticed that two pages were missing from the final number. When we reached that part of the song, I'd fumbled and improvised, but it was clear to anyone watching that I'd made a mess of it. I'd barely closed the piano lid and gathered my things when Mr. Williams burst into the alcove red-faced and shouting. When I finally managed to get a word in edgewise to explain that the pages had been missing, he'd motioned violently toward the piano bench. "You fool! Why didn't you look in there? If you do anything like this again, you're finished!"

He'd stormed off, leaving me shaking. Finally, I opened the bench, and through my tears I saw the two missing pages.

Why on earth hadn't they been in the portfolio where they belonged?

From the direction of the stage came footsteps and then, "Don't take it to heart. He's always bawling at someone." The voice was feminine and musical, with a slight accent.

I looked up, blinking the tears back.

The young woman from the trapeze act stood at the threshold of the alcove. While she had been flying through the air, she looked lithe and powerful; up close she was petite and very pretty. Her long black hair was still coiled in braids around her head; her expression was sympathetic, and her eyes were dark and sparkling.

My attempt to recover my poise failed, and her lips parted in surprise. "Why—you're a woman!"

I swallowed hard and nodded, too wretched to even attempt the lie.

"Don't worry." She came close enough that she could murmur. "I won't give you away. It's hard enough for us. If I could masquerade as a man, I would. But we get paid more if I'm in this." She glanced down at her pale pink costume, which, in contrast to Sebastian's severe black one, left her legs and arms bare and was embroidered with sparkling threads.

"And I get paid more if I'm in this," I said, gesturing to my masculine garb.

She laughed.

I nodded toward the curtains through which Mr. Williams had vanished. "Does he really always shout like that?"

"Every night that I've been here," she said airily. "I remember once I was late to the stage. He all but had a *fit*, I tell you! He looked like a rabid dog, with spit flying out of his mouth. And the horrid names he called me." Her delicate eyebrows rose. "I thought Sebastian was going to hit him."

A rueful laugh escaped me. "Well, I can't hit him. I need the money."

"So do we," she said cheerfully. "So does everyone, I dare say. But he'll forget it by tomorrow."

"I hope so."

She gave a crooked smile that revealed small white teeth. "My name's Marceline. What's yours?"

"Nell. It's short for Elinor."

She tipped her head toward me, her eyes thoughtful. "Well, Nell, I'll see you tomorrow. And really, don't worry about old Williams." With a graceful little wave, she turned away and went to stage left where her brother was waiting, coat in hand.

I'd felt so grateful to her. I might not even have had the courage to return the following night if it hadn't been for her kindness.

As the hospital door closed behind my friend, I blinked back the tears pricking at the corners of my eyes. What vile person had beaten her and dumped her in that rotten little street? And where was Sebastian? Had something similar befallen him? Did he have any idea what had happened?

I waited until a light appeared in the room used for admitting new patients. I imagined the night nurse settling Marceline in a bed; then, feeling relieved that she was safe for this night at least, I started for home.

Chapter 2

I woke to the muted clanging of copper pots on the stove.

I had been lucky last night: when I'd returned home, Matthew's bed had been empty. And judging from the clanging, Peggy had returned this morning, which must mean that her daughter, Emma, was feeling better. So, my first feeling of the day was one of relief.

The morning sun glowed through my curtains, and the bells of Grosvenor Chapel rang the quarter hour. In the light of day, and surrounded by familiar sounds, my anxiety about Marceline was somewhat allayed. I had the utmost confidence in Dr. Everett, for over the years, I'd seen him perform what some might call miracles upon even his most feeble patients, and Marceline was young and strong. Still, I longed to know for certain that she'd recover.

The thought nudged me out of bed. I went to the washstand and poured water from the ewer into the basin. As I splashed and dried my face, I considered how and when I should try to see Marceline.

Matthew usually left by ten o'clock, after which I would

practice for four or five hours while Peggy was occupied in the kitchen and the bedrooms. After I finished at the piano, she cleaned the parlor and the study, while I went for a walk or to the shops. There was part of me that longed to visit the hospital this morning, but Peggy would be certain to ask where I was going and why. And what excuse could I give to Dr. Everett for appearing unexpectedly and inquiring about a particular patient? No, I decided. It would be best if I were to follow my usual routine. If I started for the hospital at half past three, I'd arrive after Dr. Everett's afternoon rounds, when he would have seen Marceline, but before tea, which he always took precisely at half past four. I could steer the conversation toward new patients to find out her prognosis; and if Marceline was by chance awake and able to talk, I might even be able to visit her. Maybe she'd be able to tell me where to find Sebastian; assuming that her brother was all right, he must be mad with worry about her. But without Marceline's guidance, I'd have no idea where to find him.

Though she and I had become good friends, I knew very little about her brother other than that he was a year younger than Marceline and very strong. They had been raised by their grandparents and trained by the great trapeze artist Jules Léotard himself at the Cirque D'Hiver in Paris. When a fire destroyed their theater, they came to London and styled themselves "The Flying Tourneaus."

I opened my armoire to find my trousers in a heap on the floor. In my exhaustion the previous night, I must have missed the hook. With a sound of annoyance, I caught them up, brushed off the dust, and hung them, hoping they wouldn't be too crumpled this evening. Then I buttoned myself into my blue day dress and headed for the stairs, where the clattering sounds from the kitchen rose to greet me.

Peggy had been our housekeeper since before I was born; now she kept house for us and for Dr. Everett, three days each, with Sunday her day of rest. Lately she'd come less often because her daughter, Emma, suffered from consumption and was having one of her bad bouts. Now Peggy would be like a dervish trying to put things back to rights here. Wanting to take some of the burden from her, I'd dusted the parlor, polished the furniture, and thoroughly cleaned the kitchen after yesterday's tea. But by her accounting, the house would be at sixes and sevens. Admittedly, in the exacting light of morning I could see a layer of grime on the front windowsills. It was impossible to avoid dust, even if the house was shut up every hour of the day.

I entered the dining room, where my brother was drinking his tea and already several pages into his newspaper. The erratic din emanating from the kitchen rattled my nerves, but I suppressed my discomfort. Matthew, who was rarely agitated by anything, seemed not to notice it at all.

"Good morning," I said.

"Morning, Nell." He smiled and handed me my newspaper.

I sat down, poured myself tea, added sugar, and laid my paper flat.

And then, as was our wont, we were silent for some time, turning our pages. Reading the papers with my father and brother every morning had been part of my *disciplina logica*—my "logical education"—which, in lieu of the more traditional womanly skills of needlepoint, drawing, and French, emphasized mathematics, science, Latin, geography, and politics, among other things. After Father had passed away, Matthew and I had kept up the habit, and I liked the familiar beginning to every day.

Peggy's tall, spare frame appeared at the door, her arms akimbo.

"Did the coal man come yesterday?" she demanded without pre-amble.

I put my finger on the margin to hold my place and gave Matthew a questioning look. His clear blue eyes met mine, and he shrugged in reply.

"I don't think so," I replied. "Was he supposed to? Usually he comes Saturdays."

"But he shorted us last week, and he told me he'd deliver the balance yesterday! For mercy's sake!" She pursed her lips in disdain, but before she could start toward the kitchen, the doorbell rang. Her eyes sparked. "That'd better not be him, coming to the front door." And she stalked off to answer it.

Matthew raised an eyebrow. "Surely he's not that much of a fool," he said under his breath, and I stifled a laugh. More likely it was a message from Scotland Yard for Matthew.

My brother had begun his career in uniform at L Division, in Lambeth, five years ago and risen rapidly from constable to sergeant to inspector, whereupon he'd transferred to the Yard last year. He had gained a reputation for being strong, clever, and unflappable, with the ability to work longer hours than other detective inspectors, being unfettered by a wife or family. He had teased me recently, saying it was fortunate that he merely had a younger sister to manage, and on most days I wasn't an inordinate amount of trouble. His jest had made me cringe inwardly, as my nighttime excursions would certainly cause him—at the very least—an inordinate amount of worry. The fact was, I hated keeping secrets from him. But I'd squelched my guilt with the justification that my playing at the music hall wasn't doing anyone any harm, and it wasn't for much longer.

Peggy reappeared in the doorway, a scowl on her face but no note in hand. "Beggin' your pardon, but it's a constable, and he's very stubborn. I told him that I could deliver a message, as you're eating breakfast like civilized people *do* at this hour, but he says it would take too long to put in writing, and he has to see you himself."

"Hm," my brother said and removed his napkin from his lap.

"Matthew, you could offer him a cup of tea," I suggested hastily. "It's still early. It would be the decent thing to do."

He snorted. "That is a truly pitiful attempt to mask your nosiness."

"Well, we've never had a visit from a stubborn constable before," I retorted.

He gave me a look of good-humored indulgence. "All right, Peggy. Let's have him in."

The constable was a thin fellow of around one-and-twenty, with red spots in his cheeks, a sharpish nose, and a top hat that he held in front of his chest. He wore the blue swallow-tailed coat of the Metropolitan Police, with its high neck and a row of buttons down the front. The coat rode a bit wide across the shoulders, as if he needed to grow into it.

"Why, Hodges!" Matthew said with some surprise.

The constable bobbed in my direction and looked abashed. "Sorry, Miss." He turned to Matthew with the air of deference that always made me feel a mixture of amusement and pride in my brother. "Mr. 'allam, I'm turrible sorry to interrupt your breakfast. Wouldn't do it if it warn't important."

"Of course not. What's the trouble?"

"A man found dead, down by the river just west of Waterloo Pier."

I knew that pier; it wasn't far from the Yard, on the north bank of the river, in the curve closest to Soho.

Matthew's gaze sharpened. "You found him?"

He nodded. "On my rounds, though I wouldn't 'a seen 'im at all, except I heard two boys shoutin', and one of 'em asked if 'e was dead. I couldn't see 'em at first because there was a wall on that part of the embankment." He raised his hat. "So I used this. It was still mostly dark, but I could see something wot looked like a bloke near some broke-up crates."

"You used your *hat*?" I blurted out.

Matthew arched an eyebrow but didn't rebuke me.

The constable nodded, flipping the article over so I could see. "It's shored up with cane, so's we can step on it. It's come in tol'rable useful more 'n once."

"Yes, I'm sure it has," I said faintly.

He turned back to Matthew. "I ran round to where 'e was layin' and saw 'e was beat bad, blood everywhere."

Unbidden, my mind leaped to Marceline, and I had the unsettled feeling that coincidence sometimes gives.

"We turned 'im over, so we could see 'is face," Hodges continued. "That's when I seen 'ow it was just like the murder wot 'appened near St. Luke's."

"St. Luke's, in Soho?" I asked, turning to Matthew. That was Peggy's church, and it was only a few streets from the Octavian.

"Yes." Matthew gave me a look and lowered his voice. "I'm not sure Peggy heard about it, as we kept it out of the papers, and I have no intention of bringing it up. She has enough to worry about with Emma." Matthew turned back to Hodges. "How was it similar?"

"Well, you remember, 'is face was beat summat awful, and 'is right 'and 'ad the three middle fingers broken." He held up his own fingers. "I didn't see it on this bloke till we turned 'im over. And I remembered wot you said: that if I ever saw it again, I was to find you direc'ly."

I thought of Marceline's bloody hands. I hadn't observed them closely enough to tell if the bones were intact. "What is significant about broken fingers?" I asked.

Matthew pantomimed holding a fan of playing cards. "Conventionally, it's been a punishment used for gamblers who didn't pay their debts."

"A warning to others," I said.

"As it were."

"O' course, like you said 'afore, it might not be for gambling," Hodges offered. "Could just be a—a trick, like. To 'ide the real reason they was killed."

"When did the murder near St. Luke's happen?" I asked.

"A few days ago," Hodges answered, seemingly appreciative of my interest. "Same sort o' thing as last night. The poor man was stripped down to his skiv—well, down to—well, down to not much a'tall"—he averted his gaze from mine and the bits of color in his cheeks darkened—"with 'is 'and wrecked, and beat so's 'is face was pretty much gone. 'Twas lucky that somebody came for'ard right away and told us who 'e was."

Matthew pushed back from the table, and I followed them to the front door, my mind drawing various, if somewhat tenuous, connections between the two murders and Marceline's attack. My face must have revealed the tenor of my thoughts, for the constable bent toward me, his face twisting with regret.

"Sorry to 'ave disturbed you, Miss," he said. "I know this ain't the sort of thing that sits well with breakfast."

"Oh, I'm all right. It's just—just such a grisly thing," I said.

"It is," replied Hodges earnestly, as he donned his tolerably useful hat. "Most as grisly as I ever seen. Even worse'n that time wot I pulled a dead man out of the Thames with 'is eyes et out of 'is 'ead."

Chapter 3

$\mathcal{P}$romptly at half past three, I donned my boots and coat and walked toward Charing Cross at a quick clip.

Most voluntary hospitals in London did not accept patients with mental diseases; nor did they take children, incurables, or patients who were infectious, with child, or truly destitute. It was a testament to Dr. Everett's standing in the medical community—or to his gifts of persuasion—that he'd convinced the hospital's Committee of Benefactors to establish a ward in which brain diseases in patients of any age or condition might be treated.

When I arrived, I entered through the main hall. To the left of it was the receiving room, where dozens of patients were examined daily by the inquiry officer and then either admitted to a ward, treated for minor injuries, sent to the dispensary, or directed to the outpatient benches, where they would wait to be seen by a consultant. Dr. Everett's dominion was in the north wing, on the second floor of four, and I climbed the central stairs, passed through two archways, and paused at the threshold of the long, narrow room, made in the newly adopted "pavilion" style, that was the women's ward.

Because Dr. Everett believed that a pleasant environment was conducive to mental health, the walls were painted a soft yellow, and pairs of windows both enabled cross-ventilation and let in the light all day long. The wooden floor was polished, and two black stoves in the center aisle cheerfully kept off the chill. The room held thirty beds, fifteen on each side, with their metal headboards set against the walls. A few had free-standing curtains, not unlike those at my piano alcove, for privacy. Near the back of the room, Dr. Everett was tending to a patient with a bandaged head and broken arm. Her name was Grace, and she'd been admitted last week, having been thrown from her husband's carriage. He caught sight of me in the doorway and beckoned. As I approached, I scanned the room; so far as I could tell, Marceline wasn't there, but she might be behind a curtain.

I bent to greet Grace, but her eyes only wandered vacantly to the ceiling above me with no noticeable change of expression. I felt a stab of pity, and the smile I'd intended for her slid off my face.

"Nell, my dear," Dr. Everett said, "I was just about to have tea. Why don't you go to my office? I'll be there in a moment."

I nodded agreement, but as I left the room, I adjusted my steps to peer surreptitiously around the curtains, my anxiety increasing as I neared the last bed.

Marceline wasn't there.

Fear gripped me. Was it possible that she'd died in the night? Striving to remain outwardly calm, I started down the corridor to Dr. Everett's office, wanting desperately to ask someone. But what pretext would I give for inquiring whether a nameless young woman had been unceremoniously deposited at the hospital the previous night?

As I passed the door to the children's ward, I halted. Could she have been assigned to a bed there? She was small for being seventeen, and I could see how she might be taken for several years younger. I took a quick walk through, smiling at the patients who seemed well enough to notice, until I reached the end of the row, where a beige curtain partitioned off a bed. Through the gap between two panels, I glimpsed thick black hair on a pillow. My heart leaped. I looked in hopefully and gave a sigh of relief when I saw Marceline.

Nurse Aimes, who had been with Dr. Everett for as long as I could remember, was setting aside the portable sphygmograph used for measuring the pressure of arterial blood. She caught my eye and put a finger to her lips. I nodded and remained silent. But as she bent over her chart to make notes, I stepped inside the curtain so that I could observe Marceline more easily.

I had to stifle my gasp. Her eyes were covered by a white bandage that encircled her head, and another bandage wrapped under her chin, keeping it immobile. Her hair was a tangle, matted with bits of dried blood. What little I could see of her cheeks and mouth was discolored and swollen, and her hands were swathed in bandages to above the wrist. The bedclothes were barely disturbed, and she looked even smaller than usual. I could see why someone had mistaken her for a child.

When Nurse Aimes stepped outside the curtain, I followed and asked softly, "What happened?"

"I dunno," she replied, her mouth pursing in vexation. "Poor thing was brought in last night by a cabdriver. He said there was another bloke, too, but he ran off. I dunno if I believe that; my guess is that the driver was the one who beat her senseless, the worthless blackguard."

I kept my face neutral. "Well, at least he brought her here."

"Yes, and the doctor has done his best, o' course. I imagine she'll pull through." She checked her gold pocket watch. It was an unusual thing for a woman to carry, but I knew it had been a gift from her father. "The doctor'll be taking his tea shortly."

"Yes. He asked me to meet him in his office."

She pursed her lips again. "Perhaps *you* can make him take more than ten minutes for it."

I smiled. "I'll try."

DR. EVERETT'S OFFICE was as familiar to me as a room in my own house, for I had often come here to read or study as a child. As I got older, I would sometimes help him with his books or notes for his research. Glass-fronted cabinets held shelves filled with sturdy white skulls, delicate eye sockets, and brains in clear jars. On the walls hung framed drawings of the muscles and nerves of the face. Standing on a black marble pedestal in the corner was an old phrenology head done in plaster, its parts labeled with Roman numerals, which Dr. Everett kept as both a curiosity and a humbling reminder of how fallible science could be. Along one wall were cases of books, several of which he or his colleagues had written. Some discussed mental diseases and their treatments, while others outlined the merits of a practical education for boys and girls alike. Along the other wall stood wooden files full of case histories.

One of those histories belonged to my mother, Frances, whom

the doctor had treated for two years before she abandoned us to pursue a career as a pianist in Europe.

I had no memories of her, as I was only an infant when she left, and my father refused to speak of her afterward. But when Dr. Everett felt I was old enough to understand, he explained that there was a disease, first described by Aretaeus of Cappadocia in the first century, in which mania and melancholy alternated with each other. He had let me read the scientific papers by the French doctors Jean-Pierre Falret, who had identified it as "circular madness" in 1851, and Jules Baillarger, who in 1854 named it "*folie a double forme.*" By all accounts it was often passed down from parent to child, bred in the bone or the brain, as it were, but Dr. Everett believed he had discovered some means for countering it. That was why he had drawn up a curriculum for me, which limited my literary reading and piano practicing to works that were cheerful and pleasant, and he had spoken to me regularly about the importance of avoiding excesses of emotion. As he explained to me, any situation that caused either fright or great excitement could be the initiating event in a cascade that might devolve into the illness that lay latent in my mind.

So all my life I had tried to tamp down my feelings, as if with an inward una corda pedal, which on the piano shifts the action so the hammers strike one string instead of two, or two instead of three, making the sound softer. I often found myself having to strive for the equanimity that came more naturally to Matthew, but I did my best. The one area in which I skirted the doctor's advice was my music. I hadn't limited myself on the piano to lullabies and the like, though I was careful to keep that from him.

"Good afternoon, Nell," came his pleasant voice behind me. "Contemplating Mr. Stirling's brain, are you?"

I turned away from the cabinet to smile at him. "Admiring his lovely cerebral cortex." I came forward and kissed him on the cheek. "Hello, Doctor."

He was a rather short and sturdy man, neatly dressed, with small, deft hands, a head of thick graying hair, a tidy mustache and beard, and silver-rimmed spectacles. He nodded appreciatively at the table. "Our tea. I'm glad of it, as I haven't had a bite since breakfast. It's been a busy day."

Beside the tea tray lay the mail—several circulars and, on top, an envelope that bore colorful foreign stamps with little moons. For as long as I could remember, Dr. Everett had collected an array of peripatetic friends. As he described them himself, they tended to be eccentric, in both their mental habits and their foreign travels, which made them all the more interesting.

He removed his coat, hung it carefully on the back of his chair, and sat down.

My eye was caught by his cuff links, which looked Oriental in design and had a red stone in the middle. Usually the doctor wore only the plainest sort. "Are those new?"

He glanced down, and his expression changed to an almost bashful smile. "A gift from a former patient. Aren't they intriguing?"

"They're beautiful." I drew my usual chair closer to the table, so I could reach the tea things. "I saw Nurse Aimes just now. She was with a new patient."

"Yes, an awful case. Poor young woman."

I settled the cups into the saucers and lifted the lid on the pot to be sure the tea had steeped fully; the doctor liked it strong. "Why is she in the children's ward?"

"She was put there last night, and there's no reason to move her just yet. She's small and slender, but her craniofacial bones suggest she's at least sixteen or seventeen. And her muscular development is unusual, as if she were a ballerina, perhaps, or accustomed to strenuous physical practice."

I poured tea for us both. "You've no idea who she is?"

"No. The cabdriver who brought her had no idea at all." He reached for his teacup.

"But she'll recover, won't she?"

I'd sought to keep the urgency out of my voice; still, he shot me a curious look before he dropped two sugars into his tea and stirred. "I hope so. Her vital organs are fine, and that's in her favor. A ruptured spleen or a punctured lung would be very serious, especially given that she'd been out at night and her body temperature was below normal when she was brought in. She has a badly wrenched shoulder, some severe injuries to her face and her back, including a possible fracture in her jaw, cuts and contusions on her wrists and hands, and four cracked ribs—but those will all mend in time."

"Are her eyes all right? I saw they were bandaged."

"That's only to avoid aggravating the symptoms of concussion." He shifted in his chair. "From her injuries, it seems that she rolled into a ball to protect her torso for as long as she was conscious. Of course, it meant that whoever did this had access to her head, and there is evidence of several strong blows. I had to put twelve stitches in her scalp."

Twelve stitches, I thought, feeling sick. *No wonder there was so much blood.*

His eyebrows rose over his spectacles. "Much to my relief, there was no sign that she was violated."

My breath caught in horror at the thought, but I said only, "Thank goodness."

"What is a bit curious to me, from a medical standpoint, is that the nurse spoke to her in English this morning, but although she seemed to understand, she replied in French." He frowned. "Unfortunately, this suggests that her brain has broken partially free from its usual connective fibers. She probably also has a hemorrhage, and she may lose her sight or her speech for a few days—and part of her memory, possibly even permanently."

Suddenly the tea was bitter in my mouth, and my stomach turned. I set down the cup abruptly, keeping my eyes averted and refolding my napkin to conceal my agitation.

He seemed not to notice and reached for a triangle of sandwich. "I'm just glad she was brought here and not somewhere else. There've been half a dozen articles in the *Lancet* the past year describing various hospital treatments for concussive injuries—most of them inane, based upon nothing more than meager instincts and inchoate knowledge. Giving ice-cold baths, hanging people upside down, administering potions verging on poisons. Pfft!" His eyes sparked behind his spectacles. "Do you know that Dr. Freyn has been sticking magnets up people's noses, with the idea that it will realign the compass that he thinks is in the brain?"

"That sounds particularly absurd," I agreed.

"Of course it's absurd—not to mention dangerous!" He bit into his quarter sandwich rather more energetically than necessary.

"What will you try first?"

"Rest. I've given her some laudanum for the pain, so she can sleep. And we're monitoring her objective symptoms, of course—blood pressure and pulse and so on. In a day or two, she may be able to speak. I don't want her to attempt it yet; if her jaw is fractured, that could injure it further. Time enough when she's better to find out what happened."

"Provided she remembers," I said, feeling apprehensive.

He dabbed his mouth methodically with his napkin. "If, in fact, there has been damage to the parts of the brain that house memory, the best thing we can do is to find someone familiar to her, usually a relation, to help recover it. But of course, we can't find that person until she's able to speak. It's rather a conundrum."

My heart skipped a beat. Last night, I'd only thought to find Sebastian so that I might let him know that Marceline was alive and in the hospital. But now, there was a second reason to find him: to help Marceline recover.

But how? And what if he had been beaten as well—perhaps left for dead—

And then, suddenly, a thought that cut through me like a rush of cold water: *What if Sebastian was the man who had been killed by the docks?*

"Nell?" Dr. Everett was peering at me, concern on his face. "Are you all right? You look peculiar."

"Yes, of course," I managed. "It's just . . . just quite awful."

"I know." He selected another quarter sandwich. "I sent a message round to the Yard first thing this morning, to ask Matthew if anyone had made any inquiries about a missing woman of her description, but he said not. And as we have no idea who she is, there isn't much the police can do. If the cabdriver is to be believed, he found her on the corner of Brewer Street. Matthew says this is the fifth time in the past fortnight someone has been beaten and left for dead in Soho."

"Fifth," I echoed faintly. "Well, I know Matthew has been working a great deal. I barely see him these days." Suddenly I wanted to drop this topic. "She'll be safe here, at least."

"Naturally." He buttered a piece of scone. "No one will suspect her presence. *Tutius est ut invisibilia.*"

"Yes, invisible is definitely safer," I agreed. But I was thinking, *Until I find Sebastian, I'm at least familiar.* Casually, I added, "I'd be happy to sit with her, if you think it would help. She might feel comfortable with someone her own age."

"Quite possibly. You've always had a good way with patients." He wiped his fingertips on his napkin and tapped the newspaper at the side of his plate. "Did you happen to see the papers this morning? They published the list of attendees for the August meeting of the British Association for the Advancement of Science. It's in Bristol this time, so I will certainly try to go, especially as my friend Dr. Martyn will be discussing his new research on the anatomy of skin. Although I must say, I find some of the topics rather esoteric." He unfolded the newspaper. "Ah, yes. I think I shall not attend Mr. William Baily's lecture on a new species of *Labyrinthodont amphibia* found in the coal at Jarrow Colliery in Kilkenny."

"Goodness," I said. "I'm imagining some sort of beastly frog with a maze of teeth."

He looked at me over the top of his newspaper. "Well, don't worry, my dear. Mr. Baily is an archaeologist, so I believe it's extinct."

I laughed, and with that, our conversation turned elsewhere.

But all the way home from the hospital, my thoughts ticked with the persistence of a metronome between two concerns: how I might go about locating Sebastian without alerting anyone as to why, and—given the attacks—whether I should go to the music hall at all.

Chapter 4

*B*y that evening, I'd dismissed the possibility of not going to the Octavian. Drummond and Mr. Williams would never keep a performer who left them in the lurch. And how would I find another position? It had only been by the best of luck that I'd found this one, walking into the Octavian the same afternoon that the other pianist left.

Besides, I was fairly certain that I could limit the danger by going to the Octavian early—even earlier than Stephen had asked—taking the longer way home, through streets that were better lit, and keeping my eyes sharp about me.

I opened the armoire and reached to the back, groping for my men's clothes. I hung my dress on a hanger, then took out the long swath of fabric I'd cut from a worn bed-sheet. It was nearly a foot wide, and I wound it three times around my chest and tucked the end under my arm. Being thin, I hadn't much to conceal, but still. Then came my white shirt—the smallest I could find, with a snug, stiff collar. I drew on my trousers and buttoned the placket closed. My hairpins were stored in a jade box that one of Dr. Everett's patients had brought back from China. Putting my hair up so it would fit under my hat was a tedious process, but at last it was done. Then I donned my coat, took my portfolio from behind some books, and went downstairs.

All of my old sheet music was on a shelf in the study. I sifted through the stack until I found three pieces that I thought Stephen might be able to use and slid them into my portfolio. As I started to leave the room, my eye fell on the desk, and I paused. In the top left drawer, we kept a revolving pistol that had belonged to Father, who had served for years as an officer in the navy. When he was alive, he had assembled a collection of several fine firearms as well as some rare swords. We'd sold most of them the previous year at auction, where they'd brought a good price, but Matthew had kept one pistol for his occasional use. Managing a gun had not originally been part of my logical education, but after Matthew had joined the police, he'd taken me to the country and taught me how to load the bullets into the chambers and shoot with some accuracy.

I opened the drawer and unwrapped the gun from the felt. It slid into my grasp, the ivory handle smooth against my palm, the heft reassuring. But where could I carry it? It wouldn't fit in my music portfolio or even the pockets of my coat. And what if I lost it and Matthew noticed its absence—which he surely would at some point? That would be impossible to explain. I rewrapped the gun and put it back in the drawer.

As I passed through the hallway, I took the umbrella out of its stand. It didn't look like rain, but I felt reassured by both its weight and its pointy tip. In the kitchen, I took the key from its hiding place behind a pot, locked the back door behind me, and stepped into the unlit alley. Ours was the second house from the corner, where the alley began. The house to our right was unoccupied at the moment, and I'd never once encountered anyone on my way out.

Small and sedate, Dunsmire Lane was tucked into the fringe of Mayfair. On either side of the cobbled road stood a row of well-kept homes, gracious and inviting, with short sets of mottled marble stairs leading up to glossy black-painted doors. Covering parts of the upper windows were rectangles of fine black ironwork that, as a child, I'd thought looked like lace writ large. Through some lower-story windows I could see chandeliers, luminous and sparkling; elsewhere, the curtains had already been drawn for the night. It was easy to imagine the families inside, dressing for dinner or reading the papers. Where the footpaths met, a few crossing sweeps still lingered, their brooms between their hands, signaling that they were ready to brush the refuse out of a lady's or gentleman's way for a sixpence. From somewhere above came the muted sound of a piano, and I recognized the first prelude from Bach's *Well-Tempered Clavier*. At once delicate and lively, measured and familiar, it was a fitting accompaniment to the street.

On the other side of Regent Street lay Soho, which, like most of London, was a palimpsest, its purpose having been overwritten several times. Three hundred years ago it was a royal park for Henry VIII's palace of Whitehall. A hundred and fifty years later, it had become the French Quarter. Now, it was home to people from many different countries, to small theaters and seedy brothels, cheap eating houses, and shops that catered to the poor. Here young boys, their hats tacked with the sticky strips and carcasses of flies, sold flypaper; prostitutes lurked, their slack mouths ready to twist into smiles of false desire; costermongers shouted the prices of their wares from carts and wagons. The street was strewn with the detritus of the day—horse droppings, decaying fruit, brown paper wrappings, and slats from broken crates, which would be gathered for fuel by nightfall.

I turned down Beakman Street, right at the corner, then left onto Wickley Street.

The farther I went, the more I felt I had frightened myself unnecessarily. There was no sign of danger. Dozens of people passed me, poor but ordinary men and women carrying their bread for dinner, clutching packages to their chests, holding the hands of their children. The lamp man was just lighting the gas street lamps. The cat's meat man's hoarse cry came over the wall: "Cat's meat! Last bits of the day! On a skewer, come and buy!"

I wished I could avoid the dimly lit yard behind the Octavian, but it had been impressed upon me that no matter what the time of day, I was never, ever to enter by the front door. I crossed the empty yard and tried the door, but as I expected, it was locked. I knocked loudly, and when no one answered, I banged with the handle of my umbrella.

Sid Lowry, one of the young men who helped manage the stage properties, pushed the door open a crack. "Christ, Mr. Nell! What the bloody 'ell be ye doin' 'ere so early?"

"I'm meeting the violinist. We're going to find some songs for him to play. Why? What's the matter?"

His eyes were shifting left and right around me. "Nought. Never min'." He ran a forefinger inside his cheek and flung some foul-smelling tobacco paste onto the dirt. "Old Drummond's been sittin' in his office drinkin' worse'n usual all afternoon. If you know what's good fer ye, you'll stay out o' his way."

"I always do."

He gave a snort, and I slipped past him, down the ramp, and up toward the piano alcove.

Behind the curtains, someone was playing the piano. Scales in the key of C, the first one any pianist learns.

Was Stephen here already? It was easy enough to imagine him sitting at the instrument, his elegant hands on the keys, his fine hair falling over his brow.

Then I realized that although the E was still flat, the B had been restored. Had Mr. Williams hired someone to tune the piano after all?

The scale stopped abruptly, and I heard a low grunt of annoyance. I shifted a black panel of curtain just enough to see that it was Jack Drummond's head and shoulders under the propped-up piano lid.

I swallowed a groan. If Jack wasn't careful, he could wreck the action or the pegs for good. I drew in my breath to stop him—

And then, with a wave of surprise—and something like shame—I saw that he knew exactly what he was doing. His left hand reached over the music rack to play the E again and again, while his right hand, which held some sort of instrument, moved inside the wooden cabinet.

He was completely engrossed in his work, and it altered his entire expression. Not that his face was ever hard, or cruel like his father's; it was just shuttered, as if he'd learned early on to keep his thoughts and feelings to himself. Now, his dark eyes were intent on the strings, and his black hair fell every which way. A smile quirked the side of his mouth when the note tuned true.

"There you go, you bugger," he said under his breath, but in satisfaction rather than annoyance. He bent closer to the strings.

Another minute of tuning, and he went back to the keyboard and played the octave. As he came back around the piano, I must have moved the curtain slightly, for he halted in midstep. "Who's there?"

I stepped into the alcove, letting the curtains fall back in place, and spoke in my usual rasp: "It's just me."

"Oh, hullo." He bent under the lid again, and his voice came out muffled: "You're early."

"And you're tuning my piano."

"As you said, it needed it."

I watched as he made another minute adjustment to a peg. "I shouldn't have assumed you didn't know how to do it. I'm sorry."

He didn't reply.

"You should have corrected me," I added, more sharply.

The rebuke made him look up, and our gazes caught and held. He rested an elbow on the rim, his expression thoughtful, even measuring. Then he gave a brief smile and a shrug. "Maybe. But 'twas no matter." He turned back to what he was doing. "I didn't take offense."

I set my portfolio on the bench and began to unbutton my overcoat. He plucked one of the strings. "If you want me to finish, it's going to be a while. The soundboard's gone soft, and the rain's made it worse."

"That's all right. There's plenty of time. I came early to help the new violinist choose some music."

"Mmm." He went around to the keyboard and played the scale. The E was a little too high now, but I didn't have to say so because he'd heard it, too. He frowned and ducked back under the lid.

We had our piano tuned regularly, but Mr. Kinsey was a fidgety man who had said he wouldn't work with some chit hovering over his shoulder, so I'd never seen it done. Here was my chance. "Do you mind if I watch?" I asked tentatively.

"Course not."

On the piano bench sat a dented wooden box of tools, open, so I could see inside. The device he was using was one of several he had that were about a foot long, with a pale wooden handle and a long metal piece, almost like a knitting needle, bent into an L at the top.

"Are those your tools?" I asked.

"My uncle's."

"And what's that called?"

"Tightening wrench."

It was on the tip of my tongue to ask if tuning a piano required that he speak only two words at a time, but I wasn't sure how he'd take being teased, so instead I asked, "Was it your uncle who taught you?"

"Yes." He fished in the box for a tool that looked like a crochet hook. "He owns a shop over on Samson Lane." He waved at the keyboard. "Play the C scale for me, would you?"

I went to the bench and ran my hand up the octave. The E was exactly right.

"Now the next octave."

I did as he asked. The A seemed even flatter than before.

"Put down the damper pedal." And then as an afterthought: "Please."

I pushed it with my foot. "What for?"

He rummaged in the box and drew out some little spongelike wedges. "So I can place these. They separate the three strings. Makes it easier."

I held down the pedal until he told me to let it up. Then I went round the side of the piano. He had tucked wedges in under two of the three strings. He picked up the tightening wrench and placed his left forefinger above the A key.

"I can do that," I offered.

"All right. I'm going to keep turning, and you keep playing it, every few seconds."

I went back to the keyboard.

It must have taken a dozen tiny movements of the wrench before he seemed satisfied.

I played it again. "But that's too high."

"I know. That's how you set the pin. You turn it a little high and then release it. Remember I said the soundboard's gone soft? So this is the best we can do. Now we have to do the other two."

Bit by bit, I heard the A come to a true tone through all three strings.

Jack was remarkably patient. The whole process for that one note took nearly ten minutes. Eighty-eight keys on a piano. No wonder Mr. Kinsey charged a small fortune every time he came.

Finally, Jack nodded to me. "Try it now."

I played a scale, then an arpeggio. "The upper notes are more responsive, too," I remarked, surprised and pleased.

"I put some new felt in," he said. "That won't solve the sticking problem, but it'll help."

"Thank you." I smiled up at him gratefully. "It's much better."

I played the opening measures of the prelude by Bach that I'd heard earlier. The right side of his mouth tipped into a smile as he settled the tuning instruments back in the box. I had a feeling he recognized the piece.

Midphrase, I stopped. "It was good of you to do this."

"I would've earlier, but I've been busy this month." He folded some bits of felt into neat squares. "I heard what you said once, about how playing flat keys was like having splinters under your fingernails."

"Yes, it is," I said, surprised that he remembered. I watched him put the felt away in a leather pocket. "Sometimes I even change the notes, so I can avoid the bad keys."

His eyes were on the wire he was coiling. "I know. I've heard you."

If he'd noticed that, he must have a good ear. "Do you play yourself?" I asked.

He shrugged and tucked the wire into a small envelope.

"Do you?" I pressed.

"I used to."

"Who taught you? Your uncle?"

I was sitting on the bench, looking up at him, and I saw his expression change before he turned away to close up the box. His answer came over his shoulder. "My mum. My uncle François is her older brother. She played even better than he did, till she died."

So his mother had played the piano, like mine. And he'd lost her. As the similarities struck me, I felt quite suddenly that I understood his reticence and the shuttered expression he often wore. "I'm so sorry. When was this?"

He wiped his hands with a rag. "Eleven years ago. I was ten."

I felt a pinch of envy. "I wasn't even a year when I lost mine. She was a pianist, too."

His eyes showed a flicker of sympathy. "That must be hard, to have lost her so young."

I gave the easy answer: "My brother feels it more than I do. He remembers her."

He folded the rag into a careful square. "Who taught *you* how to play?"

"I had a tutor named Johann Moehler. He died last year."

"Sure. I knew him."

I started. "You did? That's rather a coincidence."

He shrugged. "Not really. My uncle and I used to tune all the pianos at the Academy. Mr. Moehler kept one there."

I rubbed absently at a scratch on the F-sharp, remembering. Strict and exacting, Mr. Moehler had never been demonstrative, but we'd been alike in our profound commitment to music, and when he passed, I'd lost not only my instructor but also my plan; everything had changed afterward.

"He was a good teacher," I said at last.

"Obviously. You play very well."

I couldn't help a wry smile at that. "Not that the audience here appreciates it, necessarily."

He gave an answering grin.

Impulsively I said, "Jack?"

"Hmm?"

I wanted to ask if he knew where I might find Sebastian. I remembered, like a scene glimpsed in passing, Sebastian and Jack talking companionably together after a show. It wasn't surprising that they'd be friends; they were nearly the same age, and, though they were both somewhat reticent, they carried themselves with the same air of confidence—a confidence that I sensed derived at least in part from being physically able to meet the challenges of their daily life. But as I thought of Marceline in the hospital, some instinct held me back.

Hurriedly, I groped for a different question. All I could come up with was the one I had tried to ask Mr. Williams the night before: "Who is Mr. Ace?"

Jack looked puzzled.

"Mr. Williams said he was the reason the crowd was so riled yesterday," I added.

His face cleared. "Oh, you mean Jem *Mace*. He's a bare-knuckles boxer. He beat Iron Hands Kelly yesterday."

Even I'd heard of Iron Hands Kelly, one of the most famous fighters in the illegal sport.

"I didn't see it myself," he said, "but I heard it took twenty-two rounds. So it's not surprising some of the blokes were riled, if they came straight from—"

The black curtain swung aside.

It was Stephen, and his eyes darted from me to Jack. "Well, hullo!"

I felt the interruption like the twang of a broken string.

"Hello, Stephen," I said. There was a long moment when neither man said a word, so I added hastily, "Have you two met?"

Jack shook his head, his expression pleasant. "You must be the new violinist."

"That's right. And you're Jack Drummond, the owner's son." Stephen's voice was cool, even churlish, and I couldn't help but stare.

Jack also looked surprised, and a bit mystified. "That's right."

"Jack has the piano almost working properly," I said, trying to smooth away the awkwardness.

"Ah, yes. I've heard you're good at fixing things up for people," Stephen said, and though his expression was bland, there was a peculiar note in his voice. Jack's eyes narrowed slightly, and for a brief moment, as the two of them studied each other, they reminded me of two stiff-backed dogs circling in the street. But then Jack turned away, and Stephen said to me, "Shall we begin?"

Jack picked up his box of tools. "Thank you," I said to him.

With an oblique, inscrutable glance at the two of us, he pushed aside the curtain and was gone.

From behind me, I heard Stephen's voice: "Careful around him."

I felt myself bristle. "Why? He was perfectly pleasant."

He cocked his head in a way that suggested I was being a fool. Nettled by his condescension, I persisted: "Why would you say that?"

"Well, for one thing, he's a brawler from Seven Dials. He used to earn his living boxing in one of those illegal places on Monmouth Street, and he has a quick temper to go along with his fists." He set down his violin on a chair. "For another, he sticks his nose in and tries to cause trouble for people, just for the fun of it."

I drew back. "I thought you said you didn't know him."

For a moment, it seemed he stiffened, but it could just have been a pause as he thumbed the hairs on his bow and began to adjust the tension. "I don't." He glanced around my alcove. "You're out here, so you don't hear what people say. But everybody talks backstage."

I laid my hands restlessly on the keys, played a few chords. "Well, it was nice of him to tune my piano."

"It's his job to mend things around here."

"Yes, but a piano is different."

He raised an eyebrow. "Then maybe his industriousness has to do with fancying you."

I looked up in astonishment. "You think he fancies men? Don't be daft."

He snorted. "I knew you were a girl the minute you cried out last night on the stairs. You think he doesn't know, too?"

"I thought you realized it when you shook my hand," I said slowly.

"If we're splitting hairs, I had a *hunch* when you cried out and was only certain afterward. But I'm guessing he knows."

"Well, he's never hinted at it—and if he fancied me, as you say, wouldn't he give me some sort of wink?" It was true I didn't know much about men, but it seemed likely.

"Maybe he has."

I sighed. This conversation was absurd, and I was ready to be done with it.

I took up my portfolio and set it on the music rack. "I brought three pieces. What do you want to play first?"

He came to my side then, close enough that I could smell him—the scent of smoked tobacco, the slightly musty wool of his coat. "I'm sorry," he said. "I didn't mean to pick a quarrel. I just don't want you taken in after you've been so good about helping me. And you look pretty tonight, like an English rose." Then he grinned and touched my hat. "Even in this old thing."

His teasing made me laugh a bit, and the moment of annoyance was past. He nodded approvingly toward the music for "The Gambling Gents": "It's just the song for this crowd." He bent to take his violin out of its case, speaking lightly over his shoulder. "Three blokes cheating another out of his winnings."

We practiced together until it was time for the show to begin, and he was thoroughly pleasant, even playful. But what he had said about Jack nagged at me and reinforced my sense that I was right not to have asked about Sebastian. At least not yet.

But who else was there to ask?

I was still mulling this over when the blue curtains swooped up, and as I struck the opening chords, I thought: *What about Mrs. Wregge?* She was as kind and chatty a soul as there ever was. She might know who Sebastian's friends were, or where he and Marceline had lived.

And so, after the final act, I went upstairs to the costumes room, where I found her sorting through a pile of spangled bodices.

"Mrs. Wregge?"

"Yes, dear?" She looked up with a bright smile.

"Have you heard anything about what happened to the Tourneaus?"

"'Fraid not." She peered at me. "You were friendly with Marceline, weren't you?"

I nodded.

"Well, I daresay they'll be back at some point," she said. "They usually are."

"Did they ever mention where they lived, or—or maybe where they worked before here?"

She tipped her head. "Weston's, I think it was. By St. Vincent's. But if they've moved on, they could be anywhere in London, or even Manchester by now. There's halls up there, too."

I heard a noise behind me, and from behind a wardrobe stepped Stephen, shrugging into a formal black coat. "Oh, hullo, Ed." He stepped in front of Mrs. Wregge's foggy mirror and turned to her. "Is this better?"

She began twitching the shoulders this way and that, barely acknowledging my thanks as I left.

Tomorrow evening, maybe I'd visit Weston's and see if I could find someone who knew where I might find Sebastian.

Chapter 5

As I entered the dining room the next morning, Matthew didn't glance up from the newspaper, and there was a rigid set to his shoulders that I recognized.

I leaned beside him to find the headline. Halfway down the page, there it was: "Man Murdered, Scotland Yard Close to Apprehending the Killer." Quickly, I scanned the article. Matthew's name was in the third paragraph as the detective inspector.

"They gave your name," I said. He hated that.

"I know. That's one of the few facts they managed to get right."

The rancor in his voice made me study him more closely. Matthew, usually imperturbable, was both angry and worried. His face was drawn, and the grooves around his mouth were deeper than usual.

"I'm sorry." I sat down and poured us both tea, as his cup was empty. "Does this concern the man who was killed by the river?"

"Yes, in a way. Although he's only a part of it." He

closed his eyes for a moment, and when he looked at me again, his gaze was full of uncertainty. "I don't know, Nell. I think I may be making a colossal mess of things."

I stared. I had never seen him like this—not even when he first joined the police in Lambeth.

"The worst of it," he added, "is I'm at odds with everyone at the Yard."

"Everyone?"

"Well, not William."

He and William Crewe had come over to the Yard from Lambeth together. They'd each saved each other's lives at least once, and Matthew considered him his closest friend. I liked him as well; he was a forthright young man, friendly and clever.

"I'm glad to hear you've one ally, at least," I said. "But what's happened? Why are you at odds with the rest?"

"I think I've discovered something peculiar. But no one else seems to agree, and when I brought it up to Barrow, I was all but given a pat on the shoulder and told to toddle back to my desk."

Barrow was his superintendent, a man who had been hailed ten years ago for having rooted out bribery at the customs houses and who had subsequently been reassigned to Scotland Yard. He was greatly admired, although Matthew found him humorless and somewhat aloof.

"And now they think I'm the bright-eyed new detective, bent on making my cases appear more momentous and complicated than they are so that I might gain a promotion for solving them," he added with a groan.

"Oh, Matthew." I touched his arm. "Anyone who knows you wouldn't think so."

He looked unconvinced.

"Well," I continued, my tone practical, "*I've* never known you to be fanciful, so I imagine there's something to whatever you're seeing. What are the proper facts?"

"You won't mention it to anyone, of course," he said hesitantly. "It's all still a muddle."

"Matthew! I *never* do. You know that."

He balanced his teaspoon delicately on his forefinger and spun it so the silver glinted in the sunlight coming in the window. Once, twice, three times around. Finally, he set it down. "I believe there may be an organized group of very adept thieves that break into houses and shops here in London."

"Adept," I echoed. "It sounds as though you admire them."

"Well"—he gave a hard little smile—"they're proving a worthy adversary, at any rate."

I settled back in my chair to listen.

"When I first transferred," he began, "I saw the thefts around London like everyone else—just a flurry of crime that happens when too many people are crowded together and desperate enough to steal. And the items that were taken varied: jewelry, ivory, handkerchiefs and cloth, fine pens and pipes, silver, money, pieces of porcelain and carvings, even small paintings. There seemed to be no rhyme or reason to it." He leaned in on his elbows, his expression intent. "But when I started reading some of the reports side by side, I noticed the patterns. I saw it first with the houses: the thieves would rob two or three houses in a particular area, and then they'd move on, not coming back for months. But sometimes we missed it because if the houses were in different divisions—say if the street ran from Kensington to Marylebone—the reports from F Division and D Division came in separately."

"You mean that you have to connect the houses by both date and location," I said slowly.

He nodded. "From the few witness accounts, I gathered that the thieves worked in small teams—a lockpick, a lookout, and a housebreaker or two. Sometimes they came off the roof from an adjacent house, or up a trellis. Oftentimes, they seemed to know things about the family—when they had dinner, say, or when they were leaving for the theater, which suggested they had watched the house in preparation. But they're well trained in other ways, too. What made me sure of it were the objects they left behind."

"You mean things too large to carry?"

"No, Nell. They take the diamonds and leave the paste. They take the silver and leave the plate. They know the difference, as sure as any pawnbroker."

I stared.

"I didn't see it in the reports," he continued, "because of course we don't tend to note down what *wasn't* stolen; in most cases, that would be absurd. But at a burglary on Bedford Square last month, the thief—or thieves—had taken only the real pearls and gold out of the girls' bedrooms; they left the rest. And they were so unobtrusive that nobody would've known it had happened if one of the daughters hadn't asked the other to return a necklace she'd borrowed." He shook his head. "When it comes to shops, the thieves take goods that are easy to pawn and hard to trace. As with the houses, they break into two or three shops each night—and don't go back to the same street for months."

I frowned, trying to take in the scope of this. "So you think groups of thieves are coordinating their crimes, in some sort of organized circuit all over London?"

He gave me a wry look. "Now you sound like Barrow."

"Sorry." I grinned. "I promise I won't pat you on the shoulder."

"He says that given the number of thefts in London, it's easy to select a few particular ones and find a pattern in them. To him, my theory is merely a contrivance—and the more attention I pay to the patterns in my mind, the less likely it is I'll catch the thieves in front of me." He shrugged. "He's so sure, he had me convinced. At first."

"But not now?"

"No. Last week, I found someone who hinted that I might be right. A man named Powell. He was the one killed near St. Luke's. Hodges mentioned him."

"I remember," I said softly.

"Powell was a star-glazer, someone especially trained to break in through shop windows without shattering the glass. He told me that he belonged to a small group centered in Bethnal Green." He ran his hands through his hair with a sigh. "It makes me wonder if they're organized around the rookeries at St. Giles and Seven Dials. Maybe Devil's Acre as well."

"Why did Powell confess all this to you?"

He paused, and I sensed he was measuring just how much to tell me. "He is in debt to some dangerous men. He offered to talk if I'd help him and his family stay out of their way."

I caught my breath. "I—see. Did he say anything else?"

"Not really. But when I asked if there were efforts to coordinate thefts, he didn't deny it."

I must have looked skeptical, for he added, rather shortly, "What he said was, he couldn't tell me any more, or he'd be dead."

"And then he was killed," I said slowly.

Matthew's jaw was tight. "Those dangerous men aren't known for their patience, and he owed them a great deal."

"Have you told anyone at the Yard about Powell?"

"No."

"Why not?"

His eyebrows rose. "And present them with what? The words of a dead man? That's just hearsay. I'm not going to say another word until I can show some evidence."

"I understand." I shifted in my chair. "Do you think there's a chance someone found out that Powell talked?"

He frowned. "I was careful, same as always. We met in two different places, and I took every precaution to make sure I wasn't followed. So I doubt it."

"Powell's fingers were crushed, weren't they?" I asked.

"Yes. It seemed punitive—certainly gratuitous, given that he was killed. I haven't found anyone who can confirm he was a gambler." He sighed. "Kendrick, the man Hodges came about yesterday morning, never gambled a day in his life. He was a churchgoer, if you can believe it."

It took a moment for me to absorb the significance of his words—that it hadn't been Sebastian who'd been killed at the docks. Before Matthew could notice my profound relief, I picked up the newspaper and read the concluding paragraph. "It says that you're close to finding the killer."

"We're not," he said bluntly. "My guess is they said that so as not to disgrace Barrow. The papers like him." He glanced up at the clock and shoved away from the table. "I need to go. I'm due there in half an hour."

I rose as well and followed him into the front hall. "Matthew, if you're right about this group, and the person who killed these men thinks that you're getting close—"

"I know." He took his hat off the rack and turned to me. "I'm being careful, don't worry. And I've been taking extra precautions to be sure that I'm not followed here. I'd never forgive myself if I put you in danger."

Something caught in my throat at his words, making it impossible to speak. Here he was, doing all that he could to keep me safe. And here I was, putting myself in danger several nights a week.

He smiled, a real smile, and put a reassuring hand on mine. "Don't worry. It's going to be fine." He opened the door and turned back. "But bolt the door behind me."

THAT AFTERNOON, I went to the hospital again, made my way to Marceline's bed, and stood by the curtain. The large bandage that had covered both eyes was gone, but her right eye and the area over her right temple were still covered by a thick white patch, and the bandage supporting her jaw remained. I thought that she might be sleeping, but as I stepped closer to the bed, her left eye flickered and she turned toward me.

I had braced myself for this, but still, I had to fight to keep my expression cheerful. Most of her face was badly swollen. The bruises on her forehead and cheeks were plum and greenish yellow. At least the blood was gone from her hair, which had been put into a thick braid. I was glad the nurses hadn't done what might have been simpler and cut it all off.

I drew the curtain closed before I approached the bed. I didn't want anyone to witness our reunion; it would have invited a dozen questions. Bending toward her, I touched her arm, which was one of the few places that seemed unharmed. "Hello, there."

Her uncovered eye widened in surprise. She recognized me, or almost did. I guessed that she was trying to match my voice to my appearance, for she had never seen me with my hair down or in a dress. She blinked several times, and then a light came into her eye—and I sensed wonder and relief.

I sat carefully on the edge of the bed so as not to jostle her and kept my voice soft. "Marceline, the doctor says you're not to talk until your jaw heals. So perhaps you could just nod, or shake your head. And if you get tired, don't worry, I can come back later. All right?"

She nodded almost imperceptibly.

"You're in a ward in Charing Cross Hospital." I hesitated, unsure of what I should ask. "Do you remember the night you were brought here?"

A cautious shake of the head, no.

"I was on my way home from the Octavian," I said, watching her for any sign of distress. "It was quite late, and I found you in an alley. You'd been badly hurt, so I hired a cab and brought you here." I paused. "You don't remember any of it?"

There was a long pause, and then I thought I saw a look of dawning memory.

"I couldn't stay," I continued, "but I made sure you were brought safely inside by the night guard. And I brought you *here* because Dr. Everett is a family friend. His specialty is brain and head injuries. It was the best I could think of."

The look in her eye softened with what seemed like gratitude.

"But Dr. Everett doesn't know that I know you," I said. "He doesn't know I play the piano at the Octavian—he would never approve—and he doesn't know it was I who brought you here. Do you understand?"

A small nod.

"Do you know who did this to you?" I ventured. "Did you see them?"

It had been on the tip of my tongue to remind her that my brother was a policeman and might be able to bring them to justice, but the fear that sprang into her eye warned me against it. She flinched under the covers, and I could almost sense her pulse beginning to race. "It's all right," I said quickly. "You don't need to think about that now." I tried another topic, something more pleasant: "I'm sure you'll want to see Sebastian. Do you know where I can find him?"

But this seemed only to terrify her further. She gave a low, guttural cry from the back of her throat, her entire body went rigid, and a sheen of perspiration broke out on her upper lip.

Dismayed, I said, "Marceline! Please, don't upset yourself." I laid my hand on her arm. "I only want to help, honestly. I won't do anything without asking you first, I promise."

Slowly, the tension in her frame began to abate. "I haven't told the doctor who you are," I murmured. "I wasn't sure if it was safe. Do you want me to tell him?"

A tiny but definite shake of the head. I wished she had said yes. But I swallowed that down. "Then I won't." She simply stared, her dark eye wide, and I sensed there was something she urgently wished to convey.

"I know it's frustrating that you can't speak," I said sympathetically. "But Dr. Everett said it should only be a few days. And at least you're safe here. I wanted you to know that much. When you're ready, I'll do anything I can to help you. All right?"

A small crease formed at the corner of her eye, a hint of what would have been there if she'd smiled. I leaned over and kissed her forehead gingerly, to the side of the bandage. "Get some rest," I whispered and left the room.

I met Dr. Everett in the hallway just outside the ward. "Why, Nell. Good of you to come. How did she seem to you?"

"She's frightened. But I told her where she was and reassured her that she was safe. She seemed to understand." I paused. "I said I'd come back when she's able to talk. She seemed to appreciate that."

He nodded, satisfied. "If she can trust someone here, it's more likely she'll accept treatment. That's all we can hope for at this point."

We bid each other goodbye, and I turned away, feeling uncertain that I'd done the right thing in promising to withhold Marceline's name, for I knew that Dr. Everett always put the patient's best interest first. I consoled myself with the thought that Marceline would soon be able to speak for herself.

I made my way back to the front door and onto the footway that bordered Agar Street, mulling over Marceline's expressions and gestures. She was clearly against the idea of me contacting Sebastian, from which I gathered that she didn't want him to know where she was. But why?

A sudden thought stopped me cold: *Was Sebastian the one who had done this to her?*

Every instinct I had said it couldn't be. Yes, Sebastian was physically powerful enough to inflict this sort of injury; I'd seen his taut body arc and somersault in the air and watched him catch his sister, bearing both her weight and his with only one hand. But from what I'd seen, the two of them seemed intensely protective of each other. Wasn't the trapeze act itself a testament to the trust that was between them?

But perhaps it was precisely that—an *act,* with the trust merely an artifice that vanished offstage, like Amalie's French accent.

Chapter 6

$\mathscr{I}$t was Monday afternoon. I'd been at the piano for nearly six hours, and practicing was going badly. I found myself distracted—by thoughts of the audition, nine days away; of Marceline, mute and fearful; of Matthew, upon whom the long hours were beginning to tell. That morning at breakfast, he had darkening circles under his eyes and a hoarse cough from all the hours in the nighttime air.

I played the same measures of the Chopin over and over, working hard to find the proper touch in D-flat major for the arpeggios, those delicate downward flutters of notes like clear water over stones. But the harder I tried, the more muddy and murky the measures became—and at the next chord, I heard the *ping* of a broken string.

I let out a cry of frustration.

"Nell. Please. Stop."

The words came like three semibreve notes held over-long, as if there were fermatas over them. I twisted around to see Dr. Everett standing on the threshold with an expression of shock and worry that made him look years older than he was. I felt my mouth go dry. After a long moment, I said, "I didn't know you were there."

"Peggy let me in. She was leaving for an errand." His voice was toneless. "I'm sure you didn't even notice her departure. You were"—a pregnant pause—"perilously engaged in your Chopin."

I winced. "Yes, I was engaged. But not perilously so. I was just playing."

He came toward me swiftly, abandoning all pretense of calm, and fixed me with his gaze. "Just *playing*?" His voice was ragged. "You looked positively fierce, Nell! You should have seen your face. And the tilt of your head, the curve of your body over the keyboard—it's exactly like hers! When I came in, I thought I was seeing a ghost." He rubbed the heel of his hand over his forehead. "I had no idea you were playing in such a way. But then again, I haven't heard you in years."

"I play at the hospital sometimes," I said defensively.

He glared at me. "Soothing melodies for the benefit of the patients! And Christmas carols to raise funds! Don't pretend you don't know the difference." He shook his head in disbelief. "God only knows what a piece like that is doing to your brain! It's violent."

It's not violent, I thought. *It's passionate and magnificent.*

But I knew he said this out of concern, a concern I'd accepted gratefully for years, understanding that he had felt partially responsible for Matthew and me after my mother left.

I rose from the piano bench. "It's just one day of practice that didn't go well. It's not usually like this." When he didn't answer, I added in a more conciliatory tone, "I know you're worried. But only half of my brain is my mother's. And thanks to you and—and Father, I've had a logical education to balance me, and I—I know what to look for."

He threw up his hands. "That's absurd! No brain can examine itself objectively!" He leaned forward, his eyes narrowed behind his spectacles. "That piano is a dangerous partner for you, Nell. And I think you're being willfully obtuse about it—not to mention deceitful."

Stung, I drew back and remained silent as I fought down waves of hurt and mortification. He bit his lip, recovering his composure. Then, as if he'd made up his mind about something, he removed his coat, went to Matthew's usual chair, and gestured for me to take the one opposite. "Please, Nell."

I did as he asked, bracing myself for a stern lecture.

He began, in a voice laden with sorrow more than anger, "I believe this is in part my fault." In my surprise, I said nothing, and after a moment, he added, "My fault that you don't fully understand the danger that you are in."

I opened my mouth, and he raised a hand to stop my protest. "Oh, I know you've read the scientific papers. And I've observed you over the years as you have learned to mitigate your feelings so that you show less than you feel and perhaps even feel less than you might."

Somewhat mollified, I nodded.

"When you were younger, you took it on faith that I knew what was best for you. But now that you are nearly grown"—he stopped himself with a wistful expression—"I beg your pardon, you *are* grown. But as you were a child for so much longer than you've been a woman, it's not been my habit to think of you as such. I daresay in my mind, you are still thirteen, or thereabouts."

I couldn't help but smile. "I daresay there's parts of me that *are* still much as they were at thirteen."

He looked rueful. "Not many, my dear. But I see now that I

have done you a disservice. I believe I was right to provide you first with medical information about your mother's disease—scientific theories and abstract generalities—but at some point I should have shared the specifics of your mother's condition. Yes," he said heavily. "I see now that I was wrong not to tell you."

"I don't agree," I protested. "Your reticence was perfectly understandable. You didn't want to cause me pain, and I'm sure some of the—the specifics aren't pleasant."

"Nor did I want to frighten you unnecessarily." He spread his hands in a gesture of openness, or perhaps defeat. "But perhaps the other reason I held back is that with respect to your mother's case"—a long pause, and a deep breath—"I failed utterly. And frankly, I didn't want to see the blame in your pretty blue eyes." His own eyes were sad. "They're a good deal like hers, you know."

"Doctor—"

He put up a hand to stop me again, but this time I ignored him, my words coming out in a rush: "Whatever you did for her, and for me, please believe that I *know* it was done with the best of intentions, and with all the medical knowledge available. I could never blame you for trying to help her—and for helping my father afterward," I said earnestly. "I have a great deal to thank you for."

A thin smile. "That is kind of you, Nell. And I do believe you mean it. But if you want to show your gratitude, you will listen to me now. Because I could not bear it if your mother's disease came upon you, when a few words from me—however unpleasant and unwelcome—might prevent it." He hesitated, his expression irresolute. "Mind you, there are things I didn't even tell your father . . . didn't even put into my case notes, because I never wanted him to know."

The room was silent, except for the clock at my elbow, which was ticking more steadily than my heart. Finally, I said, "I understand."

He went to the decanter at the sideboard and raised it to pour himself two fingers of whiskey. After a swallow, he rested both the glass and his right forearm on the mantel and turned to me, his manner reminding me that he was not only a doctor but also a lecturer at University College.

"Before I undertake a course of treatment, I speak with people who knew the patient before the disease manifested itself," he began. "In your mother's case, there were several family members to whom I could appeal—your father, of course, but also Frances's own aunt Louise, who had known her since birth and was thus most valuable. By her account, Frances had always been a lively and talented child, with a tendency to exaggerate her own emotions, but no more so than is usual for imaginative children. Your mother showed a remarkable talent for the piano early on, and her parents fostered it with lessons, and bought her that"—his eyes flicked to the piano—"for her sixth birthday. There was little in her young adulthood to suggest what would happen later." He turned the glass thoughtfully on the mantel. "As you know, she met and married your father when she was nineteen."

I knew what he left unsaid: *the age you are now.*

"He left for the sea, and shortly afterward, she realized she was with child," he continued.

"Matthew," I interjected.

He nodded. "When your father returned six months later, he noticed a significant change in her. She seemed depressed in her spirits, so he called upon me. I prescribed some tonics, advised a daily hour of exercise out of doors, and administered a few other therapies—all benign, but none effective in her case. Her depression only deepened. I believe we all hoped that it was merely an effect of her condition. That when the baby came, she would naturally improve."

"And did that happen?"

He hesitated. "Not exactly. Oh, she became more animated after Matthew arrived. He seemed to be the distraction she needed. But what I saw as elevated spirits was really the onset of the mania—although I had no way of knowing that." He rubbed at his brow unhappily. "Oh, perhaps I should have suspected, but I think I was so relieved—for her and for your father—that I blithely believed that she had been cured due to my wise and benevolent care." His tone was derisive.

It pained me to see him raking himself needlessly over the coals. "I'm sure you did everything possible—"

"No, I didn't," he said sharply. "I certainly didn't observe her symptoms as closely as I might have." A pause, and then he recovered his poise. "I beg your pardon, Nell. I know you mean well. But I've had years to reflect upon this. Hindsight truly does provide a remarkable clarity."

I remained silent, and after a moment he drained his glass and set it down soundlessly. When he spoke, it was with the air of someone determined to confess the worst.

"For nearly two years, her symptoms seemed milder, or perhaps we began to accept her fragility as normal. She seemed reasonably happy and our concerns—still quite nominal, mind you—abated. Peggy had been working as a housekeeper here since their marriage, but her husband, Joe, had died; and when your father was scheduled for another tour of duty at sea, he asked her to come stay here with Emma, so that she could help more with Matthew."

"And to keep an eye on Mother, no doubt."

He nodded. "Particularly because it soon became apparent that Frances was again with child—with you. And the trouble began anew. During the six months your father was away, the cycles of melancholy and mania increased in frequency. At times she could barely rouse herself to come to the breakfast table, and worst of all, she showed no interest in Matthew. Other times, she laughed too heartily and talked in a hurried, erratic fashion, becoming impatient with us when we didn't understand. She had trouble sleeping, and it became clear to me that there were two initiating symptoms that were easy to observe." He ticked them on his fingers. "If she began to stay in bed longer than ten hours at a time, it signaled an oncoming phase of melancholy. If she began to play the piano for more hours than she was sleeping, that signaled oncoming mania." His expression was grave. "To me it seemed that the instrument fed her illness."

"*Fed* it?" I echoed.

"Even when she was at her most stable, it exacerbated your mother's moods, multiplied their severity, so she went from sad to miserable, or from happy to ecstatic. When the mania struck, she stayed up until two or three in the morning, playing feverishly and composing new music—only to tear up everything she'd written. Peggy would find shreds of paper all over the carpet."

His words felt like knives carving into some soft part of me. But I couldn't parry them. How could I? I had never known the woman he was describing.

"As you can imagine, I was reading everything I could on the disease. I consulted with other physicians and tried various treatments." His expression was bleak. "But nothing helped. So finally, we sent for your father."

I could only imagine my father's feelings, being far away and receiving a telegram telling him Mother was ill again and asking him to come home.

"He returned by the next ship, of course." He grimaced. "I was here to meet him. You and Matthew had been removed to your aunt Margaret's house. Your mother had spent two days in bed, refusing to get up even to relieve herself, soiling the bedclothes and lying inert when Peggy tried to help her."

My mouth went dry, imagining my mother in such a state and my father returning home to find her so.

"We went into her room together, expecting to find her in bed. But by then she had begun to come out of her melancholy. She'd stripped the soiled linens, and she ordered your father out of the room. Then she behaved lasciviously, removing her clothes, and insisting that she had long desired me." His voice was matter-of-fact, but his eyes were averted. "It was a secondary symptom of the disease, of course. She had no more desire for me than a cat for a dog."

Sign of the disease or not, I felt the blood hot in my cheeks and a tightness in my throat. No wonder Dr. Everett had taken such pains to try to prevent this disease in me.

"I managed to sedate her," he continued, "but when the medication wore off, she lay in her bed, curled up like a child, saying she no longer wanted to live." He spun his empty glass slowly. "You were born shortly after, and we all hoped that what had happened with Matthew would happen with you. But instead, she became still worse."

He saw something in my expression that made him pause. It seemed to me that he thought better of what he was about to say. After a moment, he resumed. "You were only a few months old when she entered a manic phase that seemed more fierce than usual. I begged your father to have her admitted to my hospital, but he couldn't bear the thought of her being away from her children. She began to proclaim that England was the wrong place for her genius—that she belonged in Vienna, Paris, or Munich." He bit his lip. "And then one evening, when your father was gone for an hour, she packed her clothes and her music. Peggy was upstairs in the nursery with you, and when she heard your mother's footsteps in the hall, she came out, carrying you. She saw your mother heading down the stairs, dressed warmly and holding a portmanteau. Peggy called to her, and then she heard Matthew ask Frances where she was going."

He stared into midair, as if he were picturing all of it, as I was. "As Peggy came to the top of the stairs, she saw Matthew on the landing, trying to keep your mother from leaving. But Frances pushed him aside, and he fell to the bottom, breaking his arm in the process."

With those words, I felt as if I'd been struck myself. I'd grown up seeing the scars below his left elbow. I knew that he had broken his arm. But I hadn't known all this.

"She didn't even look at him. She just strode out the door." He turned the glass several more times. "Naturally, Peggy stayed with you and Matthew. Your father arrived home shortly afterward, at which time he contacted the police. Detectives managed to trace her to a steamer, where she had booked passage to Calais under an assumed name. Your father went after her, but to no avail."

His tone signaled that this was the end of his narrative; and I let go of the breath I'd been holding.

He looked at me sorrowfully. "Now do you understand why your father and I devised the special education for you, and why I have cautioned you against excessive feeling of any kind? And why, when I hear you play as you just did on that thing"—he gestured toward the piano, the snap of his wrist suggesting that he would shove it out of the room if he could—"can you blame me for being frightened for you?"

His words had created a cold fear in me, one that began at my spine and ran along my every nerve. "I understand," I said. "Of course I do."

A look of relief came over his face. "Thank God."

"Have you ever told Matthew any of this?" I asked quietly. "Is he in danger?"

He shook his head. "I believe he remembers enough of your mother's behavior to need no warning. Besides, his brain isn't like yours. He's much more like your father, as you know. Eminently practical—at times even phlegmatic—not to mention tone-deaf. And he is past the dangerous age."

"How can you be so sure?"

"Not only is the disease inherited," he explained patiently, "but there is evidence that the age of onset is passed from parent to child as well. So if your mother's symptoms began to emerge at nineteen and became full-fledged at twenty-three, it is virtually guaranteed that the disease will appear in her children at that time, if it appears at all. Matthew, being twenty-five, is past danger. But you are not." He straightened up, leveling his gaze on me. "Nell, I want you to give up the piano. Not forever. Just for the next few years."

Something like an iron band tightened, hard, around my heart. I sat stunned and silent.

"Nell? I want you to promise me."

I spoke through the lump in my throat. "I . . . can't."

His eyes widened, and he removed his spectacles, pinching the bridge of his nose between this thumb and forefinger. "You cannot tell me that playing piano is worth your sanity."

"Of course not, but . . ."

He flung his arms out in a gesture of frustration. "But what? You said you understood!"

"I *do* understand," I said earnestly, "and I promise to be careful. If I see any of the symptoms you saw in Mother, I'll stop immediately."

He glared at me. "So you *don't* understand. The very disease precludes you from being able to stop yourself. Don't you see?"

I felt tears rise to my eyes.

"Oh, good God." He gave an exasperated sigh and turned away to rest both hands and his forehead on the mantel.

We were silent for several long minutes.

Finally, he turned back with a resigned expression. "Well, you have been raised to reason for yourself; I suppose I am to blame for that, too." His voice was bitter with disappointment, and I could hardly breathe for unhappiness.

"I'm sorry," I said, my voice breaking. "I have no wish to cause you worry. I'll come to you the minute I see any symptoms of sleeplessness, or—or lying abed for hours. Truly, I will."

He pursed his lips. "If you must practice, will you at least promise me that you will try to do so with patience and moderation—and some restraint?"

"Yes." I felt so relieved, I would have promised anything.

"Very well." He studied me for a moment. "We will talk about this again in a month."

I nodded.

A sigh rose from deep inside his chest, and he shook his head.

"This wasn't even why I came here. To lecture you, I mean. I came because the girl asked for you."

Marceline's name almost escaped my lips, but I caught myself in time. "She did?"

"Well, not in so many words. She asked for the girl who plays piano." His head tipped and he looked at me searchingly. "How did she know that?"

"Oh—well, I told her," I said. "Only because I was trying to speak of something that wouldn't upset her. It's rather difficult to hold a conversation with someone who can't reply." I managed a smile.

He frowned. "It's an odd thing. She doesn't seem to remember anything from the night she was injured, or much of the last few days. But she remembered that single fact." He peered at me, and I nearly squirmed under his scrutiny. Then he shrugged. "Unfortunately, she seems quite wary of the nurses and me, and downright terrified at the idea of the police. So I'm glad she feels at ease with you."

"I'll come see her, of course."

"Not today, as I have some treatments planned. Tomorrow would be best."

I nodded.

He started for the door, and I followed. I removed his coat from the rack, and I helped him into it, one arm at a time, then handed him his hat. He took me by the shoulders and kissed my forehead, an unusual mark of care. I saw the worry in his eyes— and I understood it wasn't only for me; he was fearful that he hadn't said enough, or the right sorts of things.

It made me want desperately to reassure him. "I'm glad you

told me, for you've put me on my guard in a different way, truly, and I—I understand so much more now."

He gave a small smile. "Well, the good thing is that you can't play any more today; there is a blessing in a broken string."

I returned his smile, relieved that he had recovered enough to make a joke.

After he left, I stood with my hand on the door. I'd been playing the Chopin for months, with seemingly no ill effects. I'd even had a few experiences lately—such as finding Marceline injured—that had severely frightened me, yet I slept deeply and ate well and felt no desire to stay up all night or withdraw to my bed. I hadn't noticed anyone struggling to understand my speech; nor did I feel impatient conversing with people.

But perhaps it would be wise to change to practicing the more measured, delicate Mozart for a while, just to be sure.

I sent a note to Mr. Kinsey about the repair. He might not come for a day or two. But if I couldn't practice anymore at home, I could at least practice later at the Octavian.

Thanks to Jack, I had a piano that was reasonably in tune.

THAT NIGHT, I went to the Octavian early. The door was still closed, so I knocked, and after a moment, Sid Lowry opened the door and stepped aside. "Violinist was here 'afore, but 'e left again."

"It's all right, Sid. I'm just early."

I reached the alcove, turned up the lights, and removed my overcoat.

It wasn't until I sat down on the bench that I saw the single long-stemmed white rose on the fallboard. This rose was nothing like the ones we sold here. It was a large bud, pale as sugar, with a thread of red on the petals. The green stem was very dark—almost black—thick and freshly cut. I picked it up and inhaled. Its perfume was luxurious and exotic, about as far from the stink of cheap cigar smoke and spilled gin as one could get. I touched the leaves, feeling their silken coolness, and remembered Stephen's bit of flattery, about me looking like an English rose. Sid had said Stephen was here earlier. Could he have left the rose, perhaps out of gratitude for my help?

I set it beside me on the bench and opened my portfolio. The hall was completely empty; the doors wouldn't open for at least another hour. I laid out the pages of the first movement of the Mozart sonata, the Allegro moderato, and played it through once, more slowly than usual, finding my way to the section that was giving me some trouble. When I found it, I paused, took a breath, and reminded myself of the promises I'd made to the doctor: *patience and moderation,* I thought. *And restraint.* Besides, frustration such as I had felt that afternoon with the Chopin would do me no good.

Over and over, I played the twenty-two measures. I wanted the melody to come trippingly and lightly, without sounding hurried, and finally my fingers caught all the notes exactly as I wanted them, including a troublesome D that my fourth finger didn't always find as fully as I wished. I breathed a sigh of satisfaction and then, to set the measures back into place, I played the first movement in its entirety before I stopped, content with it and pleased with myself. It was only a short session of practice, but I felt that, had Dr. Everett been there watching, he might have been reassured.

"That isn't in the show," came a man's voice.

I looked up from the keys. Jack was standing at the curtain, a pair of wrenches held in one hand and an absorbed expression on his face that sent a peculiar flutter through me.

The silence hung between us as we looked at each other. "How long have you been listening?" I asked, remembering at the last second to alter my voice.

"Isn't that one of Mozart's?"

I kept my surprise to myself. I wasn't about to be caught underestimating Jack again. "It's his sonata in C major."

He came into the alcove and let the curtain close behind him. His dark eyes were thoughtful. "You weren't just playing. You were practicing."

I made no reply.

"I won't tell anyone," he said. "Do you have an audition?"

I nodded, reluctantly. "For the Royal Academy."

A look of understanding lit his face. "Is that why you're playing here? To earn tuition?"

"Yes."

"So you'll begin in the fall."

"If I'm accepted."

He frowned. "Why wouldn't you be?"

I hesitated. I wasn't going to tell him that of the twenty students enrolled last year, only three were women. But he seemed to be waiting for an honest reply, and at last I uttered part of the truth: "They've never admitted anyone my age."

To my relief, he didn't laugh, and when he replied, his voice was neither falsely reassuring nor condescending. "Well, they certainly *have* students your age. And I'm not the judge my uncle is, but I'd say that you're as good as any of them, if not better than most."

"I guess we'll see," I replied, unsure how to accept his compliment. I gestured to the wrenches in his hand. "What are those for?"

"Oh, the piano," he said carelessly, pointing the wrenches toward the pedals. "The damper was sticking yesterday, so I thought I'd thump it a few times."

I gaped. "What?"

He laughed, a warm sound. "I'm joking. The wheel was loose on one of the unicycles."

"Oh!" I couldn't help but laugh back.

Through the black curtains came the sound of the front door opening and the usual shouts and scrapes of the chairs against the floor as the audience began to crowd inside.

"Aren't you supposed to be at the door?" I asked. "Fending off the pickpockets?"

He shook his head. "Sid's there. I'm tending to the bar tonight. I just finished unloading a crate of wine."

"Jack!" Mr. Williams bellowed as if on cue. "Where the devil are you?"

Jack gave me a look that was equal parts amusement and exasperation and drew an eyebrow iron corkscrew, with a bit of cork blunting the sharp end, from his pocket. He waved it at me, and then he parted the curtains and was gone.

Chapter 7

That night, Stephen's act was very well received, with shouts and cheers at his final bow. He gestured toward me in thanks; but we didn't exchange a word until after the show, when he drew the curtain aside.

"Hello, Nell." His eyes were glittering, and there was an air of ebullience and triumph about him. He laid a hand on the fallboard and bent toward me, his mouth close to my ear, so he could be heard above the racket of the stage properties being wheeled off. "They loved us tonight, did you notice?"

I shifted away from him and nodded. "They were singing along."

His eyes fell on the rose that still lay on the piano. I touched it. "Did you leave this for me?"

He grinned and raised an eyebrow. "I told you, you're like an English rose. Do you like it?"

I felt a twinge of disappointment that I didn't pause to reflect upon. "Yes, thank you." I smiled. "It's lovely."

Surreptitiously, he leaned forward again, almost close enough for a kiss, and touched a piece of hair that had escaped my pins. "Careful there."

I pushed the lock back up into my hat.

"I can't have you getting fired," he said as he returned to standing. "You don't even know how much luck you've brought me. Say, can you dine with me tonight?"

I looked up from tying my portfolio. "I don't think so. It's late."

"So? You've been here for hours. You *must* be hungry."

At the thought of food, my stomach made a perceptible complaint.

"There, I can tell you are by your face. Come with me." His voice became persuasive. "Please. It's my way of saying thank you."

I hesitated. Matthew had been coming home well after midnight for weeks. But . . .

He glanced toward the stage, where Sid and the others were dismantling the scenery from the final act. "It's perfectly respectable, you know," he said, his voice low. "Two blokes having dinner after the show."

"I know. It's just that my brother gets home from work, and I need to be there."

"What time is he usually home?"

"Not until at least one," I admitted. "Lately."

"I'll have you home by midnight. I promise," he wheedled.

My stomach growled again. "All right," I relented and followed him out of the alcove.

We'd almost reached the door to the street when it opened and Jack appeared. Seeing us, he stepped back and held it wide for us to walk through.

"Hullo," Stephen said and moved so that he and I were farther apart.

Did I imagine it, or did Jack's eye note Stephen's rose under the ribbon of my portfolio? But he simply nodded and said, "Night."

Something about his tone of voice brought a flush to my cheek, and I was glad for the cool night air. Perhaps Stephen sensed my agitation because as we entered the Mews, I felt him dart a series of oblique glances toward me, and his exuberance faded, replaced by a covert scrutiny. I had a moment of misgiving, suddenly wishing that I were heading home to have a plain bowl of bread and milk and go to bed. It was on the tip of my tongue to say so, but just at that moment, Stephen asked, "You're becoming friendly with Jack Drummond, aren't you?"

His voice carried a challenge, and I had the sense again, as I'd had on Thursday night when the three of us were in the alcove, that Stephen had feelings about Jack that seemed out of proportion to the circumstances. My curiosity kept me walking beside him.

"No more than with anyone else here," I said. "Why?"

He shrugged the question away.

"No, Stephen, really," I said, unwilling to let the matter drop. "You seem to dislike him a great deal, though I can't imagine you've had much to do with him."

"You're right, *I* haven't," he acknowledged. "But—well—I didn't tell you the other thing I heard about him. That he has a habit of striking up—er, friendships with the women performers. And if they don't like it, he has Mr. Williams fire them."

I stopped dead and stared at him, a sick feeling roiling inside me.

"It happened last year with a singer." His expression was apologetic, as if he regretted having to tell me. "I'm only saying this to put you on your guard."

We had reached Regent Street, and I was grateful for the noisy rumble of carriages and cabs that precluded talking. I understood the warning Stephen wanted me to take from this. But could the story possibly be true? It didn't seem to fit with what I knew of Jack. And I could practically hear Matthew's voice in my ear: *This is the problem with hearsay; the best it can do is to introduce all sorts of suspicion, and at least half the time it's false.*

When at last we turned onto a quieter street, Stephen said, "You look like you don't believe me."

"It's not that I don't believe you. But it's an ugly story," I said. "I'd hate to think anyone would abuse their influence that way."

He snorted. "There are a lot of ugly stories, and plenty of his kind abuse their influence, as you say, to hurt decent people."

The strain in his voice suggested that he had received this sort of treatment himself, and recently enough that the injury was still raw.

"Well, let's never mind them for now and enjoy ourselves," I said lightly. "Where are we going?"

He seemed glad enough to take my cue and smiled down at me. "Don't worry. You'll like it. The chef studied with Urbain Dubois, who worked for the Hohenzollern family, and the food is excellent."

We crossed into Mayfair, and he led me up a street that was broader and finer than mine, with elegant porticos set back from the footway. He stopped at number 74 and pushed open the door.

It had once been a house but had been converted to a fine

eating establishment. A thick Turkish carpet covered most of the marble floor of the foyer, an electrified chandelier sparkled overhead, and the rooms to my left and right held tables set with fine white linen and silver candlesticks that shimmered in the light from the wall sconces. Somewhere a quartet of string instruments played a concerto that I'd never heard, performing it so well that I wondered how Stephen seemed not to notice it. But then again, he'd been here before. As we waited for the proprietor, I surveyed the diners—the men in black coats and the women with their bare shoulders and glittering jewelry—and suddenly became aware that Stephen, in his own elegant coat and trousers, was dressed far more suitably than I, in my secondhand music hall attire.

Feeling the blood rise to my cheeks, I muttered under my breath, "Stephen, I don't belong here."

"Nonsense. If you're with me, you belong. I used to come here all the time with my father."

There was no time for me to answer, for the maître d'hôtel came toward us. A look of consternation flashed across his face, but was replaced immediately by a polite smile: "Good evening, Mr. Gagnon."

"We'll sit in the back room, please, Wilson," Stephen said, with the air of someone accustomed to being given his choice here. Again I found myself wondering why on earth this man was playing violin at a music hall for a few pounds a week. I couldn't remember ever having met anyone so full of contradictions.

Wilson stiffened, and his voice became even more proper: "I'm afraid that room is full."

Stephen's eyes narrowed. "You mean my father is here."

The maître d's face remained impassive. "I think you would be more comfortable in this side room." He gestured to the room on our right, and I prepared to follow him. "I have an excellent table near the fire—"

"We'll sit in this room," Stephen said, pointing to the left.

The maître d's lips tightened, and he inclined his head. "Very good. Please come with me."

He seated us at the lone unoccupied table, only large enough for two, near a window. I felt the draft immediately as we sat down. Why the need to sit in this room, at this uncomfortable table? And why would the maître d' be so intent on keeping Stephen and his father apart? Nonplussed, I drew my napkin onto my lap before I realized that the waiter had intended to do it for me.

He laid the white cloth across Stephen's lap, and as he turned away, Stephen's expression grew obdurate. "I'm sorry about that. But I want to see my father. And this is the only way I can. He'll have to walk through this room to get to the front door."

He must have seen how I felt about serving as a pretext for coming here, for he hastened to add, "I would have come alone, if you'd said no. I haven't seen my father in over a month. And he usually has a late dinner here on Mondays."

"But why can't you see your father when you like?"

"Because he's disowned me. Cut me off without a shilling, as they say in novels."

"Disowned you?" I echoed skeptically.

"It's a rather long story, and not even particularly interesting—"

The waiter interrupted to serve us wine, and as Stephen went silent, I heard a particularly beautiful passage from the quartet.

Impulsively, I asked the waiter, "What is this piece of music?"

He finished pouring before he answered. "I don't know. But I can find out if you'd like."

"Yes, please."

He left us, and I took a sip of wine. Matthew and I rarely had it at home, and I savored the tang of it across the front of my tongue, the warmth as it slid down my throat.

"I'd like to tell you—if you really want to hear it," Stephen said.

It took me a moment to realize that he was referring to his story. And though his tone was diffident, I had the growing impression not only that I'd been brought to dinner to hear it and sympathize but also that I was being conscripted into some private drama of Stephen's designing—rather like one of Hamlet's players, an unwitting accomplice in catching the king.

"Of course I want to hear." I sat back and arranged my napkin in my lap. "Especially if it has to do with how you ended up at the Octavian."

My genuine interest reassured him, and his eyes dropped to the wineglass that he was turning in a slow circle on the table. When he finally looked up, his expression was sober, even sad.

"You told me you live with your brother," he began. "Do you get on?"

"Yes, mostly."

"Well, I have a brother, too—a very smart, charming elder brother—and we don't. The truth is, he's always been my father's favorite." He shrugged. "But it's to be expected. They're very much alike."

"What's his name?"

"Alfred. Same as my father—and his father." He took a sip of his wine. "Back in the thirties, my grandfather began a shipping company. It did quite well, but when my father took over, it grew from four vessels to twenty. That's when he began to move in better circles, which is where he met my mother, who is a relation—

albeit somewhat distant—of the Earl of Hardwicke. About eighteen months after they married, my brother Alfred was born."

"How much older than you is he?"

"Two years." He paused. "We're as different as night and day. He was always a fine student, especially in maths and history, and from the start, he was intrigued by my father's business, whereas all I cared about was music. I played my mother's piano from the time I was only two years old. When I was five, she bought me a violin and took me to Monsieur Rambeau. Do you know who he is?"

I shook my head.

"He's one of the best violin teachers in London. His family fled France during the Revolution."

"Of 1848?"

"Of 1789. His grandparents came with the clothes on their backs, a violin, and a gold ring, which—so the story goes—his grandfather pawned for a new bow the minute he got to London, so he could fiddle in the street for their supper." An admiring smile crossed his lips. "At any rate, I began to study with him, and when it became clear I had talent, my mother spoke to my father about sending me to the Royal Academy. At first he refused to even consider it. His business holdings had grown so large, he felt he would eventually need both sons at the helm. His idea was that my brother could manage the financial end of things, and I could do some of the traveling required because I have an ear for languages. But my mother prevailed, and though my father refused to put more money than was absolutely necessary toward my 'useless fiddling,' as he called it, he allowed me to go to the Academy when I was twelve." He paused for a moment, his eyes distant. "Everything was quite brilliant, until my sixth year, when a lie was spread that I'd organized a gambling party to steal my best friend's violin."

I stared, surprised by this odd turn to the story. "Why would anyone do that?"

He shook his head. "I've no bloody idea. I wasn't even allowed to confront my accuser. I was simply thrown out."

"But that's absurdly unfair," I said. "Surely there must have been a way to appeal, or—"

"They had what looked like proof. A pawn ticket among my things—that I'd never seen before—and the word of another one of his friends." He shrugged, but his voice gained a bitter edge. "So I went to work for my father. I had no choice. Every day at seven o'clock, I accompanied him to the office, and every night I dreamed about escaping. All those numbers and dollars and crates and pounds of tea and bolts of silk." A short, hard laugh escaped his lips. "I tried to care, but I just couldn't. And then I made a bookkeeping error and lost nearly five hundred pounds."

My hand flew to my mouth. That was an enormous sum.

He winced. "I know. It was terrible. But—if it did nothing else, it showed that I had no business being there in the first place." He leaned forward, his expression earnest. "Don't you see? If my mind was so far away that I was going to make a mistake like that—well, I was never going to be any good at it!"

I found myself agreeing. "What did your father say?"

He sighed and sat back in his chair. "He was furious, of course. I told him the only thing I cared about was the violin, and he told me I could go to the devil, or wherever I liked, but he washed his hands of me. So my mother gave me some money, and I found a room with a friend I'd known at the Academy. I played for a while in a quartet at the Golden Bough."

I nodded. It was one of the smaller music halls in London, patronized by those who liked classical music.

"But then it was time to move on, and I didn't find a place right away. So I busked at Covent Garden until Mr. Williams found me."

"You've had a rotten run of luck," I observed, feeling genuinely sorry for him.

A flicker of a smile appeared. "Well, it seems to be changing. I think the Octavian is a good place for me—at least for a while. And I have you to thank for it."

I smiled in return. "Well, if I helped you, I'm glad."

At that moment, our first course, a fish soup, arrived. As the waiter set it down, he murmured, "I asked about the music, sir. It is a new work by a composer named Dvořák. Number five in F minor, and it was composed last year."

I'd heard of Dvořák but not this piece. I committed its name to memory, to find later, and thanked the waiter with a smile.

As I had not eaten since teatime, the smell of the broth made the saliva come into my mouth, and I applied myself to it eagerly. The soup was creamy and thick, and the pieces of fish came apart, sweet and salty, against my tongue.

Stephen seemed as hungry as I was, and we ate in silence for several minutes. Finally, I wiped my mouth with my napkin and said, "Well, forgive me for saying so, but it seems rather hopeless. If your father is determined to think the worst of you, why do you want to see him tonight?"

"Because he wants to pretend that I don't exist . . . and I—"

He shook his head and the words came out in a rush: "I just want to tell him that I don't need his money—I don't even *want* his money. What I'm making at the Octavian is plenty for my needs . . . and"—his voice dropped so I had to lean forward to hear the rest—"all I want is to be his son again."

There was a plaintive tone in his voice that struck me as self-pitying; but then I considered the resentment and frustration I would surely feel if I had been unjustly thrown out of the Royal Academy and imagined it would color every story I told, too.

"I understand that," I said gently. "I hope he can forgive you."

He nodded and set aside his spoon. "Now, I don't want to talk about all this anymore," he said. "Tell me about your studies."

"Oh, my story isn't anywhere near as engrossing as yours," I said. "I had lessons with Mr. Moehler until he passed away, and now I'm hoping to study at a conservatory someday."

His eyes lit with interest. "Here or abroad?"

"Here, I think. I wouldn't want to leave my brother. He's my only family."

"Is he a musician, too?"

I smiled, amused at the thought. Matthew wasn't quite as tone-deaf as Dr. Everett said, but he couldn't play a tune to save himself. "No. He works at Scotland Yard."

Stephen gave a quick, involuntary movement. "Really? Is he a detective?"

"Yes. He's been there for about a year now. He was in uniform before that—"

Suddenly Stephen's eyes jerked away from me, and his hand, which held his wineglass, stopped on its way to his mouth. I turned to find the object of his gaze. Walking through the arch-way from the back room was a tall, prosperous-looking man with slightly stooped shoulders and silvered hair. His face was impassive, but he was moving quickly and purposefully toward the door. I glanced at Stephen and my suspicions were confirmed: Mr. Gagnon knew exactly where his son was sitting.

I watched as Stephen rose and moved to intercept him, his face hopeful. "Good evening, Father," he said and laid his hand on the older man's arm. I saw them both in profile, and it was as if they were mirror images—one older than the other, but with the same high forehead, the same fine cheekbones, the same chin. Then Stephen said something I didn't catch, and a look of contempt came over his father's face. Mr. Gagnon spoke a few words that erased Stephen's smile, then continued toward the door without a backward glance.

Stephen stood still for a moment, seemingly taken aback. I saw that several other diners in the room were watching, and some had raised their napkins to conceal their amused expressions. After a moment, Stephen noticed them as well. The blood rose to his cheeks, and his spine stiffened just as the maître d' appeared at Stephen's elbow to direct him back to our table.

He sat down and took a large swallow of his wine. I watched him carefully for a moment before I spoke. "I'm sorry, Stephen. What did he say?"

"To stop embarrassing him in public," Stephen replied shortly.

It seemed another instance of his father's injustice. "That hardly seems fair. It isn't as if you assaulted him or started a row in the middle of the room. You simply tried to speak to him."

His eyes were dark with fury, and I realized with a start that his face wore the same expression I'd seen the first night at the Octavian, when the crowd had jeered him.

His fingers tightened on his wineglass. "He's *never* been fair.

But this is the end of it. I shan't take any more pains with him." He looked with disdain at the last of the soup, congealed in the bowl. "I'm not hungry anymore. Do you mind if we leave?"

"Not at all." The other patrons were still glancing our way, and I didn't relish the scrutiny.

Stephen paid for our dinner, and in a matter of minutes we were outside, in the chill night air.

"I'll get you a cab," he said. "What's your address?"

"Dunsmire Lane, number fourteen."

"This way." We walked together toward the corner, and he raised an arm.

He seemed wrapped in his own bitter thoughts, and I suddenly felt weary to the bone and wishing I'd never come. We stood together in silence until a cab stopped. Stephen gave the address, and I wished him good night and climbed in, relieved to feel the jolt of the wheels against the road.

The church clock struck three times. I held my breath, waiting to hear nine more chimes for midnight. But there was only silence.

"Driver," I called. "What time is it?"

"A quarter to one," came back at me.

I groaned, realizing the folly of what I'd done.

Well, one thing was certain, I couldn't have the cab rolling up to my door. "Driver! Could you let me off at Cork Street instead?"

"Aye. Same to me."

"And please hurry!"

The cab rattled a bit faster over the cobbles, and then drew up. I climbed out, paid the fare, and scanned Cork Street. There was no one about—only a cat prowling along the wall, its eyes shining in the darkness—and no lights on inside our house.

Did that mean my brother was still at work? Or already in bed? Or—the worst possibility—had he found me missing and, terrified of what might have happened, gone out looking for me? The last thought had me running the rest of the way to the back door.

I turned the key in the lock with painstaking care. My heart pounding, I stole inside, closing the door so the sound was barely audible. I held still and listened. Nothing.

In the dark, I hung the key in its proper place, took off my boots, and made for the hall in my stocking feet. In my haste, I nearly knocked over the umbrella stand. I snatched at the rim and set it upright with shaky fingers. That would just do it, if Matthew were home—the copper cylinder crashing to the floor, him flying downstairs in his nightshirt, finding me in my masculine garb—

But as I rounded the banister, I saw that the coatrack was empty, and I gave a sigh of relief.

Boots in hand, I started up the stairs. I'd just reached the landing when the clock struck the top of the hour, and behind me I heard the key turn in the front door. I took the remaining stairs two at a time and dashed into my room. Frantically, I flung the boots under my bed, fumbled my hat off and under my pillow, and got between the covers.

I heard Matthew's footsteps come up the stairs and pause in front of my door. And then—what made him do it tonight of all nights, when he had never done so before, to my knowledge?—he opened the door and looked in. My back was to him, so all he could see was the lump of my body and my hair. Something about him waiting there made me want to squirm, but I held myself still.

At last I heard my door close, followed by his, a muted echo of mine, at the end of the corridor.

Chapter 8

As I'd promised Dr. Everett, I went to the hospital the next day. In the foyer, I was handed a note in his hand, asking me to come to his office. I went reluctantly, dreading a continuation of our argument. But I found him standing at his desk, preoccupied with sorting a tall stack of papers into piles.

"Ah, Nell." He waved me toward him. "I wanted to speak with you before you go in to see our anonymous patient."

He sat down, his hands interlaced at his waist, a frown of concern on his face as he looked up at me. "This morning, Mr. Oliven told me something odd that happened last night. After I left, a man came to the guardhouse, asking if a girl had been brought here last week with injuries. He had a description of her, and a name: Marceline Tourneau. He says she's an acrobatic performer, from a circus in France, and he claimed to be her father."

Feeling my heart begin to race, I looked down and began to undo the buttons of my coat to conceal my consternation. So far as I knew, Marceline had been raised by her grandparents. Was this man really her father? Or merely pretending to be? Either way, it was someone who knew her and knew of her injuries. What if this was the brute who had injured her? And how on earth had he known to come here?

I sat down and draped my coat across my lap. "Was he admitted?"

"No, of course not. Aside from the fact that it was after visiting hours, Mr. Oliven didn't like the looks of him. And when he was refused entry, the man became irate and threatened to break in. You can well imagine how that went."

Yes, I could. Mr. Oliven was not only a burly man with a formidable expression and a bellowing voice; he carried both a truncheon and a pistol, and he took his responsibility for the safety of the hospital and its inmates with absolute seriousness.

Dr. Everett rubbed at his temple. "Apparently the man cursed Mr. Oliven roundly before he left, threatening that he'd be back."

"Has he returned?"

"Not yet. But the day guard has an eye out, and I sent a note to Matthew, asking if we might get a bit of extra attention from the police."

"Matthew?" I echoed in surprise.

"Well, yes." His eyebrows rose. "It's the simplest way. Not that I need to tug on that string very often, thank goodness. The last time was when that wretch was throwing rocks through our windows. Do you remember him?"

I nodded perfunctorily. "The girl doesn't know, does she, about this man coming?"

"Oh, she's the last person I'd tell. But I do wish we could discover if that is indeed her name and profession." He frowned and tapped his forefinger to his lips. "It's been nearly a week, and she's making progress, but her head is still healing. If we push her too hard to remember, she could become frustrated or frightened and suffer a relapse. On the other hand, she may recall a good deal more than she is admitting."

"What can I do to help?"

"Well, it's splendid how quickly you've earned her trust. This morning, she reiterated that she didn't want to speak with anyone until she saw you." His smile conveyed genuine admiration, and I felt a pang of shame at my deception.

"Perhaps it's because I'm closer to her age. And I'm not anyone official," I suggested.

He shrugged. "At any rate, her jaw is healing and the swelling is down. I have her on a low dose of laudanum for the pain, so she may be a bit sleepy. But it's safe for her to talk."

Safe. The irony of the word was as bitter as horehound on my tongue. I had a feeling Marceline would never be safe from dangerous men so long as she *could* talk. But of course, that's not what Dr. Everett meant. At any rate, I simply nodded, and slipped out of his office, leaving him to his papers.

MARCELINE'S EYES WERE BOTH UNCOVERED NOW, and Nurse Aimes was applying salve to one of her hands before she rebandaged it. I couldn't help but stare; the skin on Marceline's palm was torn to bits. I imagined her trying to grasp a trapeze bar and winced as I realized that both of us relied on our hands to make our livings.

"Hello, there," I said.

Marceline smiled a bit and Nurse Aimes said cheerfully, "Good afternoon, Nell." She finished wrapping the hand in gauze. "There. Is that better?"

Marceline nodded. "Thank you." Her voice wasn't much over a whisper, but she was trying.

Nurse Aimes beamed down at her and patted her shoulder gently. Then she looked over at me. "You are in charge of getting some broth into her."

"Yes, mum." I sketched a mock salute and shot a small grin toward Marceline.

Nurse Aimes left, drawing the curtain around the bed, and I perched on the edge of the bed. "How are you feeling? You look much better."

She nodded. "I am. People have been very kind."

I glanced over at the tray with the bowl. "Do you—?"

"Please." Her brown eyes were intense, serious. "I'd rather talk first."

"All right."

"Tell me what happened the night you brought me here."

Quietly, so we couldn't be overheard, I recounted it in as much detail as I could remember. When I finished, I fell silent, just watching, as she worked to order the events in her mind.

Finally, I asked, "Marceline, what happened before I found you?"

A shudder ran over her, and she looked away for a moment.

My voice was a whisper. "Who did this to you? Was it Sebastian?" I hated to think of it, but I had to ask.

Her eyes widened in indignation. "Of course not! He would *never* hurt me."

"I'm sorry." I rested my hand gently on her arm. "I didn't mean to doubt him. It's just that when I came last time, you made it quite clear that you didn't want me to find him—and I thought . . ."

Understanding flashed across her face. "No, it's nothing like that. I don't want him found. But that's because I'm afraid *for* him, not *of* him." She swallowed. "You said you'd help me. Will you?"

"Of course, as much as I can," I promised.

A frown knit her brows. "I'm not sure about everything that happened."

"That's all right. Just tell me what you can."

"I had left our flat, and I was walking to the Octavian," she began slowly. "It was just half past six, or a bit later. Two men came toward me, and before I knew what was happening, one of them had put his hand over my mouth and pulled me into an alley. The other followed."

"Where did they take you?"

"To a house not far away. They dragged me upstairs to a room that I could tell was right under the roof because the ceiling was peaked, and I could see bits of light through the cracks. The room was long and narrow, with wooden crates stacked several deep at the far end and a few chairs and a stove. There was a metal pole, and a small rectangular window."

"What did they want?"

She gave me a look. "At first I thought they wanted . . . to . . ."

A lump formed in my throat. "I understand," I said hurriedly, so she wouldn't have to say it.

"But they didn't want me." She paused. "They asked me where Sebastian was."

A shiver went down my back. "What did you tell them?"

"Nothing, of course." Her eyes met mine, and I could see her fierceness shining there. "I knew some places that were likely. But I'd have let them kill me before I told."

"So they beat you," I whispered.

She nodded. "They tied me to the pole."

I turned away, swallowing down the bile that rose in my throat. "Good lord, Marceline."

"He's all I have," she said simply.

The very rawness of her words made tears burn at the corners of my eyes. "I know," I said, my voice ragged. "I feel the same way about my brother."

She nodded.

"Did the men say what they wanted with him?" I asked.

"Just that he owed them something. They didn't say what."

"Money?"

She shrugged.

"But if it was money, why not just say so? Or ask if you had it?"

"I don't know. But I do know that Sebastian has been keeping something from me. He'd go out at night sometimes, not tell me where. And we had more to spend than we were used to."

"Do you think he was gambling?"

Her face screwed up in denial. "No. That's not like him."

But the tension in her shoulders told me that this train of thought was distressing her, so I shifted topics. "How ever did you manage to escape?"

"They left me, and I sawed the rope off on a sharp bit of the pipe."

"That must have taken hours!" I was aghast at the thought of her locked in that room, trying to free her hands, all the while listening for the men coming back.

"I don't remember, honestly. I just knew I had to do it. I think it took an hour, maybe two. And there was a small window. I couldn't open the hasp, it was so rusted. So I broke the glass and climbed across the roof. There were shingles, so it wasn't slippery."

Broken glass and shingles.

"No wonder your hands are torn to bits," I said. "How did you get down?"

"A drainpipe. My hands slipped, and I must have fallen." She shook her head. "I don't remember anything else until I woke up here."

Not for the first time, I said a silent prayer of thanks that I had found her.

Nurse Aimes popped her head in and pursed her mouth disapprovingly when she saw the untouched tray. "It's not going to be any good cold, you know. Here, let's get you up." She deftly adjusted the pillows so that Marceline was almost sitting normally, and I tucked the napkin over her waist and removed the cover from the bowl. I dipped a spoon in, and Marceline opened her mouth obligingly.

"Is it still warm?" Nurse asked.

Marceline nodded after she swallowed. "It's very good."

Nurse paused to watch a few more spoonfuls go in. Then she seemed satisfied and left us again.

"Is she a friend of yours, too?" Marceline asked, a little wistfully.

"I suppose she is, yes," I said, somewhat surprised by the question. "I've known her for years. She's a good sort." I paused. "Would it be all right if I told her your name? Right now, they call you 'our anonymous patient.'"

I saw another hint of a smile, but she hesitated.

"Just the doctor and Nurse Aimes?" I suggested.

She nodded.

I smiled. "Toast?"

She nodded again, and I buttered it for her, then watched as she ate with extreme care, taking small bites and chewing gingerly, as if she were trying to find the way it hurt least.

Getting the soup and toast into her took the better part of half an hour, and by the time she'd finished, she seemed to feel both physically and emotionally more at ease. I hoped that she would be open to what I had to say next.

I set the tray aside. "Marceline, I know you don't want me to go looking for Sebastian, but what if I were to contact a friend of his? Someone you trust, who might know where he is and could get a message to him secretly?"

She opened her mouth to protest, but I reminded her gently, "He has to be half out of his mind with worry. Especially if he's in danger himself and can't go looking for you."

A moment passed, but at last she nodded. "I need to think of someone."

The anxiety was apparent on her pale face, and as if on cue, Nurse Aimes reappeared and assessed the situation at a glance. "That's enough for today, Nell. You need your rest, little lamb." She waved both her hands, as if to nudge me out.

"Come back tomorrow," Marceline begged. "Won't you?"

"Of course," I said lightly, though inwardly I felt the urgency of the situation like a heavy weight in my stomach.

I left without saying goodbye to Dr. Everett and walked home slowly, turning over all that Marceline had said.

Chapter 9

$\mathcal{M}$y key turned too easily in the front door; the locking bolt hadn't been engaged. Still, distracted as I was, it took me a moment to register the sight of Matthew's untidy brown hair over the top of the chair in the study.

As I unbuttoned my coat, I called out, "Matthew, what are you doing home at this hour? You never come home for tea."

He didn't reply, and as I entered the room, I saw that he held a glass with an inch of whiskey in it balanced on the chair arm.

Alarmed, I touched his shoulder. "Matthew?"

"Mr. Kinsey was here," he said, his voice subdued. "He fixed your piano."

"Yes," I said, puzzled. "The string was broken."

He managed a strained smile. "Were you at the hospital? I saw Dr. Everett yesterday. He said you've been helping him with one of the patients."

My heart jumped a bit. Surely that was not the reason he was home, to check on me. "Yes, I was."

"He asked me to take her statement when she's well enough to talk. She was attacked in Soho."

I sat down on the chair nearest to him. "Is that what's bothering you?"

He was silent for a long moment, contemplating the amber liquid in his glass.

I bent forward to catch his eye. "You can confide in me, you know," I said offhandedly, to make it easy for him to refuse. "If you've no one else."

Normally that would make him smile, even just a little. But his expression remained somber. "I think perhaps you're the only one I *can* tell."

His dejection tugged hard at me. I touched his arm. "Then I'm listening."

"I'm worried there's a snitch at the Yard."

I sat back in my chair. "Oh, Matthew." I knew how much he had come to trust his fellow detectives, and how much the idea of a traitor would hurt him.

"I know." He rubbed a hand over his face, hard, as if he were scrubbing it. "I've only been there a little over a year. Who am I to question anybody?" His expression was pained. "But I don't know how else to account for things that have happened. And I feel as though I should have realized before this."

"Most of us don't scrutinize the people close to us," I said gently, "at least, not unless we're overly suspicious by nature. But what's happened?"

"Do you remember what I told you about Powell?"

I nodded.

"I assumed that the reason he'd been killed was because one of the men he owed got impatient with him. The fact that it hap-

pened before our second meeting was just a terrible coincidence."
He took a sip of his whiskey. "But now I'm beginning to wonder
because it happened again, Nell—and I swear I took every precaution. In and out of doors, crossing alleys, turning back two
and three times. There's no way I could have been followed."

"By 'it happened again,' do you mean the dead man—what
was his name—Kendrick?"

"No. I never met the man. I mean his wife." His voice was
bleak. "I finally found her on Sunday, and she was willing to talk
to me. But she also wanted passage out of London."

"Of course. She must've been terrified that whoever killed her
husband would come after her."

He nodded. "We arranged to meet at a public house near Spitalfields Market yesterday afternoon. But she never appeared, and
now she's gone missing."

"Maybe she left of her own free will. Maybe she was too afraid
to wait for you."

His eyes met mine. "I went to her home. There were dishes in
the sink, and there was a packed suitcase beside the door, full of
clothes and a few pictures."

"You mean keepsakes that she'd take with her," I said slowly,
"if she were leaving for good. Except she was taken before she had
the chance."

He sighed and ran a hand through his hair. "I've asked her
neighbors, but they didn't see anything. My guess is it happened
Sunday night or very early yesterday morning."

I bit my lip. "Who knew you were meeting with her yesterday?"

"The only person I told this time was William."

I started.

No wonder Matthew was upset. I hated the thought, too.

"Did you ask him?"

He gave me an incredulous look. "You can't exactly ask someone if he's secretly working for a ring of thieves and betraying things you tell him in confidence. Might be a bit insulting, don't you think?" He swallowed the rest of his whiskey.

"Well, yes, I suppose. But wouldn't he prefer to have a chance to explain?"

"But what if he *is* the snitch, Nell? Then all I've done is alert him." He stood and paced restlessly around the room. "Not to mention it feels like a rotten betrayal on my part, even thinking it—but then again, if it's true, he's not the person I've thought he was."

"Nor I. But Matthew, are you *sure* no one else knew?"

He took a deep breath. "That's the only reason I'm still giving him the benefit of the doubt. I wrote it in my notes, which I kept in a locking drawer in my desk. But I left it unlocked—briefly— yesterday when I stepped away."

"Aren't you supposed to turn the notes in?" I knew that a few months ago, that practice had become required as the detective divisions began centralizing their cases.

"Yes."

"Where do you keep the key?"

He bit his lip. "It's with me always. And if someone picked the lock, there'd be scratches on the brass. I looked for those."

"Does anyone else have a copy? Barrow?"

"No. And he wouldn't be involved in something like this. In his twenty years of service, there hasn't been a whiff of scandal connected to the man."

"Well, I think you owe it to William to ask him. You've been friends for five years. That has to count for something."

He nodded and stared into his empty glass, his expression despondent. "People say this happens. That at some point in your career as a policeman, you will be forced to choose between your duty to the job and your loyalty to a friend, or a family member, or your own pocket." He shook his head. "I just never thought it would be William."

"Do you want to invite him here to talk? Would it be easier? For privacy, I mean."

"And maybe he wouldn't be quite so much on his guard." He winced. "It seems an underhanded thing to do."

"I'm sorry, Matthew. This is rotten."

"And now Mrs. Kendrick." His face was fixed in despair. As I knew he would, he was blaming himself. Under his breath, he said, "God only knows what they've done to her."

I thought of Marceline, and I, too, feared for this woman I didn't even know. For a moment we were both silent. Finally, I asked, "If it's not William or Barrow, who do you think is likely? Which detective would be useful to an organization like this?"

Matthew poured himself another drink, albeit a smaller one. "There's McFarr. He grew up near the docks, like William, and he still has friends there, so he knows a good deal about shipping and smuggling. And last week, the River Police found two ships carrying bilge plates with stolen goods."

"What's a bilge plate?" I asked. "It sounds like a special sort of dish."

He smiled briefly, as I'd hoped he would. "Not that kind of plate, Nell. Bilge plates are large metal pieces that attach to the outside of the ship, below the water line. They create a sort of pocket against the hull, where goods can be transported secretly."

"All right, so that's McFarr. Who else?"

"O'Neill. He knows the rookeries of London—especially Seven Dials and St. Giles. He has connections to brothels, fences, and pawnshops." He thought for a moment. "And there's Bidwell. He's in charge of finding counterfeiters and very diligent about it. He's arrested twenty-four pairs of them in London in the past year."

"Pairs?" I asked.

He shrugged. "Counterfeiting is much easier with two sets of hands. Most of the time a man brings in his wife because she can't testify against him, and she can't be charged. She can say she was working under his direction, so she's protected."

Another time I might have laughed at the vagaries of the law. "So you have three possibilities, aside from William. Do you have a feeling for which it might be?"

He shook his head and sipped the last of his second drink. "I've been wracking my brains, Nell. I can't see how to navigate this."

"And you don't want to steer your boat onto the rocks."

He glanced at the clock, dragged himself to his feet, and picked up his coat. "Not least because if I steer the wrong way, I may well be pitched out."

Chapter 10

On Wednesday morning, Marceline was sitting up bolstered by pillows. The bruises on her face were beginning to fade, and she had some sparkle in her eyes. Her hands were still bandaged in gauze, but she seemed more cheerful. She even managed a lopsided smile.

Nurse Aimes put me in charge of helping Marceline drink some tea and eat a soft-boiled egg, which I began to do, carefully.

"How are things at the Octavian?" she asked between sips.

"Much the same," I said. "The piano is finally in tune. Jack did it."

"Jack? Well, good. That thing was dreadful." She gave me a keen look. "Does he know you're a woman?"

I hesitated. "He might. But he hasn't said so."

"Jack's a good sort." Her expression softened. "He's always been kind to us, even the first time, when we made mistakes."

My hand paused with the spoon. "That's right. I'd forgotten this was your second engagement there."

She nodded. "The first time was last August."

My mind jumped to Stephen's story about Jack. I wondered if Marceline knew anything about it.

"What's the matter?" she asked.

"Well—it's just . . ." I paused. "I heard a rather nasty bit of gossip about Jack, and it seemed out of character. You might know the truth about it." Briefly I relayed what Stephen had said.

She brushed the idea aside with a bandaged hand. "Oh, that wasn't Jack. It was Mr. Williams."

I felt a surge of relief at her words. "Are you certain?"

She nodded. "Her name was Rosalie. She's Amalie's cousin, I think. But she didn't want anything to do with old Williams. So he tossed her out, and told everyone it was because she was a drunk and unreliable, just so she'd have a hard time finding another position." She wrinkled her nose. "He's a disgusting pig of a man."

I shook my head, equally appalled. But I was thinking that this would go a long way toward explaining why Amalie loathed him so. And while this wasn't proof that Jack had *never* injured a woman in such a way, it made me feel a little better.

"He's quite unlike your Dr. Everett," she observed. "I don't remember ever meeting a man who was so proper and dignified. Although he's also . . ." She hesitated. "We have a word in French, *excentrique*. It means—"

I laughed. "I know what you mean. We have it in English, too. Eccentric."

She smiled and shook her head to refuse the last bit of egg. "When he came to see me yesterday, he told me that he was a close friend of your family, but when I asked how you met, he said I would have to speak to you."

"Well, he *is* a friend, that much is true." I set the egg cup down on the tray and reached for my tea. "Do you remember I told you that my mother left when I was very young?"

"Yes, to pursue her music."

"What I didn't tell you," I said slowly, "is that she'd had a mental disease for several years beforehand. Dr. Everett tried to treat her, but he wasn't very successful. He still feels guilty about it. It's why he's quite watchful and protective of me."

Her expression became understanding. "To make up for her leaving."

"Well, yes. But he's also afraid I may have inherited the tendency for her illness. And the fact that I play the piano like she did . . ."

"Oh! I see." She gave me a probing look. "And you? Are you afraid?"

"Yes, sometimes."

Her eyes were full of sympathy. "That would be frightening. Not to be sure of your own mind."

"I suppose it's rather like you working without a net," I said, trying to make light of it. "That first night, I couldn't even watch you two, though I got used to it."

"Ah, that's not frightening." She shook her head dismissively. "It was just play for Sebastian and me as children. The only difference now is we're paid."

It was the best opening I was likely to get. I offered her some more tea and asked, "Did you think any more about sending a message to him?"

Her eyes lowered, and her bandaged hands lay still on the blanket. "I *did* think of someone." Her voice dropped to a whisper, so I had to lean forward to hear. "His name is Jeremy. If you could tell him that I'm all right, he'll let Sebastian know. Sebastian trusts him."

"Where can I find him?"

"He works at the *Falcon*."

"The newspaper?" I asked, surprised.

She nodded. "Jeremy helps one of the newspapermen, Mr. Flynn. And if he's not there, Mr. Flynn will know where he is. But you can't tell Mr. Flynn anything—"

"No, of course not," I agreed. "I'll only talk to Jeremy."

Her eyes were anxious. "Just tell him I'm all right. Don't tell him where I am. Promise me. I don't want Sebastian coming here. I want him to stay hidden."

I laid my fingers on her arm. "I promise."

I took a hansom cab into Whitechapel, grateful that the driver knew precisely where the offices were, for the journey took us through some dodgy areas and a tangle of alleys. I could tell we were approaching the Thames, for the stench of the river grew stronger.

In Prescott Street, the cab drew up at a tall, square building, all of brick. At the roofline perched an iron sculpture of a large black bird, its wings outstretched. From where I stood it looked more like a crow than a falcon, but so be it.

I climbed the few stairs to the front door and hammered with the knocker. The door was opened promptly by a man carrying a package under his arm. "Hullo," he said in some surprise. "Be ye the girl from Mason's?"

"No. I've come to see a boy named Jeremy. I have a message for him."

"Jeremy? Jeremy Marcus?"

"I suppose so. Does he work with Mr. Flynn?"

"Shore. 'E works with Flynn." He jerked his head over his shoulder. "Upstairs. Just ask anybody. 'E's been in the archives all day."

"Thank you."

I started up the wooden steps. The entire building seemed to rumble with a myriad of noises plaited together—clunking, banging, shouting, clicking. I reached the landing and peered into a long room. At a dozen canted wooden tables, men stood laying metal type for what must be the evening's paper. There was a good deal of banter and cursing and calling back and forth, until one of the men caught sight of me.

"What ho! Who's this?"

Several men turned toward me. I had a vague impression of mustaches and grins and, as I stepped all the way into the room, the pungent smell of men's sweat.

"I'm looking for Jeremy Marcus," I announced to the group.

"Jeremy? What'd he do to deserve you?" shouted one.

Another told him to shut his yawp and smiled pleasantly at me. "Upstairs, Miss. Mr. Flynn's up thar. He'll know where Jeremy'll be." He beckoned to a boy at the end of the bench. "Sam! Show the lady."

The boy shambled toward me with a lopsided smile. "This way, Miss."

I stepped carefully in Sam's footsteps, as the stairs to the upper floors were even more decrepit than those at the Octavian, with several treads missing altogether. Finally, we reached the landing, and he took me down a hall, past several rooms where men sat engaged in conversation or paging through old issues of the paper. The air smelled of decay, and the light coming through the windows illuminated the dust hanging in the air.

He stopped when we reached a windowless room, where the only light came from two bright lanterns on either corner of a large desk. Behind it stood a man, bent over some pages that were spread in front of him, so my first impression of Mr. Flynn was the top of a head with dark brown hair thinning in an oval pattern.

Wordlessly, Sam gestured for me to go in, and then he vanished.

I cleared my throat. "Excuse me. Are you Mr. Flynn?"

He looked up. A round face, intelligent in expression, with a small turned-up nose and eyes of an unusual olive green. They swept me up and down, not lecherously but impersonally, as if to catalog my appearance and any odd details, before he answered, "Yes, I'm Flynn. Who are you?"

"I'm looking for Jeremy."

His mouth twitched in acknowledgment that I hadn't answered his question. "Well, he's out. Can I help you?"

"I'm afraid I need to speak to him directly."

He shrugged and gestured with the end of his pencil to a chair by the wall. "You can wait if you like. Shouldn't be long."

He returned to his task and ignored me. His eyes darted from paper to paper, his right hand making notes. I noticed that he was missing the tip of his index finger. Not that it seemed to slow his progress any, but I couldn't help wondering how it had happened.

At last a young man appeared at the door. He looked to be about fifteen, or perhaps a bit older. He had a thin, wolfish face,

bright brown eyes, and cheeks flushed pink, as if he'd been running, and he brought the oily smell of the Thames into the room
with him. His coat was too long, and threadbare at the cuffs, but
his boots were stout, and he looked well fed, if wiry. In the same
impersonal way as Mr. Flynn, he looked me over as he crossed
into the room.

I stood. "Are you Jeremy?"

Mr. Flynn's right eyebrow rose; I realized he'd thought we
knew each other.

The boy sniffed. "I am. Who be you?"

"Can we talk privately, please?"

He pulled a face at Mr. Flynn. "Shore." He made a theatrical
gesture for me to precede him into the hall, then directed me to
one of the empty rooms.

He didn't shut the door but stood facing me with his hands in
his pockets, his gaze frank but not insolent. "What's *your* name,
Miss?"

I waved a hand. "It isn't important. Do you know a young man
named Sebastian? Sebastian Tourneau."

He tipped his head as if trying to recall, then shook it. "Don't
think so."

I felt a stab of surprise, and then my heart sank. "You don't?
Are you quite sure?" He stood staring indifferently at me. "I was
told . . ." I stopped. How could Marceline have been mistaken
about this? "Never mind, then. I must have the name wrong."
I started toward the door, my heart hammering. I'd blundered.
And now I had let Jeremy know something—just the smallest
scrap of information, yes . . . only a name . . . but still . . .

"Who sent you?" came his voice, abruptly, as I reached the
threshold.

I turned back.

The nonchalance had vanished, and his expression was wary and dead serious. "Tell me that, if'n you won't tell me your name."

"His sister."

Pain and disbelief flashed across his face, and he made a sudden movement—not toward me, but it caused me to flinch all the same.

"You're lying," he said fiercely, between gritted teeth. To my surprise, tears had sprung to his eyes. "Marceline's dead."

"No, she's not! She's hurt—badly hurt. But she's alive."

"'Ow do you know?"

"Because I'm the one who found her in the street and took her to—to—someplace safe. I saw her just this morning."

His lips parted, and he stared at me, blinking hard. "When'd you find her?"

"Wednesday night."

"Where?"

"In an alley in Soho."

"Where is she now?"

"I can't tell you that. She asked me not to—to protect you, as well as Sebastian. She doesn't want him coming out of hiding. All I'm allowed to tell you is that she's safe, and she's mending."

At my evasion, his eyes narrowed. "Why should I believe you?"

I'd had enough of the interrogation. "For goodness' sake! How else would I know your name and how to find you, if she hadn't given it to me?"

"'Ow do I know she gave it to you by choice?" he snapped back.

His point was a fair one. I sighed and provided a gesture of good faith. "My name is Nell Hallam. I play piano at the Octavian, where she was performing with her brother, and we became friends. She—and I—just want to let Sebastian know she's all right."

The mistrust faded from Jeremy's face. I waited, and at last he gave a faint nod. "I'll tell 'im. If'n I see 'im."

"Is he safe? She's worried about him, too."

"I ain't 'eard otherwise."

"And do you think you can find him?"

A shrug. "Mebbe. Can you come back Sunday, around midday?"

"Here?" I asked, surprised.

"'Ere's safe enough. Nobody'll connect this place with you, or with either o' them."

"Sunday, then, at noon." I put my hand on the doorknob, my mind already on the rickety stairs I had to climb down.

"Miss, is she really all right?" came his voice from behind me.

I turned back once more. His guarded demeanor had given way to undisguised worry, and I felt a sudden wave of warmth toward him. "She will be. She's had her wounds tended to and has a clean bed and good food. She's mending."

His mouth curved in a genuine boyish smile that made his whole face light up. "Good."

Chapter 11

As had become my cautious habit, I went to the Octavian early on Wednesday night and spent the hour before the show practicing. No one interrupted me, and when I heard the front doors open, I changed one set of music for the other. But my mind was elsewhere, and for the first time ever, I found myself playing the finale of the show without being able to recall much about what had preceded it.

Afterward, I gathered my things as usual and went down the stairs to the back corridor. As I passed Amalie's dressing room, I heard her throaty laugh in the pause between the scrapes of heavy properties being moved in preparation for the next show—and then a man's voice, smooth and well-bred.

Was that Stephen? I thought, pausing.

Well, the two of them had a right to spend time with whomever they pleased. It was none of my concern.

And then, from behind me, came Drummond's voice, menacing and slurred with drink: "What the hell're you still doing here?"

For a panicked second, I thought he was talking to me, and I whirled around. But there was only his bulky shadow, grotesque in the light cast by a lantern on the wall. It was getting larger, though, and I had no wish to be anywhere near his line of sight. A few steps away, an old slatted door formed a small tricorner space near the stairs, and I slid behind it.

Peering between two slats, I saw that Drummond had a pair of raffish boys by their collars, and he was dragging them toward the ramp that led up to the street. I didn't recognize the boys, though I thought I knew by sight the dozen or so who worked here, selling roses and cigars, emptying the ashtrays, and sweeping the aisles during the show. As a rule, the hall boys were decently dressed; these two must be pickpockets who'd managed to slip in somehow.

With the pounding and scraping sounds overhead, I couldn't hear what he was saying to them, but I could distinguish their features. One was perhaps ten years of age, the other a few years older; neither one wore shoes. The older boy seemed to be explaining something, and his thin arm pointed toward the front door. Drummond listened with an expression of disbelief and then, without warning, knocked their heads together twice. The suddenness of it shocked me, and I nearly cried out. The boys fell to the floor on their hands and knees, the younger one sobbing. Drummond gave the older one a kick and proceeded down the hallway toward my hiding place. I didn't move a muscle, not even to breathe, and he passed by without a glance.

A few more steps, and he'd be at his office—and I would go to those boys—

Then Stephen emerged from the far corridor. I gave a small sigh of relief and nearly slid out of my hiding place—

"Drummond," he called.

The older man turned back. "There you are."

The ease between the two men froze me in place again.

Stephen glanced at the two boys huddled together on the floor and stepped around them without the slightest change of expression.

The band of cloth around my chest suddenly felt tight.

The pair walked to the end of the hallway and turned left, toward the rooms that were used for properties and such. Their shadows, cast by lights in the next hallway, stretched onto the wall, two long dark pillars that shrank and then vanished.

I let out my breath in a ragged exhale. *What was Stephen doing with Drummond? And how could he have looked at those boys and done nothing—not even said a word to them?*

My heart pounding, I came out from behind the door as warily as a rabbit coming out of a hole and hurried over to crouch beside the two boys on the cold floor. The younger boy was curled on his side, clutching his head. The older one was on his hands and knees, his breath coming in gasps. He had blood running from a cut over his left brow.

I put one hand on the older boy's shoulder and kept my voice to a hoarse whisper. "Are you all right?"

He looked up blearily and wiped his sleeve over his thin face. "Who are you?"

"I play the piano here. I saw what Drummond did just now." I reached inside my coat for my handkerchief. "Here." I offered the bit of white cloth. The older boy eyed both it and me with suspicion. Without taking it, he turned to the younger boy, who still lay on his side, his eyes full of tears. He had an ugly red scar, as if from a burn, across the side of his mouth, and when the older boy leaned over him, he let out the smallest whimper and said a few garbled words.

The older boy understood him, though, and nodded. *Brothers,* I thought, as I looked at them in profile. But what had happened to the younger boy's mouth? That scar looked painful, though not fresh.

I held out the handkerchief again to the older boy. "There's a pump on the Mews where you can wash that cut."

"We're a'right." Still on his knees, he shifted closer to the other boy and pulled gently at his shoulder. "Come on, Gus. We got to be gone 'afore he comes back."

Though they clearly didn't want my help, I felt unwilling to leave. I rose and watched uncertainly by the lantern's light, and my eye was caught by a U-shaped scar on the older boy's bare heel. *It's no wonder,* I thought, *if they're going barefoot in the London streets.* "What happened to your foot?" I asked. "Did you cut it?"

"Nah." He pulled Gus to his feet, and they started up the ramp. The younger one—Gus—was still rubbing his head as they reached the door. It squeaked open and closed and they were gone, leaving behind a cold, damp gust of air.

I bent to pick up my portfolio where I'd dropped it. I desperately wanted to be gone myself. What I'd just seen had put a lump in the pit of my stomach.

"Nell!"

With a gasp, I turned.

Stephen stood there, his smile fading as he studied my face. "What's the matter? You look like you just saw a ghost."

"Nothing. You startled me is all."

His eyes narrowed. "It's nearly eleven o'clock. What are you still doing here?"

The echo of Drummond's snarled words felt uncanny. But I pushed the thought aside and shrugged. "I forgot my portfolio and had to come back for it. Stupid, I know."

My self-deprecatory laugh sounded thin to me, but he nodded and smiled. "I looked for you after the show, you know. I've just come from upstairs. Someone told me they thought they'd seen you headed that way."

I couldn't help but stare at how sincere he appeared, at how his head was inclined just enough to suggest an easy rapport between us, at how his gaze didn't swerve a hair away from mine. In that moment, rendered silent by a welter of feelings I couldn't even name, there was part of me that wished I could snap back a retort that shamed him for his outright lie.

But what I'd seen just now—Drummond with those boys, and Stephen on easy terms with Drummond—wasn't merely the backstage seediness of a music hall; it was callous and brutal. The same instinct that had pulled me back behind the slatted door to avoid Drummond now made me smile up at Stephen and say, "Oh, the stagehands were moving something across the alcove, so I took the other stairs."

"Ah!" He seemed to accept this explanation.

"But I'm late now. As you know, I have to get home."

"Yes, your brother."

I nodded in agreement. "Good night, Stephen. I'll see you next week." At the top of the ramp, I turned back to see him watching me with a slightly puzzled expression. I gave him a cheerful wave with my portfolio and pushed at the door.

So long as I was in the yard, I kept up the pretense of hurrying home. But as I rounded the next corner, I had to stop, lean my back against the wall, and take a few deep breaths before I walked on. I made my way from one gas lamp to the next, their light above me distorted and diffused. By contrast, the individual moments of the wretched scene I'd witnessed appeared in my mind with the clarity of daguerreotypes. Drummond's face, his eyes blazing and his mouth working . . . the boys trying to speak, their faces full of terror . . . the older one with the blood on his forehead, so full of distrust that he refused my handkerchief . . . the younger one trying to speak, and that ugly puckered scar across his mouth . . . and Stephen's rotten indifference—

There was a high-pitched scream from a horse—human shouts of warning—the pounding of hooves—

I was in the middle of Wickley Street, and like a complete fool, I froze in place and turned toward the sounds. Out of the mist came a pair of horses, running at me, the lanterns on either side of the cab swinging wildly, the carriage careening from side to side as it came. I dodged one way and then the other—the horses seemed to follow my course like devils—the hansom drew near—was nearly upon me—I tried to run, but my boot slid on the wet stones—

A quick movement behind me, and two strong arms whirled me out of the way as if I weighed no more than a cat.

Chapter 12

I cried out as the horses flew by, the carriage wheels jouncing against the cobbles—and in seconds, all I saw were the two lanterns bobbing crazily through the mist. Then the darkness closed behind them, and the only lights came from a single gas lamp nearby and some public houses open late.

The man—for it was a man who had grabbed me—still held me, not painfully but firmly. My hands were on his chest, and though it was as broad and unyielding as an oak door, I could feel his heartbeat coming as fast as my own.

"Are you all right?" he asked finally, his arms loosening.

It was a voice I recognized.

I drew back. "Jack!" My eyes searched his face. "What are you doing here?"

His face wore the guarded expression I'd seen often enough. "It's lucky I was. Are you all right?" he repeated, studying me as if searching for injuries.

"I'm fine. Just . . . just frightened half to death." But the fear was already giving way to anger. "What was the driver thinking, racing his horses through here like that? What sort of fool would do such a thing?"

"There wasn't one—a driver, I mean—at least not one who was sitting upright."

"You mean he'd fallen asleep?"

"Or been thrown out. I don't know," he said abruptly. "I was looking at you."

He was still looking at me—and belatedly I realized I had spoken to him in my own voice. I'd given myself away. But there was no surprise in his expression. So Stephen had been right: Jack had known all along and never said a word.

I stiffened and pulled away from him. Instantly, pain shot from my ankle all the way up my leg. I let out an involuntary cry and nearly fell, and his arm was back around me in a minute.

"What is it?"

I clutched at his arm. "My ankle. My God." The pain was so sharp I could barely breathe, and tears sprang to my eyes. He only hesitated a moment before he swung me up into his arms and began to walk. I bit my lip so as not to cry out from the spikes of pain shooting up toward my knee. I'd never fainted in my life— but I felt so sick that I was close to it then.

Jack pushed a door open with his foot, and we were in the dining room of a public house, warm from a robust fire and smelling of roasted beef and onions. Most of the tables were occupied, and suddenly it occurred to me how strange we must look. A man carrying another man—coming into a public house—they probably all thought I was drunk—

"Everything all right, Jack?" someone called.

"Fine," he answered but didn't stop. He carried me between two long benches where people sat with their tankards and lowered me into a chair beside an unoccupied table. Clumsily, I maneuvered myself to a comfortable position, and he drew another chair close and bent down, using one hand just below my calf to keep my foot from touching the floor. His dark eyes met mine. "We need to take your boot off."

Now that I was sitting still, with the weight off my ankle, the shooting pains were diminishing to a heavy throbbing.

His other hand was poised over the fastenings of the boot. "Would you like me to help you?"

"Yes, please."

"Tell me when you're ready."

"Go ahead." I wrapped my hands around the sides of the chair.

He undid the five buttons, and as I watched I remembered how scrupulous he was with the piano, his fingers patiently moving over the strings. But even with him pulling carefully, I couldn't stifle a sharp inhale as the boot came over my heel.

He glanced up. "Sorry." His hands felt around the ankle joint gently. "I don't think it's broken, but it's swelling. I'm going to see if they have any ice."

"Jack—you know this place?"

"The Bear and Bull. Some friends own it." He rose, ducked under a wooden panel that separated this room from the next, and disappeared through an archway.

The room wasn't overly spacious or elaborately decorated, but it was well kept, and the floor was cleanly swept. A fire glowed in a massive stone hearth, and above the mantel was the head of a bear, mounted so its teeth were showing. It would have seemed more menacing if its ears weren't ragged and the fur weren't patchy along the neck; it had rather the scruffiness of a well-loved children's toy.

Well, there is the bear, I thought; but though I craned my neck, I saw no sign of a bull.

Along one wall ran a wooden bar, long enough to accommodate a dozen stools, a few of which were occupied by young men talking and laughing over their late suppers. Couples sat at several of the small tables, and a rather noisy trio of men sat at a larger table in the corner, playing cards. One of them shot me a look and nudged his friend. I felt myself flush, and wishing Jack would hurry back, I kept my eyes fixed on the archway, breathing a sigh of relief as he emerged. Beside him was a young woman, her lustrous fair hair coiled into a thick bun. His dark head was bent toward her pretty face, and she was smiling up at him, her hand on his arm. He gestured toward me, and she cast a quick glance, then they vanished together behind another door.

He returned to the table alone, unwrapping two narrow slabs of ice from a rumpled towel. "We're lucky, the iceman came this morning. Thank God for Norway." He sat down in the chair and rewrapped the ice more neatly. "Where does it hurt most?"

"On the outside."

He supported my lower leg again with one hand. "Can you move your foot? Up and down?"

Cautiously, I flexed my stockinged foot. "It hurts, but yes."

He looked relieved. "It's just sprained, then."

With his other hand, he carefully applied the ice along my foot.

I felt the color creeping into my cheeks, and I wondered if he was as embarrassed as I, for he kept his eyes down, as if his attention were wholly absorbed in holding the ice just so.

Finally, I could stand it no longer. I asked, in my own voice, "How long have you known?"

He looked up then, and I was grateful that he didn't pretend not to understand me. "Since your audition."

I didn't remember him being there, but then again, I'd been nervous because Mr. Williams had hovered beside the piano bench, plunking page after page of music in front of me and scowling the entire time.

"You never said anything," I replied, a note of accusation in my voice.

He shrugged. "If you wanted me to know, you'd've told me."

"Does anyone else know?"

"I've no idea," he said frankly. "Mr. Williams might, but you're so good that he'll look the other way so long as you keep up the pretense."

I bit my lip. "What gave me away at the audition?"

"Afterward, when you thought you were alone, you bent to pick something up, and your hat fell off. I saw your hair, all pinned up." A half smile crossed his lips. "And your face really is too pretty for a boy."

He said it so matter-of-factly that I almost couldn't take it as a compliment. But though there was a glint of humor in his eyes, there was also warmth—and as his gaze held mine, my breath caught. A wave of shyness and gratification and surprise came over me, and I fell awkwardly silent.

But to my surprise, he appeared quite at ease, as unselfconscious as he'd been when I found him tuning my piano. He seemed in no rush for me to reply, and after some minutes, something of his naturalness transmitted itself to me, like a new chord in my ear, along with the possibility—amid all this feeling—of forthrightness and a lack of restraint. An unfamiliar space seemed to open inside my chest, and I regained enough self-possession to gather my thoughts, the first of which was how on earth Jack Drummond happened to be in Wickley Street not half a dozen steps from me tonight. I didn't want to appear ungrateful, but I wasn't going to pretend it wasn't odd, either. "It's rather a coincidence that you were close enough to pull me out of the way of the carriage."

He made a noise that might have been an assent and kept his eyes averted.

"I heard your father lived in Seven Dials," I prodded. "That's nowhere near here."

He shifted the ice slightly. "That's true."

"You don't live with him?"

"No."

I remembered the evening when he tuned my piano, how I'd had to drag answers out of him. "Where do you live?"

He adjusted the ice again, carefully. "Off Everling Lane."

"So Wickley Street isn't on your way home."

He remained silent.

Suddenly, I had a sick suspicion that I'd wholly misread his character. "Were you—were you spying on me?"

His head shot up at that, and his expression was incredulous, and then indignant. "God, no! I wasn't *spying* on you—at least not the way you're meaning. I was just keeping watch to be sure you'd get home safely. Just until Regent Street. I figured once you were in Mayfair, you'd be all right."

I was still gaping at this answer when the girl who'd given Jack the ice came over to the table. She gestured toward my foot. "How is it?"

"I think it's just sprained," Jack said.

"Thank you for the ice," I spoke up.

Her mouth opened in surprise. "Why, you're not a bloke. I thought you was, from your clothes."

"No," I said. "I play piano, so I have to pretend."

An odd expression came over her face. "At the Octavian?"

"Yes."

She gave me a cool, appraising look, then turned away, laying her hand on the back of Jack's chair. "We've got your favorite stew tonight. Mum made it this afternoon."

Her rebuff had all the delicacy of a vaudevillian shove. To her, Jack was a familiar and treasured friend, and she wanted me to understand that any special care being shown to me was only out of deference to him.

"Are you hungry?" Jack asked me.

I nodded.

Jack looked up. "Thanks, Sarah. Two bowls. And some bread, if there's any left."

"All right, then," she said. "Ale for the both of you?"

"Thanks."

Still, she hesitated by the table. There was a peculiar note, of caution or a hidden care, in her voice: "Ben'll be sorry he missed you. We've *all* missed you, Jack. Mum was just asking about you t'other day, and—"

"I've been working a good bit at the piano shop," Jack interrupted.

"Oh!" She smiled broadly. "I expect your uncle will be in later." She tipped her chin toward the back of the room. "He lost a bit last night, might want to earn it back."

Jack gave a knowing laugh, and her cheeks dimpled before she turned away.

I remained silent during this exchange, recognizing that there was a long shared past that underpinned their conversation and sensing that Sarah was rather pleased at excluding me. But when she was gone, Jack readily explained, "Ben is Sarah's brother. My uncle and I have known the Connors forever, and he plays cards with those three blokes over there most nights." He shifted my foot gently and moved the ice to the top of the ankle. "How does it feel?"

"Better," I said. And before my shyness stopped me, I added, "You're being very kind. I'm—sorry I accused you of spying."

"It's all right."

"First you fix my piano, and now you're fixing me."

That made him look up. Our gazes snared again, and there was a moment of silence, during which I wondered if I'd made too much of what he'd said and done. Then a smile of unexpected sweetness curved his mouth, and it struck me that with his ugly cap off, and at ease among his friends, he looked wholly different. Long dark lashes, a curly tangle of black hair, a mouth that was at once firm but expressive. And eyes, dark as strong coffee, that sparkled in the changeful light from the fire. I felt a queer lurch inside me. No, this wasn't the same taciturn young man from the music hall—not by a country mile.

"I thought you'd want this for your foot," came Sarah's voice. "Leastwise while you're eating."

Both of us jumped.

Sarah was holding a pillow and looked apologetically at Jack. "Sorry. I didn't mean to come at you from that side."

With a scrape across the wooden floor, she dragged another chair to our table and plunked the pillow on top. Carefully, Jack shifted my foot over to it. The pillow was less comfortable than his hands, and as Sarah vanished, I bit back the smile I felt forming. Was Jack as conscious as I of Sarah's maneuver?

"I've got a bad ear," Jack said to me.

I bent forward, thinking I'd misheard him. "I beg your pardon?"

"I don't hear so well out of this one," he repeated and tapped his left ear. "That's what Sarah meant."

In my surprise, I fumbled a response: "Oh—I never would have guessed—I mean, you tune pianos and . . . how did it happen?"

He shrugged. "I was born with it, so I've never known any different. I thought it was what everyone had, until I was seven or eight."

The way he said it, I couldn't help but laugh. "Well, how would you even know to ask?"

"Exactly." A grin. "Fortunately, the other one works just fine."

"Jack Drummond." An older woman stood before us, hands on hips, smiling down at him. Her thick white hair was pulled into a bun at the back of her head, and she had green eyes, the same color as Sarah's. "It's been weeks."

Jack was already rising to kiss her cheek, and she pulled him toward her in a hearty embrace.

"Hello, Mrs. Connor. How are you?"

"I'm right as can be," she said and glanced at me, "and glad to see you—and your friend."

"This is—" Jack began, but gave a short laugh and turned to me. "I don't even know your real name."

"Nell Hallam."

I saw him take it in, replacing the name *Ed Nell* with this one.

She was already extending her hand to pat my shoulder. "A pleasure to meet you, dear. I'm Mrs. Connor. What happened to your foot?"

"It's my ankle, actually. I twisted it trying to get out of the way of some horses. There was a runaway cab."

"Oh, dear." She looked at Jack. "Where were you?"

"Wickley Street," he said. "Not far."

Her eyebrows rose. "Well, I've heard of wild horses dragging people places. I s'pose I should be thankful for them, seeing as they steered you here. Your uncle should be in soon."

"Sarah said he lost money last night."

"Yes, Josef was with them." She wiped her hands gently on her apron. "Now, I'll go see about your supper."

I watched her vanish into the kitchen. "Who's Josef?"

He sat back down. "One of my uncle's friends."

"Lucky at cards?"

"Unlucky at life, mostly."

I waited for him to explain.

"He has money troubles, but none of them are really his fault. He came here from Poland ten years ago, and the first thing that happened when he got to London, he was robbed on a train. Then his father got sick, and his wife. That took most of the savings he'd brought with him." He shook his head. "He lent the rest to his brother-in-law for a venture that fell apart. So *vingt-et-un* is my uncle's way of helping him."

Now I understood. "Because he won't accept charity."

A nod. "My uncle used to loan him money—but then Josef was so ashamed of not being able to pay it back that he started avoiding him."

I smiled. "So to preserve his friend's pride, your uncle loses at cards. Does everyone else at the table collude in the scheme?"

Jack shrugged, a smile tugging at the corner of his mouth.

Sarah arrived with two steaming bowls of stew, a loaf of bread wrapped in some brown paper, and a plate with butter and some kind of yellow cheese. "Careful, it's hot."

I placed my palms on either side of the bowl and shivered as its warmth spread into my hands. The stew smelled of butter and beef, potatoes and onions. I ate slowly, savoring the first mouthful as Jack ripped the bread and handed me half. It was the sort I liked best, flavored with rosemary and soft as down on the inside. I tore a small piece and spread the butter thick, then added the cheese. And in that warm, welcoming room, filled with the companionable noises of clinking dishes and muted conversation, we talked easily and without restraint. About how he'd met the Connors when he and Ben smashed into each other on their bicycles; about Matthew and Peggy and Emma; about tuning pianos with his uncle at the Academy and my upcoming audition; about his most eccentric customers, including the lady who insisted that her lapdog be present for tuning sessions because he had an exquisite ear for tone—"Which would be fine," Jack concluded, "except that he bites my ankles while I work, which slows things up a bit." I was already laughing when he added, with a bemused look: "And I have to schedule my visits around the dog's naps."

How had I ever thought Jack was surly, or even shy? In its own way, his manner was as easy and companionable as Matthew's.

"Jacques, *mon fils.*"

We both looked up.

A man of about fifty rested his hand on Jack's shoulder. Like Jack, he was sturdily built. His brown hair was flecked with gray, and his hands were swollen at the knuckles, as though he had worked them hard for many years. But his expression was cheerful, and he smiled affectionately at his nephew.

Jack stood and embraced him. "*Bon soir.*" He turned to me.

"This is my uncle, François Bertault. Uncle, this is Nell Hallam, the new pianist I told you about. She hurt her ankle in the street, so we stopped here."

I smiled up at him and held out my hand. "How do you do?"

His eyebrows rose, and instead of shaking my hand, he bent over it with playful gallantry. "*Mademoiselle,* you deceived my first glance with your costume."

Jack drew a chair from another table for his uncle and sat back down in his own. "Please join us."

"For a minute, I will," Mr. Bertault said, flapping his damp coat behind him and taking the seat. "Then I have to go play cards with those fools." He turned to me. "So you are the new pianist."

"Yes. Did you know that Jack tuned the Pleyel for me?"

"But of course. He borrowed my tools."

"That's right," I said, remembering the box. "I can't tell you how much I appreciate it."

"He says it needs a new soundboard. The one in that piano there is"—he rubbed his thumb against his fingertips—"soft like soap. Drummond won't bother to replace it. However, Jacques can keep it in tune for you. He's better than I, especially now that my hearing isn't what it was." He tugged his ear and leaned toward me, his eyes bright with humor, and said in a conspiratorial stage whisper, "Of course, he was not always so good at it."

I played along and feigned consternation. "He wasn't?"

"The very first piano he worked on—bah! The poor thing! *C'était horrible!* He made it worse every day!"

Jack gave a sigh and rolled his eyes toward the ceiling.

"Of course"—Mr. Bertault shrugged—"I was not going to let him loose on any good pianos. He was just a child—"

"Uncle, I was fourteen."

Mr. Bertault shook a forefinger in the air. "This piano had bad veneer work and broken keys and strings. *C'était un véritable gâchis*—a wretched mess—hardly worth saving. But the lady who wanted to sell needed the money, and I didn't want to hurt her feelings, so I bought it from her. And I put this one"—he waved toward Jack—"to work on it. It was like a stone rolling downhill! First the veneer, then the keys, then the strings—and after a week, not a single note was in tune with the next."

Jack ripped a piece of bread. "Because you twisted the pegs back out every night."

His uncle threw back his head and gave a shout of laughter. "But it was good practice, was it not?"

Jack assented. "It was."

Mr. Bertault turned to me. "And where have you studied your piano?"

"Only at home, with Mr. Moehler. Jack said you knew him before he died."

"Of course!" He shook his head unhappily. "A brilliant man—such fine technique! His death was a terrible loss. I knew him at the Academy."

Jack added, "My uncle knows most of the teachers and students there."

Unbidden, Stephen came to mind. I wondered if Mr. Bertault knew him—and what he thought of him.

A shout came from the corner: "François, are you playing or not?"

"Ah! They need me for the foursome." He stood up and made a small bow in my direction. "A pleasure, *Mademoiselle*." With a wink for both of us, he left.

"He calls you Jacques," I said. "Is that your real name?"

"Yes. My middle name is François"—he tipped his head in his uncle's direction—"for him."

"Is it true, he used to undo your work on purpose?"

Jack grinned. "For practice. That piano he was talking about, it *was* beyond repair. He bought it for me to learn on." He shook his head. "And my God, he made sure I learned—everything from sanding to matching the color of the ivories. He had me take apart and put together the action on a key until I could do it blindfolded."

"Does he have children of his own?"

His smile faded, and his eyes went to his uncle for a moment. "No. I think he would have had them gladly. There was a woman he wanted to marry, back in France. But she was in love with someone else."

"That's too bad. He seems like the sort who should be married." He assented, somewhat absently, and I searched for a different topic. "When did you start truly mending pianos, not just practicing on the bad ones?"

"I don't remember exactly. But I remember the first one he let me work on, an upright. It wasn't terribly expensive, but it belonged to a family he knew. I was trying to be so careful, and I ended up scratching the soundboard—a big scrape, right across."

I winced.

"I felt terrible. I dreaded telling him"—he stopped, and his thumb rubbed at a knot in the table's surface before he continued. "Well, I told my uncle he could take it off my wages. And then he said something that surprised me."

"What?"

"He told me that he owed me more than money could repay." His expression was pensive. "My mother was his younger sister, you see, and he loved her very much. Not long after she died, he moved here from France to teach and open the piano store. He asked me to keep him company, and to keep him away from the whiskey bottle, so I did. He told me if I hadn't, he'd have died." He glanced over at his uncle. "I think he was giving me too much credit, but—well, he believed it."

I swallowed. "He was lucky to have you."

"I've been lucky to have him, too."

In the way he said it, I thought I could read the truth—that his uncle probably provided a refuge from his father sometimes.

A song broke out at the table, sung lustily in French by all four men. I smiled at first, and then I realized it was vaguely familiar. "Why, that's one of the songs Amalie sings!"

"That's right."

"What does it mean?"

"It's a song about life as a gathering of opposites. You've probably heard the English version." He leaned closer and sang a huskier, quieter version of the melody that was being bellowed at the corner table, but with the English words: "Life is a mix of betwixt and between, of boats and carriages, deaths and marriages, lilies and thistles, and wiles and whistles, of silver and sixpence, today and a week hence . . ."

When he finished, I sat back. "I've never heard that version. I had no idea that's what Amalie was singing about. I wonder where she learned her French."

"I taught her," he said simply.

I stared. "You did?"

He smiled. "Amalie's not her real name, and she doesn't really speak French. But back when she was looking for work, she knew it was something that would set her apart. She has a near-perfect memory, as well as a perfect ear."

"She has new songs every few weeks," I said. "Do you teach her all of them?"

He nodded.

"That's kind of you."

He shook his head, as if to correct me. "After my mother died, my father wasn't well, and Amalie's family looked out for me. It was mostly Amalie, though, who mended my clothes and made sure I ate. She told me she had three younger brothers already, so she didn't even notice." A faint smile. "It wasn't until later that I realized she said that so I wouldn't feel beholden. But I know what I owe her."

I felt my perception of Amalie shift. "How long has she been singing at the Octavian?"

"Since it opened, so seven years. Her father died when she was seventeen, and they needed the money."

So Amalie is twenty-four now, I thought. But seven years? That might explain some of the weariness I saw in her face when she wasn't onstage. "And did you convince Mr. Williams to hire her?"

"I didn't have to; he was lucky to get her. She probably should've gone to the Academy herself."

"Did she want to?"

"I think so. But she's happy now, married and all."

"She's married?" I blurted out.

"Sure. Has been for two years."

I felt my view of Amalie realign yet again. And I realized something else, too: if Jack had in fact injured her cousin, Amalie wasn't the sort who'd forgive him. Now I knew, without a doubt, that Stephen's story had been false.

The French song finished with a boisterous chorus and a good deal of laughter. Some of the people at other tables clapped, looking amused.

We were silent a moment, with Jack lost in some private thought and me trying to decide whether to broach what I knew would be a difficult subject.

"Jack."

He took the last bite of his stew and wiped his mouth with the napkin. "What?"

"Tonight, back at the music hall, I was on my way out, and I—I saw your father. There were two boys with him—and he was terribly angry with them."

"Two boys?" he repeated, his voice carefully neutral.

"I assume they were pickpockets. The younger one was called Gus, and he had a scar here." I touched the side of my mouth. "He seemed to have difficulty talking."

Jack nodded. "Rob and Gus. They're brothers."

"You know them?"

"I've seen them around."

"Do you know how Gus got that scar?" I asked.

"He was stealing a hot potato from one of the stalls in Covent Garden." His voice flattened. "When he got caught, the owner shoved it in his mouth and made him hold it there."

I was silent at that, horrified.

"What were they doing?" he asked.

"They were leaving—I think. But your father was—well, he was yelling at them."

"Yelling?"

"He hit them," I admitted, and then added, more softly, "He frightens me."

The minute the words were out of my mouth, I wished them back in. Jack looked away toward the fire, his whole body rigid. He was angry, but also ashamed and—it seemed to me—uneasy.

"I'm sorry." I reached an impulsive hand out, though I pulled it back before touching him. "I'm truly sorry. He's your father, and . . ."

His gaze came back around to me. "And what?"

"And—well," I floundered. "I wouldn't find it easy to hear something like that about a . . . a relation."

"It's no matter," he said tonelessly. "I know who he is."

"But it does matter. It's not my place." I swallowed. "We were having such a nice time, but now you look . . ." My voice trailed off. "You look like you used to at the Octavian. Closed off." He said nothing, and I added hurriedly, "There, you barely say a word and until the other day, when you were fixing my piano, I might even have called you sullen. But here, you're so . ... different."

"You're different at the music hall, too," he retorted. "You're a man there, and a woman everywhere else."

"But that's because I *have* to pretend."

"I know." He watched the fire for a moment, and as the tension eased out of him, he looked back at me with a sigh, seeming resolved to explain. "My father wasn't always like he is now. Back when my mother was alive, he was happy. He'd laugh so loud it would hurt my ears."

And he changed when she was gone, I thought, picturing my own father.

He pushed his plate aside and set his elbows on the table. "My mother grew up in a small town not far from Toulon, and she caught influenza as a young child. It made her lungs weak, and from then on, she was prone to illness, especially during the rainy season. When she was twenty-two, she met my father and moved here to be with him, and though she wasn't sickly, she wasn't what you'd call strong."

"What was her name?"

"Eugenie. Here in England everyone called her Jane." His expression lightened, as if even saying her name brought a measure of happiness.

"Where did you live?"

"Not far from here. I went to school in the mornings, and then I'd help my mum with chores and go on errands for the baker and the butcher down the street in exchange for good bread and meat. That's how I know Mayfair. I had manners, they said, so they'd usually send me when there was a delivery 'cross Regent Street."

I smiled to think of a young Jack running around the streets of Mayfair.

"The winter I was nine," he continued, "my mum got sick again. It was her lungs, just what the doctors said it would be. At first it was just a touch of flu, like most folks. But with her, it turned into pneumonia. By September, she was gone."

"I'm so sorry," I whispered, my heart aching for him.

"What about you?" he asked. "How did your mum die?"

I laced my fingers in my lap, considering what to tell him. Everything about this evening made even a lie of omission feel wrong. Finally, I said, "I told you I *lost* my mother, and that was true." My voice caught a bit. "But she didn't die. She ran off."

To my relief, he didn't look disgusted or appalled at the idea of a woman who would abandon her husband and children.

"Where did she go?"

"To Europe. To become a professional musician. Before she left, my mother was ill. Not like your mother, I mean. She was . . . she had a disease in her brain. I don't remember her myself because I was so young, but she vacillated between mania and melancholy, and during one of her worst times, she became fixated on the idea that her genius required her to go to Europe. So she left, and my father couldn't find her."

He raised an eyebrow. "What does he think of you playing?"

"He passed away." I picked up my spoon and put it inside the empty bowl. "My father changed, too, afterward. Oh, he was always fair to us—my brother, Matthew, and me, but he was"—I searched for the right word—"distant, and resigned, as if he just couldn't bring himself to care about much."

"Your brother's older?"

I nodded. "By four years. I feel like I was raised more by him and our housekeeper and our doctor than by my father." I paused. "Dr. Everett is the one who had concerns about my playing. He believed my mother's illness was exacerbated by it, which is why he designed a practical education for me, to balance out the music." I couldn't quite meet Jack's eyes as I added, "Although recently he reminded me that I still need to be careful. He heard me playing Chopin."

"Do you feel you're like your mother?" Jack asked.

The frankness of the question brought the blood to my cheeks. "I don't have any delusions about being a genius, if that's what you mean. And I've never had a night when I couldn't sleep, or a day when I didn't want to get out of bed. But I do lose myself at the piano sometimes. Hours will pass, and I won't even notice. That worries me."

"Well, for what it's worth, I've been around pianists my entire life, and I think they all do that."

Before I could answer, the mantel clock struck, startling us both.

I stared in dismay at the two hands pointing, one nearly straight up and one down. "Oh! Jack, I'm sorry. I have to go." Still sitting in the chair, I struggled with putting on my coat, and he reached around to help me find my sleeve. "Matthew doesn't know I play. He doesn't even know I'm not home some nights."

His eyebrows rose. "How've you managed to keep it from him?"

"He works late."

He stood up, dug in his pocket for some coins, counted them out, and set them on the table. "What are you going to tell him about your ankle? You can't hide that."

"I'll have to say I was out for a walk and fell, or . . . well, I'll think of something. And I can take a cab. I'll just have it stop at the corner. I can hobble from there."

He put on his coat. "I'll come with you."

"You don't have to," I said.

He said nothing, only bent down to pick up my boot.

Sarah came over to our table. "You're going, then?"

He looked up. "Afraid so. Say hello to Ben for me, will you?"

"I will." She picked up our dishes and stepped away. But she was still watching us as he picked up my boot.

Yes, I thought. *I think Sarah cares for Jack a good deal more than he realizes.*

He made the opening as large as he could.

"Do you think it will go back on?" I asked.

"We'll leave it unbuttoned at the top. The swelling's not bad, what with the ice and keeping it up on the chair. You should be able to walk on it in a day or two."

"I hope so. I need to get back to the Octavian on Monday."

"Let's try." He slid the boot on, and I felt the swollen part of my ankle push against the sides.

He put out his hands to help me up. He was right: the injury was already better, without the shooting pain, though it was still tender. Leaning on his shoulder, I could manage, and we half walked, half hobbled through the front door. I think he bore most of my weight the entire way down Wickley Street, but being at least half a foot taller than I, he had to stoop to help me.

We paused at the corner, where the street crossed Howland, at a gas lamp. The metal of the post felt cold to my perspiring hand.

"We can rest a minute." He straightened up.

"The problem is I'm shorter than you are. It's so awkward—"

He was standing quite close to me. "Is it?" A smile played around his mouth. "I was just thinking it was rather a pleasure."

My heart thudded once, hard, but not a single coherent phrase came to my mind, much less out of my mouth. I stood there dumb as the metal post I was leaning against.

When he spoke again, his voice was flat but not unkind. "You must be exhausted. Wait here. I'll find a cab at the corner. There's no reason for you to walk anymore."

With that, he left me, my insides churning with uncertainty. He returned in a hansom cab pulled by a plodding brown horse. It stopped beside me, and Jack climbed out, helped me over the wheel, and got back in. He looked at me expectantly, and when I said nothing, he said, "I need to tell him where to go."

"Oh! Of course. The corner of Cork and Dunsmire." Jack repeated the words to the driver, and the cab began to move.

He kept to his side of the seat, his elbow on the edge of the window, and looked out. His silence was hard for me to read, but if I had to guess, his thoughts were at least partially occupied elsewhere. Still without speaking, we crossed Regent Street, and the gas lamps became more regular, the streets smoother and quieter, the *hic-hac* of the horse's shoes rhythmic on the cobbles.

Finally, I made myself speak, determined not to have my silence misunderstood for indifference. "Jack." I cleared my throat. "I'm sorry. I'm not very good at talking when I've more feelings than I can say at one go."

I couldn't see his face in the shadows, but his voice was easy as he said, "I understand. I don't mind."

"But I'm very grateful for what you did tonight—and dinner was lovely."

To my ears it sounded inadequate, but it seemed to be enough. He turned, and as the light from a street lamp fell through the window, I could see he was smiling. Though neither of us spoke, a kind of wordless exchange occurred that felt as confidential and comfortable as our conversation at the public house, and my heart lightened in my chest.

We reached the corner of Cork and Dunsmire. The cab stopped, and Jack helped me out, slowly, so I wouldn't knock my ankle on the step.

Jack spoke to the driver. "Wait for me. I'll be just a minute."

The driver grunted in return.

"I need to go down the alley," I said. "My key is to the back door."

This time when he picked me up, I put my arm around his neck; when he set me down on my back doorstep, he didn't step away.

"I'll check on Rob and Gus tomorrow," he said.

Had that been what he'd been thinking of in the cab?

"And, Nell . . ." A hesitation, as if he were making up his mind about something. "I'll keep your secret. Don't worry about that. But for now, don't come to the music hall before half past six, and go straight home afterward."

I stared, surprised. "Why shouldn't I come before half past six?"

"Just trust me on this, all right?"

"All right," I echoed.

He touched my shoulder. "Take care of your ankle." A quick smile, and he was turning away.

"Good night," I called softly after him. I wasn't sure if he heard.

I watched as he strode away, his hands jammed into his pockets, his long coat flapping behind him, his dark head down. The wind made a hollow, high, whistling noise that echoed against the backs of the houses.

As I unlocked the door, the bells of Grosvenor Chapel tolled midnight, the tones deep and somber and familiar to my ear.

I found myself grinning like a fool as I ascended the stairs in the dark.

Chapter 13

$\mathscr{M}$y dream felt so real, I could have sworn that I heard glass smashing and had tumbled out of a carriage onto a dank and desolate street overrun with rats.

I came awake with a gasp, flat on my back, my eyes wide open, my heartbeat fast and unsteady. The room was still dark, and I sensed I'd only been asleep an hour or so. I sat up, my every nerve on fire. But all was silent, and the coolness of the air in my room was reassuringly normal and bracing. I took a few deep breaths to clear the nightmare and terror from my mind. Slowly, I lay back, burrowing into the warm blankets.

And then I heard a noise downstairs, and I sat up again. This time I pushed the covers off and fumbled for the matches at my bedside, finding the box and lighting my candle with unsteady hands. My mantel clock said half past two, later than I would have guessed, and I gave a sigh of relief. It was wholly likely that it was Matthew downstairs. Had he just come in? Or was he simply unable to sleep? That wouldn't surprise me.

Without thinking, I dropped my feet to the carpet. The pain in my injured ankle sent me back onto the bed with a soft moan. I ran my fingertips carefully over the area; the outer part of my foot was swollen and tender. Gingerly, I tried to take a step and realized I'd need some sort of support. Fortunately, we had a cane, from when Matthew had injured his knee a few years ago. He'd borrowed it from Dr. Everett and never given it back. I wrapped myself in my dressing gown and, hopping and hobbling, opened my door and made my way to the hall closet. I pushed aside some clothes, groping until my hand found the cane's curved ivory top. A bit too tall for me, but it would do. With one hand on the wall and the other grasping the cane, I headed toward the stairs, my bare feet silent on the carpet. Halfway down I paused on the landing, from where I could see Matthew's coat on the rack and a light coming from the study.

Carefully, I made my way down, and as I entered the room, I opened my mouth to say, "Matthew, are you all right?"

But it wasn't Matthew. It was a woman in a black cloak.

I let out a small cry, my hand tightening instinctively on the cane. She was standing still, facing the doorway, as if she'd been waiting for me. Her figure was slight, but I couldn't see her features, for a black hood covered her hair.

"Who are you?" My words came out just above a whisper.

"I need to speak to the inspector." Her voice was hoarse, and she broke into a raspy cough that made her double over. When she stood up again, she pushed back her hood, and I saw that she looked frightened.

"Inspector 'Allam," she insisted. "Is he here?"

"He's upstairs. But who are you?" I asked again.

There was the sound of a door opening above, swift feet on the stairs, and Matthew was behind me in a rush. I heard his quick intake of breath. "Thank God! You're all right."

I looked up to reassure him that I was fine—and realized he was talking to her, not to me. As he went toward her, the lamp-light caught the shining grip of Father's revolving pistol, which he'd tucked hastily into the back of his trousers. My eyes fixed on it, and I felt myself go very still. Matthew had been anticipating trouble tonight.

But this woman wasn't trouble. She raised her hands to cover her face and began to cry, with wracking sobs that shook her entire frame. Until then, her hands had been concealed by her cloak. Now I saw that her right hand was cut, and blood was drip-ping down toward her wrist.

"Your hand!" I exclaimed. "What happened?"

"I 'ad to get in," she said between gasps.

Matthew grasped her gently by the arms, for she had swayed toward him as though she were about to faint. "Nell."

I nodded and limped to the kitchen. By my candle's light I could see the broken pane in the back door, and realized that the smashing of glass in my dream had been real. Even in the few minutes since she'd entered, the night air had turned the kitchen cold. Shivering in my wrap, I put the kettle to boil, and fetched bandages and some yarrow and calendula from the cabi-net. While the tea was steeping, I ground the herbs together, adding a bit of water to make a paste that I put on a saucer. I stowed the bandages and tweezers in my pockets so I could still use my cane, and I returned to the study with the saucer and teacup.

She was slumped in a chair. Matthew was on his knees build-ing a fire. Father's gun was on the desk.

"Here, let's get you out of that cloak," I said briskly, setting the tea down. "It's wet." Obediently, she rose to her feet, untied the ribbons at her throat—they were damp and difficult to pull apart—and hung the garment next to Matthew's coat in the hallway.

"How did you get in?" Matthew asked.

"I smashed the winda' in the door." She lifted her chin, and her expression was both defiant and ashamed. "I knocked, but no one came."

"It's no matter," Matthew said, "but I'm going to get a board to cover it. Meanwhile, Nell will see to your hand."

He left the room, and I picked up the gun, opened it, and checked the chambers. The first was empty, for safety, as he'd taught me; the others were full. The sight of the bullets made my chest tighten, but I left them in place, slid the gun into the desk drawer, and picked up the cup of tea, putting it into her good hand. "Here. Let's start with this."

She sipped at it. "Ach!" she said in surprise.

I looked up from the bandages I was unraveling. "Is it too hot?"

"No. Just I'm not used to 'avin' sugar."

Crouching beside her on a stool, I took her right hand in my own. "Do you feel any splinters from the glass?"

She moved her hand tentatively and winced. "There's one 'ere. That's all, I think." She pointed, and I used the tweezers to remove it, then began applying the paste of herbs across the gash on her palm.

The sound of a hammer striking nails startled us both, and I paused in my bandaging. Her hand was shaking, and mine wasn't quite steady, either. But I continued on and tucked in the ends. "Is that better?"

"Yes," she said gratefully. "I'm much obliged. And sorry for breakin' in. I just didn't know what else to do, and I thought I 'eard someone comin' in the alley."

"What's your name?" I asked as I began to wind the unused bandage.

"Nancy," she said. "Nancy Kendrick."

I concealed my surprise as I finished putting my supplies in a tidy pile. No wonder Matthew had been relieved, and the poor woman was desperate to get in. She was probably running for her life. I straightened and reached for my cane. "Matthew will be back in a minute. Would you like more tea?"

She shook her head. "I been enough trouble to you."

"Not at all." I smiled, wanting to reassure her.

I met Matthew in the hallway. "I've bandaged her hand. But she looks near starved. I'm getting her something to eat."

A touch on my shoulder. "Thank you, Nell."

"How did she know to come here?" I asked.

"I told her she could get me a message here, in an emergency." He hesitated. "I probably shouldn't have given her the address, but—"

"It's all right," I interrupted. "I don't think she could hurt a flea, although she startled me half out of my wits just now."

He pointed at the cane. "What's wrong with your leg?"

"It's nothing," I said. "I just twisted my ankle a bit."

Frowning, he opened his mouth to question me further, but just then Mrs. Kendrick coughed.

"Go on," I said and gave him a push toward the study. "I'm fine. She's not."

Back in the kitchen, I hastily assembled a tray with bread and butter, some cheese, a plate, and a knife. I didn't want to miss a word she said.

As I entered, I saw that Matthew had lit two additional lamps, so the room looked more cheerful. He had also pulled two chairs close to hers, so we could all be close to the fire. Mrs. Kendrick looked less anxious, but her face showed her exhaustion. She looked down at the teacup and spoke under her breath. "I'm sorry to be a bother."

"Not at all," Matthew said. "I thought you'd been taken. I went to your house and saw the suitcase."

She nodded, her eyes large. "I did that so it'd look like I 'ad been. I knew 'twas the only way they'd stop lookin' for me."

Understanding and even admiration crossed Matthew's face. "That was clever of you."

"Oh, I ain't clever." She gave a small, bitter breath of a laugh. "I've just not got much left to lose. But you told me you'd 'elp me get away, if'n I told you what I know."

I looked at Matthew in surprise. That sort of bargain didn't sound like him.

"I said that I'd get you out of London in any case," he corrected her gently. "But I'd appreciate anything you could tell me."

She flushed and looked ashamed. "True," she muttered. "I just thought you meant t'other."

"Mrs. Kendrick, you can tell me nothing at all, and I'll get you on a train tomorrow morning."

Tears sprang to her eyes. "I ain't used to people lettin' me choose."

"Why don't you eat something," I interjected.

She took up a piece of bread and nibbled at the crust before setting it back on the plate apologetically. "My stomach ain't been right, but I'll 'ave more by and by."

I set the tray aside, and she settled back in her chair. Her bandaged hand lay in her lap, while her good hand held the cup.

"Well, you prob'ly know that the thievin' ring's near as big as London i'self. The man at the 'ead of it's named Tierney. Least-wise, that's what 'e calls 'i'self."

Matthew nodded encouragingly.

"'E calls it 'the Fleet,'" she continued, "and 'e's divided it into districts called 'ships.' Each one 'as its own cap'ain and crew. The crews are trained, you see."

"Who trains them?" he asked.

She averted her eyes, her expression unhappy. "Men like my 'usband, though it's not 'ow 'e begun."

"You said there are districts that he calls 'ships.' Do you have any idea how many?"

She shook her head. "Tierney keeps 'em all separate, so they cain't talk to each other. But from what 'arry tol' me, there's at least seven, spread out from the Cut in Lambeth up to Euston Station."

I felt my mouth go dry. That was an enormous portion of the city. Hundreds, if not thousands, of streets.

"And what do the ships handle?" Matthew asked.

"Most anything worth stealin'. Some go for shops, some for 'ouses. Each ship collects its own lot, and then it's sorted and sent out for sellin' or smugglin' or meltin' down, dependin' on what it is. So all the jewelry goes one place, 'andkerchiefs and clothes another, silver, copper, porcelain, paintin's and such, little bits o' art, and trifles all have their own."

"Trifles?" I asked.

"Cigar cases, snuffboxes," she replied. "But there are new things all the time. Last month, 'twas fans. The boys were taught to look for ones made of bone and ostrich feathers. Soon it'll be summat else."

"How do they choose the houses?" Matthew asked. His voice was mild, even gentle, which told me how closely he was listening.

"It's mostly the servants wot tells 'em."

Matthew's eyebrows rose.

"A servant from one place passes the word 'bout when a family'll be gone, and where the valu'bles be," she explained patiently. "They get ten or even twenty pounds back, depending on if'n they give the name of another servant at a different 'ouse who'll do the same. D'you see?"

I stared, shocked by the level of organization such a plan would require. Matthew managed to reply, "I do, thank you." He mulled everything for a moment. "But what about your husband? What did he do for the Fleet at first?"

Her eyes wandered to the fire, and it took her a minute to answer. "'E were a silversmith 'afore we came to London, so when he couldn't get a job 'ere, bein' Irish, 'e worked for a ship in Whitechapel that 'andled silver. Candlesticks, cutlery, pitchers, tea trays, them sorts of things. Some got smuggled 'cross the Channel, but a good bit was melted down and turned into 'alf crowns and sixpence."

"Not pounds or threepence?" I asked, naming the other silver coins.

"Nay. Sometimes shop folks won't take pounds from a stranger, and threepence are worth only 'alf o' six and just as much work." She was beginning to relax, warming to her subject. "Most anybody can pass 'alf crowns and sixpence, 'specially in 'otels and places where there's foreign folks wot carry coins instead of notes. 'Nd the ships for copper make the pennies and farthin's."

The fire had begun to drop down, and Matthew rose to add more coal to it.

"How does one counterfeit a coin?" I asked, partly because I was curious and partly to keep her talking. "Do you know?"

"Well, I ain't done it m'self, mind you, but 'arry's tol' me often enow." She sipped at her tea. "First, ye take a true coin and grease it with tallow or suet. Then you make a mold round it, using plaster of paris, and clamp it together." Her hands came together around the imaginary coin. "Once the plaster's dry, you pour the silver into the collar, let it cool, and open the mold. Then you cut off the gat—the little bit that sticks out where the silver was poured—and file it down. Then you plate it, usin' a batt'ry with acid and cyanide, and last, you rub it with some lampblack and oil." She gave a small sniff. "If'n it's too shiny, you can't pass it."

"Where are the ships set up?" Matthew asked as he returned to his seat.

The animation faded from her face, and her brows knitted together unhappily. "I dunno. 'Tis the one thing 'arry never told me. For my own good, 'e said. But I've often thought on it. Tierney sells to pawnshops all over London. Maybe some ships are above the shops or somewhere close. 'Twould make sense, wouldn't it?"

"Yes, that's a good thought." Matthew nodded. "Is there anything else?"

She bit her lip and shook her head, her expression anxious. I thought I understood why, and Matthew was quick to reassure her.

"You've given me more help in this half hour than I've had in months," he said kindly. "Now, why don't you try to rest for a few hours. I'll get you on the train first thing. You can tell me where you want to go when we get to the station."

Relief came over her face, but I felt profoundly sad for her. With her husband dead, she might get out of London, but what then? Where would she find work? I hoped she had relations somewhere who would take her in.

With a look at Matthew, I rose and took a blanket from the cabinet. "Here, Nancy, why don't you stay by the fire, where it's warmest."

She nodded, docile as a child, and let me tuck the wool around her.

I picked up her teacup, and Matthew followed me to the kitchen with the tray.

"Well, that was an earful," I said quietly.

"Yes, rather." He popped a hunk of bread in his mouth.

"Why did you have Father's gun? Were you expecting her, or someone else tonight?"

He swallowed and met my gaze. "I didn't expect anyone in particular—certainly not her. But there was a black mark on the bottom of our door yesterday. Didn't you notice it?"

"No," I said, puzzled. "What sort of mark?"

"About so long." His hands sketched a length of about a foot. "It was used in Lambeth two years ago, as a warning to police. Two of the detectives looking into a contraband shipment at the customs house wouldn't let it alone."

I studied my brother. "What happened to them?"

"They were found dead in the river a week after the mark appeared on their doors."

I felt the blood drain from my face, and I grasped his arm.

"Matthew." It came out hoarsely. "Do you think someone in the Fleet made the mark?"

The lines around his mouth deepened, and his hand gave mine a quick squeeze. "Maybe. I think it's more likely that whoever did it knows I served in Lambeth, and that I know what a black mark means." He paused. "Don't you?"

Someone in the Metropolitan Police, and likely someone at the Yard, trying to frighten him.

Perhaps he saw how shaken I felt, for he led me to one of the stools and gently pushed me down. "Do you know who the snitch is yet?" I asked.

"No. But at least I'm certain it isn't William."

I let out an uneven breath. Thank goodness he could still trust his friend, if no one else. "What makes you sure?"

"Because someone is trying to throw suspicion on him." He leaned against the table and crossed his arms over his chest. "Yesterday afternoon, a woman came into the Yard looking for him. A rather beautiful prostitute." He grimaced. "She told the sergeant that William owed her money for services."

"A prostitute came to the Yard, wanting to be paid?" I asked, incredulous.

He let out a snort. "She didn't *say* she was a prostitute. She claimed she had done some sewing for him—said that Mr. Crewe owed her for three pairs of pants, and he wouldn't be welcome back in her shop until he paid up. But it was clear enough what she meant."

"And you're supposed to suspect that William is in debt and might be selling police information to pay what he owes her?"

"It looks that way." He unfolded his arms and reached for a

piece of cheese. "But her photograph is in one of the books we have of known prostitutes, and I know William well enough to know that there's no way he'd betray Mary. They're engaged, and he adores her. I said as much to several of the men, and it was passed off with a good chuckle."

"What did William say when he heard about it?"

"He was alarmed and angry, naturally. But it gave me the opening I needed."

"How did he take you asking?"

His smile was both rueful and relieved. "Like a friend. He understood why I asked. In fact, he thanked me for it, as you thought he might. And at least now he's on guard." He sighed and turned to stare at the boarded window. "I wish you could stay somewhere else, at least until this is over."

"Oh, Matthew. Where would I stay? Besides, I don't want to leave you here alone."

"I know," he said wearily. "I'm just saying I wish you didn't have to be here."

I swallowed. "I'll be careful."

He picked up Father's revolver. "You should go back to bed. I'll have her out before dawn. But I want to let her sleep for a few hours. She looks done in."

"So do you," I said. "In fact, I could stay up—"

"Please don't argue, Nell."

The strain in his voice made something inside my chest twist. "All right, Matthew, if that's what you want." I rose and gave him a kiss on the cheek, the way I used to when I was young.

Back in bed, I lay still, my nerves on edge. But after an hour of silence—broken only by the church's chimes on the quarter hours—I climbed out and went downstairs to peer into the study. Mrs. Kendrick was fast asleep, her feet on a footstool. Matthew lolled in a chair, the pistol across his thigh.

Silently, I wrapped myself in a blanket and kept watch for all of us, until five o'clock, when I heard the first rumble of carts across the cobbles. I woke them, then, and they were gone minutes later, out the back door, into the gloom.

Chapter 14

*W*hen Peggy arrived at half past seven, I was alone and sitting in the study. Naturally, she wanted to know both what I'd done to my ankle and what had become of her window. I told her an approximate version of all that had happened, including the reasons for Matthew's worry, and it seemed that afterward the pots rattled around the kitchen more vehemently than usual. Shortly after nine o'clock, the glaziers arrived to measure the opening, announcing that Matthew had sent for them.

By the time they left, my exhaustion had taken hold, and I was heading upstairs to snatch a few hours of sleep when Peggy found me. "Nell?"

"Yes?" I said, stifling my yawn.

"Come with me, child," she said abruptly, and swallowing a sigh, I followed her back to the kitchen.

"Black marks and broken windows and strange women appearing in the night! For mercy's sake, we might as well be in Belfast, with spies all round and the bloody Catholics murthering people in their beds." Peggy took a towel off a bowl and took out four potatoes. She pursed her mouth. "And then we have you, sneaking out at night in men's clothes."

It took a moment for her words to penetrate my tired brain.

She snorted. "Well, at least you've the decency not to deny it. Is that the truth about how you hurt your ankle?"

"How long have you known?" I managed.

"Since two Wednesdays past. I came back because I forgot my umbrella. And there you were, crossing Cork Street." She found a knife in the drawer. "Frightened me at first."

"Frightened you," I repeated. "Why?"

She merely looked at me as if I were being purposefully obtuse.

"You mean, you thought I might be *leaving*?" I asked incredulously.

She shrugged. "I admit, it didn't seem likely. For one thing, you warn't carrying so much as a satchel. And for another, I remembered how you'd had those smudges under your eyes some mornings, and I guessed it warn't just the one time. I thought on it, and figured you'd be back."

I swallowed. "Of course I'd be back."

"And so you were." Her deft hands started on a potato, the skin coming off in a long strip. "And I warn't going to say anything, but now that this has happened"—she nodded her head toward the window—"I want to know where you're going and what you're doing. And if you don't tell me, I'll tell Matthew, and he'll make sure that's the end of it."

I sat down on a stool and leaned against the wall. I couldn't tell her everything, but I'd confess some. In a way it would be a relief.

"I have an audition with the Royal Academy."

She looked up from the potato. "What's that to do with you going out at night dressed like a man?"

"To earn the tuition, of course. There's no point in trying unless I can pay for at least the first year. So I . . . I took a position."

Both eyebrows rose.

"I'm playing piano in a music hall a few nights a week." I paused and added, reluctantly, "In Soho."

The knife clattered onto the table, and her mouth fell open. "For mercy's sake, Nell!"

I plunged on. "I know—and when Matthew told me about the attacks, it scared me, too. But I always go when the streets are still busy and the shops are open. There's someone who guards the back entrance for the performers, so I never stand outside. I take lighted streets all the way home, and I'm back by eleven every night—well, most nights—and it pays *well*, Peggy—very well. Another month or so and I'll have earned all the money I'll need for the first year."

Her lips were pressed together so tightly they were white.

Silently, I took another knife from the drawer, reached for a potato, and started peeling, just to have something to do besides observe the anxiety, exasperation, and dismay that were taking their turns on her countenance. She took out a sharpening steel and drew her knife across it half a dozen times. The sound always made my nerves go taut, and she knew it.

"Peggy, please don't be angry."

She pointed the knife at me. "If something had happened to you one of those nights, we wouldn't have had any idea where to begin looking. A music hall in Soho wouldn't've occurred to any of us, that's sartin."

I peeled the potato carefully, so the strips of skin mounded in a tidy heap. "I know."

"Was it really worth risking your life? Just to go to the Academy?"

"It's all I've ever wanted, to play piano," I replied quietly. "You know that."

"But you can do that in your own parlor!"

"Not if I want to continue learning," I protested.

We stood there, the two of us, just looking at each other for a long moment, until finally she gave a sigh of capitulation and began dicing the potatoes into quarters and then eighths. "Well, then. Are you ready?"

I felt a wave of relief that I wouldn't have to argue further. "I think so. I'm playing Chopin and Mozart, and mostly they're all right."

"But?"

"But even if I play well, I may not get in."

She frowned. "Why not?"

"I'm old, for them. The Academy says they take applicants until they turn twenty—so officially, I'm still eligible for another month. But most students start when they're ten or twelve. In fact, I inquired, and they've *never* taken anyone over sixteen. I've a feeling the judges are going to laugh at me because I'm the oldest person they've ever seen."

She dropped the potato pieces into a bowl. "They aren't going to laugh when they hear you play."

"And then I worry that I've chosen the wrong sorts of pieces. I can hear them now: 'Oh, not the Mozart *again*.'"

"Hmph." She sifted through the bowl and put aside a rotten bit. "When is it? The audition."

"Next Wednesday afternoon."

Her hands paused. "Less than a week? No wonder you've been so scattered lately." She covered the potatoes with a towel and set the bowl aside. "Fetch the peas, would you? They need shelling."

I removed the sack of peas and two small dishes from the cupboard while she began to knead the bread dough. I drew the stool forward so I could keep the weight off my foot and began to separate the peas from the pods. We worked in silence for a minute or two, until she asked, "What happens if you get in? What are you going to tell Matthew and Dr. Everett?"

"I don't know. But there's no point in telling anyone unless I do."

She tipped her chin toward the bowls. "You're mixing them."

I looked down. She was right. I'd put some of the peas back in with the pods. I fished them out and began again. "You know that Dr. Everett stopped by the other day. He caught me practicing and gave me a good talking-to. He's worried that playing pieces like the Chopin will be what pushes me into Mother's disease." I swallowed, wanting to ask but half afraid of the answer I'd receive. "Do you . . . do you see her, in me?"

Her capable hands folded the dough on the worn wooden table before she answered. "I don't know, child. I can see your likeness to her, that's sartin. Not just your talent, but the way a fire truck with four horses could run through the room while she was playing and she wouldn't have noticed." She flipped the dough again, and a puff of flour rose. "But there are other parts of her that you don't seem to have at all."

"Really?" I heard the hopefulness in my voice.

"Oh, I know the doctor says it was a disease in her brain, and he's the one who's been to university, so p'rhaps he's right. But you have to remember, he didn't know her except the last four years, and those were the worst of it. He warn't called in until she was beyond what regular folks could manage." She turned the dough again. "Besides, Dr. Everett's a medical man, with his own partic'lar way of thinking. To him, it looked like a disease no one could help, like rickets or scarlet fever, that began when she was nineteen or thereabouts. But that don't take sartin things into account."

I shelled the last pea and pushed the bowls aside. "Things like what?"

Her expression became regretful. "I'm not one to speak ill of the dead, but from the time Frances was a mite, her parents made an uncommon fuss over her playing. And I daresay she got used to it. People said she loved her piano, but there's part of me thinks she loved people looking at her and praising her just as much. By the time she was eleven or twelve, there were plenty of evenings when her parents would invite people over to hear Frances, and they'd all declare they'd never seen the like, and she should be sent away to special places for lessons so she'd be as famous as Jenny Lind and such. It made her all flushed and excitable. Even after people left, she looked"—she frowned—"hectic, like she had a fever. Sometimes she could scarce go to sleep at night, she was so riled up."

"Maybe that was part of the disease," I said. "An early symptom."

"Maybe," she said, sounding unconvinced. She floured the dough again. "I could understand her being headstrong and too wrapped up in herself at that age; but she didn't grow out of it like most folks. I saw her governess try to bring her round. But when Frances complained, her parents dismissed the poor woman." She sighed. "Oh, Frances could be pleasing when she wanted, and she was pretty, o' course, and plenty clever, that's sartin, but by the time she was sixteen or thereabouts, your grandparents warn't quite sure what to do with her and left her mostly alone."

"You think their behavior is to blame for her condition?" I couldn't help the note of skepticism that came into my voice.

She dropped the dough onto the pan and looked up at me, her expression matter-of-fact. "A girl might like biscuits and sweeties, but those can't be the only things you feed her."

"No, I suppose not. It just seems that mere overindulgence shouldn't bring about a disease."

Peggy's expression became stubborn, and I knew not to press the point further. Instead, I yielded with a small laugh. "Well, at least I can't say I've experienced that sort of spoiling."

"No, I'd say not."

I ran my thumb absently over the edge of the table, feeling the nicks in the wood. "Dr. Everett believes that Mother's playing fed her moods."

She sighed. "I don't know if I'd say it that way myself, but she *was* excitable at the piano, and certainly by the end, the piano was like a poison. It made it so she could scarce think of anything else."

"I wonder if she ever thinks about us now." The words slipped out of my mouth before I quite realized I'd thought them.

She paused in the act of opening the rag cupboard, and her expression softened. "Sometimes I think to myself that she must. Maybe at nights, when she's quiet, or doesn't have much else to occupy her." She chose a rag from the pile and shook out the folds. "If ever you're a mother, you'll know how it is, loving your child. Why, I'd set down my life with no more thought than set-tin' down this rag, if I thought it would cure Emma."

Her words brought stinging tears to my eyes.

"And that's why I can't believe your mother didn't have some place in her that loved you, that might've showed itself, except it got covered up."

I felt a pang of self-doubt. "Do you see any signs of that in me? The inability to love people?"

She came close then and, in an uncharacteristic gesture, gently tucked a loose piece of hair behind my ear. "No, child. Seems to me, you have your attachments, same as the rest of us."

I smiled. "Well, I'm certainly not going to go running off to Europe. I wouldn't leave Matthew for the world. Or you, or Dr. Everett."

"No. And that part of you is like your father. He ran off, as you say, to look for her, but we all knew he'd come back."

"I wonder what would've happened if he'd found her."

"Oh, he found her, all right." Her tone was acerbic.

I blinked. "What?"

Dr. Everett didn't know this. Did Matthew?

"He went to Paris and found her in the papers," Peggy said. "With a photograph and all, listed as a performer, using her mother's name. Then he found out she'd paid for her passage by selling some of her dowry silver the week 'afore she left. He'd thought her leaving had been the work of a moment, but she'd been planning it all along, sly as a fox. You can imagine how that made him feel. Like a fool."

"But he wasn't a fool! He trusted her, as he should have. She was his wife."

"Some would say, more's the pity." She shook her head dolefully. "Marriage is a tricky business. It's the most important choice you can make, and most people make it when they're too young and plum silly, thinking someone's worth loving just because of the way he's dressed, or some such nonsense."

"You were young, and it worked out happily," I reminded her.

That brought a smile. "He was a good, sturdy sort, my Joe was. He warn't some fancy man with a few coins in his pocket and a pretty face. He was practical, with prospects, and he took care of me." She gave the counter an absent swipe with the rag. "Made me laugh, too. There aren't many of his sort left, so far as I can tell."

"Well, I hope I find someone like your Joe," I said. "Fortunately, I have a few years before I need think of it."

Peggy's face altered, and I knew what that small pinch of pain around her mouth meant. Emma didn't have a few years, and she'd never marry.

I could have bitten my tongue off. "Peggy, I'm sorry. That was stupid of me. I'm so sorry."

"Don't be silly. It's sartinly not any of your doing." She shook her head. "It's time I got on with the dusting." But before she left the kitchen, she let her hand rest on my shoulder, and I squeezed it in return.

I picked up my cane and went upstairs to bed. But whereas an hour ago I would have fallen asleep instantly, now I lay with my eyes open, and it wasn't only because my ankle was throbbing.

For my whole life, all I'd had of my mother were stories about her—stories that allowed me only to sketch her with the barest outlines. Peggy had added new contours to the picture. Her account differed a good deal from Dr. Everett's, but her details seemed so credible that I sensed the truth might lie somewhere in between. It wasn't lost on me, however, that the one aspect they agreed upon was that Mother's piano playing was dangerous to her. Their belief gave me a hollow feeling under my ribs. I fell asleep hoping desperately that the piano would never be a poison for me.

Chapter 15

For two entire days I remained quietly at home, using my cane, putting ice and poultices on my ankle, and observing the glaziers as they replaced the window not once, but twice, because the first pane they brought cracked not a minute after they'd installed it. Dr. Everett stopped in to check on me, and so I asked him to tell Marceline what had happened, and that I'd come to see her as soon as I was able.

Eventually, I grew fidgety and found my confinement irksome, especially as the feeling of wanting to see Jack again pulled on me like one of his tightening wrenches on a pin.

To my relief, on Saturday morning, my ankle was sturdy enough that I could walk without pain. Jack had told me that he spent that day at his uncle's piano shop, so after I finished practicing, I went upstairs and opened my armoire, debating my options. My brown poplin dress was my prettiest one, with lace at the collar. But the blue lawn brought out the color of my eyes. I put on the blue, looked at myself in the mirror, and nearly changed it for the brown before I shut the door firmly. Yes, it was the first time Jack would see me in a dress, but I was being ridiculous. I wrapped a thin gray shawl around my shoulders and set out.

Thick white clouds shifted overhead against the blue, and though it might rain later, the breeze felt cool and pleasant. I began at the end of Samson Lane and walked east. It was a well-kept street, with neat storefronts that displayed their wares in their windows: The Bluebird Patent Candle Company, with its tidy rows of hanging ivory tapers and the fragrances of vanilla and tallow wafting onto the sidewalk. The York & Co. Hat Shop, with men's dark top hats in the small-paned windows on one side of the door and ladies' frilled and feathered concoctions on the other. The J. Salloway Tea Company, with a small crowd outside, the mothers looking on indulgently as the children clamored for the biscuits that a young man was doling out from a tray. The Kittley Bakeshop, whose hot cinnamon buns dusted with sugar almost made me pause. Eager to set out, I hadn't eaten much breakfast.

Five minutes on, I came upon a store with the sign M. BERTAULT, FINE PIANOS on a neat brass square beside the door. There was a large plate glass window at the front, washed perfectly clear and framed by a reddish wood that was polished to a high gloss, as if to promise that an old piano might regain its luster here.

Through the door, I saw a room with perhaps a dozen pianos, most with their lids lifted; Mrs. Kendrick's revelations notwithstanding, they made me think of a fleet of ships sailing before the wind. Beside one piano stood Jack with a customer who had a narrow face, a Gallic nose, and only a fringe of dark hair around his ears. At the moment, he was laughing, and Jack's hand rested companionably on his shoulder. Then the man sat down on the bench, and Jack raised the fallboard to reveal the keys.

I felt a fluttering under my ribs as I put my hand on the brass doorknob. It turned with a silent smoothness that I imagined customers found as reassuring as the elegant front window. A bell tinkled over my head, and I closed the door gently behind me.

Jack's eyes flicked toward me, caught, widened in surprise, and held. Then came an unhurried smile that sped up the fluttering and made my limbs feel as if they were no longer connected to me in quite their ordinary way. He gave an almost imperceptible tip of his head toward the man seated at the piano. I nodded back to convey that I'd wait, and turned to survey the shop.

It didn't look large from the outside, but I realized that this room was only the first of several. Its walls were painted a muted blue that set off the wood veneers. On the far wall two windows hung with patterned silk curtains flanked a door that probably led to a back alley with dustbins. To the right was a staircase leading up to the second story; to the left was an archway into another room. I didn't want to hover where Jack was, so I walked into it and found myself facing instruments in various states of repair: uprights, grands, a few clavichords, and some harpsichords. Along one wall was a wide workbench, upon which lay steel wires of different thicknesses, strips of felt, pieces of ivory, spare black keys, and piano legs. It made me think of an operating theater.

"Good afternoon, *Mademoiselle*," came Mr. Bertault's voice behind me.

I turned and gave him my best smile. "I'm dressed as myself today, Mr. Bertault."

His eyebrows rose in delighted recognition; one would think I was a long-lost friend instead of an acquaintance of a few min-

utes. "Ah! *Mademoiselle* Nell!" He took my hand and bent over it.
He glanced back to the front room where Jack was still with the
customer, and his voice became apologetic. "Jacques is busy for a
moment. Perhaps—"

"Please don't interrupt him," I said hastily. "He knows I'm
here. I don't mind waiting. And I don't want to take you away
from your work, either."

"Nonsense. I shall make a tour with you. Come."

I let him steer me toward a group of grand pianos near the back
of the store. "Are you repairing these?" I asked.

"Yes, although some, like this one"—he gestured to a particularly shabby instrument by the wall—"are . . . what do you call
them when the end is inevitable?"

"Hopeless causes?" I supplied.

"*C'est vrai.*" He waved a hand. "Not worth either the time or
the money. But it is hard to turn someone away."

I remembered what Jack had said about his uncle losing money
to Josef on purpose. Here was another example of his kindness.

"Here." He took my arm to lead me toward a piano with gold
scrolling on the blond wood cabinet. "What do you think of this?"

"It's very pretty," I said hesitantly.

"Yes, it's very pretty." His lip curled. "Good for someone who
wants to look at the piano and not play it."

I pointed to a plain one. "And that one?"

"A Bechstein, but it needs a new soundboard. Jacques will do
it for me this week." He patted the edge as if it were a friend's
shoulder. "What kind of piano do you prefer?"

I raised an eyebrow. "One that's in tune."

"Ah!" He gave a shout of laughter as if I'd said something very
clever. "You don't ask much."

"I suppose not." I looked around the room. "I've a Broadwood at home."

"Ah! A fine English instrument." He led me to a piano with a black lacquer cabinet. The fallboard was down, and he drew it up. "Jacques just repaired this one. Would you like to try it?"

I played a chord, separated the four notes, and rejoined them. "The action is different from mine. The keys spring back faster."

"It's a piano that requires a strong touch," he said. "But you do not look feeble."

I sat down and ran my hands through some harmonics. Then I played them again, astonished by the way the notes connected. "It's wonderful!"

His eyes gleamed with approval. "What do you hear?"

"It doesn't hesitate. Every note is clear as water. What was it like when it arrived?"

"Very bad. This one has traveled from France, and an ocean voyage is one of the worst things you can do to a piano." He sat down on a nearby bench. "Play something for me, *chérie.* My sister used to play for me, and I miss it." He waved his hands. "With these, I cannot play anymore."

Mindful of the presence of customers, I chose the first movement of Mozart's Sonata in E-flat Major, an adagio. It was neither too short nor too long and was generally pleasing to the ear.

When I finished, I looked up to find him studying me with a puzzled expression.

I took my hands off the keys at once, feeling embarrassed. He had heard scores of brilliant musicians play; perhaps I sounded amateurish to his ears. "Is something wrong?"

He shook his head hastily. "Of course not. Jacques said you played well—but if he only heard you play those bits for the show, he could not know. You play *very* well. Why are you not studying at the Royal Academy? Or do you have a tutor?"

"I haven't had one since Mr. Moehler died, I'm afraid."

He sighed. "Ah, yes. Now I remember. Have you considered what you will do, now that Johann is gone?"

"He didn't have time to find me a new teacher. And the two I approached said they couldn't take me."

He rubbed his chin, considering. "But they are not the only two tutors in London. Perhaps I can help you."

"Well, I'm also not the usual age of most students."

"I know some for whom that would not be an obstacle. My friend Jane Talbot, for example. I could speak to her."

Seeing he was not going to let the matter drop, I smiled and bent toward him. "Actually, I have an audition at the Royal Academy next week."

His face brightened. "Ah, *bien*!" He slapped his palms onto his knees. "I do not need to convince you, then. On Wednesday, isn't it? And you would begin in the fall?"

"Yes."

"Tell me, what are your two pieces?"

"Mozart's Sonata in C and Chopin's Scherzo number three."

His eyebrows lifted. "*Vraiment*? They are both difficult to play well. Many people think that sonata is simple, but I have heard it butchered, especially the left hand. Now, the Chopin . . ."

He broke off and took my left hand in his. Knowing what he was looking for, I stretched my fingers wide, and he smiled. "*C'est bon*! Some of the chords are very difficult, but your reach is long."

"I still have to stretch," I admitted. "And not just my hands. It's

the hardest piece I've ever played. Some days when I'm practicing, I can practically hear Chopin turning in his grave, moaning
about stupid English girls tinkling away in their parlors."

He threw back his head and laughed heartily. "Let me hear it."

"Oh, I don't know if your customers want to listen to—"

"Please. Just the first two parts, if you would. I want to hear
what you are stretching for, as you say."

He looked so earnest, I couldn't refuse him. "All right." I took
a deep breath and set my fingers back on the keys.

I played the first section in C-sharp minor and the second in
D-flat major. Then I turned to see his reaction.

His eyes had been closed for listening, and a moment after I
finished, he opened them. I had played without any noticeable
errors, and I was prepared to see at least mild approval in his expression. But although he smiled, it seemed a trifle forced.

"Your technique—it is *very* good." The overly hearty note in
his voice opened a dark pit of fear under my ribs.

"You say that as if something else is not."

He rubbed a hand over his face. "Pardon an old man—"

"You're not old," I broke in, my heart sinking at the thought
that he was trying to soften his criticism by disparaging himself.

He pursed his lips. "Frankly, my dear, if you weren't so very
talented, I wouldn't bother saying anything. But yes, I think there
is something missing from your playing."

I had to swallow before I trusted myself to speak. "Very well.
Tell me what's wrong. If I'm not going to get into the Academy, I
want to know why."

"Oh"—he waved dismissively—"I don't think it will keep you
from getting in. You're very proficient."

I breathed again. "But what is it? What's missing?"

"Why, I think you are missing *la susceptibilité*." His voice softened: *"Oui. C'était la susceptibilité, Mademoiselle."*

I had no earthly idea what he meant. "Susceptibility to what?"

"You play with poise—with reserve, perhaps born of esteem." He touched his fingertips to his chest. "But Chopin, of all composers, was a man who was intimate with his piano. It was the means by which Chopin conveyed his sentiments to the world— the longing he had for fulfilling love, the pain of his illnesses, the grief of his tragic exile."

I nodded. I knew of Chopin's vexed romance with George Sand, his tuberculosis, his emigration from his beloved Poland.

"But he understood that the piano has its own voice as well, which he was compelled to heed. It *held* Chopin's notes"—his hands formed a cup—"and then refined them, enlarged them, so that they resonated in his ears and stirred his heart. You play with almost perfect correctness but with the susceptibility"—he pushed his open hands away—"out here, as if the piano is not allowed to speak back to you, to make its impression upon you in return."

I felt a growing dismay, for I was beginning to have an idea what he meant.

"My dear, all of music is a reach beyond borders and across the ages. A daring attempt to touch those we do not know, but whose feelings we know in the deepest parts of our hearts because they are our own. Thus, the passions, the pains, the—the sensitivities of the composer and the instrument, all must not only be acknowledged but celebrated." He leaned toward me, his brown eyes intent. *"Comprenez-vous?"*

I swallowed. "I think so."

"Then why do you not play so?"

The note of agitation brought sudden, stinging tears to my eyes. He drew back. "*Merde*," he said under his breath.

I looked away and fought to compose myself.

He sat down heavily next to me on the bench, and I shifted to make room. "Oh, *chérie*." All the fierceness had faded from his voice. "It's a stupid tongue I have in my head." A linen square, thin and soft from many launderings, was pushed into my hand and I pressed it to my eyes. "I'm sorry. I've no right to speak to you that way."

I met his sorrowful gaze. "Of course you do. You only mean to help me, and you're not wrong. I do keep susceptibility, as you say, at a distance. I just never knew you could hear it as something missing in my playing. Mr. Moehler never said so. In fact, he didn't approve of pianists—especially women—who imposed their own feelings on the work. He said it was selfish and disrespectful to the composer, a sign of the pianist's desire to be applauded, when a true musician should want to be almost invisible, transparent, to let the music come to the fore."

He frowned. "But that is impossible! Even the most brilliant pianist cannot hold himself wholly apart. There will be inflections, be they ever so faint. Not because a pianist desires to be seen—the way a man parades in Hyde Park to show off his new coat—but because our brains and hearts inform our playing, and the sounds we hear affect us. To think that one can avoid *that*—well, it's—it's—"

"Naive?" I said tentatively.

"*Mais, oui.*" Mr. Bertault made a noise in the back of his throat, a rumble of a cough. "Did you ever hear Johann play Beethoven's Ninth?"

I nodded, remembering. "It was brilliant."

"Brilliant." He nodded as well, slowly. "Sparkling as polished silver, but cold. His piano was like a mute thing, silent in the face of an onslaught. Beethoven would not have played it so."

"He was a good teacher," I said defensively.

"A fine teacher," he agreed. "Or your technique would not be what it is. But for someone such as yourself, he was missing"—he brought the thumb and forefinger on his right hand nearly together—"just the smallest piece. It's not his fault! He didn't know. It was not in his heart to be humble, to be open to the collaboration between player and instrument. And I could not have explained it to him, as I have done just now, and have him understand what I meant. You"—he pointed—"know how to listen."

His kindness brought a lump to my throat. I dropped my eyes to the keys and ran my thumbs along the ivory edges, feeling the gaps between them. Finally, I said, "My mother—she was a pianist, too, but she was ill, for a long time."

"Ah, that is very hard." His tone was subdued, and I sensed he was thinking of Eugenie.

I looked up. "She was ill in her mind," I amended. "She had what a French doctor calls '*folie circulaire*.' The tendency for it can be inherited, you see, and her doctor believed the best thing for me would be to avoid all extremes of feeling, particularly at the piano, as that is what seemed to make her condition worse. He heard me the other day, working on the Chopin. I was playing so vigorously that a string broke, and it distressed him very much. But I am trying—I've always tried—to be careful."

"And your mother? What happened to her?"

"When I wasn't quite a year old, she ran away to Paris. She never came back."

A heavy sigh. "I see. From the way you looked just now, I thought she might have died."

"That might have been easier to bear." It came out of my mouth before I had time to think how it might sound to someone who had lost his only sister. Stricken, I wadded the handkerchief tightly in my hand. "I'm sorry. I didn't mean—"

His eyes held compassion. "I know what you meant."

"It was nearly twenty years ago. You'd think it wouldn't matter anymore."

"Nonsense. It will always matter." The gentleness in his voice made my eyes burn again. After a moment he added, "I am glad you told me, for I understand now. And I would like to hear you play again. But not the Chopin, *chérie*. Try something that feels like play to you, instead of work. Perhaps something peaceful, of which your doctor would approve."

It took me a moment to swallow down the tightness in my throat, the sting in my nose, and to think of a piece. Finally, I picked Brahms's "Wiegenlied," something I could play as easily as I could navigate my house in the dark.

A dozen measures in, he murmured, "That's it. Let the piano speak back to you. You've nothing to fear from a conversation as tender as this."

I did my best, and at the final note, I looked up.

"*Mon Dieu!*" Mr. Bertault's eyes were wet. "Did you feel the change?"

I had, and as tears pricked the corners of my eyes, I nodded. "But does it sound any different?"

"You play with what the French call *la tendresse,* and it strikes here." He tapped his chest with his right fingertips.

"Mr. York says you play like an angel," came Jack's murmur, close.

Startled, I turned to the opposite side of the piano and hastily wiped my eyes. Jack's eyebrows rose, and he looked uncertainly from his uncle to me.

"And now," Mr. Bertault said with a sigh, "I will leave you to visit."

"Thank you," I said, reaching out. "For saying what you did."

A quick squeeze of my fingers, a smile that deepened the lines around his mouth, then an apologetic look at Jack, and he turned away.

"My uncle doesn't usually make people cry," Jack observed.

My laugh was shaky. "I just came to say hello to you, and instead I received a lesson."

"A welcome one?"

"Yes. It was just—unexpected." What Mr. Bertault had said was still resonating like a held chord, for I had experienced the alteration in my playing almost physically, somewhere between my brain and my heart and my hands.

"How is your ankle?" Jack asked.

"Fine. I walked from home."

"I'm glad you came." A brief teasing smile flickered over his mouth. "You look pretty in a dress."

I felt the warmth rush to my cheeks. "Thank you."

He extended his hand to help me up from the bench. "Would you like to see something unusual? It just came in this morning." He led me to a baby grand that stood in the corner. One leg was badly scratched, the wood veneer was dull and peeling, and pieces were torn off of what was once exquisite wooden beading around the edge.

"Look inside," he instructed.

I peered under the lid and felt my eyes widen. Etched inside, in black ink, were rows of what looked like names, letters, and numbers.

"It belonged to a family named Lavin," Jack said.

"The writing is so elaborate."

"This part is in Cyrillic." He ran his forefinger along some of the ink that had faded. "This other part is in French. It's their entire family tree," he said, touching each name in turn. "Vadim— that's the father, Agafya, the mother—and here are the five children, and their children. You see the birthdates?"

I nodded. "Who were they?"

"Russian royalty. They left Moscow in the eighteen thirties, and their daughter eventually settled in Paris."

"There's an inscription," I observed. Our shoulders brushed as I leaned forward. "But I don't read French."

"It says, '*Ce piano est le cœur de notre maison.*' This piano is the heart of our home."

I went to the keyboard and played a scale. It was horribly out of tune, and some of the notes didn't play at all.

"You can restore this?" I asked, doubtfully.

He nodded. "It's not so bad."

"Jack, my boy."

We both looked up. A middle-aged man with a stoop and a cane stood in the archway. He raised his hand and waved to Jack.

"I'll be back," Jack said to me. "Mr. Wendell." He took the man's elbow and led him to an easy chair in the corner of the main room. I had to smile. It was the same kindness that his uncle had showed me. Jack was more Monsieur Bertault's nephew than he was his father's son.

I bent once more inside the piano. I could read some of the names but not all. Antoine. Étienne. Another Antoine. And then Mr. Bertault was at my side again. "I'm sorry, my dear. Jacques will be with this customer for some time. While he's busy, would you like to see my second passion?"

I must have looked a bit wary, for he laughed. "Don't worry, I won't make you cry again. Come with me."

My curiosity roused, I followed him through the archway and to the back door. He reached behind a bookshelf for a brass key, unlocked the door, and pushed it open.

I stood at the top of a set of stone stairs and gasped in wonder. I had anticipated a drab alley. What I found instead was a garden that would have been beautiful anywhere in the world. Here in London it seemed as magical and enchanted as something out of a fairy tale.

Enclosed by the dull brick walls of the buildings around it, the square space was brilliant with flowers of every color—scarlet and plum, gold and pink, white and pale blue, at once as lush as wild-flowers in a field and as delicate as a painting by Redouté. There were four slender trees, one for each corner, whose limbs, graceful as those of dancers, cast moving shadows on the brown earth. Two neat graveled paths crossed in an X, their meeting place marked by a white ceramic birdbath. A winged cherub with a dimple in his cheek sat on the edge and tipped a copper urn into the basin. The scent of roses was thick and heavy as incense in a church.

Behind me, Mr. Bertault gave a mischievous chuckle. I turned and laughed with him. "You relish the surprise, don't you? I'm sure no one suspects! How could they?"

"They don't," he agreed. "And you're right. I like my small joke, but I only play it on my friends. And it is best in June, with the roses."

We walked down the steps onto one of the paths, the gravel crunching under our feet. Pale bricks marked the edges of the flower beds, and I bent first to examine the delicate lavender phlox at my feet, then to smell the peach roses behind them. Next came bushes of peonies flanked by dark pink roses that were mostly buds, except for one that had laid itself open wide, so we could see the golden heart. The petals were like silk, the green leaves verdant, and the fragrance sweet without being cloying.

"These are the Pink Ladies," Mr. Bertault said.

"They're beautiful. How did you grow all of this?"

He gestured around. "Plants like alchemilla and phlox and ranunculus all grow easily this time of year. But the roses are from clippings from our farm northeast of Toulon. It's been my family's business for years, beginning with my great-grandfather."

I leaned forward to smell one of the yellow ones. "Who runs it now?"

"My two older brothers. My sister and I were quite a bit younger, and we were sent to a conservatory together. But whereas she had genius, I had only some talent. I quickly realized that I was far more interested in the mechanics of the piano—the strings, the wood, the tuning." He held up his hands. "These ugly fingers may not look like it, but they are quite adept."

I smiled. "I'm sure they are."

"I worked on pianos in France for some years, and when I came to England—more than ten years ago, now—I started looking for a place where I might both fix pianos and keep my roses. And once I found this and established the shop, I traveled back to fetch some cuttings. They were fragile, of course. At first, I wasn't sure they'd survive." He gave a shrug. "This climate is not so hospitable, but I keep them carefully watered and blanket them with soil and straw in the winter to protect them from freezing and thawing. That's what kills them, you see."

I walked on to the next bush, covered with small yellow roses edged in orange, like miniature sunsets. "What are these?"

"Golden Amours." He pointed to some white roses a bit farther on. "And these are some of my favorites. *Les Cœurs Noirs.* The Black Hearts."

"Why call them Black Hearts when they're so white and pretty?"

He cupped an open bloom and turned it toward me so I could see the heart, the color of deepest night, inside. "You see?"

I looked more closely at the bush. Most of the blooms were closed, or barely open, white roses, with threads of red veining the petals, and with leaves of green so deep they were almost black.

They were identical to the rose that had appeared on my piano.

Keeping my voice casual, I said, "They're beautiful. I don't suppose they're common."

"No. I'm the only one who has them here in England, so far as I know."

I could feel my pulse thrumming as I touched the petals. My mind was busy reassembling the events on the night that Jack had left the flower, and so I only caught the tail end of Mr. Bertault's sentence: "Would you like to hear it?"

I tore my eyes away from the rose. "I beg your pardon?"

"The story about the roses," he said patiently. "It's a romance, of a sort."

"I'd love to hear it," I said.

"*Alors.* Once there was a girl named Désirée Clary who lived in Marseille. Have you heard of her?" I shook my head. "She was a French silk merchant's daughter, a beauty, with black curling hair and dark eyes, and when she was younger than you, she was Napoléon Bonaparte's first love." His expression turned regretful. "But her brother Étienne didn't approve of the young upstart soldier, who had been born in Italy and wasn't even French, especially as he would be going off to war and might never come back."

He clasped his hands behind his back, looking down at the flowers. "Now, as you'd expect, Napoléon was not to be thwarted. He came to Désirée one night in disguise, borrowing his groom's clothes to conceal himself, so that he might declare his love and ask for a secret engagement before he left for the front. Young Désirée promised herself and waited for him. However, by the time Bonaparte returned to Paris, his ambitions had grown, and he abandoned her in order to marry the widow Joséphine de Beauharnais, who had not only a small fortune, you see"—he raised one finger, then a second—"but also political connections."

"That's rotten."

"Poor Désirée was heartbroken. Of course, eventually she fell in love with a different French general and became queen of Sweden—so we must not feel too much pity. But Bonaparte had this rose cultivated expressly for her, to remind her of their early love. When she was crowned queen, he sent her an entire bouquet."

"I see. They're called Black Hearts because he was opportunistic and faithless," I said dryly.

"Or because, in his heart, he never stopped loving the black-haired girl. Some find the story romantic." He gave me a wink. "To me it suggests the value of being able to disguise yourself effectively when circumstances require."

I laughed and drew my shawl closer around me as we walked on. The sun was dropping and the breeze had turned cool.

Thinking of Stephen's lie about the rose, I realized I had the perfect chance to find out if there had been any truth at all in what he'd told me about himself. "Mr. Bertault," I began haltingly, "Jack told me that you knew most everyone at the Royal Academy. Did you know Stephen Gagnon? He plays violin at the Octavian now."

He looked at me, and his guarded expression was very much like the one Jack sometimes wore. "*Oui*—I knew him." A pause, and then, in a careful tone: "Is he a friend of yours?"

"An acquaintance, I would call him."

He looked relieved. "*Ah, bien*." He stopped in front of some crimson blossoms that ran riot over a wooden trellis and plucked out a dead twig that was tangled in the stems.

"Did Jack tell you that Stephen had come to the Octavian?" I asked.

"Yes. Jacques never met him at the Academy." He twirled the twig absently. "But they had a friend in common."

"Stephen told me he was thrown out because of a false rumor."

"Bah!" He turned, and his scowl was almost as bitter as one of Drummond's. "There was nothing false about the rumor. He's a rat and a cheat, and that's the truth." His vehemence startled me, and I remained silent. After a moment, he looked at me apologetically. "It's no matter, *ma chérie*. He won't last long at the music hall. I've no admiration for my brother-in-law, but he's no fool. He'll discover what sort of man Stephen is soon enough."

But Stephen is exactly the sort of man Drummond likes, I thought.

"Could you tell me the truth about why he was thrown out?"

I asked as I sat down on a nearby bench. "I—I've a particular reason for wanting to know."

"Very well." He sat down on the bench beside me. "I also taught piano in France for several years before coming to the Academy. Did Jacques tell you that?"

I shook my head. "No. But I might have guessed."

That brief, sideways smile, both wry and mischievous. "Because I cannot resist giving lessons, eh?"

I laughed. "Because you know precisely what needs to be said to make your point."

"*D'accord*. Well, sometimes it falls on deaf ears." He shrugged. "When you teach, you come to recognize the different kinds of students. There are some, like you, who are humble and willing to learn. They work hard; they listen; they build their skills, piece by piece. Then there are some whose parents have sent them to a music school to get them out of the way, or to find them something to do—which is a foolish waste, but there are plenty of bourgeois families with more money than sense." He paused. "And then there are those who have talent—sometimes exceptional talent—but they're lazy, or arrogant, or too sick in the soul to learn. Stephen was one of those. From the first year, it was clear he was bored by the practice, the routine. And although desire is important, practice is what takes one from goodness to greatness, *n'est-ce pas?*"

I nodded.

"*Bien*. So, two years ago, Stephen seduced one of his family's maids."

I caught my breath.

"His father—who is very strict and proper—was disgusted by his behavior and threw him out of the house, along with her."

"That's hardly an equal consequence," I said with some asperity. "She wouldn't be able to find another position without a character."

"*C'est vrai*. And of course Stephen wasn't the sort to make a provision for her."

"That poor girl."

"Unfortunately, it's not an unusual story. Not for that sort of gentleman." The derisory note was heavy on the final word.

"What happened after that?"

"Stephen's mother supported him for a while, with what she could, and it might have all been forgotten with time. But he was extravagant, and when his debts began to heap up beyond what he could pay, he began to gamble."

"And he fell further into debt?"

"Not at all. He gathered a group of young men to play with and managed to fleece one of them in particular. A boy named Andrew Palmer, who also happened to be a friend of Jacques's. Stephen lured him in so deep the poor boy was desperate, until one night Stephen threatened to expose his debts to Andrew's father unless Andrew gave up his instrument."

I stiffened. "The violin."

"Yes. An extraordinary one. A Guarneri." He inclined his head toward me. "Do you know the name?"

"No."

"Giuseppe Guarneri, del Gesù was a master violin maker in Italy in the early seventeen hundreds. A rival to Stradivari, though to my mind Guarneri was a superior craftsman. He made violins with a sound to make the angels cry. Worth hundreds of pounds— some of them thousands."

The breeze was swirling fallen leaves and petals into fractured circles on the ground.

"So Stephen virtually stole the violin," I said.

"And pawned it, then lied about how it had happened. Denied threatening the boy." His nose wrinkled in disgust. "But you see, Andrew had told Jacques, and Jacques had confided in me because he was worried about his friend. Jacques had never met Stephen, and he didn't even know his surname, but I knew enough to assemble the truth, and I told Principal Bennett."

The breeze set the ends of my shawl flapping, and I clutched them closer. "Do you think Stephen knows the part Jack played?"

He considered this. "Possibly. If he discovered that Andrew and Jacques were friends." The reason for Stephen's attitude toward Jack was becoming abundantly clear.

"Very little of the story he told me resembles yours," I said.

"But you don't seem surprised."

"I suppose I'm not."

The back door swung open with a drawn-out squeak, and I saw Jack's silhouette in the doorway, the light from the store behind him. "I need to oil that door," Mr. Bertault sighed. "There's always something that needs fixing, it seems."

"Jack would do it for you."

"He does too much for me already." He looked up at the sky and clenched and unclenched his hands. "It's going to storm. I can feel it in my joints."

Jack walked down the three steps into the rose garden. His black hair blew across his brow, and he pushed it out of his eyes as he came toward us. "Mr. Wendell's gone. He was our last appointment for the afternoon. Do you want me to lock the door?"

Mr. Bertault rose and drew out his pocket watch. His broad thumb pushed the button to open the case. "*Mon Dieu,* it's after five o'clock. Your friend Nell has been patiently indulging my regrettable habit of boasting about my roses. I've probably bored her to tears."

I shook my head. "It's been perfectly lovely."

Mr. Bertault put his watch back into his pocket. "I have to see Mr. Anders before six. Was Mr. Wendell pleased?"

Jack nodded. "He said it was what he wanted."

"Hmph. Crotchety old man. He gave *me* nothing but trouble about it." He reached for my hand and raised it to his lips. "*Au revoir, Mademoiselle.*" He turned to Jack. "Don't forget to leave the note and the pages for Madame Sayer. She's coming by tomorrow morning, first thing."

"I have them ready," Jack said.

"Goodbye," I said, and gestured around me. "And thank you."

Mr. Bertault smiled. Then he walked to the door, closing it behind him, and Jack and I were left alone. Above us, the clouds were scudding more quickly, the storm on its way.

Jack slid his hands into his coat pockets. "He likes you. He doesn't usually share his garden."

"He was being kind." I walked toward the Black Hearts. "Jack . . ."

He followed me. "What?"

Gently, I touched one of the blooms. "The rose on the piano was from you. And I never thanked you because Stephen told me—or let me believe—it was from him."

"I figured as much."

I swallowed. "Your uncle told me the truth about him." The wind gusted harder, and I shivered as I met his gaze. "You knew, didn't you?"

"Not on his first day. But when I mentioned him to my uncle, he told me that it had been Stephen who'd cheated Andrew."

"Why didn't you say something? Why didn't you warn me what he was?"

"Because I barely knew you—and it was hardly my concern."

"But I barely knew *him*," I protested.

"What if you thought I was telling you those things to steer you away from him, just so I might have a chance?"

There was a long silence. Finally, I said softly, "Why did you even want that chance? After all, as you said, we barely knew each other then."

I'd inadvertently placed a faint emphasis on the last word, and his smile told me he'd heard it. "Sometimes it doesn't take long to know enough about someone," he replied. "For me, it happened the day we tuned the piano."

"Because I helped you?"

"No. Because you didn't want to be misunderstood."

I stared, mystified.

"When you saw that I knew how to tune the piano, you said that I should have corrected you. You were annoyed because I'd let you think something false about me. Do you remember?"

I nodded.

"I liked that you were honest about something that small." His voice became quiet. "That's really the only thing that matters, isn't it? That two people can tell each other the truth."

He stepped close enough that his breath was warm on my cheek, and his hands came out of his pockets to cup my elbows. I felt the warmth through my thin dress. My heart was slamming inside my chest, resonant as a bass drum, and I couldn't speak. Then one of his hands slid down to hold mine.

My fingers looked pale against his brown ones, and I could feel the calluses across his palm.

Two birds trilled. A door blew shut somewhere—

And then he was turning my face up to his, his arm was around me, and his mouth was on mine, his kiss fierce as one of Beethoven's symphonies and yet tender as a lullaby I knew by heart. The breeze swirled chill and damp around us, but where his skin touched mine, I could feel the quick heat of him, and when he finally let me go, we stood just staring at each other. My breath was coming ragged, and every nerve, down to my fingers, felt as if it were on fire.

"It's raining," he said, his voice hoarse.

I tipped my head back and felt one large drop and then another. Nothing delicate about them. They were the harbingers of a full-on rainstorm, and I hadn't even noticed.

"Let's go in." He held my hand and took a step toward the door. But I stood rooted to the spot, suddenly overcome by a feeling taking shape deep inside my chest.

He looked puzzled. "What's the matter?"

For once I wasn't tongue-tied by a commotion of sentiments; there was only a clear sense of longing. "I don't want it to be just this, Jack."

Understanding lit his dark eyes, and a slow smile curved his mouth. He shook his head. "It isn't." And then his mouth was on mine again, and perhaps it began to rain in earnest, the drops plinking into the fountain; perhaps the wind bent the roses to its will; perhaps the four trees quivered, etching an ephemeral calligraphy upon the walls beyond; or perhaps not.

All I knew with any certainty was him.

Chapter 16

*T*he next morning at breakfast, I must have run my eyes twenty times over the same story in the *Record*—something about the ongoing strife between Christian peasants and Bosnian chieftains in a little-known region of the Ottoman Empire. But I was thinking about Jack and trying to keep my happiness—a live, sparkling thing—from showing all over my face. The last thing I wanted was Matthew questioning me.

Jack and I had made plans to go to the museum in the afternoon, but first I had to go to the *Falcon* offices. It was Sunday, and I hoped that Jeremy had some good news for Marceline.

"Dr. Everett told me I could see Marceline this afternoon," Matthew said.

The echo of her name from my own thoughts startled me. "Really? Already?"

"He says she's able to talk, and he's not concerned about disturbing her memory any longer, so I can take her statement." He folded his newspaper back into order. "He also said she's wary of police but seems to trust you. He thought it might be best if you were to introduce me."

"Of course." I could easily imagine Marceline feeling more at ease if I were there to vouch for him.

"Could you meet me at the hospital around one?"

I nodded. The newspaper offices, the hospital, and then the museum. I flexed my foot under the table and said a silent thank-you that my ankle was healed.

WHEN I PUSHED OPEN THE DOOR OF THE *FALCON,* Jeremy jumped up off a chair as if he'd been waiting for me for hours. "There you are! Thought you might'a forgot."

"Of course not." I frowned. "I'm early, you know. It's not even noon."

He sniffed and jerked his head toward the stairs. "Come on, then."

I handed him my umbrella to carry, drew my skirts out of the way of my feet, and followed him up. "Were you able to find Sebastian?"

"Yah. 'Ow's Marceline?"

"Much better."

We reached the top of the second flight of stairs and headed down the hallway into the warren of ill-lit rooms. He directed me into one of them and stood with his feet planted and his chin lowered doggedly. "Now, you got to tell me where she is."

I sighed. "No, Jeremy. She doesn't want Sebastian or anyone to find her. She thinks it's dangerous, and so long as she asks me not to, I'm not going to tell you."

"It's all right. I don't need to know," said a voice behind me.

I spun and saw Sebastian in the doorway. The breath came

out of me in a rush. "Sebastian! Oh, thank goodness, you're all right!"

At the Octavian, I had only ever seen him in the full-length black leotard he wore for the trapeze act. Now, he was dressed in ordinary clothes that partially concealed his lean, muscular frame. His long dark curls had been cut very short, which altered his appearance a good deal. But there was no camouflaging the grace and deliberation in his movements. As he entered the room, I was reminded of a panther I'd once seen on exhibition at the zoo in Regent's Park. He removed his coat and dropped it onto one of the wooden chairs. With his shirtsleeves rolled to the elbows, I could see the muscles in his bare forearms. There was power there, held in abeyance, and I realized, as I hadn't before, that Sebastian could be dangerous if one came up against him.

But just then his expression was that of an anxious brother, and he wrapped his fingers so tightly around the edge of the chair that the knuckles turned white. "How badly was she hurt? And how did you know where to find her?"

"I didn't," I replied. "I wasn't even looking for her. I was on my way home from the Octavian last Wednesday night. I heard a cry, close to where Brewer meets Regent Street. So I stopped to see— and—and there she was."

"Was it very bad?" His eyes were locked on mine.

I hesitated. I'd already discerned that he was blaming himself; I didn't want to add to the weight of his guilt. "She's better now, Sebastian. She's going to be fine."

"Tell me the truth," he said, so sharply that I flinched. "I want to know. What happened?"

Reluctantly, I relayed both what Marceline had told me and Dr. Everett's catalog of her injuries. His face paled as he listened, and by the end he was ashen. He turned and hit the wall with the outsides of his fists, then laid his forehead against them. His breathing stuttered, and at first I thought he was suppressing tears, but then came a string of what sounded like French curses.

I glanced at Jeremy, who was leaning rigidly against a table. His arms were tight across his chest, and his eyes flashed with the same fury.

There were three chairs in the room. I wouldn't have trusted the one in the corner to hold a cat, and Sebastian had thrown his coat onto the second. I pulled the remaining one away from the wall, sat down, and waited. After some minutes, I said, in a voice that I hoped sounded calm and resolute, "Sebastian, I want to help both of you."

Slowly, he came to the chair and sat down. He rested his elbows on his knees, his head in his hands. His short hair made me think of a shorn lamb.

"Sebastian, do you know why she was hurt?"

"I can guess," he muttered.

"She didn't tell them anything," I said.

He looked up. "I know *that*," he said grimly. "If she had, I'd be dead."

"Do you know who it was?"

He sent a quick, oblique look at Jeremy before he met my eyes. "You say she's going to be fine. But how do you know? You're not a doctor."

"No, I'm not. But she's been seen by one, and he's said so."

"So, she's at a hospital," Sebastian said.

Jeremy gave a soft cough, and I sensed that it was intended as a warning.

"Sebastian," I said sternly, "you need to stay away from her."

"Why?"

I saw the stubborn set to his jaw, and I sighed. But I had an idea how I could convince him. "Because the people who are looking for you might be watching the hospital."

Jeremy coughed again, but I kept my eyes on Sebastian.

"I haven't told Marceline," I continued, "because I didn't want to worry her, but a few days ago, a man came looking for her. He spoke to the guard, and he knew her name. He claimed to be her father."

Sebastian's every muscle tensed. "What?"

"He wasn't admitted, and the other guards have been warned about him. But—"

"But someone else could try, or they could break in—"

My voice rose over his. "I suppose they could—but you're the one they want, not her. If they believe she's in the hospital, they don't need to get in. They just need to keep watch and wait because they expect at some point you'll come to see her."

I watched as he digested that. At last he nodded. "When will she be able to leave?"

"I don't know, but not yet," I replied. "I'll get word to you when she can. Do you have someplace you can go? Somewhere away from London?"

Jeremy interjected, "Mr. Flynn says 'e'll 'elp get them away, soon as Marceline can walk."

"Will you be able to get her out of hospital?" Sebastian asked. "Without anyone knowing?"

"I'm sure we can find a way to do it discreetly," I said. "But there aren't any secret passageways, if that's what you mean."

He frowned, dissatisfied with my answer.

"When it's time, she can come 'ere." Jeremy pointed his thumb in the direction of the river. "It's easy 'nough to get a small boat to the docks if'n you want to get out o' London."

"Would you go back to France?" I asked.

"Maybe." Sebastian stood and went to the window. He seemed lost in his thoughts, and we were all quiet.

Finally, I rose and picked up my umbrella. I didn't want to be late meeting Matthew. "I'll tell her you're all right. Is there anything else?" I expected him to ask me to tell her he loved her, or something like it.

He turned. "Marmalade."

"Marmalade?" I repeated, confused.

He nodded. "Just tell her I said 'marmalade.' She'll know what it means."

Chapter 17

It was a few minutes past one when I arrived at the hospital. As I approached the gate, I caught sight of Matthew on the other side of the street, a short distance away. It gave me the opportunity to see him as I rarely did, and it struck me that were he a stranger, I wouldn't imagine that he was a detective. With his leisurely stride and his tendency to pause at shop windows, he seemed like an average man out for a midday walk.

Suddenly Matthew turned to the side, just for a moment, as if he glimpsed something behind him. A prickling sensation began at my neck, making its way down my arms. Did he suspect someone was following him? I scanned the crowd in his wake: a few women, a few men, two boys, more men, one with a cane. I saw no one who seemed to bear any particular interest in my brother, and as he approached, I saw no signs of anyone slowing down or observing him.

"What are you staring at, Nell?" he asked as he came close.

"Nothing, thank goodness. I don't see anyone following you."

His eyes widened slightly in surprise, but he smiled. "Glad to hear it."

We entered the hospital together, and I led him up to the ward and Marceline's curtained bed.

But the bed was empty and made, the corners hospital crisp.

My thoughts raced. Could something have happened to her? But surely Dr. Everett would've gotten word to Matthew or me at once if that were the case. I went outside and found Nurse Aimes. "Where is Marceline?" I said, not even trying to hide my alarm.

"Marceline?" She smiled and pointed down the hallway. "She's walking."

And indeed, there she was. She had a cane and was making her way slowly and gingerly, with the upright posture and steps of a dancer.

"Good lord, she's just a child," Matthew muttered.

"She's seventeen," I corrected him. "She's just small. Wait here. I'll bring her to you, all right?"

He nodded, and I started toward her. As I drew close, I saw that her hand was at her side, but more as if she were protecting her ribs than feeling pain.

"Marceline," I said quietly.

She smiled at me. The bandage on her temple remained, but the bruises on her face were less, and the swelling at her jaw much diminished. "Hullo, Nell."

"I'm so glad to see you up and about. Does walking hurt your ribs?"

"Not so very much."

I turned to accompany her. Very softly I said, "I found Sebastian."

She froze. "He's all right?"

"He's fine," I reassured her. "I promise. Not a mark on him."

The relief brought tears to her eyes. "You saw him? You spoke to him?"

"At the *Falcon*. Jeremy helped, just as you said he would." I paused. "He asked me to pass you a message. 'Marmalade.'"

To my relief, a puff of laughter came from her lips, which I was glad to see. "What on earth does it mean?" I asked.

"It was the name of our cat. She was orange, like marmalade, and the nimblest thing. Sebastian always said I reminded him of her. Marceline, marmalade. Silly, really." Her smile faded. "I expect he told you that so I'd know you'd really met him and were telling the truth."

"Probably."

Her expression was apologetic. "If he knew you better, he'd trust you as much as I do."

"Oh, I'm not offended! I'm glad he trusted me with that much. He's terribly worried about you. He insisted I tell him about your injuries."

She winced. "You also told him I'm much better, didn't you?"

I nodded.

She laid her fingers on my arm. "Thank you, very much."

I kept my voice low. "Jeremy suggested that when you're able to leave here, you meet Sebastian at the *Falcon* offices, in Prescott Street. There are boats you can take down to the docks."

"I wonder when I'll be well enough."

"You're already doing so much better," I said encouragingly and put my hand over hers where it rested on the cane. "And now—I have to ask you something, and it's rather a favor."

"Of course," she said, surprised.

"Do you remember I told you that my brother, Matthew, is a policeman?"

Her expression became cautious. "Yes."

"He wants to meet you."

"Nell . . ."

"It wasn't my idea," I added. "He heard about you from Dr. Ev—"

"Why would Dr. Everett tell him about me?" she broke in.

"Because Matthew is investigating a series of attacks in Soho the past few weeks; he's looking for a pattern."

She nibbled her lower lip, considering.

I lowered my voice still further. "Marceline, I've told him nothing about you—or the Octavian. He still doesn't know I play there, and he doesn't know you have a brother. He thinks we met here at the hospital."

She turned to look toward the end of the hallway where Matthew stood. "Is that him?"

"Yes." I tried to reassure her in terms she'd accept: "And just as much as you trust Sebastian, I trust him."

"All right," she said simply. I squeezed her arm lightly, grateful.

Marceline and I walked toward him, and as we drew close, I wondered if his height and bulk would feel intimidating to her. But she seemed to have taken my words to heart, for she smiled up at him. "Hello, Matthew. Nell says you want to ask me some questions. I'll tell you everything I can."

"Bless you," he said frankly. "I don't hear that very often." He looked over at me. "Dr. Everett says we can sit in his office. No one will disturb us there."

"Would you like a wheeled chair?" I asked.

Marceline shook her head. "The walking is good for me."

At Marceline's slow pace, we made our way to the office. I was so used to the doctor's collections that it hadn't occurred to me just how odd the room would look to Marceline. Her eyes darted around to the preserved brains, the phrenological head, and the anatomical drawings before they met mine. "How curious all this is."

I laughed. "Yes, I know. *Excentrique,* remember?"

The three of us sat down, and Marceline hooked the curve of the cane around the arm of her chair. The only sign of tension was in her back, which was ramrod straight.

Matthew sat back in his chair—not lounging exactly, but composed in his manner. After a moment, he began in that easy way he had: "I'm sure Nell's told you that I'm a detective. I'm looking into a series of attacks that happened in Soho recently because I've a feeling they are connected. I know this might be a painful subject, but anything you can tell me about what happened to you will help. And please, take your time."

And with that, he waited for her, his hands folded comfortably across his waist.

I breathed a silent sigh of relief. Not that I was surprised, but Matthew had managed this perfectly. Her shoulders relaxed, and after a moment, she said, "I work as a trapeze performer, with my brother, at the Octavian—the music hall in Soho. Do you know it?"

"Yes, I do. It backs onto Hawley Mews, doesn't it?"

She nodded. "I was on my way there on Wednesday night when I saw two men coming toward me. They dragged me into an alley and through a door, and up several flights of stairs."

"Do you remember which alley?"

A quick glance at me. "I think it was somewhere in Brewer Street."

I felt myself tense. If she continued to look at me, Matthew might guess that I knew more about this than Marceline was telling him. I hoped he would ascribe it to her looking for reassurance rather than corroboration.

"Why do you think so?" he asked.

"Because that's near where I live, and they didn't take me far." She hesitated. "There is a greenish awning at the shop nearby."

He nodded approvingly. "You have a good memory. Go on. What happened next?"

"They took me to the top floor of a building. It was a room, long, like an attic, with crates at the end, and a metal pole, where they tied me."

"What did the men want?"

"They wanted to know where my brother was."

"Why?"

"I don't know. They didn't say."

"What can you tell me about them? How did they look?"

She thought for a moment. "One of them was tall and broad, like you, with brown hair, and very strong, like an adagio."

"An adagio?" He looked at me. "That's a musical term, isn't it?"

"It means a slow tempo," I said unhelpfully.

"It's also a man who juggles girls onstage," Marceline explained with a small smile. "This man spoke a foreign language. I think it was Polish, or German. He had a squarish head and a small mustache, and one of his ears was crinkled."

"And the other man?"

"He was also tall but thin. Bony but strong. He had his hands on my wrists, and I felt his fingers, biting in." She touched her cheek below the right cheekbone. "He had a scar here, like a four-pointed star, and reddish hair."

A casual observer wouldn't have seen the impression that made upon Matthew: his expression didn't change, his eyes didn't widen, his body didn't tense. But there was a moment of stilled breath, and suddenly I felt as if the air had been charged with electricity.

"And when they tried to make you talk," Matthew said gently. "Did they use their fists?"

"One of them had a stick, about so thick"—she put her thumb and forefinger in a circle—"polished and rounded at the end."

"Which one was that? The adagio or the other?"

"The other one, with the reddish hair." She hesitated. "There wasn't much of it; he was going bald. But he had some around the sides, by his ears."

He nodded. "Did you tell them anything?"

She shook her head, soberly. "I knew if I did, they'd use it to find my brother."

He tipped his head. "And why did they let you go?"

"They didn't. There was a rough bit of metal on the pipe, and after they left, I scraped the rope against it till it wore through. And then I climbed out the window, crossed the roof, and found a drainpipe I could slide down."

"I can't believe you did that with broken ribs and all," I said. It was no less impressive, hearing it the second time.

"It's a remarkable feat, even for an acrobat such as yourself," Matthew agreed, his tone admiring. "How did you come here?"

She kept her eyes fixed on him. "I don't remember. Dr. Everett said I was brought in a hansom cab and left with the guard."

"Mr. Oliven," I supplied.

His eyes narrowed briefly. "And you remember nothing else?"

She shook her head. "That's all." There was a moment of silence, and she touched her cane uncertainly.

Matthew took the hint and rose, offering his hand to help her up. "Thank you. You've helped me a great deal," he said, with a warm smile. "Please let me know before you leave the hospital. I'd be happy to help you in return, in whatever way I can. Truly, I would."

Then he looked at me. "I need to see Dr. Everett for a minute. I'll meet you out front." He gave us one last smile and left the room.

She waited until he was out of earshot, then she took a long slow breath and turned to me. "Was that all right?"

I nodded. "He meant it when he said you helped him—and that he'd help you."

"I just hope he can catch them." Her eyes flashed with her usual spirit.

We made our way back to the ward, her steps slowing as we drew near. I could see how fatigued she was, and I adjusted my pace to hers. Finally, she reached her bed and sank down on it with a sigh.

"You're getting stronger every day," I said. "I'm sure you'll be able to leave soon."

She looked up at me, her smile showing her small teeth. "You've been such a good friend through all this."

Impulsively, I leaned over and embraced her. When I let her go, her eyes were glistening with tears, and she laughed shakily.

I gave her my handkerchief with a smile. "I'll see you tomorrow."

She nodded and lay back against the pillow, giving me a wave goodbye.

I walked out to the foyer to find Matthew. He held the door open for me, and I asked over my shoulder, "Was that helpful?"

"Very." He halted on the footway and took my elbow. "Have you anything to add, Nell?"

I returned his gaze. "Why do you think I would?"

He glowered at me. "Don't dodge the question, Nell. What has she told you that she didn't tell me?"

I should have known Matthew would guess at least this much. "She's afraid her brother has gotten mixed up in something he shouldn't," I said with a sigh. "I don't know what it is—but I think she was afraid you were going to press her about him."

He nodded, seeming to accept my explanation, and started to walk.

After a moment, I ventured to ask, "You looked as if you recognized someone from the description she gave."

"Did I?" he said blandly.

I gave him the same scowl he'd just given me, and he shrugged. "I could be wrong. We'll see."

"Do you think her attack has anything to do with the others?"

"Yes. But not in the way I'd expected." He paused at the street corner, and I could see his mind was already elsewhere. "Thank you, Nell. I'll see you at home." And then he was striding away.

Chapter 18

After I left the hospital, I headed toward Cromwell Road. A few blocks from the South Kensington Museum, it began to sprinkle, and I put up my umbrella.

Knowing it might rain, Jack and I had made plans to meet there so we'd be indoors. It was also—as Jack said wryly—one place in London where we could be fairly certain we wouldn't see anyone connected with the Octavian.

I lowered my umbrella to shake off the raindrops as I came close to the entrance, which admitted a steady stream of Sunday museum goers. I made my way through the door, scanning faces in the crowd until I found Jack's. A smile lit his face as he saw me. He put out his hand to carry my umbrella, and crowd or no, he leaned over to brush my hair with his lips. I tucked my hand inside his elbow as though I'd been doing it for years, and we made our way out of the throng.

"The last time I was here was with my uncle over a year ago," he said, as if we were merely continuing a conversation.

"I used to come with my father before he died. His favorite section was the inventions from the Great Exhibition."

"Let's start there, then." We moved toward the first court. "Your audition is in three days. Are you nervous?"

I felt my stomach tighten at his words. "Yes. Although your uncle was very kind and reassuring. He seems to feel I'll pass."

"He told me what he said to you about your playing. He felt horrible about making you cry."

"Oh, *he* didn't make me cry." I shook my head. "Not really. I hope he knows that." We paused before a voting machine, and I continued, "I expect the reason I was crying is that for years I've been told that I need to restrain my feelings, not only by my doctor but also by Mr. Moehler, and I've done so, for the most part. But there was your uncle, wanting to know why and opening up the possibility of doing it differently." I sighed. "I love the idea that I could play with what your uncle calls 'susceptibility.' To feel the influence of the piano upon me. I'm just . . . not sure I can."

"Safely, you mean."

I nodded and walked toward the enormous telescope, roped off in the center of the room, and peered up at the metal structure that towered above us, with its metal dials and odd levers.

"What if you were to try?" Jack asked. "You have people who would keep watch and let you know if you began drifting into danger."

"Yes, I do." I kept my eyes on the placard that listed the telescope's dimensions and made my voice light: "Are you offering to help?"

"Well, you've already caught me spying on you once," he said soberly.

Chagrined, I looked up—only to find him repressing a smile. I poked at him with my elbow. "That's rotten of you, to cast that accusation up to me."

He just laughed, and we moved on, halting in front of a player piano.

Jack read aloud: "The first to use light springs to read the roll and to employ a mechanical amplifier. Eighteen fifty-one, Pape, England."

"Now this is what the Octavian needs," I said.

"Until there's a new act that needs to be worked in at the last minute," he replied.

I snorted.

"I assume you'll stop playing at the Octavian once you're accepted?"

"If," I corrected him. Then I considered his words. "You know, I hadn't really thought about it."

"But you've an idea what you'd like to do after the Academy, don't you?"

"Well . . . somewhat."

"Would you want to play with an orchestra, at the Monday Popular Concerts at St. James's, something like that?"

I said nothing for a long moment. I'd never admitted my ambition out loud to anyone, but at last I said, "It's probably more than I should hope for, but yes. I saw Arabella Goddard play there once. Mr. Moehler had an extra ticket—or at least that's what he told me then. I have a feeling now that he bought it for me. She was going to tour abroad, and he wanted to be sure I saw her before she left."

"When was this?"

"Three years ago. She played Beethoven's Concerto in E-flat. I could hardly breathe, it was so magnificent. And I wasn't the only one affected. The two men next to me were crying, and the papers the next morning were full of praise." I quoted one of them: "'Such fullness of tone, such breadth of style, and sustained elevation of sentiment, we have never met with before, except in the happiest efforts of our greatest male pianists.'" I smiled. "I guess that's when I began to imagine what it would be like."

We crossed the threshold into the Oriental Court, whose rooms featured works from China, India, and Japan. The walls were hung with paintings, scrolls, and cases of ornate weapons, and we made our way through desultorily until we reached the last room, where my eye was caught by an object at the far end: a large, multicolored sculpture of wood in the shape of a tiger mauling a man who was lying flat on his back.

"What on earth is that?" As I drew closer, I could see that the tiger's teeth were bared and at the man's neck. "Tippoo's Tiger," I read from the card near the tiger's left foot. "'Made for Tipu Sultan, ruler of Mysore (seventeen eighty-two to seventeen ninety-nine). A mechanism inside the tiger's body causes the European man to lift his arm and emit wails of pain.'" I frowned, remembering. "The Siege of Seringapatam was in seventeen ninety-nine, so I guess Tipu was killed by the British soldiers."

"If that isn't a symbol of India's resentment against the British, I don't know what is," Jack said. "Look at those incisors."

"Rather pointed," I agreed. "Both the reference and the teeth."

We were on our way out when he paused by the door in front of a glass case. Inside was a life-size wooden figure of a man upon which hung a lavishly embroidered red-and-gold silk kimono. A broad band of black silk encircled the waist, and from the sash hung a pipe and a small carved wooden turtle with a laughing man riding on his back.

I leaned close to the glass. "Japanese kimono, seventeenth century, with obi, pipe, and decorative turtle netsuke." I studied the exquisitely detailed figure. "Net-suke. I've never heard of that before."

"It's pronounced net-skay," he corrected me. "Usually they're made of ivory or stone. They're used to hold items on sashes."

I couldn't help but laugh.

Jack's eyebrow rose. "What?"

"It's just that you sometimes surprise me with the things you know."

For the briefest moment, there was a peculiar look on his face, but then he smiled back. "My uncle has a friend who collects them. The pipe looks like a bassoon, don't you think?" When I didn't answer, he added, "We should start back. I need to be at the Octavian in an hour."

We dawdled a bit on our walk homeward, strolling in companionable silence when we weren't conversing. At Cork Street he handed me my umbrella and squeezed my hand. "I'll see you tomorrow night."

He left me then, and I wondered, not for the first time, how on earth I was going to explain to my brother how we met.

Chapter 19

*T*he next morning, I woke to a house that was silent and peaceful, with the rain spattering my window. I took a deep breath in and let it out contentedly. I'd have all day to practice and rest before I performed. I rose, dressed, and headed downstairs, but as I reached the landing, the front door opened and Matthew entered and collapsed his drenched umbrella. His expression grim, he dropped a newspaper on the table and shrugged out of his coat.

"You're up early," I observed.

He looked up. "I wanted to see what the papers were saying."

"About what?" Silently, he handed the paper to me, and I opened it so I could see the front page.

It was the morning *Record*. In the middle of the lower half was a woodcut of a scene: three grand houses behind wrought iron fencing; on the footway stood a plainclothes detective beside a uniformed policeman carrying a bright lantern. Each loomed over a thief lying facedown. I looked closely. Yes, I'd say the detective bore a fair resemblance to Matthew. The headline read: "House Robbed in Westminster; Scotland Yard Baffled."

I wrinkled my nose. "Did the paper get it right?"

"No," he said. "Are you hungry? I want some coffee this morning, and I'm half starved."

I folded the paper, tucked it under my arm, and followed him into the kitchen. While he started the fire, I filled the pot for the coffee. He sliced some pieces off a loaf of bread and put cheese on a plate, and I prepared some soft-boiled eggs.

"Let's eat in here," he said. "What Peggy doesn't know won't hurt her."

I poured a cup of coffee for him, and sat down opposite with one of my own. "I assume the plainclothesman in the picture is supposed to be you?" I said, teasing him a bit. "They've made you look like a giant. You positively tower over the thieves."

There was no answering glint of humor in his eyes. "They were just boys, Nell. They fell off a three-story roof. We found them dead on the pavement."

The smile slid off my face, and my cup rattled onto the saucer, coffee splashing over the rim. "Oh, my God. Matthew. That's dreadful."

Matthew pushed his plate away. "The younger one couldn't have been more than ten, a scrawny little thing. Just bones under his clothes." He pressed the heels of his hands into his eyes as if he were trying to rub the image of those two boys out of them. "There was blood everywhere. With the rain, it had turned that bit of the street pink."

A hard lump formed in my throat, and I swallowed it down. "Where in Westminster?"

He took his hands away, and his tired eyes met mine. "Pentwick Street. The rain last night probably made the roof slicker than usual. Their feet were bare—they must have slipped."

"Were they . . . part of the Fleet?"

"I think so." He groped inside the pocket of his trousers. "They had silver in a sack, and one of them had this." He held the small object between his thumb and forefinger. It was barely two inches tall, pale gray stone, in the shape of an animal. "Curious little thing, isn't it? I've never seen the like before. Maybe it's this month's new trifle, as Mrs. Kendrick said. I'm going to take it to someone I know. I'm hoping he can tell me something about it."

With a feeling of misgiving, I held out my hand, and he put the little figure in my palm. It was a fox, with a bristly tail curled around its front paws, its ears cocked, and its face so finely etched that I could see the creature's tiny nostrils and the line of the mouth.

"Matthew, I think this is a piece of netsuke," I said carefully. "I've seen some at the museum recently. How fine it looks, with all this detail about the face and ears."

His eyebrows rose. "Bully for you, knowing your treasures. What's netsuke?"

"It's from Japan. People used to hang them off their sashes. For decoration, I suppose, but they also hold objects, such as pipes. They can be made of wood or ivory, too."

"And you've seen it at a museum," he said slowly. "I suppose that means it could be worth a good bit."

"I imagine so."

Matthew made an unhappy sound in the back of his throat. "Yet again—something new, something we haven't seen before. That, and the scars on their feet."

"What scars?"

"The boys had been branded, like cattle, Nell. It was in the shape of a C, right on their heels."

I felt the blood rush out of my face, and suddenly I was very cold. In my mind's eye, I was back in the corridor under the Octavian, staring at the mark on Rob's heel. I'd taken it for a U, but it could have been a C.

"I'm sorry. I know it's vile. I shouldn't have told you."

The coffee roiled my stomach, and a wave of nausea came over me. "No—it's all right. It's just—it's wretched."

He nodded. "I've no idea if it's connected to the Fleet. They could just as easily have had the marks before they joined, and in that case, God only knows what the C means. Christchurch? Covent Garden? Or Crow, or Chiv, or Crapped, for all I know."

I was only half listening. *Could the two boys have been Rob and Gus?*

"It could also be a U." Matthew stood and paced to the window. "I'd give anything to begin to break the Fleet apart—even just a few ships. To think of the captains using boys that young." He took a deep, controlling breath. "The good news is—I found someone else who might be willing to talk. I just wish I'd found him three days ago. The boys might still be alive."

My words came through dry lips: "Who is it?"

"A man named Avery. He's a fence." He turned. "William found him, actually. But this time we're not taking any chances. The minute we finish talking to him, we'll put him on a train. He'll be gone by tomorrow night."

"Out of London?"

"Yes." He glanced around the kitchen with an apologetic, hesitant look. "I've a lot to do today."

"Don't worry, I'll wash up," I said quickly, wanting him away so I could think without him watching me. He gave a smile of thanks, patted my shoulder, and headed toward the front door. I sank back onto the stool, my fingertips pressed to my mouth.

What if the mark on the bottom of Rob's foot meant he was part of the Fleet? And why had he been at the Octavian that night? Could it be possible that the music hall is the site of one of the ships?

The front door closed, and I snatched up the paper to read the article:

Within London, close courts and stifling alleys lie at no large distance from elegant streets whose denizens may fancy themselves far from the haunts of vice and villainy. But almost nightly, residents of one fine house or another discover their error. Young thieves with the talent and daring of circus performers risk life and limb to gain access to these homes by any means, in order to steal treasures, including bits of silver, jewelry, baubles, and such other small items as can find their easy market. Under existing jurisprudence, children between the ages of seven and fourteen are deemed incapable of forming criminal intentions, but there are vicious men who are well able to step into the breach—men such as those immortalized by Mr. Dickens in the character of Fagin, who find and train children to carry out their felonious plans, with this great advantage: that the children will often have their prison sentences commuted to workhouse terms, and death sentences commuted to transportation. But what sort of commutation exists for the child who dies as a result of such criminal acts?

Such was the sad event of last night, at approximately eleven o'clock, when two young boys fell from a steeply pitched rooftop on Pentwick Street and met their tragic fate. The owner of the house, who wishes to remain anonymous, was gone from his residence, with his wife and two daughters; at home were a maid, the butler, and two footmen, but they were all abed and saw and heard nothing. Uniformed police and detective inspectors from Scotland Yard were at hand to examine the bodies and retrieve the stolen property. Their countenances wore expressions of pity for those forced by cruel men to pursue such activities, and one reflected that this sort of crime harkens back to previous decades in this century, when flash houses dispersed young boys nightly to pillage the city.

There was more, but it provided no further details about the crime, or the boys. No mention was made of the brands, and, fortunately for Matthew, his name was left out of it.

If the Octavian was one of the ships, did that mean that other ships were based in music halls as well? There were hundreds of them in London, scattered in every borough. Now that I thought about it, music halls were admirably suited to being used by the Fleet: the thieves could stay there during the day and leave at night, when the halls were needed for their usual purpose. And if other music halls were like the Octavian, there were no doubt various rooms where the stolen goods could be stored and counterfeiting equipment set up.

I read the article once more, and this time, the comparison with circus performers struck me as I refolded the paper and laid it aside. Was this what Sebastian had become involved in? I pressed my hands to my temples, trying to put my thoughts in order.

Like dozens of other acts in London, Sebastian and Marceline had made the rounds of music halls and theaters. If the Fleet was tied not just to the Octavian but to other music halls as well, Sebastian could have found and joined a ship anywhere.

If so, did Marceline know about it? Given her agility, who was to say she wasn't part of it as well? She'd certainly be as adept as any boy. She'd crossed a roof and slid down a drainpipe after she'd been beaten nearly unconscious.

I went back to the sink and mechanically began to wash up from our hasty breakfast. But I was already forming a plan. First, I had to find out if my guess was right—that the Octavian was one of the ships. And I couldn't go at my usual time at night; by then, the boys would be safely away. I needed to go this afternoon, and I couldn't risk being recognized as Ed Nell.

I needed to go as myself.

Chapter 20

*T*hat afternoon at half past two, I left the house with my heart thudding under the thin wool of my dress. I wore a hat, and I carried a small reticule and my umbrella, which I was grateful for by the time I reached Regent Street, as the clouds were darkening overhead and a breeze was picking up.

I entered the yard behind the Octavian. As I expected, the back door was locked. For the first time since I came to apply for work, I went to the front door, a big black door with a brass knocker. Silently, I turned the knob; it, too, was locked. How on earth was I to get in?

"It ain't open for hours yet. What be ye wantin' in there?" I turned and saw a grizzled man of fifty or so, hunched forward at the waist and with a cap shoved back to reveal a thatch of gray hair and a bulbous, red-veined nose.

"What be ye wantin' in there?" he repeated.

"Oh . . . I . . . I was . . . that is, I heard they were looking for singers."

The man squinted up at me skeptically. "You lookin' for work, then?"

I nodded absently and went to the window to the left of the door to look in. But the inner shutters were closed fast.

"You're a likely lookin' lass. I know a way you could make more'n you'd make for just singin'."

I turned. "I beg your pardon?"

His liver-colored lips spread over yellow teeth. "A lass pretty as you could fin' good work easy. Wouldn't have to sing, neither. 'Ave you tried over at Mrs. Belvedere's?"

"Mrs. Belvedere's? Is that another music hall?"

"Nae. It's for gentlemen wot be likin' fine ladies like yourseln, not the common lot—an' they're willin' to pay the extra shillin's." His hand shot out as if to grab my arm. "Mrs. Belvedere pays the best of anybody—"

Now I understood, and I jerked back. "Get away from me."

"Aw right, aw right." He put his hands up. "If you be lookin' to work at the Octavian, ye can find Mr. Williams over at the White Swan." He looked me up and down. "Dare say 'e'll be glad to 'ave ye, if ye can sing."

"I'll come back later," I said, backing away.

His lips pursed. "Suit yourseln."

I gathered my skirts and returned to the back entrance, praying that a delivery would come and require the door be opened, or someone would come out the door. A lone tabby cat, its coat matted, came toward me with a mewling sound.

And then I heard the bolt inside slide. I dodged behind a stack of crates and watched. Out came two young men around my age. I didn't recognize them, but I wasn't going to miss this chance. They closed the door, but I didn't hear it lock, and the moment they were out of sight, I put my hand to the knob. It slid against my damp palm. I wiped my hand against my skirt and tried again. This time it turned.

Never mind that it was daytime; inside looked the same as always in the uneven light from the sconces. But absent were the noises of entertainers preparing, the banging and scraping of properties being moved, and the boisterous commotion of the audience. All was silent except for the creak and bang of old pipes.

I hesitated at the stairs that led to the piano alcove. There were no large rooms in this part of the hall. If the boys were anywhere, it would likely be upstairs near where the musicians kept their instruments. I made my way to where the spiral staircase wound to the second story and started up—but then I heard faint noises coming from somewhere behind me. Neither Drummond's office nor the property room were large enough for a group of boys, but I followed the sounds. Halfway down the hall, I turned to be sure I was alone. The sight of my own misshapen shadow on the wall startled me, and I gave myself a mental shake. *For goodness' sake, Nell, you can't be scared of that.*

I crept past Drummond's door. There was no light behind the opaque window.

Cautiously, I went to the door of the property room and pushed it open a crack. There was no one inside, only shelves littered with paraphernalia, a ladder with its rungs hanging askew, and trunks, crates, and barrels piled any which way. But the voices were louder here and interspersed with the clink of metal against metal. I closed the door, and when my eyes grew used to the darkness, I could make out a crack of yellow light perhaps a foot above where the floor met the far wall.

There was a room hidden beyond this one. And if the sound was anything to go by, there were at least a dozen people inside it.

I crept carefully toward the back. Surely there was another entrance to the room, probably from the back alley. But maybe there was a door here as well. I felt in every direction for a knob but only managed to brush some crumbling plaster onto the floor. At waist height, there seemed to be a horizontal indentation an inch deep, but if there was a door, the hinges must be on the other side. Which meant that if I pushed, it would open into the room, and I'd be discovered. Frustrated, I ran my fingers above where the light was emanating and found two indentations, roughly two feet apart. My heart leaped; perhaps it worked like a window. Very gently, I pushed upward and was rewarded by the small crack enlarging. I knelt down and put my eye to it.

Boys. Nearly two dozen of them. Some only seven or eight years old, but most of them older. They looked slightly better fed than pickpockets, most of them, and some even wore clothes that had a faintly prosperous air—but from the way they fit, I'd guess they had them secondhand. Some of the youngest had bowls of what looked like soup with beans and bits of bread, and they were sitting cross-legged on the floor, hunched over their meals, scooping hungrily. One boy finished his meal and applied his tongue to the bowl as well as the spoon.

"Cor! You got bloody nerve, lickin' like that," said an older towheaded boy. He stretched out his hand. "Gi' me the damn bowl! You be done with it, ain't cha?"

The younger boy threw him the bowl and spat, "Take it, then!"

The towhead stood up with a curse and took the bowl over to where a boy was doling bean soup from a large pot on a black stove. The server dipped the ladle twice and passed it back.

The boy beside him protested: "I say, he got two dips—"

The one who was serving the mess growled, "And if you brung in what he done las' night, you would, too. Now shut up about it!"

The towheaded boy came to a spot not far from me, sat with his back to the wall, and spooned the meal greedily into his mouth. As I watched, the scene was repeated again and again, the boys eating and passing on their dish, until everyone had been served.

The young man leaning against the reddish-brick wall was clearly in charge. As the last few boys were finishing their meal, he went to the center of the room. "Aw right, git on! We've our four 'ouses tonight, and Peter's got the lay of 'em."

The room quieted. My heart was thudding hard in my chest, and my mouth was dry.

A small boy near me took one last swipe with his forefinger and dropped the bowl beside his feet. Then he crossed his legs and sat quietly, looking for all the world like a pupil waiting for his teacher to begin a lesson. He turned his head toward the boy beside him, and I saw the scar on his mouth. It was Gus.

I couldn't help it; I gasped aloud. Still, with the shuffling and noise in the room, I'd have sworn he couldn't have heard it— and yet he swiveled around, his eyes scanning the wall. The towheaded boy noticed and followed the direction of his gaze.

Could they see me through the crack? I stayed perfectly still, hoping not—but the towhead pushed up from the floor, his hands already reaching toward the sliding panel, and shouted for everyone to be quiet—

I jumped up, stumbling as my boot caught my skirt. My eyes had adjusted to the light inside the room, and the darkness around me seemed complete. I bumped against one of the large trunks, and in the relative silence of the room beyond, the thud roared in my ears. My dress snagged. I kept on and felt it tear, but at least my sight had adjusted and I could see my way back to the door. As it shut behind me, I heard the scrape of wood against wood. I pulled my skirts above my ankles so I wouldn't trip, ran down the hallway, past Drummond's door, right into the back hallway, up the stairs—

Footsteps behind me—and then a boy's voice: "Wait! Stop! Who are you?"

I pushed open the back door and shoved it closed behind me, my eyes blinking against the brightness of day. Gasping, I ran through the yard and the Mews, toward the shops. There wasn't enough of a crowd for me to lose myself in, and no chance I could outrun the boys, not in my skirts.

Looking about, I ducked into the baker's and took my place near the front window, hidden behind a selection of pastries and meringues. From there I could catch my breath and watch.

I kept my eyes glued to the place where the Mews met the street. Twenty seconds, thirty, forty—the entrance to the Mews remained empty—fifty, sixty—surely they'd have come running through by now if they were coming—

Just as I was beginning to hope I'd escaped, three of the older boys and the towheaded one came around the brick wall into the street. One of them was holding my umbrella by the handle, and my heart gave a thump. It was just an ordinary black umbrella with no name on it, but it was their proof that someone had been watching them. The towheaded boy looked up and down the street and shook his head. Talking rapidly, he put his hands up above his head to show my height and perhaps the shape of my hat. The others listened closely. Then the four of them separated in a practiced motion, one into each of the four streets that led away from the music hall.

My fingers were trembling, but I untied the ribbons of my hat, slipped it off, and let it drop to the floor behind a stool. I looked myself over. There was nothing else I could think of doing to change my appearance. At least my dress was a very ordinary shade of brown.

It was my bad luck that the sharp-eyed leader headed in my direction, up the other side of the street. He pulled his cap lower and stopped to light a cigarette. His eyes scanned the windows of the shops on my side, and I drew back from the storefront, my heart tripping. He sauntered along, the cigarette cupped inside his hand to protect it from the breeze. At each shop, he glanced in through the paned windows and then turned to survey the street. My guess was that he'd work up one side of the street and down the other. He gazed only briefly into the barber's, ducking his head under the sign "Singeing done here for sealing and strengthening the hair." Next was the milliner's window filled with lace, ribbons, and all manner of hats. He peered in, put his hand on the door, and went inside.

Now was my chance.

I dug into my reticule for the few coins I'd put there—thank God I hadn't dropped that!—and civilly asked for three rolls. I took one out of the bag and munched on it to conceal my face as I walked down the street. Just like any other girl in Soho who'd missed a proper tea.

And then I saw one of the other young men—the one with reddish hair—coming straight at me. He'd just passed a tailor's shop, barely taking the time to look in. I turned immediately into the next doorway and found myself in an apothecary, such as I used to visit with Dr. Everett sometimes. It smelled like the one near the hospital, a mix of bitter, sour, and sweet. On a high shelf were the dark green bottles with fluted sides for poisons. Below the shelves were cabinets with wooden drawers: Syphovit, Syphomet, Spongic, Subaer, Aluta, Emplastr . . .

The apothecary, a man of about forty, looked up from his bench, where he was using a pestle on some green substance in a bowl. "Can I help you to summat, Miss?"

"Yes," I said, casting my eyes along the bottles. "Some glycerine, if you please, for my mum." There was a mirror above the workbench, and in it, I could see the red-haired young man standing outside, peering in through one of the glass panes.

Please just pass by, I thought.

But he remained where he was, even though the apothecary took a long time putting the glycerine in a small vial. And with each passing minute, I felt more like a mouse caught in a hole, with a cat waiting outside.

But I didn't like being a mouse, and suddenly I was angry. This young man outside would expect me to look guilty, timid, and afraid of being caught. He'd expect me to want to get away from him.

By the time the apothecary finished wrapping my vial up in brown paper, I was ready. I'd seen Maggie Long do it often enough, strutting and winking at the men in the audience, as if she meant it, for half an hour at a time, performance after performance. Surely I could manage something of the sort for a few minutes.

I took the package, paid the threepence out of the last coins I had, smiled brightly at the apothecary, and thanked him loudly enough that the young man would have heard. As I expected, he was waiting for me outside the shop, just to the right of the door. He was taller than I, and his narrowed eyes held an accusation.

"Why, hello," I said, smiling up at him. I let my eyes rake him suggestively from his cap down to somewhere around his waist and back up. "You look awfully healthy. What might someone like you be wanting in here?"

His eyebrows lifted uncertainly. "Thought I might 'a recognized ye, that's all."

"I saw you watching me through the window." I winked and didn't wait for his answer. "It's all right, you know. I don't mind, only you might have come in and introduced yourself." I rested my free hand just for a moment on his arm; I didn't want to overplay it. "I work at Mrs. Belvedere's of the evenings. My name's Adele. You can ask for me special, if you like."

"Sorry." He stepped away from my hand, his cheeks flaming. "Like I said, thought you was someone else." He continued up the street, took a quick look in the baker's window, though the owner was swinging the CLOSED sign into the door. He turned and saw me watching him still. I gave a warm smile and a wave of my fingers before I turned, walking with a sway that made my skirts swing.

But once I'd reached Regent Street, I paused, my hands clutching at the far side of one of the fake pillars. I closed my eyes for a moment and took a breath. There was no doubt that the Octavian was part of the Fleet.

And then came a thought that buckled my knees.

That night at the Bear and Bull, Jack had told me Rob and Gus's names, and how Gus had gotten his scar. If he knew that much, then he had to know what they were doing at the Octavian, and about the thieving ring that was being run from the basement of his father's music hall. How could he not?

Like notes in a scale, other hints of the truth fell into place: Jack telling me not to come early to the Octavian, behaving very differently at the music hall from when he was away from it, knowing about netsuke at the museum.

But just how much did he know, and how deeply was he involved?

"Miss, are you all right?" came a woman's voice close to me.

I looked up to see a woman of about Peggy's age peering at me in concern. "Are you ill?"

"No, I'm fine. Thank you." I pushed myself away from the pillar and continued on toward home.

Just because the Octavian was a ship didn't mean all of the ships were in music halls. But if they were, this was the very piece of information Matthew needed. And yet—how could I tell him when it might mean Jack would be caught? Knowing my brother, I was sure he'd figure it out sooner or later—most likely sooner, given that he'd found that man Avery. And if he did, how could I warn Jack without betraying Matthew?

Chapter 21

I made my way slowly up the steps of our house and drew my key from my reticule. The glycerine slid from my numb fingers. As I grabbed for it, I fumbled the bag of rolls, and they fell. No matter, they'd served their purpose. Mechanically, I picked up the bag from the step, turned the key in the lock, and went inside. I set my parcels on the table by the door. The newspaper from the morning was still there, open to the woodcut of the two dead boys. I felt a wave of revulsion, and my hand groped for the banister. Swallowing down my nausea, I climbed one step, then another.

I was halfway up the stairs when Peggy came into the hallway and looked up at me in surprise. "Nell! There you are!"

I turned toward her but said nothing.

Her eyes went wide. "For mercy's sake, child! What's the matter with you? You look ill!"

"I've a terrible headache. I need to lie down."

"D'you want some tea?"

"No," I said, almost desperately, and climbed the last few steps. "I walked too far today. I just need to lie down."

"Walked too far?" Her voice, skeptical, trailed me up the stairs. "Since when've you ever been sick from walking too far?"

But I didn't answer. I made my way down the hall and into my room, careening toward the bed. The nausea hit me again. I reached for the chamber pot—blessedly empty—and the roll I'd eaten in the street came back up.

Knowing Peggy might check on me, I feigned sleep and waited until I heard the front door close before I changed into my men's clothes. Ten minutes later, I was making my way along the back alley. I didn't know how I could perform tonight as if nothing was wrong, but I had to see Jack.

I arrived in Soho at a quarter past six, but though I lingered near the yard of the Octavian and circled the music hall, I caught no sight of him. At half past seven, Sid Lowry finally appeared at the back door. I asked him where Jack was. He didn't know.

Jack wasn't in the piano alcove, or either of the upstairs or back hallways, or the instrument room.

With fifteen minutes until curtain, I hurried to my place, hoping against hope I'd find him, or some sign of him. But no. It was still empty, except for the piano, its wing down, the fallboard closed. My hands were shaking as I unbuttoned my overcoat and hung it on its usual nail. I lifted the wing and propped it on the stick; then I raised the fallboard. But it fell back down with a slam that made the blood stop in my veins.

I couldn't do it. I couldn't get through these next two hours unless I talked to him first. I left my music on the stand and ran back down the stairs. Maggie was in the corridor, her usually smiling face sullen.

"Maggie, have you seen Jack?"

She shrugged. "What's the matter? You look peculiar."

I swallowed a retort. "Have you seen him at all tonight?"

"Sorry," she said sourly, as she turned away. "I got my own bloke to look after."

Any other time, I'd have asked her if something was wrong, but now I hurried to Amalie's room and knocked.

"Who is it?"

"Ed Nell."

She opened the door and peered through the crack. "Can I come in?" I asked.

"So long as you don't mind if I finish dressing." She kept herself behind the door and locked it behind me.

She wore only her white chemise and drawers, thin white garments that concealed little. A few months ago, I might have been embarrassed by her lack of modesty, but now I saw that this was a practiced role, put on night after night, with very little of her true self in it. I glanced around the room, at a costume dangling from a hook on the wall, a full-length mirror murky at the corners, a chaise longue upon which lay some undergarments and scarves. She made her way back to the dressing table and sat down. In the light from the two lamps, I could see the faint lines at the corners of her eyes and between her brows, and her cheeks looked a sickly yellow rather than a flirtatious pink.

"What do you want?" she asked.

I stood behind her, so that I could see her face in the mirror. "Have you seen Jack tonight?"

She snorted and began to twist her hair in a coil around her head. "No. Why?" In her accent, it came out "Woy."

"I need to talk to him is all."

"You don't need to keep up the pretense of your voice." Her eyes darted toward my chest, and she gave a small, knowing laugh. "Not much to show it, but I know you're a girl, and you're here because you want to go to the Academy." With practiced fingers, she inserted half a dozen pins into the coil to fix it in place.

A pinprick of doubt; and I had to ask, "Who told you?"

"Stephen."

Naturally. Ashamed that I'd suspected Jack, even for a second, I merely said, "Ah." Mindful that she was Jack's friend, I felt it was only right to say, "You might want to be careful about him."

She met my eyes in the mirror and let out a laugh that sounded genuinely amused. "You're giving me advice? That's rich. Don't worry, I've seen his sort before."

"What sort is that?"

"The sort who's told so many lies he's begun to believe them." She inserted four sparkling combs into her hair. "Shiny as silver on the outside and black as rot in his heart. That boy's his own, and that's all."

The accuracy of her assessment surprised me, though I suppose it shouldn't have. "I beg your pardon. I didn't mean to insult you. It's just that it was a while before I saw through him myself."

She turned around to face me. Her expression had softened some. "No need to be begging my pardon. But I've been here nigh eight years, and I've seen plenty of folks come and go, including liars like Stephen, and two-bit tarts who think somebody in the audience'll marry 'em if they lift their skirts, and even some hopeful sorts like yourself. Eight years ago, I might'a been much the same as you, thinking this would only be for a year or two, till I made enough money to do something else." A pause, and she shrugged and smiled. "Life has a way of changing plans, sometimes for the worse, sometimes for the better."

"Jack told me you could've gone to the Academy, if you wanted," I said. "That you have a perfect memory for words and songs."

Her hands paused in the act of taking her costume off the hook. "He's a good bloke," she said finally. "Always has been, even when—"

A hard banging at Amalie's door startled us both. Amalie shouted, the Cockney thick on her tongue, "Who the blasted 'ell *is* it?"

A man's voice, demanding, "Is Ed Nell in there?"

I opened the door, careful to keep whoever it was from peering inside.

Sid Lowry's furious eyes met mine. "What the devil are you doing? The curtain was supposed to go up ten minutes ago! Williams is going to tan yer hide!" He grabbed my arm, dragged me into the corridor, and shoved me in front of him.

I stumbled up the stairs. The crowd was already rumbling and hissing, the air loud with catcalls and whistles, cries of disapproval and disdain.

I came through the curtain, sat down, and began to play. For the first time in my life, the keys felt dead to me, my fingers worked like soulless machines, and the sounds of the music hall came as if from a distance, much farther away than the fear rising to a crescendo in my brain.

I GOT THROUGH THOSE TWO HOURS SOMEHOW. The minute I finished, I shoved my music into the portfolio, snatched up my coat, and hurried to the back hallway. I came upon Sid. "Have you seen Jack?"

He looked at me strangely. "He's out back. Just came from—"

But I was already gone, slipping in something wet on the ramp, grabbing for the wall, pushing at the door. The catch was stiff, and my fingers turned and twisted. I let out a small cry. *For pity's sake, just turn—*

The door jerked open and I fell into him. "Jack." I buried my face in his chest, and his arms were around me at once.

"Nell! What's the matter? Amalie said you were looking for me, so I waited . . ."

I pushed back, away from his chest, and stared up into his face. But my thoughts were such a muddle I couldn't speak. The two lanterns on either side of the door lit most of the yard. He drew me around the corner, to a place where we could be in the shadows but still see each other. Then he put his hands on my shoulders and turned me toward him. "Now," he said. "Steady on. What is it?"

I swallowed. "Jack, I know about your father . . . and about the boys who live here . . . and . . . and what they do." His eyes widened, his lips parted, but he kept silent. I swallowed again, knowing I had to ask, but not sure I wanted to hear the answer he was going to give. "How much are you involved in this?"

A long pause, and then, quietly: "What do you guess?"

"I'm guessing . . . I'm hoping . . . that it's as little as you can be." My voice cracked, I was so desperate to have him confirm my version of the truth. "And that you're only involved because of your father."

He dropped his hands off my shoulders and shoved them in his coat pockets. The world shrank to those few square feet of ill-lit dirt. Finally, I could no longer stand it. "Jack. Just tell me.

You said it was important that two people could tell each other the truth."

"It is, and I'm not going to lie to you. But I *can't* tell you unless you promise not to tell anyone. Not even your brother"—he cocked his head—"although maybe he knows a good bit already."

"I've told him nothing, Jack, I promise." I leaned back against the brick wall, glad to feel its sturdiness against my spine. I swallowed down the feeling of disloyalty to Matthew. "And I won't tell him anything you say now."

"All right, then." His eyes locked on mine. "I've wanted to get quit of it since last year, and I'm in it now less than I was. But I came here of my own choice. I needed the money."

"But you were working for your uncle—"

"Not enough."

"—and earning your living as a—as a boxer."

He looked a question.

"Stephen told me."

Jack's mouth twisted. "Well, he's right. I did, for a while."

"Why did you stop? Did you get hurt?"

"No."

"Were you arrested?"

"No."

I felt as if we were back to that first day in the alcove, when I had to drag answers out of him. "Then *why*?"

"Because they asked me to throw one."

"Throw *what*?"

"Lose a match on purpose," he said patiently, "without making it obvious. I didn't know that everyone has to do it eventually."

My breath caught.

"The money's in the betting," he continued. "And the odds were on me that night, by a fair bit."

"So people who bet against you had something to gain if you lost."

He nodded. "Old Helms—he ran the place—he told me if I didn't throw the match, I was out. I fought for *him*, he said, not to please myself. He knew I'd hate it, and I think he expected me to quit right then. But I wanted to stay."

"You didn't want to go to work for your father."

"It's not my father. It's who *he* works for."

Tierney, I thought.

He shifted his weight, keeping his hands in his pockets. "Once you get in his pocket, you don't get out. So I planned to do what Helms asked—except it didn't work."

"Why not?"

"I was up against a bloke from Bethnal Green. Not a bad fighter, but I had at least two stone on him, and he was still green. After a while I dropped my guard a bit, acted tired, left myself open a few times so he landed a few." Jack's words came in a rush, as if he wanted to get them away from himself. By contrast, his body was motionless. "And then I threw a hook that I thought he could dodge. But he walked right into it and didn't get up."

"What happened to you?"

"Helms tossed me out, of course. Said I was worthless if I couldn't follow the simplest bloody directions." He pressed the toe of his boot absently in the dirt. "But the more I thought about it later, the more I wondered if it was an excuse. Helms liked me—and I'd earned him a fair bit. But there was something else at stake. Helms was afraid of something."

Suddenly I thought I understood. If Tierney wanted Jack to work for him, he passed the word to Helms and backed it with a threat. I shivered. "So you left boxing, and came to work for your father."

He nodded. "I never recruited the boys, or trained them, if that's what you're asking. But I'm in charge of keeping track of the nightly take, making sure it gets where it needs to go— pawnshops, the docks, the railways." He hesitated. "Not that it means much, but the last year or so, I've been helping the boys when I can. I get them extra food, make sure they've got shoes and clothes and medicine if they get sick. My father doesn't care, so long as I pay for it out of my own share."

His voice was low, and I heard in it the note of guilt that carried a plea for me to understand. But the image of the two boys dead on the pavement was fresh in my mind. I felt a wave of frustration and sadness and anger toward Jack that, together with my affection, made it so I could hardly breathe. We were silent for several minutes, until he broke it, his voice rough. "Nell, say something."

I took a deep, ragged breath, and what came out was half a wish and half a warning: "You can't do this anymore, Jack."

Even in the slanted light, I could see his eyes dark with torment. "Don't, Nell."

"Don't?" I stared. "What do you mean, *don't*? I can't let you— you *can't* believe what your father—what you and your father are doing is right—"

"Damn it, Nell!" His voice was almost savage, his eyes searching mine. "Don't ask me to betray my father. I can't do it. I tell you, I won't."

My mouth fell open. "But these boys are getting killed, doing what they're doing! They need to be somewhere they'll be treated decently—not forced into dangerous places like roofs and gutters and God knows where else!"

"And where do you think they came from?" His expression was a mix of impatience and disgust. He shook his head and turned away from me, pacing about the yard in semicircles. "Most of these boys came out of the rookeries, Nell. Most of them were stealing before they got here—only they were starving and getting beat half to death, no matter what they brought back at the end of the day. And plenty of them were killed working that way, too, don't think they weren't. Rob and Gus had two older brothers. One of them worked for a ratcatcher, until he got bit and died. The other was strangled and thrown into the Thames for not handing over a shilling he found on the street. For keeping it in his pocket."

The lump in my throat made it hard to speak. "That's . . . that's horrible, Jack, I know. But that doesn't mean they should be *here*. Why aren't they somewhere safe—"

"Like where? Workhouses? Orphanages? Do you know what they do to boys in those places?"

I flinched at the sharpness in his voice. "At least they feed them—and—"

"They hurt them, too. And sometimes they bugger them." His eyes had gone black, and there was something queer and cold in his voice that told me this was something he knew, not from any sensational newspaper story, but in his bones.

My mouth was dry. "When were you in an orphanage?"

"After my mum died. My father was in prison for debt. They sent me to St. Lucien's, near Seven Dials. The second night I was there, I was sleeping on a straw pallet with two other boys. We'd

spent the whole day, twelve hours, refilling jars of shoe polish."
He stopped, and I waited, my breath shallow. "Sometime around
midnight two men came and stood at the end of the bed. To this
day, I don't know why they didn't take me. But they took those
other two boys instead."

"Oh, dear God," I whispered. Part of me wanted to ask him
to stop.

"There were rooms upstairs kept empty for it."

I felt bile rising into my throat. I put my palm over my mouth
and swallowed hard.

"The boys came back an hour later," he continued. "Wouldn't
say a word to me. One was crying, but he had a gag around his
mouth to keep him quiet. I had a knife hidden in my boot. It was
dull, but good enough I could cut the knot."

"And you were ten."

"They were younger." He was silent. "I left the next day, went
back to my old street. That's when Amalie's family took me in."

"Jack, I had no idea."

"I know," he said tiredly. "That's why I'm telling you. Because
you've got to understand—it may look like these boys are being
badly used—and maybe they are. But they're also getting two
meals a day and someplace to sleep."

I tried once more. "The police are going to find out what happens here, you know. Sooner or later."

"Maybe." He said it bitterly. "It just means the boys'll go back
out onto the street. My father'll hang, and if I'm caught, I'll be
right there along with him."

I felt the roughness of the bricks under my hands. "Not if you
get out and tell the police what you know."

He gave a short, horrible laugh. "He's my father, Nell."

"I *know*," I said between gritted teeth. "But I have to say it's hard for me to believe. I've never met two people less like each other."

He studied me for a moment. "We're more alike than you think."

I let him see the skepticism in my face. His eyes narrowed, and he shook his head. "Seems you think people are simple, like what you see of them over a few months is all they've ever been. But people change."

Stung, I drew myself up. "Of *course* people change. I'm not a fool. But if you want me to understand something different about your father, then you have to tell me. Because I've never seen a *shred* of compassion or kindness or generosity in him. Not even toward you."

"All right," he said simply. "I'll tell you." He moved to lean against the wall next to me. "When my mother was dying, the doctor said she'd do better if she could sleep upright—so my father held her, every night, all night, against his chest. I remember how shiny and pale her face was because she'd sweat, even in her sleep. He'd hold a cloth over her mouth, so she could cough into it, and he'd wash out the blood in the morning." He paused. "The doctor said my mother needed help digesting her food, and that her stomach could only tolerate fresh meat and bread. So my father would go out and buy the best he could find. He'd come home and cut it up tiny, stand at the stove and soak it in broth in this old, dented pot we had. Then he'd spoon it into her mouth, like she was a babe." Finally, he looked at me. "She was sick for months, Nell. Sickness costs money. And time. My father lost his job at the docks for all the days he took off. Eventually, he went through all our savings. He sold everything we owned—our pictures, our silver, a ring his father had given him." Another pause. "Everything except her piano. He kept it. Do you know why?"

I shook my head.

"Because he knew that if she woke up and saw it gone, it would make her cry."

My tears came so fast that my eyes burned. In that moment, my heart ached for all of them.

"Now do you understand?" he asked. "Never mind that he hates me sometimes. It's because I remind him of her. But I'm all he has."

I couldn't answer.

Heavily, he pushed himself away from the wall, came round to face me, and said, "I know that what he's doing is wrong." His voice dropped until it was almost inaudible. "But I won't turn him in, Nell. Not even for you." His fingers brushed my damp cheek so lightly I might've imagined it.

And then he was gone, back inside the music hall, and I was left alone in the darkness as the nighttime noises swelled and reverberated around me—theatergoers' voices and laughter, the clop of horses' hooves, the creak of wheels, the yowl of a lone cat.

I tilted back my head to blink back the tears.

A soft laugh came from somewhere off to my right. I whirled and strained my eyes to see who it was.

Just as on the night I first met him, Stephen emerged from the shadows, his fair hair gleaming. He slid his hands into his pockets and raised an eyebrow. "That was quite a scene—though I wish I'd seen it from the start. I have a feeling I may have missed some touching dialogue."

"Not everything's a bloody performance," I said, chokingly.

"Of course it is," he said.

My voice was taut. "No, it's *not*. Although maybe the lines are blurrier for you."

That stopped him, and a look of surprise came over his face as he leaned against the wall next to me, in the same place Jack had been moments earlier. I could smell the whiskey on his breath.

"What's the matter with you?" he asked curiously.

Careful, I thought to myself.

"Nothing." I made as if to leave, and he put out a hand.

"No, wait. You're going to tell me what you meant." His voice was still pleasant, but his hand was firm. He wasn't going to let me go until I told him something; I gave him what I thought was safe.

"That performance you gave at the restaurant the other night— tell me, was that for my benefit or your father's?"

He had the grace to look slightly ashamed. "Well, for my father's. Obviously."

"What do you mean, obviously? I can't tell if your story was to make me feel sorry for you, or if I was there as a prop while you confronted him."

His hand dropped from my arm. "Oh, don't get all righteous about it. He's my father, which means he damn well owes me an audience." A pause, and then he rolled his eyes. "For God's sake, we all perform. You're not that naive." He waved toward the music hall door. "Gallius Kovác's real name is David Goldman—he's a Jew from some Godforsaken part of Spitalfields, not a descendant of some Romany magician. Lady Van de Vere's the daughter of a slut, Amalie's not French, and you're not a man! This is the world we live in."

"But this is a music hall, Stephen! People in the audience *know* it's a performance. If you take that performance out to the real world—that's a lie."

He drew a French-style cigarette out of a silver case and lit it. By the light of the match, I could see that he was unmoved. "You'd have kept up your lie to me about being a man, except that I caught you out."

I shoved my hands back in the pockets of my overcoat. "We weren't friends that first night. Friends don't lie to each other."

"I've never lied to you, Nell."

"Stephen!" My voice was incredulous. "What about the real reason you were asked to leave the Academy? I heard a rather different story than what you told me."

"Oh, I'll bet you did." His voice was caustic.

"What does that mean?"

"Jack's hardly going to tell you the truth about that, seeing as he's the reason I was unfairly thrown out." He waved his cigarette, the tiny golden ember at the end tracing an arc in the darkness. "You see, he had the story wrong. The truth is, Andrew *loved* gambling. He wanted to play, came every night for a game." He shrugged. "He wasn't any good, and eventually he owed me a fair bit. Not quite so much as the violin was worth, but enough. He didn't want to admit it to his father, so he gave me the damn thing. He hated it—that's the irony. He was only at the Academy in the first place because his mother had it in her head he was going to be a famous musician." He flicked the ash of his cigarette away. "At any rate, the next morning, when he was sober, he thought better of it, so he told Jack that I'd cheated him at cards. Jack went straight to old Bennett, and I was out on my ear." A hard laugh. "And then I got here, and he didn't even know who I was. That's how little he cares about ruining people's lives. Let it be a lesson to you before you get in too deep with him."

It was on the tip of my tongue to correct him, to tell him it had been Mr. Bertault who'd gone to the principal; but while Stephen was speaking, I'd noticed how quiet the yard was. This quarter of Soho was nearly empty for the night, and I wanted nothing more than to get away.

He took a last long draw on the cigarette before he dropped it into the dirt. "You see, Nell? There's always another layer to the story. It's like an onion. Sometimes you have to peel a bit. Do you believe me?"

"I don't know. I don't know what—or who—to believe anymore." I rubbed at my forehead, suddenly exhausted. "Things aren't clean-cut."

A pause, and then in a lighter voice: "They can be, you know."

I gave a short laugh.

"Really." His face was bent toward mine, with no hint of mockery in his eyes. "Haven't you ever thought about getting away?"

"Getting away?"

"Of course! You don't have to stay here if you don't want to. Not with your abilities. You could go anywhere." He took out his cigarette case again. "Leave this place."

"You mean the Octavian?" I asked.

"Well, yes." He lit a new cigarette, and I smelled the sulphur and ash. "This place, with its sordid little crimes and petty backstage theatrics. Neither of us belongs here, playing the same tired show over and over." He grimaced. "But I meant London. It's a bad place for people with talent. Too many scavengers with their hooks into us, with their own ideas about what we should and shouldn't be doing." He drew on his cigarette, then blew the smoke aside. "Even if you get into the Royal Academy, you're going to hate it. For the first few years, you'll be in classes, practicing things you've already done, the same pieces students have played for years. And you being a woman, they're going to curb you so hard, you will barely be able to breathe. Believe me, they've got their own way of doing things."

I could hear the faint slur that whiskey had put in his voice. "What do you suggest?"

"Remember I told you my family has friends in Europe? Well, last week my father told me he'll give me money to leave England. I've all but made up my mind—I'm leaving for Paris soon. Why don't you come with me?"

I could only stare.

"It's not as crazy as it sounds." He waved the cigarette. "Oh, I don't mean as lovers! We'd be fellow musicians. We'd write music, meet other artists, create our own salon on the Rive Gauche." His voice became persuasive. "You'd get to play in real halls, not second-rate places like this. You could stay with my friend Heloise. She lost her flatmate, and she'd be pleased to have you."

If I didn't know better, I'd have thought he was sincere.

And then I realized that he was. He believed that his deceitfulness could just be waved away like the smoke from a cigarette. No doubt he considered himself generous, and that I should leap at the proffered opportunity.

He reached out, took one of my hands, and held it in his. "God almighty, girl. You're freezing. That's another good thing about Paris—it's warmer there."

"I'm all right," I managed.

"What do you think? It wouldn't have to be Paris. We could

try Vienna, or Salzburg, if you'd prefer. It's just that in Paris, we'd have a place to stay straightaway."

I heard the warmth and buoyancy in his voice, and with a jolt, I realized that in his mind, he was already halfway to Europe, with me in tow.

I withdrew my hand gently and put it in my pocket. "Stephen, that wouldn't work. You know it wouldn't."

"Why not?"

I heard the surprise in his voice and didn't answer at first. Somewhere in the back of my mind a warning sounded; I needed to handle this delicately. I had seen how he responded to rejection and ridicule.

He took a quick breath. "You can't mean you care for Jack Drummond! I saw the two of you together—but it seemed you were merely waiting him out. You didn't make any move to stop him when he left."

"It's not that," I said and managed a small laugh. "For goodness' sake, Stephen! Paris? I don't even speak French."

He frowned, and it was as if he hadn't even heard me. "You can't fall for that man. If you knew the truth about him, you'd know why."

"The truth?"

"Yes, the truth."

"Well, as you said, maybe it's like an onion. Maybe what you know about him is only the first layer."

"No." His voice was definite. "He's dangerous all the way to the core. Listen to me. His father's a criminal—and so is he."

Stephen knows about the Fleet, I thought.

"What do you mean?" I said. "Goodness, you sound like a character in a penny dreadful."

He bent his head toward me in a way that was almost intimate. "This is no cheap novel, Nell. Drummond runs a thieving ring. He and Jack have a team of boys who live here during the day and go out and rob houses and shops at night. All these boys you see around here? They're nothing more than his little slaves."

"But that's his father," I said weakly. "Jack wouldn't do that."

His smile was sardonic. "Oh, they're cut from the same piece of cloth. Don't think they aren't." He dropped the last bit of his cigarette into the dirt and pressed the stub with his toe. "He's as deep in this business as his father—and only going to go deeper. I've seen the logs of what they take in—and Jack's the one who writes them out." A pause. "I've heard he's been offered his own ring to run, someplace down in Lambeth."

My stomach lurched, even though Stephen was as likely lying as not. "How do you know all this?"

He didn't answer.

I pretended to be coming to a realization and let my eyes go wide. "You're in this with him, aren't you? And don't *lie*, Stephen. You said we're friends."

"All right. You want proof of my honesty? I'll tell you how I'm in it. Drummond's been paying me because I know some of the big houses."

I stared. It wasn't at all what I'd expected him to say. "You mean the houses he's robbing?"

He raised an eyebrow. "Don't look so surprised. My family moves in good circles. I've been in plenty of them." He shrugged. "Including my father's."

"You told him about your father's house? So the boys could rob it?"

"It's one of the easier ones. There's a small garden out back"—he jerked his head—"with a trellis. Family dines at eight, which means the bedrooms are deserted from eight till ten. A hidden drawer in my father's armoire contains his jewelry. There are some diamond cuff links in my brother's room. And there's a particularly fine painting in the upper hallway by an Italian master. Not large, easily portable." He gave an easy smile.

Dear God. His own family.

My instinct was warning me not to let him see my disgust. I kept my voice steady, even light. "Well, that's one way to square things with your father. What is Drummond giving you for your information?"

"A share. A trifle really, but then again, I'm not risking anything."

Yes, that's the way you do it, isn't it? I thought. *Let other people take the risks.* But I said merely, "And that way, you can't get caught."

He shrugged again. "I'm not a fool."

"Well, Drummond may be a drunkard, but you should be careful. He's no fool, either."

"I can get away from Drummond any time I want."

I let him see my skepticism. "How? Once he has his hooks in you, as you say, he's not going to let you go."

"Well, that's partly why I want to leave for Paris. And yet another reason you might want to get away from here, too. You've been playing for months. Who's to say the police might not think you have something to do with his schemes?"

I sighed. "Stephen, I can't leave London. My brother's here—and Peggy and Emma—people I love—"

He tipped his head. "But you lie to them."

"What?"

"You sneak out of the house, and none of them know." He gave a knowing smile. "Not that it's a bad thing. If you can lie to people who love you, in the service of your ambitions, that's a real skill. I mean it."

Suddenly I was filled with revulsion. Maybe if I'd been smarter, I'd have dropped my eyes, pretended that he wasn't making my skin crawl. But he saw my expression before I could hide it.

For a moment, hurt shone in his eyes. Then anger swept like a wave over his face, distorting it. "Don't look at me like that."

The streets were all but silent. I was alone in this yard with a man who calculated everything in terms of his own gains. He must have seen the fear in my face, for he began to laugh unpleasantly. And then his two hands flashed to my shoulders, and he shoved me hard against the wall.

"Let go of me!" I tried to pry away his fingers, but they were rigid as iron. "Stephen, let *go*!"

He leaned in, close enough that I smelled the tobacco and whiskey thick on his breath. "Do you want me to tell you about your ambitions?" he hissed. "Because I *know*. I saw girls like you at the Academy, desperate to make up for their lack of talent with hour upon hour of practice, pounding the keys like monkeys. And you know the reason for all that pathetic striving? Because you haven't anything else to fall back on."

He pulled me away from the wall, toward him, almost as if in an embrace. But instead he gave me a shove. My head smacked the bricks behind me, and I felt a blazing heat at the back of my skull.

And then, at last, he let go. I landed on my knees and pitched forward into the dirt with a cry. I heard the creak of the back door and his voice, thick with contempt: "Don't come back. They won't want you."

He dragged the door shut behind him and threw the bolt. I lay there for a moment, my breath coming in ragged gasps, until the sharpest pain in the back of my head began to fade. Carefully, I touched my scalp. Already there was a thickening, and a stickiness that could only be blood. I lurched to my feet, clumsily, and looked at the door that would never open for me again.

I wouldn't have cared a bit, except that Jack was behind it. And despite what he'd said, and what I'd learned, I still didn't want this to be all there was.

Chapter 22

When I woke, I could tell from the hollow quality of the house that Matthew had already left, and I was alone. I'd washed the blood out of my hair last night, but the back of my head felt bruised, and the pain seemed to wrap like a claw around to my temples. I dressed with a dreary sense of loss and loneliness. Moving gingerly in the kitchen, I made myself a cup of tea and nibbled some toast, but I felt no better. I moved slowly into the parlor and lay down on the couch with Peggy's usual remedies, a woolen blanket around me and a damp cloth infused with vinegar on my forehead.

For some hours, I slept, and sometime after midday I woke to the sound of knocking. I fumbled my way out from under the blanket and opened the front door. It was a boy with a message. I gave him a sixpence and opened the missive.

My dear Nell,

Marceline has vanished. The police have arrived, and it's been my first opportunity to send for you.

Please come if you can.

Yours, in haste, Dr. E.

I reread the few lines. "Vanished," I said aloud. Did that mean she'd been taken, or gone of her own free will?

With a sinking feeling, I put on my coat and walking shoes and started for the hospital. The additional sleep had done away with the worst of the pain and queasiness, but I couldn't remember ever being so low in my mind. It was the day before my audition. By all rights I should have been excited, or anticipatory, at least. Instead, I was overcome with the darkest thoughts, swamped with a sense of the futility of striving for anything for myself or of trying to help anyone else.

When I arrived at the hospital, I glimpsed two police constables searching around the outer wall of the hospital wing; they seemed to be inspecting the bushes and grounds. I entered the foyer and saw Mr. Oliven, his face earnest, answering questions being directed to him by a plainclothes detective. Matthew wasn't there, for which I was grateful. I didn't think I could bear his scrutiny.

"Excuse me," I said to one of the nurses I knew by sight. "Where is the doctor?"

"In his office, Miss Hallam."

I went to his office and knocked.

"Come in." His voice was irritable, higher pitched than normal, as if he'd said those words too many times that day.

I opened the door.

"Oh, thank God." He sighed. "Do you have any idea where she might have gone? Did she say anything to you about leaving?"

I shook my head. "No. Nothing."

He peered at me. "What's the matter? You don't look well."

"I've a headache, that's all." I paused. "Does it seem she left of her own volition?"

"It looks that way, although I've no idea how she managed it in her condition. Maybe she fashioned herself some wings, like Daedalus." He stood and put on his coat. "Come with me."

He led me up the narrow back stairs to the fourth floor, which was used only for storage. The few times I'd been up there, the air had been musty and still. This time it was fresh. He entered a small room, and it became clear where the draft was coming from. A windowpane had been broken, the hasp turned, and the window swung open on its hinges.

I stared at the doctor. "You don't think she climbed out this way, do you?"

"I'm forced to believe it."

"But why would she have broken the window, when she could simply have undone the hasp?"

"I believe she had an accomplice."

Of course, I thought. *Sebastian. Unless . . .*

"Are you certain it's an accomplice and not an abductor?" I asked.

"There was no sign of a struggle in the ward, the nurses heard nothing, and all of her things are gone. The only thing missing is a pillowcase, which I imagine she used as a makeshift satchel. So I believe she went willingly."

I went to the window and leaned out. There was a drainpipe, with sturdy metal brackets fastening it to the bricks. Sebastian could have navigated this easily. But Marceline, with her injuries?

"Whoever it was, was clever," Dr. Everett said. "No doubt he'd observed the hospital for some period and realized that Mr.

Oliven stays at the front gate, and the back of the building is poorly lit. Given that the floor below is mostly empty at night, no one would hear the glass breaking up here." He pointed to the bed frame at the bottom of the stack. "The police found a rope fastened there. The weight of the beds served as an anchor."

"I just hope she didn't reinjure herself climbing down," I said.

"*I* just wonder why she no longer felt safe here," he replied.

I felt a sickening regret that I'd told Sebastian about the man who'd come looking for her.

"Maybe it was because Matthew came to see her." He rubbed his forefingers into his temples, as though it would help his brain work out what had happened. "She really wasn't well enough to leave, and if she fell down and hit her head a second time, she could do permanent damage."

"Did you send for Matthew this morning?"

"I sent round to the Yard. A different inspector came. I spent the morning answering his questions." He gave one last look out the window and put a hand on my arm, so I had to face him. His eyes searched mine. "Nell, you didn't know about her leaving?"

"No!" I said honestly. "And I wouldn't have encouraged her—certainly not until she was healed. I thought she was safer here than anywhere else."

He sighed as we left the room and headed for the stairs. "Well, there's nothing more to be done, I suppose. I do hope she had somewhere safe to go, poor girl."

I WENT STRAIGHT TO THE *FALCON* OFFICES and found Jeremy in the main room at one of the long canted tables with a dozen other men. He was intent on his task of selecting type out of the partitioned wooden boxes and didn't see me as I approached. Ignoring the curious looks of the other men, I leaned in close to his ear. "Jeremy."

He jumped and turned. "Cor! Way to scare a fellow." His dark eyes shifted back and forth uneasily, but he hopped up from his stool, muttered a few words to the young man next to him, and followed me out of the room to a quiet place near the stairwell.

"Marceline is gone," I said without preamble. "Did Sebastian come for her?"

He hesitated.

"For God's sake, Jeremy, just tell me," I snapped. "I certainly *hope* it was him, climbing through a fourth-story window with a rope!"

"Yah. I'd say it was 'im."

"How did he even know which hospital?"

He shrugged. "'E followed you the day you come 'ere. You should'a guessed 'e would."

I glowered at him.

His eyes narrowed, and he leaned close and hissed, "Why are you upset? I'd think you'd be glad she got away!"

"Of course I am, so long as she got away *safely*!" I whispered back sharply. "But she was nowhere near healed. Her ribs were cracked, her hands were torn to shreds, and her head still had a dozen stitches, for goodness' sake! Do you really think she should have been climbing down a drainpipe in the middle of the night?"

He chewed on his bottom lip for a moment. "S'pose not."

I sighed. "Never mind. Did they get away safely?"

He looked troubled. "I dunno."

"*What?* They didn't come here?"

"Not yet," he admitted. "But I 'spect they will, soon as they can."

"Jeremy!"

"Wot?" His chin came up and his eyes flashed.

I groaned. "Why did he take her last night? Why couldn't he wait until she was better?"

"I'd say he was spooked by you tellin' 'im about that man who come lookin' for 'er."

My regret bit deep all over again. "Who was he, anyway? That man?"

"Dunno." He shook his head so hard that his hair flopped over his eyes. "But nobody you'd want to know. Nor me, either."

"Do you know why the men were looking for Sebastian?"

His eyes dropped to the ground in front of his boots.

"I know about the thieving ring," I said softly. "Was he a part of it?"

Still without looking at me, he nodded.

My heart sank. "Did it start when he was at the Octavian?"

"Nah. 'Afore that."

"Marceline said they told her he owed them something. Do you know what it was?"

He sighed and met my gaze. "'E didn't tell me wot, but it was sumpin' that 'e was goin' to trade for gettin' out. 'E didn't want to do it no more." He gave one of his deep sniffs and glanced toward the workroom. "Miss, I got to get back."

"Wait." I found a scrap of paper and a pencil stub in my pocket. "Get word to me if you hear from them, would you?"

"A' right," he said, stuffing the paper in his pocket.

My worry and hopelessness felt like a physical weight as I descended to the street and headed home.

Chapter 23

That night my thoughts kept me pacing. Wrapped in a woolen blanket, I went from study to parlor to spare room to kitchen and back.

Matthew was still out, and while I had become used to his irregular hours, tonight felt different. With each passing quarter hour, the knot in my stomach tightened. Eventually, I rebuilt the fire in the parlor and sat on the couch with the blanket, rising only to add coal, a few pieces at a time. The fire's warmth was no match for the coldness that came of feeling profoundly unhappy and worried and heartsick.

I shouldn't have told Sebastian about the man who'd come to the hospital, that much was clear. But I felt a wave of frustration that took shape as a set of questions for Marceline. *Why couldn't you have waited until you were healed before you left? Why couldn't you have asked me for help? Matthew would have kept you safe, helped both you and Sebastian get away; he explicitly said so. And where are you now?* I could imagine the expression in her brown eyes and on her delicate face, but of course I couldn't concoct the words that would come out of her mouth, and the idea of her and Sebastian on the streets, perhaps hunted by the men who'd hurt her before, gave rise to a fear in me that was almost intolerable.

As for Jack—at the thought of him, tears came to my eyes. I didn't know what it meant, that he'd left me there in the yard. But his explanation of his steadfast loyalty to his father was a note that rang true for me. If someone asked me to betray Matthew, I wouldn't, no matter what he'd done. Yet what pained me most was Jack's story about his father's love for his dying wife. He had told it so openly that it had slipped me inside their tragedy and shown me what it was to love someone so fiercely and deeply that the person's death would all but destroy me. It kept me weeping until I had no tears left.

Finally, I fell asleep on the couch, and the fire went out.

I OPENED MY EYES to see the room bathed in the gray light of an overcast day.

Audition day, I thought drearily.

Then I heard the door close quietly, and I sat up and peered over the top of the couch. When I spoke, my voice was hoarse from crying: "Matthew?"

He appeared in the doorway of the parlor, and I knew at a glance that something terrible had happened. The shoulders of his coat were drenched and dark, his face was ashen with fatigue, and the beginnings of whiskers shadowed the area around his mouth. Wearily, he entered the room and sank into a chair. With his elbows on his knees, his hands gripping the hair at the sides of his head, he looked as despondent and grief-stricken as he had the afternoon our father died.

"What's the matter?" I asked softly.

He didn't even look up. A shudder ran through him, though it seemed his large body was clenched with the effort to still it.

And then I realized his shoulders were shaking with silent sobs. The sight brought me to my knees beside him. I put my arms as far as I could reach around his broad back. I could feel the cold coming off him, and the wool of his coat smelled damp and oily, like the river.

At last his head came up, and he pulled away from me, rubbing at his eyes with the heels of his hands. "I'm sorry," he muttered, his voice rough.

"Don't be ridiculous," I said, but gently. "Tell me what happened."

"William's dead."

All the breath went out of me.

His expression was bleak, his eyes red-rimmed. "We went to meet Avery yesterday. He told us everything—where the ships were, transportation routes, the names of other fences, boats—things I didn't even know to ask about." A pause, and then, tonelessly, "When it came time for him to leave, William and he changed clothes."

A shiver ran over me, for now I understood.

"I gave Avery money and a character and followed at a safe distance. He made it onto the train. No one trailed him; I'm sure of it. But William . . ."

His eyes filled with tears again, and they ran unchecked down his cheeks. "I would've done it, but I'm too big. Avery's small and fair-haired."

"Oh, Matthew." My heart ached for him.

"William and I were supposed to meet back at the Yard. When

he didn't come, I knew something must've happened. I went back out to look."

"Where did you find him?"

"About a quarter mile downriver from the warehouse where we'd met Avery. Between Blackfriars Bridge and Queenhithe Dock." His fingers rubbed the tears off his cheeks. "It was made to look as if he fell through the window of a storehouse. He was half buried in the muck. Another few hours and I wouldn't have found him."

"You don't believe he fell."

"Of course not," Matthew answered. "He was raised on the docks. Besides, he had burn marks up and down his arms and bruises on his neck." He stared into midair, as if he were seeing William's body only a few feet away. "Someone tortured him before he died—and then killed him to keep his mouth shut."

My stomach tightened. "What did they want from him?"

His eyes flicked to me. "To know what we know about the Fleet, I'd say, including whether we knew about Barrow."

"Barrow?" I echoed in surprise.

"Barrow has reddish hair and a scar. And a stick this big that's round at the end." His fingers reproduced the circle Marceline had made, and his voice hardened. "That's a truncheon, Nell. You've seen mine."

I stared. "But . . . but he's a hero—"

"He has a mistress," he said brusquely. "Apparently, she's expensive. And he's paying blackmail to keep it from his wife and her family. Her father's a judge who could destroy him."

With a sigh, he stood and went to stand at the cold hearth. Silently, I rose from the floor and fumbled for the chair behind me.

"Thank God for your friend Marceline, or I'd never have looked at him twice," he added.

Suddenly I realized he didn't know. "Matthew," I said, hating to tell him, "Marceline is gone."

He turned to face me. "What do you mean, she's gone?"

"She fled last night, out of a window. Dr. Everett sent a message to the Yard."

At first, he looked dismayed, but after a moment he shrugged pragmatically. "I can't say I blame her. They know she could identify him."

"And if they know *you* know about Barrow?" Fear laid a cold finger on my heart. "What's to keep them from coming after you?"

"Nothing," he said. "Unless I go after them first."

I swallowed hard. "Who was the other man? Was it Tierney?"

"No." His expression hardened. "And Tierney's the one I really want. The important one—the root of it all." He shoved his hands in his pockets and leaned back against the mantel.

"Is there any way to prove that someone in the Fleet killed William?"

"When I catch Tierney, I'll make him tell me." His voice was casual, almost offhand. But I'd known my brother all my life; I'd never seen that look upon his face.

"What are you going to do?" It came out in a whisper.

Perhaps he saw how much he'd frightened me, for after a moment, he rallied his composure. He pushed himself away from the mantel, and his voice was dry, practical. "First, I'm going to have a wash and get a few hours of sleep. I've left a message for Mr. Winthrop—Barrow's superior—at his home, providing the bare facts and asking him to authorize a raid on the ships."

"What if he's in it with Barrow?"

His jaw tightened. "Then he'll say no, or postpone it long enough for Tierney to go underground. But I've met him a few times, and I can't see it. Besides, Tierney can't have *all* of London in his bloody pocket."

"I hope not," I said fervently.

"At any rate, I can't do anything until I hear back from him. He's taking the train in from Manchester and won't be home until half past two. I'm hoping he understands the urgency. We need to do this tonight."

"Tonight?"

He nodded. "Tierney may already have a head start on us."

"How?" The question slipped out of my mouth before I thought.

Matthew's eyes were somber. "William."

Of course, I thought, my stomach tightening. *Stupid of me.*

"I know he would hold out as long as he could, but . . ." He shook his head grimly. "And if Tierney's the sort of person I think he is, he has a plan for moving his ships and closing down all his routes to protect them. If we wait, he'll have changed it all, and we'll be back at the beginning." He shook his head, as if to say he wouldn't let it happen. "There are at least forty ships here in London. Can you believe that? I wish we knew the locations of them all, but at least we have thirteen."

My mouth went dry. Thirteen ships out of forty-some. Only a third. But still: was the Octavian one he knew of, or not?

In that moment, the words nearly slipped out of my mouth. But of course it would only steer Matthew's attention there, and make him wonder why I'd asked. Feeling guilty, and with some idea of atoning for all I wasn't telling him, I asked if there was anything at all I could do.

"You've been an absolute brick, Nell," he said, with a grateful look that only deepened my remorse. "Wake me at half past two, would you? And have some coffee ready. And something to eat,

I suppose." He started toward the stairs, pausing with his hand on the newel. "But wake me before then, if a message comes."

"Of course."

The steps creaked under his heavy feet, and I went to the kitchen and mechanically made some tea, as if that mundane ritual could reassure me of my own abilities to cope. But as I lifted the teacup, it slid from between my fingers and cracked against the saucer, and I realized I couldn't manage even this. My feet took me to the piano, and I sat on the bench for what must have been an hour. My thoughts went around and around in an intolerable circle, and I could find no way out of it. I couldn't let Jack go to prison, or hang. But I couldn't tell him about the raid, either, for it not only might send Tierney into hiding, it could ruin an investigation that had cost Matthew's friend's life and could very well endanger his own.

I STOOD IN FRONT OF THE GRANDFATHER CLOCK IN THE HALL, watching with a growing sense of resolve as the delicate hands closed upon the half hour.

I was due at the Royal Academy in Tenterden Street at four o'clock to register and then play before a panel of judges that would include the famous pianist, composer, and principal of the Academy, Sir William Sterndale Bennett. But I should be finished by six at the latest. Then I would go straight to Mr. Bertault's shop. Jack was likely to still be there, as he didn't have to be at the Octavian until half past seven. And if he had already left, I could go to the Octavian and at least get him a message that I needed to talk to him urgently. I simply needed to find some way to warn Jack without allowing him to warn anyone else. I had a vague notion of getting Jack away from the music hall after the show, perhaps to the Bear and Bull, and keeping him there under some pretext.

The clock gave a small chime, and I started upstairs to Matthew's door and knocked. There was no answer, so I knocked again. "Matthew? It's half past two."

"Thanks, Nell." His voice was gravelly with sleep. "I'll be down in a bit."

I went to the kitchen, made the coffee, cut a slice of bread, slathered on butter, and cut some squares of cheese and ham. He came down about a half an hour later, his face washed and shaved, though his collar was still undone.

"Do you feel better?" I asked.

"Some. I needed the sleep. It's going to be a long day." He was just finishing his meal when there was a knock on the door. I heard his sharp intake of breath, and he leaped up to answer it. I hurried after him and watched as he thanked the messenger, opened the letter, and began to read, a look of relief spreading over his countenance after the first few lines.

"What does he say?"

"Winthrop wants to see me at his home."

"You don't think it's a trap, do you?"

"No." He scanned the remainder of the note. "He agrees something must be done. He's already sent orders out to gather a force of uniformed police to put under my direction."

This is all happening too fast, I thought.

He turned away and entered the study. The squeak of a drawer brought me to the threshold, where I watched as he took out Father's revolving pistol and checked that the bullets were in the chambers.

"You have to take that?" I asked.

"Today I do." He closed the gun and tucked it into a leather harness under his coat.

"For goodness' sake, Matthew, be careful," I said, not bothering to hide my fear. "Will you be home tonight?"

He stood in front of the mirror to arrange his collar, and reached for his coat. "I don't know. Winthrop wants to take all thirteen tonight. If we can surprise the first few, we may find some people willing to give us the others, if they think that doing so will help them stay out of prison."

I felt the blood fall from my face. So even if the Octavian wasn't one of the original thirteen . . .

My eyes sought the clock on the mantel. It was twenty past three, and Tenterden Square was a twenty-minute walk.

Something inside me twisted. It was impossible that I could find Jack and still get to the Academy by four. And by the time I finished at six, it might already be too late. What if the police were already at the Octavian by then? I had no idea how quickly Matthew might move.

I forced myself to imagine what would happen if I missed the audition: a dry letter regretting to inform me that the Academy had filled all their spots.

But if the Octavian was one of the thirteen ships that Matthew knew about, I had to tell Jack. Jack needed to gather up any proof of his involvement and destroy it, and then he needed to stay far away from the place.

I heard Jack's bleak words in my head. *My father'll hang, and if I'm caught, I'll be right there along with him.* And the world might say he deserved it. But I knew, in my bones, that Jack was a good man, as decent and loyal as my brother.

Matthew opened the door and looked back at me, his expression troubled. "I'm sorry about all this. You look terribly worried. I promise I'll be careful."

I put my arms around him and then drew back, my eyes meeting his. "Keep your wits about you, all right?"

"I will."

And as the door closed behind him, I felt the stillness of the house settle around me like a held breath.

Chapter 24

I went upstairs to don my men's clothes. I had a feeling that within the next few hours I would have occasion to want not only the disguise but also the extra warmth of them, especially the woolen overcoat and hat.

It was well after four o'clock by the time I reached Mr. Bertault's piano store, where a small crowd had gathered out front. As I drew near, I saw that most people were dressed for a formal event, the women in fur stoles and diamond necklaces, the men in black silk top hats, carrying gilt-topped canes. I touched one man's sleeve, begged his pardon, and asked what was happening.

"It's one of Mr. Bertault's special concerts. Ignatio Rambusco tonight. He's playing at five thirty."

Rambusco?

I felt dumbfounded, but I must have merely looked ignorant, for the man said patiently, "He's a pianist, from the conservatory in Paris. He's a friend of the owner."

"Yes," I managed. "I—that is, I've heard of Rambusco."

"I heard him years ago at St. James's. He's going to play

a new piece by Liszt." He looked around the crowd. "I'm not sure we'll all be able to sit. We may have to stand near the back."

"No . . . I . . . I don't think I'll stay. But do you think I could go in—just for a minute? I need to see Mr. Bertault. It's quite urgent."

Graciously, he gestured for me to step ahead of him, and bit by bit, explaining myself to the people ahead of me, I squirmed my way to the front door and went through. I paid no attention at all to the gray-haired man who was seated at the exquisite Pleyel in the center of the room. I only had eyes for Jack—and so far as I could see, he wasn't here.

But Mr. Bertault was. He was dressed for the evening in a black coat with glittering studs in his shirtfront, and he held a glass of champagne in his hand. The moment he saw me, he excused himself to a slender, red-haired man and came toward me, with an expression of concern. "My dear Nell, why aren't—?"

"Is Jack here?" My voice caught on the words.

He gave me a searching look then led me to his office, in which were crammed a desk and two tables, all stacked with papers and strewn with bits of pianos—keys, wires, and the dozens of tiny pieces that made up the action.

He shut the door behind us and set his champagne on the desk. "What's happened? You're supposed to be at your audition, and Jack missed two appointments this afternoon. I know he had a repair at the Octavian, but he said he'd be here by two."

Maybe whatever it was had taken longer than expected. Maybe he's still working at the music hall.

I shrank from the thought of going to find him there. By now, Stephen would certainly have informed Drummond of who I really was and what I knew. God only knew what else he'd tell him. But dressed as I was, maybe I could enter as a spectator and somehow get a message to Jack if he was backstage.

Mr. Bertault bent toward me, his expression kind. "Why do you need him so? Can I help you instead?"

I hesitated, not knowing how much he knew about the Fleet.

A shout broke out in the main room. I looked through the window at the crowd and sensed their anticipation.

"Take your time. They will wait." He took a pile of sheet music off a chair and gently pushed me into it. Then he reached into his cabinet for a bottle of bourbon. He sloshed an inch into two glasses and passed one to me. "Here." A dry smile. "If you were dressed as a lady, I'd offer you wine, but dressed as you are, it should be this."

I took a sip. Both bitter and sweet, it burned all the way down. He sat in the chair behind the desk and drank his own silently. After a deep breath, I swallowed the rest, and passed the empty glass back to him. He finished his, poured himself another bit, and raised the bottle toward me questioningly. I shook my head.

"What's frightening you, *chérie*?" he said gently.

It was the kindness in his voice, and maybe the drink, that undid my tongue. "Mr. Bertault, do you know what happens at the Octavian, besides the shows?"

His expression changed, and I felt a wave of relief. He knew. I hadn't betrayed Jack, and I'd found an ally.

"*Merde*," he swore. "I was afraid of this. Does Drummond know you know?"

I winced. "Probably. Jack and I were outside talking, in the yard behind the music hall, and Stephen Gagnon overheard us."

"He also knows?"

"Not only that. He told me he's been providing Drummond with information about particular houses, including his father's."

He shook his head, his disgust clear.

"You know what he is," I added quietly.

"You need to stay away," he warned.

"I know." I swallowed. "The problem is, my brother is an inspector at Scotland Yard, and—he is leading a raid on thirteen ships tonight."

His glass paused at his lips, and his eyes met mine over the rim. Slowly he brought the glass down, set it on the desk, and looked a question at me.

"I only found out myself a few hours ago," I added hurriedly.

"Ah." He nodded and frowned, hard. "Jack can't be found there."

"Nor the records of stolen goods. They're all in Jack's hand."

He took a breath that expanded his entire chest.

I stood up. "The only other place I could think of to look for him, besides here, was the Bear and Bull."

His eyebrows went up. "*Mais, oui!* But first—try his rooms. He might be there, and it won't take you much out of your way."

"Where?"

"In Dawson Street, number seven. It's north of here, off Everling Lane. Above a cobbler. Take the staircase on the left side of the building, and it's the first you'll come to. There's a lantern hanging to the left of the door. The spare key is in the base. Just unscrew the bottom." He looked toward the other room, where the noisy chatter was punctuated by laughter. "I wish I could come with you right now, but I cannot leave this crowd . . ." His voice trailed off.

"You have to stay here." I managed a smile. "If it were any other day, I'd stay myself. I'm sorry to miss it."

He waved a hand. "Ah, Ignatius comes to play every year. He'll be back."

"If I need to reach you—"

"I'll be here. If I'm not, I won't be away long. Send a message to me when you find him." He stood and came toward me, put his hands on my shoulders and kissed me, once on each cheek. "*Il va bien se passer*," he murmured. "Jack is no fool."

"And will you send me a message, if he comes here before I find him?"

"Of course." He reached for a piece of paper and a stub of pencil. "Write your address here."

I did as he asked, and he put the slip in his pocket. Then he opened the door, and I threaded my way through the crowd. There were no empty seats and very little standing room. Champagne was being handed round in delicate glasses. People had wedged themselves in between pianos and benches, many of them smiling and talking excitedly. The famous pianist was sitting at the bench before the piano, his eyes closed, a contented smile visible between his mustache and his beard, his hands running soft arpeggios up the keyboard. Monsieur Rambusco might have been alone in the room for all the attention he paid to the audience.

I exited onto the street. I, too, felt alone, like Rambusco. But I wasn't content. I was only afraid.

I hurried to Everling Lane, and then turned into Dawson Street. It was too narrow for two carriages to pass, but the houses were better kept than many in Soho. I found the cobbler's shop without difficulty and started up the side stairs. The next building was very close, so the falling evening light didn't penetrate much below the roofline, but I could see well enough. The alley behind smelled rancid, as if the refuse had been left too long between visits from the dustman.

I reached the first landing, but the door had no handle, and three wide boards were nailed crosswise into the wood frame on either side. Another thirteen steps—unlucky—and I saw a rusty lantern, unlit, hanging to the left of the door. I knocked at the door, softly at first and then louder. When no one answered, I laid my ear to the wood and heard only silence.

I took down the lantern and gripped the bottom, twisting as hard as I could. A squeak, and it came off, the key falling at my feet—but not, thankfully, off the step. I snatched it up, fitted it in the keyhole, and entered.

One look told me that Jack wasn't here, and I saw no signs that he had been recently. The room was stuffy but cool; the morning fire had burned out long ago.

I stepped inside, uneasy with the thought that I was entering wholly uninvited.

The room was simple and uncluttered. A bed in one corner, neatly made. A stove in the other corner with two mismatched chairs in front of it. A large sturdy armoire of dark wood. A dresser, a few books on a shelf, a table, a sink for washing up.

As I closed the door and flipped the bolt, I heard a low growl from the corner. I whirled, my heart thumping with fear, bracing myself for an attack by whatever had made the sound. My eyes searched the semidarkness, but I could see nothing.

Then, from behind one of the chairs, came a shadow that assembled itself into the shape of a cat. "Oh, thank God," I whispered as I dropped the key in my pocket.

A candlestick and matches were on the table. I fumbled with the box, scraped a light, and held it to the wick. At the edge of the light sat a thin tabby, her paws as delicately placed as a dancer's, her eyes glowing like round, iridescent pools.

"Well, hello," I said, bending down and putting out my hand to her. "So you're Jack's flatmate?" In my experience, most cats are leery of strangers, but she wasn't. She walked right under my hand, so I stroked her ears and she began to purr. "Trusting thing, aren't you," I murmured. "Where's Jack?"

Her purrs escalated. She rolled over onto her back as I've never seen a cat do. "You're more like a dog than a cat." I rubbed her soft belly. "I wish you could talk."

On the table lay a copy of yesterday's newspaper and a stub of a pencil. I flipped the pages but found nothing scribbled in the margin or marked in any way. Then why the pencil? Whatever he'd been writing, he must have taken it with him—unless—

I slid my fingers under the rim of the table and felt the crevice that marked a drawer. I bent down to find the ring or the pull, but there was none. I went around to the other side and found the same. This time I pushed at it, and the drawer slid away from me, emerging from the other side of the table. Yes, there was something in the drawer—a sensational yellowback novel, one of the cheap editions sold at the railway stations. I gave a wry smile. Not the sort of book I'd have expected—I doubted it was his—but I opened the book and held it spine up to fan the pages.

Nothing.

Then I flipped to the back, and my heartbeat quickened. The

two last pages, not including the cover, had been left unprinted by the publisher but were covered in writing. The script was neat, and I brought the candle closer to read it. Columns of numbers, followed by what looked like dates and letters and amounts, written in a hand that had been taught by a Frenchwoman, not an Englishman, the ones written with an upstroke, and commas in the place of periods.

I quickly skimmed through the rest of the book, but only the last two pages were written on. Was this a cipher of some kind? A code for inventory? Or some sort of record of street addresses or locations in London? Whatever it was, clearly it was a second record, apart from the log Jack kept for his father.

The cat shoved her head against my leg, and I absently bent down to scratch her head. Her claws came up to my hand. "Ouch!" I stared. "What's that for?" She tipped her head, looking at me in a way that made me recall the story of Baba Yaga's talking cat.

I shook myself. I was in a strange situation, but this was a normal cat. She was probably hungry. With one hand, I slid the book back into its drawer; with the other, I picked up the candle to search around the floor for her bowl and found it empty. The cupboard held a parcel of cat meat and a jar of water, so I filled her bowls and watched as she bolted her meal.

How long had it been since Jack had been here?

I felt a vibration in the floor, and then heard the sound of boots coming up the stairs. My heart lifted in gratitude at my lucky timing. I took a step toward the door, not wanting to startle him—

The cat gave a vicious hiss.

I turned, flinching back instinctively. But she was at my left ankle, facing the door, her tail gone from a silky, serpentine thing to a rigid bristle. Her mouth wide enough to show her incisors, she hissed again. She might as well have spoken English: this wasn't Jack.

Panicked, I retreated several steps before my mind started to work again. I needed to find a hiding place. I scanned the room. Under the bed? No, of course not, that's the first place he'd look. The armoire would be better—it was fairly deep. In a flash I snatched the candle from the holder and blew it out. By the faint light coming in at the window, I opened the armoire door, felt my way over a wooden box on the floor, and crouched in a corner behind some long clothes. I thanked God I'd bothered to bolt the door and the cat had finished her food straightaway. There was no sign anyone had been there for hours, unless the visitor smelled the smoke from the candle that I still held in my hand.

The key scraped, and the door squeaked open. I wondered if the cat would try to escape, or if she'd lurk in the shadows and scare the intruder half to death, as she'd done with me.

Measured footsteps—the screech of a drawer—and then, after a moment, the sound of pages being ripped and a man's short laugh. I closed my eyes and bit my lip at my utter stupidity, leaving the book instead of bringing it with me.

"That was easy," muttered the voice. Was it Stephen? The utterance was so brief I couldn't be sure. A silent apology to Jack formed on my lips—but at least now the intruder would leave.

But he didn't. He stayed to keep looking, and I tracked him by the sounds. The squeals of wood on wood. Those must be the dresser drawers. A scuffle as he got down on all fours to look under the bed. Another scrape as he moved a table, or maybe a chair, forward and back.

Still nothing from the cat. We were a pair, we two, still and silent. But my legs were falling asleep.

The sounds of cupboards opening and closing. What else was he looking for?

Another minute and I began to feel the desperate need to scratch my nose, so sharp that my eyes began to water. I closed them, held my breath, and began to count the four-four time of my Mozart sonata, over and over again. One, two, three, four; two, two, three, four; three, two, three, four; four . . .

The boots scraped across the floor, and the armoire door opened.

People talk of their heart stopping, and I think mine did. Out of sheer self-preservation, that organ went silent, along with my breath—everything down to the ends of the hair under my hat. He pulled out the box on the floor, rummaged through whatever was inside, and replaced it. Then the door closed, and I heard something sweep across the top of the armoire. He uttered a snort, strode across the floor, and closed and locked the door behind him.

Painfully, I unfolded my cramped legs, climbed out of the armoire, and limped to the window to peer through. The landing was empty, but in the street below, by the fading light, I could see Stephen's shining hair, uncovered. I watched until he rounded the corner. Behind me, the cat made a noise. When I unwound my fingers from the candle, the tallow bore the mark of my nails.

I set it on the table and took the key from my pocket. Where had Stephen obtained the one he used? From Drummond? But would Drummond even have a key to Jack's room? Or had Stephen taken the key from Jack's coat?

That would be easy enough—Jack hung his coat where all the performers did, upstairs in the instrument room. The fact that Stephen came in without knocking suggested he knew for certain that Jack wasn't here, which led me to think he knew where Jack *was*. It must be nearing seven o'clock. Yes, Jack could be at the music hall. And those pages of figures? I could see it clearly: Stephen taking them to show Drummond, Jack being dragged to his father—good God, what would Drummond do to Jack if he thought he was betraying him by keeping a separate set of records, maybe to save his own skin?

Fear rose up from my chest, and I swallowed it down. The cat gave another yowl and paced around the legs of a chair, her tail curling around each in turn and letting go.

But what if Jack wasn't at the Octavian? Or if I missed him, and he came home? I longed to leave some sign I'd been here—but I couldn't think of anything I could do or leave or write that wouldn't tell someone else I'd been here, too. And what if Stephen came back again?

I went out to the landing, locked the door, turned the bottom of the lantern to put the key in—and had an idea. I pushed my fingers in under my hat and pulled out a hairpin. Carefully, I clipped it around the end of the key. That might be enough to tell Jack that I'd been here, that I was looking for him, maybe even that his uncle had sent me here and told me how to get in.

Then I was down the stairs and hurrying to the end of the street. I had planned to go to the Bear and Bull after Jack's rooms. But really, although it was the last place I wanted to go, the music hall was the center of everything. Jack might be there and Stephen as well. If his overcoat was hanging in the instrument room, maybe I could retrieve those pages before they did any harm.

I REACHED THE FAR END OF HAWLEY MEWS just as the clock struck a quarter to eight. By the time I reached the back yard, the door was closed and locked. By this time, Jack should be either at the front, keeping away pickpockets, or tending the bar. But if he wasn't, I could blend in with the audience and eventually go backstage to find someone who might know where he was.

It was Sid, not Jack, at the front door. I kept my hat pulled low and had my shilling ready. Sid didn't even look up at my face as he took it. A quick glance at the bar told me what I'd expected: Jack wasn't there. My pulse thrumming, I found a place at the back where I could observe the hall and wait for my chance.

The lights began to dim, and my eyes sought the black curtain of the piano alcove. Had they asked Carl Dwigen to fill in for tonight? Or would they make do without a piano?

The curtain swung open unsteadily. It wasn't Carl's thin, stooped figure that had drawn it back; it was a thickset man of about thirty. He took his seat at the piano, in a black coat that pulled unattractively across the back and shoulders. No doubt Mrs. Wregge had dug it up for him out of one of her wardrobe boxes. He began to play—the same music I played, of course, and it gave me the strangest feeling of both rapport and a cold pragmatism. We were both only replacements for someone else.

Then I told myself not to be absurd. Of course I was replaceable, and while I hadn't been personally appreciated for my contribution, I had been paid for it, after all.

Gallius strode onstage, Maggie in his wake, and as the crowd began to settle, I sidled along the wall toward the door that led backstage. The person I wanted to talk to was Amalie. She cared enough about Jack to listen and help me, if she could.

After Gallius and Maggie left the stage. Amalie strutted out, and sure enough, every eye was fixed on her. No one was paying the least attention to me as my fingers found the handle and tried to turn it. But it wouldn't budge. It was locked from the other side.

Swearing under my breath, I started toward a second door that was hidden behind a curtain on the other side of the hall. I wormed my way through a group of men still standing by the bar. Ale from one man's glass splashed the sleeve of my coat, and my toes were stepped on several times by heavy boots, but I kept pushing through.

As I reached the curtain, Amalie finished her song and bent low, her face tilted up so as not to obscure the view of her bosom, barely contained by her pale green dress. I felt for the handle. It didn't turn—but when I gave it a push, the door fell open, as if the latch hadn't closed properly. As roses flew like arrows toward the stage and Amalie began her last song, I slipped through the door and started down the ramp.

The usual smells of sweat and rotting plaster were tinged by the acrid smell of burned tobacco, and I wondered who had the temerity to smoke a cigar on the premises. Mr. Williams went livid if he saw even an unlit cigarette backstage.

I made my way to the wedge-shaped area just off stage right to wait for Amalie. From there in the shadows I could see both the stage and the catwalk from which two young men managed various items, including the trapezes that Marceline and Sebastian had used. The men were up there now, watching for Amalie's last bow, the signal to drop the flower petals. She exited amid the flurry, her bright stage smile vanishing immediately, but when she saw me, her expression altered again, to disbelief and even some concern. "Williams'll skin you alive if he sees you."

"I'm sure." I gestured toward the pianist. "Who's he?"

She shrugged and kept walking. "Someone Stephen knew."

I laid a hand on her arm. "Amalie, listen to me. I think Jack is in danger. Stephen's trying to stir up trouble between Jack and his father."

She looked skeptical. Hastily, I sketched what had happened at the Academy and what I'd seen at Jack's flat. "You said yourself that Stephen's his own and that's all," I concluded. "Well, you're right. No one else matters to him. Stephen doesn't see Jack at all; he just sees someone who's gotten in his way."

Her expression had been attentive for most of my recital, but at the last words, her whole body stiffened, and in the faint light from the stage, I saw her eyes widen and her lips part.

"Amalie, what is it?"

Her words came out in a whisper. "I heard him send two men out."

"Stephen?"

Her head bobbed like a doll's on her slender neck. "He told them to 'make sure he doesn't come back.' Those were his words." Another quick breath. "I had no idea he meant Jack."

"Were they Drummond's men?"

She shook her head. "They weren't anyone I'd ever seen before. But it was clear enough that Stephen knew them."

My heart gave a sickening lurch. "When was this?"

"Around five o'clock." She swallowed. "Jack and his father had a row right 'afore."

Of course, I thought bitterly. *And Stephen had seen his chance.*

"Where's Stephen now?" I asked. "Is he here?"

She was biting her lower lip, hard. "I don't know."

I released her arm. "If you see Jack tonight, if he comes back, tell him to meet me at the Bear and Bull."

She nodded. Then her eyes flicked behind me. "You should go." And she gathered up her skirts and vanished.

I turned to see one of the boys who helped with the props. His gaze skittered away from mine, and he fixed his attention on the stage.

There was part of me that longed to get away before anyone else saw me. But if Stephen was here, I needed to find him and ask what he'd done.

I headed toward the back corridor and crept past Drummond's office door. Through the mottled glass, I saw the light from a lamp and glimpsed a dark figure bent over the desk. I hoped whatever Drummond was doing would occupy him for a while. In the hallway, there were signs of fresh plaster on the wall and a gray cloth on the floor that bore the impressions of boots amid the dust.

Maybe this had been Jack's repair.

I climbed the circular stair and went to the instrument room. Fortunately, it was empty, but so were the hooks where Stephen might have hung his coat. Frustrated, I headed back downstairs, made my way to the door of the properties room, and pushed it open. Swiftly I slipped inside and closed the door behind me, then stood perfectly still until my eyes adjusted to the semidarkness. The light from the secret room made a golden sliver, the same as it had the first time. It was well after eight o'clock, so the boys would be gone by now. But the light faded and then returned, as if someone had stepped in front of a lamp.

I put my hands out in front of me, quietly feeling my way past a trunk with brass fittings, a wooden crate with a splintered edge, a dented barrel made of metal, a ladder with a broken rung. How on earth had I come in here before without catching my skirts on half a dozen things?

As I reached the back wall, I heard voices, and I nudged the panel upward, just enough to look inside the room.

There were no boys. As I expected, they had all been sent out. And no Stephen, so far as I could see, although I recognized his coat, hanging on a hook on the far wall.

But Drummond was there—which meant it had been someone else in his office just now—along with two other men, both of whom I could see only in profile. One of them wore the uniform of a River Police constable; the other was of medium height with a chest like a barrel. Three fingers on his right hand were mangled. A half-smoked cigar dangled between his thumb and forefinger.

My mouth went dry. It had to be Tierney. By the light of the room's lanterns, I saw his face. A heavy mouth and jaw, dark eyebrows, a narrow nose. He had broad shoulders not unlike Drummond's—but whereas Drummond was in his forties and beginning to gather fat around his middle, this man was all power, with none of the softness of age about him and no gray in his hair. I guessed he was thirty, or five-and-thirty at most.

The constable said, "Your shipments'll leave tonight. Lighter boats'll bring 'em down from St. Katharine's, and there's extra crew at Greenland to load 'em between patrols. The crates'll go in first. My men know what they're about."

"What time is it leaving Greenland Dock?"

"Half past one. So it'll be out of Greenwich Reach by dawn."

"Customs?"

"Barrow's seen to it."

"And if they get stopped?" Tierney asked.

"They got barrels of gin, with bills of lading all in order, as the cargo," the constable replied. "You can stop your frettin', Mr. Tierney. I wouldn't 'a taken your money if I didn't think I could do it proper. My men've been workin' the river for years, and they're no fools. They could get from the customs house all the way to Gravesend without lights if they had to."

"What about the rumor I heard tonight? That there's an inspector who's onto this?"

The constable shook his head. "Barrow would know if there was anything certain. I mean, there's guesses all the time, ain't there?" He glanced at Drummond. "But guesses aren't going anywhere without knowing when or where or who."

Tierney gave a low grunt.

"There's another storm coming tomorrow. It'll be a rough crossing," Drummond said. "And the guns are heavy."

"Aye. But Pierre knows what the boats can manage. A rough wind may make him late, but he's got two years o' workin' this run to Calais."

"Calais?" Drummond asked, surprised.

"Yah. It'll be transferred to a steamer there and be in Montenegro in a matter o' weeks."

Tierney threw his cigar on the floor. "I don't give a bloody quid where it goes, so long as we're paid in Calais, and it ain't traced back to me—"

A strong hand covered my mouth, and Stephen's voice drawled in my ear. "Well, well. Nosy Nell. You know what they say about curiosity killing the cat."

He opened the trapdoor, pushed my head down, and shoved me through.

Chapter 25

*T*he three men turned toward us. Only the constable showed any alarm. Drummond's eyes darkened, and his mouth took on an ugly curl, but he said nothing. Tierney looked me up and down, but he clearly didn't much care who I was or what I'd seen. And I understood in an instant that to Tierney, I was someone who could simply be done away with if I proved inconvenient.

Fear rolled over me like fire.

Stephen pulled at my hat. Maybe he imagined that all my hair would come tumbling down dramatically to reveal that I was in disguise, but I had it pinned up tight, the way I always did, and when he pulled, the brim caught on the pins, and he merely yanked my head sideways. I shoved his hand away and removed the hat myself.

"This is Nell Hallam—otherwise known as Ed Nell," Stephen said scornfully. "And my guess is she's the one who saw the boys the other day—when she was dressed properly, of course, in a woman's skirts. She knows all about what happens here."

With an instinct born of my fear, I knew I had to pretend to know very little—not nothing, that wouldn't be believable; but I had to seem utterly in the dark about the Fleet in order to have any chance of getting away. I needed to seem fearless, even belligerent, as if I didn't think I had any reason to be afraid of them. And, in a matter of seconds, it was almost as if doors shut inside the maze of my brain. So this is all I knew: I was looking for Jack, and Stephen was a cheat and a liar. And if I told Drummond and Tierney something about Stephen that caused them to trust him less? Well, so be it.

I shot Stephen a withering look. "You *wish* you had a chance to see me in women's skirts. You pretend to be some fine violinist, but you're a disgusting pig is what you are."

Mr. Tierney gave a small snort. "Who the devil is this?"

"She's my piano player a few nights a week," Drummond said. "Or used to be."

"She's not just that," Stephen said, and there was a raw edge to his voice that he couldn't quite mask. "She's Jack's slut."

"And what's she to you?" Tierney asked. His voice was cool, but there was something in his expression that told me he was the sort of man who discerned other people's deepest feelings and used them to his own ends.

Stephen shrugged. "Nothing at all."

Tierney's eyes flickered to Drummond's. I saw that between them existed an understanding as clear as a private telegraph, and my heart gave a small lurch. Stephen also meant nothing to either of them, that much seemed clear. But Stephen thought he was too smart or too valuable to be taken lightly or to be disposed of. I held on to that thought, keeping it in the back of my mind to use at the right moment.

"Where's Jack?" I asked rudely, as if I cared nothing for what they were doing—or was too besotted with Jack to care.

"I've no idea." Drummond's black eyes betrayed nothing. "Why were you back here?"

"Why do you think?" I said impatiently. "I asked one of the boys where Jack was, and he said he saw him plastering. So I was walking down the hallway, and the next thing I knew, Stephen grabbed me from behind and was shoving me through the properties room."

"She was standing at the trapdoor listening," Stephen interjected.

I whirled. "I was not! What's wrong with you? First you have me fired so you can bring that friend of yours in here, and now you're trying to make me out to be some sort of nosy nelly! Well, all I care about is finding Jack. And that's what you hate, isn't it? That I like him better than I like you."

An incredulous look came into his eyes. "You stupid girl. I don't give a damn whom you prefer." He turned to Drummond. "I tell you, she knows about the boys and about the Fleet. I heard her talking to Jack last night. She tried to convince him to betray you to the police."

I stared at him like he'd gone mad. "You're crazy!" I turned to Drummond. "He's playing you, Mr. Drummond."

"Shut up," Stephen said.

"Let her speak," Tierney said. "There's something here, and I want to know what it is."

I ignored Tierney and kept my eyes fixed on Drummond. "Stephen is using you, like he uses everyone. He was thrown out of the Royal Academy for cheating his friend out of a priceless violin. He stole hundreds of pounds from his father's business by pretending to make bookkeeping errors. He'll turn on *anybody* if he sees something to be gained."

I was riding a rough edge, I knew, but the only chance I had was to bluff hard. I willed my voice not to shake, even as sweat slid down my back. "He was bragging the other night that somebody named Tierney's been begging to set him up in some sort of business. He said that *you're* a drunkard and on your way down"—I looked at Drummond, but out of the corner of my eye I saw Tierney's shoulders twitch—"but Stephen's planning to take what he can get out of Tierney and then make straight for Paris. His father's so desperate to get rid of him, he's offered him money to go, too, so he'll have money from all of you."

"Shut up, you bitch," Stephen spat, his eyes blazing. He turned toward Drummond. "I said nothing of the sort about either of you."

"Wait," said Tierney. He stepped toward Stephen, his head tilted slightly. "You told this chit my name?"

"Of course not. She's making it up because she's guessed who you are." Stephen's mouth grew ugly, pressed into a sneer. "I'm telling you, she knows plenty—certainly more than you want her to." He looked over at Drummond. "That's Jack's doing."

"Not yours?" Drummond asked.

"No!"

"That's not true. Stephen told me all sorts of things." I turned to Drummond. "He told me about the two boys who fell off the roof the other night. He said they were robbing a house for you—and it was you who sent them out in the rain."

Stephen turned toward me, struck speechless for once.

I lifted my chin. "You talk a lot when you're drunk."

Tierney gave a short, contemptuous laugh that brought color to Stephen's cheeks. He turned and gave me a look of pure hate. "You'll be sorry you did this," he said hoarsely.

"Shut up, both of you," Tierney said. He nodded to Drummond, who motioned toward a hulking young man who'd been standing silently beside a crate.

"Put her in my office," Drummond said. "Tie her up, make sure the door's locked. And Lewis? Don't talk to her—not one word, do you hear? Then come back here."

My heart began to beat all out of rhythm. Drummond drew a key out of his pocket and handed it to Lewis. "Bring it back."

I tried one last time, as Lewis pulled me toward the trap-door: "Mr. Drummond, Stephen sent two men out to kill Jack tonight—"

But Drummond and Tierney had both turned away.

Lewis pulled me back through the properties room, dragged me down the hallway to Drummond's office, and shoved the key into the lock, all the while holding me effortlessly but not brutally. He let me go inside Drummond's office. When I tried to make for the door, he wrapped his arm around me again, and his hand came up over my mouth. I wrenched and wriggled, clawed with my free hand, kicked his shins with the toe of my boot, fought with everything I had—

"Stay quiet," he hissed, and by the light of the lamp I could see his expression was earnest. "I doan want to hurt you. Jack's my friend."

I stopped struggling, and when I nodded, he loosened his grip on my mouth, just enough so that I could say, "I wasn't lying when I said Stephen sent two men out to kill him." He looked at me uncertainly, and I added softly, "If you let me go, I have friends who can help."

"I cain't do that. You know I cain't." Still holding me by an arm, he reached inside a cupboard and pulled out two lengths of rope. The long piece looked new; the shorter one had stains, as if it had already been used. He examined them for frays and then used the knife to slice through the long piece. He pushed me into the desk chair and deftly fastened the rope around my right wrist.

"You shouldn't 'a come back here," he muttered.

"Jack could die. If you're his friend, let me find him."

His jaw clenched, but he continued tying my two hands behind my back, then my two ankles to the legs of the chair. Then he brushed off his hands, pulled a handkerchief out of his pocket, rolled it into a gag, and pulled it firmly around the back of my head.

A pleading noise crawled up from the back of my throat. Under his breath, he apologized, and then he was gone.

My breathing grew rough, and my arms were already tingling. I tugged at the ropes holding my hands, but they were snug, and all I achieved was the sting of a rope running a burn along the inside of my wrist.

Frantically, my eyes searched for something I could use to free myself. The room was no more than twelve feet square. A potbellied black stove squatted in the corner, its pipe rising to a hole in the outer wall, its scant fire casting a reddish light. Shelves were stuffed with rags and papers and empty bottles. The wooden desk was covered with more of the same.

The brick walls muffled everything, even the noises from the stage. No one would hear me, I knew, but I gave a cry. The sound, like that a small animal might make, sent terror running through my whole body, and I started to shake.

I closed my eyes. All I could think to do was run through every piece of music I knew beginning with the lullabies.

IT MUST HAVE BEEN TWENTY MINUTES LATER when I heard, over the music in my head, the scrape of the key in the lock.

My eyes flashed open, and I watched the knob turn. Long, cruel seconds passed. Would it be Stephen? Or Tierney?

Or Jack, come to find me?

It was none of them. A boy's face peered in, his thin body slid into the room, and he closed the door behind him silently.

In the faint light from the stove, I could see it was Rob. To-night he wore sturdy shoes, and wrapped around him was a black coat that looked warm, if frayed at the collar. He crept toward me, crouched as though making his way through a low tunnel, and he didn't even look at me—only whipped out a jackknife from his pocket, flicking it open with a practiced motion. He came toward me with it, raising it toward my face, and I must have made a noise.

"Shh," he hissed furiously. "You want Drummond to come?"

He cut the gag from my mouth, and I tried to stifle my invol-untary cough. He was behind me then, sawing at the rope that bound my wrists. The knife must have been dull, for he was hurting me, but I bit my bottom lip and held my breath until he had cut through. I turned in the chair to watch him as he sawed at the rope holding my right ankle. He sawed so vigorously that his hair was flopping left and right with each stroke.

"You're taking a risk helping me," I whispered.

"I ain't going to let Tierney kill you. Jack's t'only one ever been kind t'me, 'nd I know you're tryin' to 'elp 'im. Amalie told me."

"Stephen sent two men out after him tonight."

"I know."

The rope was cut halfway through. Pale brown threads frayed, cut, frayed, cut. All that was left was the rope binding my left leg.

"Hurry." The word slipped out of my mouth.

"What d'you think I'm doin'?" he hissed.

"Sorry."

The shorn rope dropped onto the floor, and I rubbed at my wrists.

"Don't just sit there. Git up!"

I stood up unsteadily. "When did Jack leave?"

"'Bout ha'-past four. He ain't been back." He snapped the knife closed and slid it back into his pocket. "I'll go first. If'n it's clear down that back hallway, you'll hear a cough. Then you get straight out o' here, you hear? Tierney's still talkin' t' the constable, and Drummond jus' left, but no tellin' when he'll be back. Whatever you do, don't get caught on the way out, or he'll kill you on the spot."

I rubbed my arms hard to bring some feeling back into them.

"Ready?" he asked, his hand on the knob.

"Thank you, Rob."

His eyes widened in alarm. I put a hand out. "I don't know your name if Drummond catches me. I swear."

He nodded and was gone. I waited a few seconds, heard a cough, and slipped into the hallway myself. His shoes were vanishing up the spiral stairs.

I hurried along the passageway, brushed past four broad-shouldered acrobats who smelled heavily of sweat, then ran for the back door. The door creaked open and shut, the mist hit my face, and I heard thunder like a drum roll off to my right.

Chapter 26

My first thought was to get away from the Octavian as fast as possible. Knowing that Drummond could return at any minute, I longed to run, but I held myself to an inconspicuous pace, jammed my hands into my pockets, pulled my hat low, and flipped up the edges of my coat collar.

Where would Jack be? Where would Stephen have sent the two men? And where could I go for help? I paused for a moment at the corner, undecided.

I should first try the Bear and Bull. Maybe Jack had gone there this afternoon. And if not, maybe Mr. Bertault would be there—if the concert was over—or Sarah would know somewhere else to look.

The image of Jack lying dead in an alley somewhere rose before my eyes. I gave myself a mental shake, clutched my coat closer about me, and headed south at a run.

Usually Wickley Street was a cobblestone thoroughfare, but it was almost a shallow streamed tonight, with the flotsam of the day bobbing along in the gutters. People sloshed through the puddles or kept close to the buildings, where the water wasn't so deep. I ignored the cold wetness seeping through my boots as I splashed across Wickley and ran along the side street that led to the pub.

Panting, I pushed open the door and crossed the threshold. I felt a wave of relief as the warmth of the place wrapped itself around me—the clink of pans, the snaps of the fire, the rumble of friendly talk from tables filled with people. A quick glance around told me neither Jack nor Mr. Bertault was there, but Sarah stood behind the long bar, stacking plates. I approached, and Sarah displayed the welcoming smile she gave everyone.

Then she recognized me, and her smile faded. "Why, hullo."

"Hullo, Sarah," I said between breaths. "Have you seen Jack?"

She wiped her hands on a towel that was looped through her belt. "No."

"He hasn't been in? Not even earlier today?"

Her eyebrows rose at my insistence. "No." And as if she anticipated my next question: "And I've been here since noon. What's the matter?"

I hadn't realized how much I'd hoped that he'd come here. The disappointment made me feel suddenly drained and shaken. Her expression was a mixture of curiosity and a sort of pitying amusement, as if I were some lovesick girl. It worked on me like a plunge into icy water, and I pulled myself together.

"It isn't like that," I said flatly. "His uncle's worried about him, too. Jack was supposed to be at the piano shop at two o'clock for appointments, and he wasn't—and I'm sure you know that's not like him. He wasn't at the Octavian tonight, and he's not at his rooms—"

"Well, I'm sure there's a good reason," she said. But when I remained silent, she sighed. "Why don't you sit down, and I'll fetch us some coffee." She waved me toward one of the tables and turned to the kitchen.

The terror that had driven me here at top speed was spent. Wearily, I pulled out the wooden chair and sat. A few deep breaths, and I had myself in hand. I told myself that Sarah's composure and even ridicule in the face of what might look like unreasonable concern were quite natural. Sarah didn't know anything of what I'd discovered in the past few hours. She knew nothing of Stephen's malevolence or of the raid. What's more, although the Connors were Jack's friends, he'd never given me any indication that they knew about the Fleet or his father's involvement. His secrets weren't mine to tell, and in the few minutes that Sarah was gone, I gathered the entire story in my mind and culled the bits that I wanted to share.

She returned with two mugs, one of which she put down in front of me as she sat down opposite. The coffee smelled burned and bitter, and I took a tentative sip. No milk to cut it, but she'd put plenty of sugar in. The second sip tasted sweeter than the first, the warmth burning all the way down, better than the brandy.

"Thank you," I said sincerely.

She frowned. "Look, Miss. I seen how the two of you were when you came in here the other night. And some folks would say it's none of my concern; but you aren't like each other at all, and maybe he's not around for you to find because he's come to see for himself how different you are."

Her bluntness made the color rise to my cheeks. "We're not so different."

She snorted. "That's like saying salt and sugar aren't so different because they look the same."

"Just because I'm not from hereabouts doesn't mean I don't know a good man when I see him," I retorted. "And as for Jack not wanting me to find him—well, right now I don't care *who* finds him. I just want to know that he's safe."

She gave a short laugh. "Just because you can't find him don't mean he's in danger."

"Have you heard him mention a man named Stephen Gagnon? He's a violinist at the Octavian."

"No."

"Stephen thinks Jack is responsible for him being expelled from the Academy last year. In fact, to his mind, Jack is to blame for everything that's gone wrong since, and he hates him. Today after Jack and his father had an argument, Stephen sent two men out to find someone. One of the other performers, Amalie, told me he said to 'make sure he doesn't come back.' And I think he meant Jack." I saw her eyes narrow when I mentioned Amalie; she was beginning to understand. "This afternoon I went to Jack's room, and I saw Stephen go in. He had a key, and he took some of Jack's papers."

"He had Jack's key?"

"Yes. And where would he have gotten that, if not out of Jack's pocket?"

All the skepticism had left her face, and in its place was worry.

"Sarah, do you have any idea where he might have gone? Someplace other than here or his uncle's?"

She gnawed at her lip and shook her head.

I stifled a sigh. "Do you have a piece of paper and a pencil?"

She pulled a pocketbook and a stub from a pouch at her waist, and I reached for them.

"Wait." She pointed. "What happened to your wrist?"

I looked down. There was a raw red band of flesh where the rope had chafed. I hadn't told her about being trapped in Drummond's office. "It's nothing," I said and pulled down the sleeve.

She grimaced at my evasion but remained silent as I scribbled down the only safe address I could think of.

"This is the address for our housekeeper, Peggy Greaves," I said, passing the pocketbook back across the table. "It's in Soho, not very far from the music hall. She lives there with her daughter. If you hear anything from Jack, can you get a message to me there? Or if Jack comes here—could you send him? I'll stay there tonight instead of going home."

"All right." Her brow furrowed. "Should you go to the police, d'you think?"

"And tell them what? That a grown man has been missing for barely six hours? They'd laugh at me."

But even as I answered, I felt a sharp regret. Matthew wouldn't have laughed at me; he never did. But I'd missed my chance to confide in him, and I couldn't now. Tonight of all nights, he could be anywhere in London, far beyond my reach. My God, what a muddle I'd made of this.

"Thank you, Sarah, for the coffee and for everything," I said, rising.

She walked with me to the door, her expression subdued. At the threshold, something occurred to me. "Sarah."

"What?"

"When Jack used to box—I mean, for money—was he good?"

"Very good. Why?" She looked at me unhappily. "I hope you don't think less of him for doing it."

"Of course not," I said. "I'm hoping it'll keep him alive."

Our eyes met, and she looked ashamed. "Good luck," she said. "I'll pray he's all right, and to keep you safe."

I thanked her and stepped outside. The rain had stopped, but the cobblestones were slick with puddles, and through the mist, the light from a gas lamp shone grayish yellow.

Should I go to the piano shop again?

I decided I would. It wasn't much more than a mile, and I was beginning to feel quite desperately that I wanted an ally.

I could feel the strong, sweet coffee running in my veins and putting life into my tired feet. I made my way down Samson Lane to the front door, and when there was no answer to my knock, I pounded hard enough that the bell inside the door tinkled faintly; but the entire building remained dark. Disheartened and frustrated, I debated whether I should wait, given that Mr. Bertault had said he wouldn't be gone long if he was out.

I stood shivering in the doorway for nearly an hour, until my hands and feet had gone numb. At last I gave up. Coffee and hope had run their course, leaving me cold, bone-weary, and afraid. My only hope was that Mr. Bertault had gone after Jack—and found him. Everything I'd tried tonight, every step I'd taken, had accomplished very little, if anything, toward helping anyone I loved. The thought brought tears that I didn't even try to fight as I made my way north, back into the heart of Soho, toward Peggy's home.

Colby Lane was dimly lit. Dully, I trudged the last hundred

steps and up the stairs of Peggy's house, my hand raised to knock.

But before I had a chance, the door opened and Peggy's tall, spare frame appeared, a dark silhouette against the light. Her right hand reached out and yanked me inside, shutting the door behind me and throwing the bolt.

Chapter 27

"Where on earth have you been?" Her hand was tight on my arm. She was frightened, I knew, not angry. But this is how fear showed itself in her.

I tensed. "What's the matter? Did Sarah get a message to you?"

"In a manner of speaking. But who is she, and how did she get our address—and who's this boy Rob?"

Rob? My heart leaped with hope, and my eyes darted to the hallway behind her. "Where is he?"

"He left. Said he'd be back, though." She gave a snort and looked me up and down. "For mercy's sake, you look like something the cat dragged in."

She turned and strode down the hallway toward the back of the house.

I followed her back to the kitchen. "Did he say anything about Jack? Whether he's all right?"

"Not a word. Just told me to make sure you didn't leave again." She jerked a chair out from under the table. "So you might as well sit down and have a cup o' tea." She clanked the kettle onto the stovetop, pulled down a tin, and muttered something under her breath.

"Mum? I heard the door," came a soft voice from the hallway. "Is the boy back?"

I turned. Emma appeared at the threshold, her pale hair hanging loose about her shoulders, the skin almost translucent on the hand that held her shawl across her narrow chest. I hadn't seen her in weeks, since I'd brought medicine from Dr. Everett. She was thinner than ever. In the light from the lamp, her face looked sallow, but her gray eyes—large and luminous—were still beautiful despite the consumption that was taking her, bit by bit.

"Nell." She crossed the room and embraced me.

"Hello, Emma," I said. "I'm sorry if I disturbed you."

"Not at all," she said, her voice gentle. "From what the boy said, it seemed you might be in trouble."

I glanced at her mother's stiff back. "I'm not in trouble, not really. But a friend is."

Peggy gave a snort.

Emma sat down next to me. "Who is it?"

"Jack Drummond," I said. "His father owns the Octavian."

Emma's eyes widened. "The music hall?"

I nodded. "I've been playing there at night to earn money, in case I had a chance to go to the Royal Academy."

"I told her about your audition." Peggy placed the teapot on a folded cloth and set three cups on the table along with a small tin of sugar and two spoons.

"Mum said another boy came to your house today looking for you." Emma poured tea into all three cups. "Not Rob. A different one."

I frowned. "When was this?"

"'Twas just as I left, at six o'clock," Peggy replied. "He gave me quite a turn, coming out from behind the stairs next door and asking for you." She nudged the sugar tin toward me. Mindful that sugar was dear, I started to shake my head, but Peggy pursed her mouth. "Nonsense. You always take sugar."

I spooned a bit into my cup. "What did he look like?"

Her eyebrows lifted. "I'd say twelve years old or thereabouts. Scruffy looking. He said 'please,' but there was something weaselly about him."

"What did he want?"

"Said he had a message for you, that Jack wanted to see you, and he wanted you to come to the Octavian."

By six o'clock Jack had been long gone from the Octavian. Hadn't he?

"What did you say?" I asked.

"What do you think?" she demanded. "I pretended I didn't know anything about it. I told him I didn't know where you were, but you warn't home, and you certainly warn't going anywhere near a music hall, dens of iniquity all of them, and besides that, who was this Jack who wouldn't come round to the house properly to call for you but wanted you to come meet him in that sort of place? I went on rather a bit, and he got snively, pulled off his cap and all. He said he was very sorry, but Jack couldn't come for some *very good* reason, and that's why he was come with a message. So I said that was all fine, but *I* had a very good reason that I would only give you the message tomorrow morning when I saw you."

"What happened then?"

"He left."

"Did he follow you here?"

She gave me a look. "No. I watched. He went the other way."

I bit my lip. Stephen knew my address on Dunsmire—but so did Jack. Which of the two sent him?

Peggy leaned forward. "I was no sooner here than this boy Rob turned up. He said that someone named Sarah sent him and that you gave her this address. He knew I was your housekeeper, which is the only reason I didn't throw him out on his ear."

"When was this?"

She glanced at the clock. "Nigh on an hour ago. But he left again, straightaway."

Emma leaned forward. "Does this boy work at the music hall, too?"

"He's part of a thieving ring that's based there," I said reluctantly.

Emma's hand tightened on her shawl, and I heard Peggy's intake of breath. "And you knew this?" Peggy demanded.

"Not until weeks after I'd started playing. And by then—well—"

"I understand. You didn't want to give up the money," Emma said sympathetically.

"And I'd met Jack."

My reply made Peggy groan and put her knuckles up to her forehead.

I took another sip of tea. "I went to the Octavian tonight to find him. While I was there, I saw something I wasn't supposed to." Briefly, I told them about Drummond and Tierney, and what I'd overheard.

"Guns," Peggy echoed. "For mercy's sake."

Emma said thoughtfully, "I wonder if the guns are going to Herzegovina. The papers say there's to be an uprising."

"Did the men say anything else?" Peggy interjected.

"No. They might have, except I was caught listening. Drummond locked me in his office, but Rob came in and cut me free."

Peggy put her cup down on her saucer with a clink. "Let's be plain about this. Drummond and Tierney know you heard about the guns."

"Yes."

"Then they had no intention of letting you go."

"Probably not," I admitted.

"Meaning they'll kill you now if they find you."

"Mum!" Emma exclaimed.

"She's right," I said to Emma. "But, they won't know to come here. What scares me more is that Amalie—she's a singer at the Octavian—told me that Stephen, one of the other performers who hates Jack, sent two men out after him."

Emma drew in her breath. "To hurt him?"

The alarm in her voice caused fear to surge through me afresh. "To kill him, I think," I said, my voice cracking. "Jack left the Octavian at around four, and no one has seen him since. I've been everywhere looking."

Peggy got up and poured more tea into my cup. "You still haven't told us who Sarah is."

"She's a friend of Jack's, who works at a public house called the Bear and Bull. She promised if he showed up that she'd get word to me. I gave her this address."

"Not your home address," Peggy said, her mouth pursing.

My heart sank. "I'm so sorry, Peggy. I had no intention of bringing any sort of danger to your doorstep—and I hope I haven't. But I knew I couldn't go home."

"Why not?"

"Because Stephen knows my address. One night we had dinner together, and he put me in a hansom cab."

She sat back in her chair. "And you think he remembers it."

"If that boy who came to the house was sent by Stephen, then he certainly does."

"And it's best to be safe," Emma interposed gently. "No one will think of coming here for you. I mean," she said, with a glance at her mother, "no one who wasn't sent by this girl you trust."

"Speaking of which"—Peggy looked up at the clock—"where is the boy?"

"I hope nothing's happened to him," I said.

"I want to make sure nothing happens to *you*." She looked me over. "Have you had any supper?"

I shook my head.

She rose, cut a slab of bread, and spread it with butter. I'd choked down half of it when we heard a knock at the door.

"You two stay here," Peggy said firmly.

She returned in a moment with Rob ahead of her. "This is him."

His eyes widened with relief when he saw me. "You're here, finally! Well, come on then."

"Is Jack all right?" I demanded. "Is he alive?"

His eyes darted to the bread with butter that I'd dropped on the plate and then back to me. "Yah, he's alive."

I let out a gasp of relief, and beside me I heard Emma murmur, "Oh, thank goodness."

"But 'e's hurt, and we're wastin' time, and 'e sent me to fetch ye hours ago! If you ain't going to come—"

"I'm coming," I interrupted and stood up. "Of course I am. How bad is it?"

"Got a knife cut 'ere to 'ere." His hand went from the middle of his thigh down to his knee. "He's goin' t' need a doctor."

"Nothing else?" I asked. "Just the knife wound?"

He shrugged. "Some cuts and scrapes, but nothin' to speak of."

I took a deep breath. The uncertainty of the past hours had been wretched. Knowing that Jack was alive, with a type of wound that I knew could be healed, allowed me to set fear aside and be practical. I put my arms into the sleeves of my coat. "I know where we can take him."

"Cain't be a hospital," he said. "They'll want t' know wot happened."

I nodded in agreement. "I know a doctor who won't say anything. We can stop by his club—and if he's not there, we'll go to his house."

"He won't be there," Peggy said.

I began to fasten the buttons. "At which? His club or home?"

"Neither." The shortness in her voice made me look up.

"Why not?" I asked slowly. "Where is he?"

Her mouth was set in a resentful line. "I shouldn't have to be the one to tell you. Why he didn't tell you 'afore this, I've no idea."

My hands gripped the edge of the table, and I bent toward Peggy. "You do mean Dr. Everett, don't you? For goodness' sake, just tell me. Where can I find him?" I just hoped it wasn't far away. I didn't relish the thought of having to drive Jack miles across the city.

"He has a companion." Pink spots appeared in her cheeks, but she did not look away.

The kitchen was silent except for a soft snapping inside the stove.

"From his club?" I asked finally.

"Yes."

Rob gave a snort and pulled a face, his upper teeth coming down well over his lower lip, in an effort not to laugh.

I bent my head and continued fastening my coat, my fingertips fumbling with the metal buttons, while I tried to absorb this. Should I have guessed? The fact that he'd never married; the way he bent over every woman's hand but never showed any personal interest in them—

"Who is it?" I asked.

"A man named Charles Tindale."

"Charles Tindale," I echoed. "The merchant. He was a patient, several years ago."

"Yes."

My mind assembled all the small signs of Mr. Tindale's connection with Dr. Everett—the letter with the foreign stamps, the Oriental-looking cuff links, quite possibly the jade box in my bedroom—

"Give us 'is address, then, and let's git on our way," Rob said.

Peggy turned to me. "I don't want you going anywhere alone."

"She ain't goin' alone," he protested. "I'll be with her."

"And what if you're leading her into a trap?"

"Love o' Christ!" he exploded. "I've been tearin' all over Lon'on, tryin' to find 'er—'nd makin' sure Jack is awright—'nd runnin' my fool 'ead off. I ain't goin' to lead her into any bloody trap!"

"It's all right, Peggy. He's already saved me once tonight." I drew up my collar. "He's been wonderfully brave and smart."

Rob looked surprised and then gratified. "Well, I owe 'im," he muttered.

"Tell me the address where you're going," Peggy said.

He gave a sulky look. "Thirty-six Pelman Street."

I turned to Peggy. "Do you know it?"

"I know where Pelman is. Can't say I know the number, but he's right. It's not far." Her lips came together in a thin line. "If you're going, take this with you." She reached up into a cabinet and pulled down a wicker basket. From it she retrieved a revolving pistol and handed it to me.

This gun was smaller than my father's, but the barrel was black and sinister looking.

"Cor!" Rob breathed. "That's a fine piece."

"My husband's," Peggy said shortly. She took some bullets out of the basket and held them in her cupped hand.

Some hesitancy must have shown on my face. Shooting a gun with Matthew, as part of my logical education, was one thing; loading a gun with the thought of using it was quite another.

"I'll carry it if you want," Rob said.

Peggy glared at him.

"What if she fires it off by mistake?" he demanded. "I'll end up with a hole in the back o' my head—"

"Don't worry," I said to him. I took the gun and loaded four of the five chambers. When I'd glanced up, Rob's expression had changed.

"Cor," Rob said again. "You're a queer sort of girl, knowin' how to handle a gun like 'at."

Peggy gave a sniff.

I slipped the pistol into my coat pocket. "I've left the first chamber empty, for safety," I told him. "So you needn't worry about the back of your head."

Peggy's mouth twitched. "Chances are, you just firing it will be enough to scare anybody off, whether you hit 'em or not."

Soberly, I replied, "I'm hoping I don't need to fire it at all."

I found Emma in the parlor. She was standing beside a desk, fighting a cough, a handkerchief to her mouth. When she saw me, she tucked her handkerchief away and picked up a square of paper from the desk. "Here, Nell." She held it toward me. "It's Mr. Tindale's address."

"Thank you, Emma."

"Of course." Emma put her hand on my arm.

It's so thin, I thought. I gave it a gentle squeeze. "I'll send Rob back with a message once I find Jack. I'll sign it Edward, all right? So you know I'm writing it freely."

"You have paper and something to write with?"

If I were dressed as a woman, I would have. "No, I don't."

She opened a drawer in the desk and gave me a small bit of paper and a pencil. I tucked them into the inside pocket of my coat.

Peggy and Rob were by the front door. She had given him a slice of bread with butter, and he was shoving it in his mouth. As I approached, she bent toward him. "And so help me, if she ends up hurt, I'll find you."

His mouth full, he simply nodded and turned the door handle.

The cold night air made me shiver. I slid my hand around the pistol's handle, feeling the reassuring heft of it against my palm.

And Rob and I went out into the dark.

Chapter 28

The top of Rob's head barely came to my shoulder, but he started down the street at a pace that forced me to hurry. Rather breathlessly, I said, "Tell me again, how badly is he hurt, and how long ago did it happen?"

"About six or seven o'clock, best I can figure. He was bleedin' like a stuck pig at first, but we tied somethin' around it."

"Who else besides you?"

"My brother Gus. That's why I had to leave Jack. *That's* why I wish you'd been at Peggy's the first time."

"I'm sorry. I was trying to find someone I thought could help. Where's Gus now?"

"Where d'you think? He's working—but I had to take him there." And then, under his breath, "Wouldn't 'a left Jack otherwise, but 'e's barely ten years old."

"I'm sorry," I said again. No wonder he'd been so angry when Peggy hinted that he was leading me into a trap. Rob had done more than anyone should ask of a child tonight. By the light of the gas lamps I could see the weariness and the worry in his thin, set face. I remembered how he'd devoured the bread, and I promised myself that when this was over, I'd find a way to repay him myself.

"What did you mean when you said you owed Jack?" I asked.

He cast a suspicious look at me. "Why ye want to know?"

"I'm just curious."

He sniffed. "'E's alwus been decent, not like his da. But last week 'e got me and Gus warm clothes and shoes. 'Nd he got Gus to the doctor."

I heard this with a mix of gratitude and satisfaction. Jack had not only checked on them; he'd been generous. We hurried around a corner, and I asked, "Who is this friend, whose place we're going to?"

"It's a brothel. M'sister works there." He glanced sideways, his face sullen and ashamed. "I didn't know no place else to take 'im."

I could tell he expected me to be appalled, but I said matter-of-factly, "Well, it was clever of you to take him somewhere safe that you know. It's certainly better than letting him lie outside on a night like this. He'd catch pneumonia." He didn't say anything, but he looked relieved. "Where did you find him?"

"Behind a dustbin."

So my guess of an alley wasn't far off. "Did he say anything? Who did it, or—"

"'E said there was two of 'em. Jack hit one of 'em, broke 'is jaw, he thinks, and he ran off. Then t'other one came at 'im with a knife, pulled it so fast Jack didn't even see it."

"But Jack got away?"

Rob sneezed and wiped his nose on his sleeve. "Aye. 'E grabbed the knife, stuck 'im in the arm. Then that one done run off, too."

"Dear God."

"Wot?" he demanded, his face incredulous. "Would you rather 'e got cut up?"

"Of course not. It's just awful, the whole thing. And two against one—it wasn't even a fair fight."

"That Stephen's no man," he agreed scornfully. "I niver seen such a coward—sending two men out to fight 'is battles for 'im."

"Do you—that is, did Jack say he thought Stephen did it?"

"Nah. 'E ain't the type to say. But Stephen was doin' all 'e could to get next to Drummond."

"I think Stephen wanted a ship for himself."

He snorted. "Tierney would'a seen through 'im. 'E's a bastard, and plen'y vicious. But 'e ain't stupid." That had been my impression of Tierney as well, formed from those few minutes I saw him.

Rob slowed and pointed to a three-story house opposite. "Thar's the back. Front's more for show, with gewgaws, and all lit up."

"How do we get in?"

He headed toward a set of stairs that led belowground. "Down here."

I halted. "I thought you meant he'd be in one of the rooms."

He turned back. In the light from the windows above, his face looked older than his years. Jaded, even. He studied me for a moment, as if evaluating how much to tell me.

"What is it?" I asked.

Finally, he shrugged. "The rooms cost money, see? The girls haf t'rent the rooms by the night, whether they got comp'ny or not." He waved a hand. "Tonight, all the rooms are took." He didn't wait for me to answer, but started down the short flight of crumbling steps. My hand grasped the metal railing; it was damp and smelled of rust. This entrance, with two metal doors, looked as if it were rarely used.

He hauled open one of the doors and called, "Jack! I brung her. But she's worried it ain't you. Say sumpin'."

Nothing. Rob swore under his breath. I called out, softly. "Jack?"

"I'm here," came a voice, weak but unmistakably his.

I felt a rush of relief. Grasping the railing, I started down the stairs, and then, as Rob brushed past me to go back up, I stopped him. "Wait." Hurriedly I pulled Emma's paper and pencil from my pocket. "Would you take the note back to Peggy for me?"

He hesitated, only for an instant. With a pang of regret, I realized that I'd been so overwhelmed with my own concerns that I hadn't given any thought to his. "I'm sorry. Do you have time? Are you able to manage it?"

He nodded, his expression flat. "I'll take it for ye."

I scribbled a note: "I'm here with Jack. Edward."

He stuffed the missive in his pocket. I dug into my pocket and pulled out a few shillings. "Here. Take a hansom cab if it'll help—and get yourself something to eat. Goodness knows you deserve it after everything you've done tonight. And Rob—thank you."

I put the coins into his palm and closed his cold fingers over them. He mumbled something that might have been "You're welcome" and stowed the coins deep inside his shirt.

At the top of the stairs he turned. "By the way—he ain't got pants on. We 'ad to take 'em off."

I felt my cheeks grow warm but kept my voice practical, to match his. "All right."

Then he was gone.

I slid my foot to the step's edge, feeling my way in the dark. I took a deep breath and smelled potatoes, onions, and thyme.

"Jack? Where are you?"

"Over here. Close the door behind you. I've got a light . . . just a minute . . . trying to reach it . . ."

I heard the scrape of a match and saw the flame between his hands, touching the wick of a candle. It stood in a metal holder, which he held with his finger through the ring. His other hand shielded the flame. I closed the metal door against its mate.

"Careful on the steps," he said.

I groped my way forward, my hand on the rough stone wall. The ceiling was so low that I couldn't stand up straight.

"Is there a lamp somewhere?" I asked as I reached him.

"I don't know."

I took the candle from him and raised it, pivoting slowly. The flame caught the shine of a lantern hanging from one of the wooden beams overhead, back in an alcove. I took it down off its nail and was heartened by the slosh of oil. In a moment, I had it lit; by its glow, I could see sacks of potatoes and onions along the wall, herbs hung in bunches from the rafters, and several crates with what looked like a French stamp on their sides.

I turned toward Jack, holding up the light. "Rob said you were hurt."

He nodded and gestured toward his leg. I moved closer, at first keeping my eyes away from his undergarments. But I didn't have time to worry about his modesty, or my own. The wound was worse than I'd imagined. It wasn't just the size of the gash, which was nearly as long as my forearm; there were smears of grime across it. Two dirty rags were tied tightly near the top and bottom of the gash, but the parts around them were red and oozing. Blood had made a small pool to the side of his thigh, a dark splotch against the dirt.

I tried not to show my dismay.

"It was . . . a knife," he said, with some effort.

"Do you have it still? Or a blade of your own?"

"Sure I do. Why?"

"I want to use it to cut these pieces off—"

"It's in the right pocket of my coat. Careful. There's no sheath."

I put the lantern down and felt gingerly inside the pocket, my fingers closing around a wooden handle. I drew it out and realized that before I took those tourniquets off, I needed something I could use as a bandage, something long and wide. And clean.

I bit my lip. "Close your eyes."

He looked surprised but did as I asked. I turned my back to him, took off my coat and shirt, and unwound the soft piece of sheet that I used to wrap myself. I set it down on top of the inside of my coat so it wouldn't become dirty, and hurriedly put my shirt back on.

"You can open them," I said as I turned.

He looked at the cloth. "Where did you get that?"

"Never mind. I need to tie this around your leg, which means I need to hold it up somehow. But first I need to get these pieces off. Where did Rob get them, anyway?"

"I don't know. I don't remember much about it. Why do you have to cut them off?"

"Because they can do more harm than good if they're too narrow and too tight, which I think they are." I brought the lantern closer. What had at first looked like scabbed blood was in fact a mix of blood and dirt. I let out a small groan, wishing I had water. I hated the idea of wrapping a clean cloth across that filthy wound. "Do you think they would give us a cup of water upstairs?" I asked.

"No!" His hand came out and grabbed at my arm. "I can't get Rob in trouble. Or Louisa."

I quickly scanned the cellar. Sacks, broken baskets, wooden crates . . .

My eyes jerked back to the crate with the French stamp. PRODUIT DE BORDEAUX. APPELLATION LUC-MUROT. MIS EN BOUTEILLE AU CHÂTEAU. "Bordeaux," I said. "Jack, is that French wine?"

"Sure."

I made my way to the crate, hunching uncomfortably under the ceiling. Naturally, it was sealed shut. I put my fingertips around the edge, but there was nowhere to grasp. I looked closely. Metal tacks were holding the lid in place.

I crawled back and retrieved the knife, slid the blade into the crack between the top and the side of the crate, and used it like a lever. I was afraid to break the blade, so I went slowly, prying it up a bit at the corner, then a few inches along the edge, then a few more inches until I could slide my fingers in. I pushed upward, heard the creak of metal, and felt the top lift as if it were on a hinge.

Carefully I put my hand down into the dark crate. I felt smooth glass and with a sigh of relief, I withdrew a dark, dusty bottle. The alcohol in the wine would be a natural antiseptic. It was the best thing. And a drink probably wouldn't hurt him, either.

"Jack?" I said. "I've got it. This will help."

He didn't answer. I scrambled back to him, my fingers groping for his wrist. "Jack!" I hissed.

His eyes flashed open, startlingly dark against the pallor of his skin. "What?"

"I've got some wine. I'm going to pour it on your leg, to clean it." He nodded faintly and closed his eyes again. But as soon as

I looked at the top of the bottle, I realized that I had no way to open it.

"Damn," I whispered.

"What?"

"I need to open it. This knife is too wide for the cork."

His lips curved faintly. "Left pocket of my coat," he whispered. I found the pocket and drew out his corkscrew. I'd seen it before, the night he found me practicing the Mozart. It seemed like months ago.

Carefully I cut the wax seal off the bottle, braced the bottle between my knees, and inserted the screw into the cork. It was the work of several minutes, as I'd only ever seen it done, but at last the cork was out, and I sniffed the wine to be sure it wasn't rancid.

"It's probably going to sting," I said. "Do you want some to drink?"

He shook his head.

I looked about for something I could use to brace his leg up while I worked. There was a wooden crate, half full of apples, that would do. I dragged it toward him.

"I'm going to lift your foot onto this, so I can wrap your leg."

I took his swallow for an assent, and though I shifted him as gently as I could, he let out a sharp, pained breath.

Something under his leg glinted in the light; coins, I realized, which must have fallen out of his pocket when Rob removed his trousers. I gathered them all and quickly put them into my own pocket, to return once I got him safely to Dr. Everett.

I flexed my fingers, as I did before I played, then slid the blade under the band near his knee, cutting carefully so I didn't nick him. The wound began to ooze blood, and the trickle grew as I cut the second tie. Flinging the filthy bits aside, I poured the wine

slowly over the gash. It made it look much worse, the wine stain-
ing his entire thigh the color of blood, but in the light from the
lantern, I saw the dirt flow away. When the bottle was empty, I
slid my clean cloth underneath his thigh and wrapped, wrapped,
wrapped, as tightly as I could without causing the skin at the
knee to blanch. It went around almost four full times. Finally, I
took up his knife, cut a slit horizontally, split the ends, wrapped
one around the back, and tied them together, thanking God all
the while for the number of times I'd observed Dr. Everett in the
hospital.

"Does it hurt?" I asked. "Is it too tight?"

"It feels better." He shifted slightly. "Why are you so worried
about it being too tight?"

"The blood'll stop going to the leg, and you could lose it."

"Oh." His eyes closed again. I bit my lip. How I wished Dr.
Everett were here.

"Jack. What I did helped for the moment, but I need to get you
to a doctor."

"In a minute."

I wanted to say, "We have to go right now." But he was breathing heavily, and by the light of the lantern I could see the shine
of sweat on his face. Even what little I'd done had tired him. I'd
give him his minute.

"Nell."

"Hmm?"

"I sent Rob for you."

I bit my lip. There would be time enough to tell him that I'd
been looking for him all night. So I only said, "I wouldn't want
you to send for anyone else."

Some of the tension in his face relaxed. I took up his hand. It was icy cold. "You're freezing. I wish Rob could have put you in a room upstairs."

"Costs too much." His voice was barely above a whisper. "And I don't like brothels."

I could hear he was trying to make me smile, so I played along: "I'm glad to hear it. I don't frequent them myself."

I stroked the hair away from his forehead.

"Nell."

"What?"

"Need to tell you. Need to explain."

"Shh. There's no need to explain anything. Not right now." Blood was seeping around the edge of the bandage. "Listen to me, Jack. I know this is going to be hard, but we need to go."

Nothing.

"Jack, do you hear me?" I took him by the shoulders and gave him a shake. "Jack!"

Still nothing.

So I kissed him, full on the mouth, as warmly as I knew how. That woke him.

Chapter 29

"ow far is it?" he asked faintly. "To the doctor."

"Not far. I found some coins that fell out of your pocket. We've plenty for a hansom. I just need to get you to it."

"Every time I move, I feel dizzy."

My heart plummeted. "Don't worry," I said, more calmly than I felt. "I'll find a cab and we'll manage. Will I be able to hail one out front?"

"Probably."

"All right, then." I hesitated. "But first, we have to get your pants back on. Not that I care, but I'm not sure a driver will take you without them."

I did my best to help him, and then he was sitting up, his skin slick with fresh sweat.

"Leave the door open, would you?" he asked.

I hesitated. What if someone noticed it and found him—

"I'll get as far up the stairs as I can while you're gone," he muttered.

"All right. I'll be back." I propped the door open with

a rock and went out into the alley, cutting around to the front of the house.

Four lamps, their shades dyed red, hung over the door. The lower windows were uncovered, and the room on the first floor was hung with a florid pink wall covering and gilt-edged mirrors. The light from the gas chandeliers shone through the windows on every floor though it was well past midnight, and people milled about the footway in front. A man, quite evidently drunk, was stumbling toward the lone cab.

Well, he wasn't going to get it. "Driver!" I called, bolting ahead. "I need a cab, and I'll pay double your fare."

The driver looked down from his box, his sleepy face coming awake. "What for?"

"I need you to drive round back. My friend came out the wrong way."

"That's a story I've heard before," he said with a snort. "Folks comin' out arse-backward."

"I'll pay you triple!" slurred the drunk behind me.

I leaned toward the driver and said in an undertone, "I know this bloke. He'll stiff you and make a mess of your cab. Now"—I pointed—"go round that way. I'll meet you there in a minute."

"Awright," he said and slapped the reins against the back of his horse.

The drunk cursed behind me, but I ignored him, ducking back to the alley to find that Jack had made it only as far as the first step. Lying there with his eyes closed, and the bloodstains on his trousers, he looked dead.

I bent over him. "Jack, I'm here. I've got a cab, but you have to get up the stairs."

His eyes opened slowly.

"Jack. Come on," I urged. "We have to get up the stairs. The cab is on its way."

He nodded. Bracing his hand on the wall, and with my two hands pulling his right arm, he managed to stand. He was breathing hard and leaning heavily on my shoulder, and I was horribly afraid. Maybe I should leave him here and bring the doctor to him. Maybe—

"I can make it," he whispered, as if he'd sensed my doubts.

"All right, then," I said.

His right arm draped around my shoulders, his left hand on the wall, he staggered up the next three steps. This was a kind of courage I didn't have—the courage to be in mind-numbing pain and yet to keep moving.

Five steps up and we'd be on the street. "All right, Jack. One step and then another. Lean on me, and you'll make it."

Three steps. And then a stop. I knew he was doing his best, and I prayed that the cabdriver would wait for us. Two more steps, and our feet were on the cobblestones.

"Jack, darling. The cab is right there."

The sweat was pouring off his face and his skin was ghostly pale. "Please, Jack," I whispered. "You've *got* to make it to the cab."

And I don't know how he did it. One foot, then drag the other. One foot, drag the other. Six times.

The cabdriver was there. "What's wrong with him?"

"Oh, he's fine!" I said. "This is the way he gets every time he's got his pay. Believe me, I'm used to it—though usually I pull him out o' one of the rooms upstairs."

"What's he doin' down there, then?"

"It's cheaper," I said shortly. "Now, help me get him in."

"That's not part of it."

"It is if I'm paying you double."

"What ho! Is that blood?"

"He got a scrape," I said. "It's nothing."

"Where's he going?" I gave him Mr. Tindale's address, and he replied, "Oh, ho, Mayfair! He's a fancy one, is he?"

"Just help me get him into the bloody cab!" I snapped. "Take his feet."

He let out a curse of his own as he dismounted reluctantly from his box, but he did as I asked. When we were both inside, Jack fell against me, his head on my shoulder. In the light from the lamp I could see the sweat on his brow, and I used my cuff to wipe it off.

"I can't do it, Nell," he muttered. "I'm sorry. I can't."

"Jack, you already have," I said into his ear. I tightened my arms around him as the cab started to move. "We'll be there in ten minutes. To a friend who's a doctor. And he'll help you." We went over a bump in the road, and he slumped harder into me and let out a soft groan.

"Only a little farther. We're so close—" My voice broke. "So close, darling. Almost there."

He didn't answer.

We drew up to a fine house. A light shone through a window, and as I watched, a shadowy figure crossed behind a curtain.

"Jack—we're here."

He made no sound.

I slid out from under him, leaped out of the cab, dashed up the five steps, and clattered the brass doorknocker against the plate.

Almost instantly, the door drew away from my hand, and a

man stood in his shirtsleeves, a gun in his lowered hand. I blurted out, "Dr. Everett, it's me, Nell."

His eyes met mine, darted to the cab, then back to me. "Nell."

"James?" came another man's voice, from inside.

"I'm sorry," I said. "We had nowhere else to go."

"Don't just stand there, help me with him!" growled the driver.

Dr. Everett turned and handed his pistol to the man beside him, hurried to the cab, and together he and the driver managed to get Jack across the threshold.

I started to close the door behind them.

"Wait a minute, there!" called the driver. "You said—"

I turned and dug my hands in my pockets for Jack's coins and my own. "Take this. And swear you'll never say a word to anyone."

He looked down at the silver in his hand, and I sensed his surprise. It struck me that he hadn't expected me to keep my word.

"Please," I said, my tone softening. "Not a word to the police or the madam at the brothel—*anyone*. Do you understand?"

He clinked the coins together and screwed up his face in something approximating a grin. "Well, I'll not be forgetting *you*, Miss, dressed up like a man, with a tongue like a bloody shrew." He slipped the coins into his vest pocket. "But, nah, I won't say a word. No reason to be causin' trouble."

"Thank you. Good night."

I pushed the door closed and went to the parlor, where I found Jack on the floor and Dr. Everett examining Jack's skull. I knew to keep well out of the way, and I took a moment to glance around me. Chinese paintings on the walls. A case of half a dozen samurai swords elaborately displayed against silk. A pair of large painted ceramic dragons by the fireplace. And a glass case of what, from where I stood, appeared to be netsuke.

"Bring the lamp closer, would you?" the doctor asked.

I turned to do it—and then realized that Mr. Tindale had already anticipated his request. I knelt beside the doctor.

"Now," he said, ignoring me. "A sharp knife, Charles. Scissors if they're convenient." The man left the room.

The doctor put his hand on Jack's forehead, then his chest, not even looking at me. "Is that your blood or his on your shirt?"

I glanced down at the dull smear of red. "His. I'm fine."

Charles returned with two knives. "Which one, James?" He chose the smaller one.

"I'm sorry, Mr. Tindale, for intruding," I said somewhat stiffly. "I wouldn't have—"

"Nonsense. You were right to come."

"After that boy brought Emma's note, we expected you," Dr. Everett said, feeling for Jack's wrist.

"Emma's note?"

He nodded, his eyes on his watch, timing Jack's pulse for half a minute. "Although she didn't say anything about you toting a half-dead man with you," he added and began, ever so carefully, to cut Jack's tattered trousers away. "What happened?"

"Two men attacked him. One of them cut him with a knife. It's deep. I wrapped it up as best I could."

The knife sliced away the top several layers of wrapping, revealing the wine stains and the blood-soaked bottom layer. One of his hands went to Jack's brow. "No wonder he's freezing. You should have brought him earlier." His voice held concern for Jack, but it held accusation, too.

"I might've if I'd known where to find you," I retorted, anxiety sharpening my voice.

A piercing glance. "Well, don't shine that light of truth too brightly, my dear. It's going to illuminate your mannish getup."

"James." Charles's quiet voice held a reprimand.

Dr. Everett grimaced. "Nell, get some blankets, quickly, from the armoire in the upstairs hall. Charles—prepare some warm water and some hot. I'm going to fetch my bag."

I ran for the stairs. Behind me, I heard Charles's voice, the words indistinct. I kept on, turned at the landing, and pulled two blankets from the armoire shelves, unfolding them as I went back.

"Thank you, Nell." The doctor's voice had lost its impatience, and he tucked the cloth carefully around Jack's torso and his other leg. "Now, go get yourself warm in the kitchen. Charles can help me for the next quarter hour, if I need it." I was at the threshold when his voice stopped me. "Wait! Nell, is this wine?"

I turned back. "I poured some over the cut to clean it. I didn't have any water—I thought it would be better than nothing."

He gave an approving nod. "You were exactly right."

I felt the kindness and smiled at him gratefully. He jerked his head to the left. "The kitchen's there. Charles is right. You look exhausted."

So that's what Charles had said, I thought and felt a rush of thankfulness for his understanding. Not to mention for his willingness to have his lovely parlor turned into an impromptu operating theater to help someone he didn't even know.

Still, it was with some awkwardness that I pushed open the kitchen door. Charles was at the sink pouring water from a vessel into a bowl, and we exchanged hesitant smiles.

He didn't speak; instead, he pushed a chair close to the stove before he vanished with an armful of towels and the bowl. I sank onto the chair, the warmth making me realize just how bone cold I was. I reached my hands toward the heat and saw that they were shaking and filthy.

When Charles returned, he lifted a copper pot from the shelf, filled it, and put it on the stove to boil. After a moment, he passed me a towel. "For your hands," he said.

I took the warm wet cloth and wiped my face first, then my hands. He was busying himself at the sink again, but I felt the profound silence, and the heat rose to my cheeks. *Was there any situation I'd ever found myself in that was more peculiar than this?*

Silently, he held out a hand for the dirty cloth, and as I gave it to him, I resolved to speak. "Mr. Tindale, did you know about—about me before tonight?"

He winced. "Please call me Charles. And what do you mean, did I know about you?"

"That I existed."

His face cleared. "Of course. You and Matthew both." A wry smile tugged at his mouth. "Though you're rather different from the way James described you." A pause, and then, more seriously, "You didn't suspect about me?"

I shook my head. "Peggy only told me tonight. I suppose she's known for a long time, being his housekeeper."

"Yes." He paused. "And because of Emma. He wanted Peggy to be able to reach him in case she needed him."

"Oh, of course."

For a moment, all was quiet except the spark and sizzle of the fire and the sound of water heating.

He looked down at his hands. "I suppose you're very—shocked."

I couldn't help the short laugh that sprang from my throat. "Rather." It came out more drily than I intended.

He winced again, and instantly I felt remorseful. "I'm sorry. It's just very—surprising and—and sudden." At the unhappiness on his face, I stopped and added more gently, "But I'm very grateful to you for helping us. You're being so kind."

He managed a smile. "I was his patient first, you know. I returned from Japan with a fever that made me feel almost mad—so much so that I nearly took my own life. I was two months in his hospital."

I was silent, taking this in.

He lifted the lid on the pot. "It's ready. Why don't you bring it to him?" He took down a ceramic bowl from the cupboard and set it on a tray, then filled it with several cups of water. I carried the tray to the parlor, setting it beside Jack.

Dr. Everett had already laid out his instruments and opened his needle case. "He's lost a lot of blood."

"Is he going to be all right?"

"I don't know, Nell. The one good thing is that a knife wound is easier to stitch up than something jagged. But this is deep." Dr. Everett used a sponge dipped in the warm water to wash the cut and a towel to blot it dry. It took several minutes, and he was so careful that only once did Jack flinch. Though Jack's eyes were closed, I could tell he was partially conscious. I took his hand—it was cold and limp—and pressed it to my cheek.

Charles entered with a large bowl of boiling water. The steam rose in white wraiths, and the doctor added a solution of carbolic acid. "Here." He handed Charles a needle and one of his instruments. "Dip these in."

Within seconds, Dr. Everett had the rinsed needle threaded with catgut. He gestured to the bottle of whiskey on the table. "Get me a glass of that."

I poured two fingers' worth. He nodded toward Jack. "Get it into him."

"Jack, you need to drink this." I helped him sit up a bit and put the glass near his lips.

"No," Jack said, faintly.

"Nonsense," Dr. Everett said. "I'm going to stitch you up, and I need you to stay still."

"No whiskey," he insisted.

Dr. Everett stared at him, frustrated. "I don't have any chloroform, or even laudanum here."

But I had an idea why Jack didn't want it. "I'll hold him," I said softly.

Dr. Everett scowled. "If he moves, I can't stitch."

"We know," I said.

He gave me a look. "Very well. It's on your head."

I draped myself over Jack's chest, rested my head on his breastbone, and put my hands on his shoulders. "Hold on to me, if it helps," I whispered. But his arms stayed where they were, slack at his sides.

Dr. Everett slid the needle into the skin at the edge of the wound. I felt Jack's entire body tense, but he didn't move, and he didn't make a sound.

It felt like an hour, but finally it was over.

The doctor sat back and touched his sleeve to his damp brow.

"Twenty-two stitches." He sighed. "I've done my best, but I'm afraid it's already infected. I only hope the limb doesn't become gangrenous."

A lump rose in my throat. "I'm sure no one could have done better. Thank you."

Then I bent over Jack and whispered his name. No movement, not even a flutter of an eyelid. Frightened, I laid my hand on his chest. Dr. Everett's hand jerked out and went to Jack's wrist.

"He's alive," he said. "It's just exhaustion from keeping himself still for that. He needs to stay warm and sleep." He remained on his knees looking down at Jack. "I wish I'd had ether or chloroform. It would have made it easier on him, poor fellow." He wiped his hands on a towel. "Why wouldn't he take the whiskey?"

"His father is a mean drunkard."

"Ah. *Filius sapiens erratis sui patris discit.*"

Yes, I thought. A wise son learns from the mistakes of his father.

"Now." He threw down the towel on top of the others. "I've helped your friend, and you are going to explain yourself. But first, I'm going to go upstairs to wash." He vanished up the stairs, and Charles took the soiled towels and bowls back to the kitchen.

Gently, I adjusted the pillow under Jack's head, and tucked the blankets more tightly around him. His face was so ashen that he looked older, uncannily like his uncle.

When he returned, Dr. Everett picked up the glass of whiskey Jack had refused, took a gulp, and looked at me through his spectacles. "I'm quite writhing with suspense. But we'll wait for Charles."

As if on cue, Charles appeared in the doorway, a steaming mug in his hands. "I'm here," he said mildly, "so you can stop writhing." He bent down and handed me the mug. "I thought you might want this."

I breathed in the smell of the chocolate. "This is heavenly. Thank you."

"You're most welcome."

Charles sat down in the chair and, almost without looking, took a sip from the doctor's glass. It was a mark of intimacy that left me disconcerted anew. How could I have known the doctor my entire life and not even guessed?

He gave a cough and looked at me expectantly.

I took a few sips of chocolate and set it on a low table. Then I took one of Jack's hands in both of mine. Now that he was safe, I could begin to think about how to explain the evening's events. I had a feeling that once I began talking, the erstwhile logical doctor was going to explode like the flaming powder out of Gallius Kovác's magic box.

I met his inquiring gaze straight on. "I know you're going to be angry. But please just try to listen until I'm finished." I added under my breath, "Then no doubt you'll say plenty."

He blinked several times. "Very well." Then he nodded toward Jack. "First, who is he?"

"His name's Jack Drummond. His father owns the Octavian Music Hall."

Dr. Everett's eyebrows flew up, but he remained silent.

I continued: "I've been playing piano there two or three nights a week to earn tuition money for the Royal Academy. In case I was ever accepted."

The doctor's face paled, and I talked quickly to get it over with. Perhaps there was something I could have kept back—but I was too tired to keep straight which secrets were mine and which were

Jack's. And what was the use, anyway? Surely, after tonight, he would hear plenty, between Matthew and the newspapers. So he heard it first from me, in a breathless, rather incoherent recital.

After I finished, Dr. Everett's empty glass clicked softly down on the table. He removed his spectacles and rubbed his hands over his face. "Good God, Nell."

"I know," I said miserably.

At last, he looked up with a sigh. "Do you think you'll be able to get another audition?"

His generosity brought a lump to my throat. All this, and his first thought wasn't to chide me for my dissembling but to ask *that*.

"I daresay you can explain the unusual situation," Charles said quietly. He sat with his elbows on his knees, his fingertips steepled near his mouth. "What's more important tonight is getting a message to Matthew. Because Tierney is still out there, and the best chance at guaranteeing *your* safety"—his nod included both Jack and me—"is capturing him." He turned to Dr. Everett. "Did he give you any specifics about his plan?"

"When did you see Matthew?" I asked.

"This afternoon. He came by the hospital." The doctor replaced his spectacles. "He wanted me to reassure him that if anything happened, I would take care of you. Then he told me what he was about to do."

"What exactly did he say?"

"That they were raiding the music halls in the Fleet, as many as they could find."

Charles's eyebrows rose, and he nodded toward Jack. "His injury is unfortunate of course, but it's a good thing he wasn't anywhere near the place."

"The Octavian was definitely one of them?" I asked.

"Yes," replied the doctor. "He showed me the list."

I glanced involuntarily at Jack, but he lay as if asleep. "It's an unfortunate coincidence, everything happening tonight," I murmured. "The shipment from Greenland Dock and the raid, both. I'm sure Matthew was hoping to find Tierney at one of the music halls—but now it seems that won't happen. I'm almost beginning to believe that Tierney has the luck of the devil."

Charles shook his head. "This scandal is going to upend all of London once the newspapers get hold of it. The public outcry will be enormous—not simply against Tierney and his Fleet, but the music halls and Scotland Yard. I do hope that if the raid isn't wholly successful, Matthew won't be made a scapegoat."

Jack's fingers jerked against mine, though his eyes remained closed. *Has he been conscious of all we've been saying?* In alarm, I looked up and put my finger to my lips.

Dr. Everett rose from his chair and came toward Jack, picked up his wrist again, and felt the pulse. "Slow but steady. We just have to watch in case he develops a fever. We'll know more in the morning."

"It's so late," I said. "You should go to bed. I'll stay with him, if that's all right."

Charles was already gathering up the glasses. "Of course." A pause. "What's the matter, James?"

I looked up to see the doctor frowning. "I just wish we could get word to Matthew about the gun shipment," he said. "I wonder if I might leave a message for him at the Yard."

"But whom can you trust with it?" I asked. "William is dead, and he wasn't sure of anyone else."

"Then I shall stay there until he returns, or until I know where to find him."

Charles asked, "Do you want me to come with you?"

"No, no." He waved away the suggestion. "I'll take a cab." He was already starting for the door.

The glasses clinked together in Charles's hand as he looked down at me. "Are you all right?"

"Yes. And thank you," I said. "Truly."

"Don't mention it, please." He smiled. "It's my pleasure. Good night."

"Good night."

Charles's slippered footsteps moved to the kitchen, then up the stairs.

"Nell." Jack's voice was a hoarse whisper, drawing me close. "What did he say about the Yard and the Octavian? I was fading in and out."

"The police are raiding some of the ships tonight," I said reluctantly. "The Octavian is one of them." His eyes opened all the way. "I'm sorry, Jack." I ran my hand over his forehead. "He didn't hear the name from me, I swear he didn't."

"I believe you. But he can't catch my father." His fingers moved weakly on the blanket. "You have to go and warn him."

A shiver ran over me. "Jack, I can't go back there—"

"You don't have to." He swallowed. "He'll be at Rosemary's house. My uncle knows it. Please, Nell." He tried to push himself up onto his elbows. "If you don't, I've got to go."

"Don't be absurd." I pushed him back onto the pillow. His breath was coming hard, and he was still struggling to sit up.

"Jack, stop it. Stop it! All right, I'll go! Don't upset yourself, and don't even think of moving, or you'll tear your stitches straight out." I had both hands on his chest, striving to hold him down. "If you move again, I won't go anywhere."

He gave in with a sigh and closed his eyes. I sat back on my heels. "I'll ask your uncle to help me," I said. "But what exactly do you want me to tell your father?"

"Tell him to get whatever money he can and get out of England. Go to France. My uncle's friends will help him." He opened his eyes, and the selfless concern I saw there went straight to my heart. "He can't go to prison again, Nell. It'll kill him."

I bent over and kissed his forehead.

Then I picked up my coat from where I'd thrown it over a chair, and once more I slipped out a door into the dark.

Chapter 30

To my relief, despite the hour, there was a dim light in a window above Mr. Bertault's shop.

I leaned against the door frame, pressing my hand to the cramp in my side, and knocked.

Instantly, the window overhead swung open. "Who's there?" he called out.

"Mr. Bertault!" I said, as loudly as I dared. "It's Nell!"

"*Mon Dieu!*" He shut the window.

I turned and looked about the dark street. A dog the size of a wolf skulked at the next corner. A quick lunge, a furious shake of the head, and the rat in its mouth went still. He turned and trotted away.

A moment later I saw the bobbing light of a lamp through the glass. The bolt scraped, and Mr. Bertault drew me inside. He was fully clothed, and a coat lay over a chair nearby, as if he'd just come back from somewhere, or was ready to go out. His hand was warm and steady on mine, and his voice calm. "*Qu'est que c'est, Mademoiselle?* Did you find Jacques? What's happened?"

"He was attacked and one of the men had a knife—"

A swift inhale. "*Merde!* Is he all right?"

"As well as he can be. A friend of mine is a doctor."

He took another deep breath in and blew it out. "*C'est bon.*"

"But Jack knows the police are making a raid on the Octavian tonight, and he wants me to warn his father to get out of England and go to France. He told me to come find you. He said you'd help me."

An angry look came over Mr. Bertault's face. "Bah! Drummond doesn't deserve the son he has. He never deserved either of them. Selfish as a pig, from beginning to end!"

I said hesitantly, "I think—I think Jack still cares about him because—well, because his father truly loved Eugenie. Jack said that when she was sick, he took wonderful care of her, and when it came toward the end, he sold everything but her piano, because he knew it would break her heart to lose it. That seems like an act of selflessness—or at least love."

His mouth tightened in derision. "The whole reason she got sick is that he brought her to London with its dirt and miasmas! He knew her lungs were weak. But Eugenie adored him. She'd have gone anywhere—and he should not have taken advantage of that love. He should have *insisted* they remain in France. My family could have found him work in the countryside, or even in Toulon. They could have been *happy*." He flung his hands up. "And when she died, do you know what he did? He drank himself sick. Poor Jacques was left to fend for himself for weeks— until Drummond ended up in debtor's prison, and Jacques was thrown into an orphanage. I don't care what sort of misery Drummond felt, he should have taken care of his son. And then to pull him into this Fleet business? If he'd been any decent sort of man, he'd have kept Jacques as far from it as possible. Bah! He disgusts me!"

Stricken, I had remained silent through his outburst. "I'm sorry," I whispered.

His anger left him then, and he heaved a sigh. "I know. It is a sorry thing, for everyone." He ran his fingers through his rumpled hair. "Do you know, as Eugenie lay on her deathbed, she wrote me a letter, begging me to do what I could to help him and little Jacques. So I will—but by God, I hope this is the end of it."

"If he goes to France, will he be all right?"

His mouth twisted in a bitter line. "Probably. It's easy to get lost in France these days."

I was conscious of the clock ticking on the wall. "Mr. Bertault"—I swallowed—"if we want Drummond to get away, we need to find him soon. Jack said you know where Rosemary lives."

"*Oui*." He picked up the lamp, and then turned back to me, his expression grim. "You're absolutely sure Jacques is all right, far away from Tierney?"

I nodded. "He's at a friend's—a friend who has nothing to do with the Fleet. There's no way Tierney could trace Jack there, unless he truly has second sight. And I think he'll be too busy tonight to be concerned about Jack."

The fear left his face. "Then don't worry, *chérie*. We'll find Drummond."

I followed him into his office and watched as he pulled open a drawer and drew out a gun, loaded it, and slid it into his pocket. His face was untroubled and his hand steady as he picked up the lamp.

"I have one, too," I said and drew out the revolver.

He nodded, accepting this without surprise. "Then let us go. Are you afraid?"

"Yes," I said. "But less so, with you."

He smiled then and touched my cheek gently. "Nothing will happen to you, I promise. Jacques would—as the French say— have my head." He handed me the lamp, opened the front door, glanced up and down the empty street, and locked the door behind us. Then he took the lamp from me, and we began to walk east. The wind was picking up, and the clouds scudded across the sky. The moon was nearly full; it etched the edge of one of the clouds with silver and then disappeared behind another.

"I came earlier, but you weren't here," I said.

"*Oui.* I thought of some places I might find him." A sideways look. "Nowhere I would send you."

"And who is Rosemary?"

"Drummond's mistress. She lives near Seven Dials."

I stiffened. Seven Dials was one of the most notorious slums in London.

"He lives with her?"

"Sometimes."

Mr. Bertault's hand on my elbow steered me north. The lantern he carried cast a ring of light beyond which lurked the London darkness, kept at bay like a pack of wolves. I half wanted to hurry toward Seven Dials and half wanted to run in the other direction, but Mr. Bertault walked steadily on, jiggering us across streets, always heading north and east, and soon we were on Monmouth Street. Above us loomed tall rookeries, as shadowy and moldering as I could have imagined. He didn't hesitate, but directed me into a narrow nameless alley. I heard the scurrying of rats, and a moan.

I spun toward it. "What's that?"

Mr. Bertault swung the lantern. At first I thought it was a heap of rags, but there was a matted clump of gray hair, and the figure shifted. Mr. Bertault clucked his tongue, the pity clear on his face. Turning away, he led me to a rickety wooden structure that ran up the side of a building. It began as a wooden stair, but parts of it were a ladder, and pieces of it were missing. "Only step where I step," he said, and I followed him precisely, keeping my hands on the banister until it ended in splinters.

He reached a third-story landing and hit the door twice with the handle of his gun.

From my chest rose an unbidden hope that we would never find Drummond. I knew the fury I'd see in his face when he spotted me. I wanted him gone, dead, anything—

"Who's 'ere?" came a woman's voice.

"It's Bertault. I'm looking for Nick."

Silence.

"Open the door, woman," he growled. "We have a message for him. Is he here?"

Silence again, and then the sound of a bolt sliding back. Drummond appeared in the crack between the door and the jamb. "What—?" His eyes darted from his brother-in-law to me, and then came the rage I expected. "You bloody fool! What have you done, bringing her here?"

"The girl has something to say to you."

"Ha!" His mouth opened wide, showing his teeth in a macabre smile. "First you talk to the police, now you want to talk to me?"

I spat back: "I didn't talk to the police!"

"Don't play the innocent, you little—"

"I didn't tell anyone anything!" My voice rose to be heard over his.

"Shhh," he and Mr. Bertault hissed together.

Mr. Bertault drew his gun and pointed it at Drummond's jaw. "Listen to what she has to say, and I'll take her straight out of here." His voice dropped to a whisper that was, strangely, almost tender: "And if I have to kill you to get her away, I'll do it. You know I will."

With something like a growl, Drummond jerked away from the gun, opened the door, and stood aside for us to enter. I could smell the whiskey on his breath as I passed him. I'd have rather stayed on the ramshackle landing.

The room stank of burned meat and cheap candles. A woman sat by the hearth fire, her gaze unfocused, her hand lying limply on a bottle of something.

Mr. Bertault turned to me. "It's all right. He's listening."

A look of impatience crossed Drummond's face. "You can put the gun away."

"*Non.*" Mr. Bertault stood between us, his gun hand motionless at his side.

"Speak up," Drummond said to me, his eyes narrowed.

I swallowed. "A group of police and inspectors are making a raid on some of the ships tonight. The Octavian is one of them."

His eyes blazed, and hard lines formed around his mouth. "Why are you here? Where's Jack?"

"Somewhere safe," I said.

Disgust appeared on his face, and he reached for a brown bottle on the table, raising it to his mouth. "Yes, that sounds like him. Staying out of the way. Lily-livered coward."

"Coward!" I stared, disbelieving, and my hand clenched around the gun in my pocket. "He's not *afraid*. He's half *dead*—because Stephen Gagnon sent two thugs out to kill him. They slashed his leg open, and he would've died in the streets except—except someone found him."

Finally, I'd gotten through to him. He pulled the bottle away from his mouth. "What?"

"I tried to tell you! Why would you trust *Stephen*—of all people?"

His brain may have been slow with drink, but I could tell he was thinking. "Stephen told me that Jack talked to the police—because you told him you'd leave him if he didn't."

I barked a laugh. "And you believed him?"

"Why wouldn't I? It's clear you meant something to Jack."

"Jack didn't talk to the police. He was the one who made me promise not to." Suddenly, I knew how to break through whatever cloud Stephen's lies and the whiskey had put around him. My voice sharpened: "Does the name 'Kendrick' mean anything to you?"

Drummond went still.

"He was a counterfeiter for one of the silver ships in White-chapel," I said.

His eyes narrowed, and his voice was alarmingly soft. "How do you know so much?"

"He's dead now, but *he's* the one who talked to the police. Not me. And not Jack, either."

Drummond turned away, his boots scuffing as he went to the window. In the silence, we all heard the wind wrapping itself around the wretched place, whistling through openings, banging a shutter to and fro.

I kept my voice calm: "Your son will live, provided there's no infection. But do you want to know what Jack's biggest worry was? *You.* He made me swear I would find you and warn you in time. He still loves you, although God only knows why."

Drummond turned back toward me, and his eyes were like flat black pools.

Suddenly, I felt tired. Just terribly tired. "That's why I'm here. To tell you that you need to get out of England. Go to France." I took a breath. "Tonight. If you're caught here, in all likelihood, you'll hang."

He set his bottle on the table. "You're telling me the truth?"

"I am."

"She'd hardly be here for the fun of it," Mr. Bertault said.

"That's not what I mean. What if she just wants me gone? She has reason enough to be afraid of me."

"I do want you gone," I said. "But I'm doing this for Jack's sake. Not yours, and not mine."

A flicker of pain in his eyes, and then it was gone, and his voice was practical: "I'll go. But I can't leave without the rest of my money."

The woman rose unsteadily from her seat on the hearth, came to his side, and seized his arm. "Nick, what are ye sayin'? Ye can't leave me here! Ye promised!"

He shook her off impatiently.

"Surely you have enough money tucked away here," Mr. Bertault said. "Don't be greedy. It could cost you your life."

Drummond ran his hand through his black hair and paced. "Damn Kendrick."

"It'll be light soon," Mr. Bertault said. "Make your way to Greenwich as fast as you can. That'll be far enough along the river, and you'll be able to find ships bound for France. You can lose yourself once you get to Calais."

"I can have someone bring me the rest of my money—it will only take a few hours," Drummond said. "The police'll only go to the Octavian. They'll never find me here."

"Is there any chance that Stephen knows this address?" I asked.

Drummond's expression changed.

"I'm warning you," I said. "If Stephen sees anything to be gained by revealing it, he will. I wasn't lying earlier when I told you that he'd turn on anyone. Think about what he could get if you're in jail."

"Nick," Rosemary said, her voice pleading.

"Shut up." He turned away and went into a back room. We heard the sound of a drawer scraping open and closed.

Mr. Bertault reached behind me to open the door, and a gust of the damp night air blew in.

"Wait." It was Drummond's voice, behind us. Mr. Bertault ignored him, but I stopped and turned.

To this day, I'm not sure why. I think I was hoping for some message to take back to Jack, to tell him that his father understood that Jack had tried to save him, that his father had cared about him after all, that he had at least said goodbye.

Drummond stood in the doorway to the back room, his hands full of notes. "My ledger. You need to get it from the Octavian."

I stared at him in disgust. "Are you mad? I'm not going to fetch your ledger."

"Then Jack will hang."

My blood went cold.

"It's a record of our nightly takes. It's all in his handwriting, and he signs it."

I felt a sinking in my stomach. "Where is it?"

"Top right drawer of my desk. A red book."

"For God's sake, Nick," Mr. Bertault spat then turned to me. "You know where that is?"

I nodded.

I expected Drummond to follow us out onto the landing. But instead he stood behind the threshold, just staring down the alley. Perhaps he had further preparations, but a strange thought came at me, like a shot out of the dark: maybe part of him wanted to be caught, to have it over with. What was left for him now, after all? I thought back to the ugly little room. This wasn't much. But a life in exile?

"Nell," Mr. Bertault said warningly. "Come along."

The moon was between clouds, and by its light, I followed him down those perilous stairs. The noises we made, with our boots scraping the rotting wood and the steps creaking, echoed in the close space. At the bottom, I let out my breath—I'd been holding it, in defense against the smells as much as against my fear of the stairs falling apart under me—and we started down the street. I had my collar up, and Mr. Bertault had his hat drawn low. Ahead of us, on Monmouth Street, a man in a dark coat stepped out of a hansom cab and raised his arm to pay the driver.

Even as I saw him, Mr. Bertault yanked me into a tiny alley and drew his gun back out. Silently we watched him walk by; I caught a glimpse of pale skin and a fringe of hair. No one I knew, but as his footsteps receded, I peered around the corner. He stood at the bottom of Rosemary's stairs, took out his revolving pistol, and banged it twice on the wooden rail.

Rosemary's door opened, and she looked out. "Who is it?" she hissed.

"Barrow. Where's Drummond?"

"I dunno. He left—about half an hour ago."

"Where was he going?"

"Said he'd be back by morning." She spoke the lie convincingly.

"Bugger."

He stood there for a moment, as if undecided what to do next. If my eyes hadn't been used to near-darkness, I wouldn't have been able to see his face at all, but in the light from the moon, I could. A man of about five-and-forty, with thinning reddish hair.

He strode back toward us, and I stepped backward into Mr. Bertault's protective arm. Barrow went past us hurriedly, and his footsteps faded away.

"Who's that?" Mr. Bertault hissed.

I put my mouth close to his ear. "Chief Inspector Barrow. Head of Scotland Yard. But he's in with Tierney. He's probably trying to figure out what's happening tonight. Matthew left him out of it."

We waited another minute and then made our way toward Regent Street, where we found a hansom cab. Mr. Bertault helped me in.

"Where to, guv'nor?" asked the driver.

"The Octavian."

Chapter 31

*W*hat if the police are there when we arrive?" Mr. Bertault asked as the cab's wheels rolled over a joint in the macadam, jarring us.

"We'll try to find a way around them, I suppose."

He rested his two large hands on his knees, rubbing them as if they pained him. "Are you all right?" I asked.

He turned to me and smiled wryly. "I'm an old man. I belong in bed."

I bit my lip. "Thank you for coming. I don't know what I'd have done without you."

He shrugged, and after a moment said, "I've half a mind to send you home." I opened my mouth to protest, and he raised a hand. "As Drummond's brother-in-law, I have some reason to be at the music hall he owns. But you? At this hour, and dressed like that?"

I shifted in the seat. "Even if you have a right to be there, the police aren't going to let you walk out with the ledger. Matthew will have told them to gather any papers, for proof."

"I know." He touched my hand. "Well, let's not go looking for trouble. The policemen may not have come yet."

I looked out the window. There was a faint graying above the rooftops. It would be dark for only another hour or so.

Mr. Bertault said, "What if Drummond was lying, sending us on some wild-goose chase, looking for a ledger that doesn't exist?"

I recalled the look on Drummond's face when he'd told us. "I don't think so. I'm not saying he loves Jack enough to sacrifice for him, but I don't think he'd want his son to hang, if he could save Jack without any trouble to himself."

A snort. "You mean if he could have *you* save Jack with no trouble to himself."

The cab drew up to the Octavian, and all was quiet. Did this mean the police had come and gone? We jumped out, and Mr. Bertault paid the driver as I went to the back door.

It was locked, of course.

"What about the window?" Mr. Bertault pointed over our heads. "Can you get in that way?"

"How?"

"I can put you up there, and here's a knife that might pry it open." I took the thin blade in its sheath and tucked it into the back of my trousers.

"Take off your shoes," he said. He offered me a step in his hands. My feet, in stockings, were cold against his warm skin, and he grunted as he boosted me up. "Now on my shoulder." With one hand braced against the rough brick wall, I stepped onto his broad shoulder, his hands still steadying me. I was right at the level with the window, and I peered into it, trying to see the hinges. Carefully, I reached for the knife and slid the thin blade along the crack. It wouldn't budge. I tried the other side and felt unyielding metal. I pushed up on it, then down, but it was stuck as hard as if it had been welded. I swore under my breath.

"Got it?"

"Not yet. I can't tell which side the hinges are on, and which the lock."

"Take your time."

In that moment, the thought flashed into my head that time was precisely what we didn't have—but his words calmed me, and I put the knife back on the left side. This time I slid it into the middle of the crack, and I felt something catch. I tried again, and then one more time—

The metal piece scraped and resisted the blade, but I wiggled the handle as carefully as I could—and the lock released.

Gently, I eased the windowpane in. One boost and I was through, slithering ungracefully over the sill and onto the floor with a quiet thunk.

I almost expected to hear shouts and people running toward me. But there was only silence.

I leaned back through the window and waved; he nodded back.

In my stocking feet, I ran silently down the corridor toward the stairs that led to the back passageway and the ramp that went to the door. Mr. Bertault stepped inside as soon as I pushed the door open, handing me my boots and taking back his knife.

"Any signs of the police?" he asked. I shook my head, slid into my boots, and led Mr. Bertault down the back hallway to Drummond's office. Naturally, the door was locked.

"Do you have a hairpin?" he asked.

I plucked one out of my hair.

"And another?"

I withdrew a second and felt a lock of my hair loosen. He bent down at the door and inserted both, carefully, into the keyhole. I was keeping watch, turning my head to the left and right, but there was no sign of anyone, only silence and the smell of moldering plaster. Then came a soft click, the door cracked open, and we slid into Drummond's office. I thought nothing would ever induce me to return, but there I was. I found myself averting my eyes from the chair.

Mr. Bertault went to the desk and began to rummage through the top drawer, then the next. "*Merde*. It's not here," he whispered.

"What?" I hurried over and began hunting through the papers, rags, and other rubble on the desk while he eased open the other drawers—top right, bottom left, bottom right—and even got down onto the floor to peer underneath the desk. "Nothing."

His head came up over the desk, and he pushed himself up with his broad hands. "I'll check the shelves."

I nodded. "I'm going to search the room where the boys stay. If the ledger is used to keep track of what they bring in, maybe it was left there by mistake."

He muttered an assent. I flicked a match to light a spare lamp, took it up, and headed for the properties room, all the while listening for footsteps. I pulled up the hidden panel and dropped in. The room stank of sweat, old food, and animal droppings. I raised the lantern and saw that the benches were no longer scattered around the room but pushed close together in the middle of the floor. From under one of the benches came a rat, which darted across the semicircle of lamplight and vanished behind a crate. Rats ate human flesh, I knew. The thought of the boys trying to sleep amid them made me shudder.

I began to search, working my way around the right side of the room. Most of the crates were nailed shut at the top, their sides rough with cheap wood that bore splinters. To my surprise, two of the lids were askew, so I wedged them up and peered in. I didn't find the red ledger in either crate—but what I did see stunned me, though I suppose it shouldn't have. Silver candlesticks, gold chains, shining spoons, ornate brooches, strings of pearls, gilded frames—the treasures of dozens of families across London, tumbled together haphazardly, with no more care than if they'd been in a rag-and-bone shop.

I set the lid of the second crate back in place and turned toward the makeshift table that had held the soup pot. Now it was stacked with pans, silverware, newspapers, and rags. Some of the pots still had food inside them. A rat showed its face above the rim of one of the shallow ones. I hissed at it, but it didn't jump out of the pot, merely bent its head to keep feasting on whatever scabs of food it had found at the bottom. A cold draft coming from somewhere made me shiver, but I kept on with my search. Above the table hung a set of shelves with more tin bowls, some lamps, and spoons. I ran my hand along the top of the shelves, and my fingers met something. A book. My heart leaped and I pulled it down, but it wasn't the ledger. A yellowback novel. I flipped through it for any notations, but there were none. I put it back and headed toward a wooden cabinet. I swung open the tall doors—

"You just can't stay away," said a cool voice behind me.

I spun around.

"What are you doing?" Stephen asked, walking toward me. His cheeks were red, as if from the cold, and he blew on his bare hands. The nighttime air seemed to follow him in, and I realized that the draft I'd felt earlier must have come from another entrance.

My heart began to race. But I knew that whatever I did, I couldn't let him know I was afraid. He'd relish any sort of weakness. And if I could keep him talking, sooner or later Mr. Bertault would come looking for me.

I lifted my chin. "Looking for something."

He removed his coat and hung it on a hook in the wall, without taking his eyes from me. "What the hell were you doing, trying to make a fool of me with Drummond and Tierney? You know they didn't believe you."

I snorted. "Oh, Stephen. I didn't care whether they believed me. I was just trying to save my own skin. And if you hadn't thrown me in the room with them, I wouldn't have had to."

"How did you get out of his office?"

"I'm clever."

He stepped closer. "Indeed, you are. What are you looking for?"

"A red ledger," I said candidly. "Drummond sent me to fetch it."

"What?" Surprise flickered in his eyes. He rapidly blinked it away, but I could see I'd thrown him off-balance.

I turned my back to him and made a show of shifting items on the cabinet shelves. "He told me it was in the top drawer of his desk, but if it wasn't there, I should look in here."

He grabbed my arm and turned me toward him, his eyes narrowed and his expression full of disbelief. "Why would he send *you* to get his ledger?"

"He said he needed it, and—and if I did that for him, he would tell me where Jack was."

He let go of my arm. "He has no idea where Jack is."

"How do you know?"

He raised an eyebrow, and his smile was mocking. "He's dead, my dear."

A beat. If I didn't know Jack was at Charles's house, those words would have sent me flying like a wildcat to scratch the eyes out of his amused face. But instead I said merely, "You're lying. I'm sure Drummond knows better than you where his son is."

He gave a graceful, resigned shrug. "Think what you like. You'll find out soon enough."

"Do *you* know where the ledger is?"

"Well, yes. I've tucked it away someplace safe, for my use. But I'm certainly not giving it to you. I've got it, and Drummond wants it. That puts me in a nice position, doesn't it?"

"I'll buy it from you."

He laughed softly and came toward me. There was a hard glitter in his eyes that frightened me. "I don't need money." There was the faintest emphasis on the last word.

As I stepped backward, the weight of the gun swung against my hip. How could I have forgotten it? I took another step back and another, and my hand began, surreptitiously, to move toward my pocket. "Well, you're not getting anything else from me."

He must have sensed something, for he lunged suddenly and grabbed both my wrists tightly enough that I let out a cry. He gave me a shake. "You're the one lying. Drummond didn't send you for anything. He'd no more trust you than the devil. Where is he? Where did you see him? And how did you know about the ledger?"

"Let go of me!" I wrenched and pulled, but his hands were like handcuffs. Now I could smell wine thick on his breath, and it came to me that I must have been mad to have voluntarily sat through dinner with him, that he had once been close enough to kiss me—

Maybe that thought occurred to him, too, for suddenly his

mouth was on mine, hard and punishing, and I was pushing with all my strength against him, but he had me fast, and then he yanked at my arm to throw me off-balance, and I landed on my back, with him on top of me, the gun a ridge of metal bruising my thigh. I opened my mouth against his lips to scream—and his left hand came across my nose and mouth. "Shut up, damn it!"

He was using all his weight to hold me down, and his right hand was dragging at my shirt. I felt one of the buttons give, and then another.

I twisted and writhed as his fingers went to my trousers, fighting as hard as I could, but his weight was too much for me. His palm was at my throat—I was beginning to feel light-headed. Then he drew back to pull down his own trousers—

In that instant, my right hand was free, and I fumbled for the pocket of my coat . . . found the opening—

Belatedly, he reached for my hand, but I had the gun out and pointed at his chest.

Shock froze his features. "You couldn't," he said, his voice hard.

"Get off of me," I said hoarsely. Instead, he grabbed for my wrist.

The gun was aimed at his shoulder as I pulled the trigger.

But it was the empty first chamber.

A raucous laugh burst out of him, and his hands squeezed mine so tightly that the trigger bit into my finger and I cried out in pain—

And then came a deafening roar that silenced every other sound.

He lurched sideways, his right arm out as if to prevent his fall.

And for a moment, we both stared at the blood spreading across the middle of his white shirt. Then his eyes met mine—and something like bewilderment came over his face, his mouth opening in a cry that I could barely hear. The red stain was spreading in an oval, and his hand came up over it, as if in a pledge. And then he was on the floor, slumped facedown, his fair hair falling over his face.

A cold horror came over me, and I found myself shuddering and gasping for air as if Stephen's hand were still at my throat. I shook the gun from my fingers, and it clattered against the floor. My hands on the floor behind me, I kicked crablike one step back, and then another. I couldn't take my eyes off him.

Full of disgust—for Stephen, for myself, for the gun and the blood—for all of it—I tried to cry out but couldn't. I wanted nothing more than to get out of my own skin. Then Mr. Bertault's bulk filled the hidden door and came through it, faster than I'd have thought possible for someone of his size. "Nell!"

He took in Stephen at a glance and crossed to me, his hands on my shoulders, pulling me to my feet and then in a fierce embrace. "I heard the shot. Did he hurt you?" I shook my head against his chest, my eyes still on Stephen.

"Look at me, Nell. Not at him. Look at me." He drew away and took my face in his hands, his brown eyes intent. "You mustn't blame yourself for this."

And then, outside, we heard noises. They could be costermonger carts. Or they might be the police. The sound jolted me, and he was speaking quickly: "I couldn't find the ledger. Everything I found is in Nick's hand, not Jack's. Where else? Never mind Stephen now. There will be time to think of him later. Think, *chérie*! They're coming."

I closed my eyes with a feeling of hopelessness, knowing how large this music hall was. Three stories, dozens of nooks and crannies, tables, properties, boxes, rooms—

My eyes flashed open. "The instrument room upstairs. Stephen leaves his violin there. Maybe in his case?"

I was halfway through the hidden door when I remembered. "The papers!"

"What?"

Keeping my eyes averted from Stephen, I ran to his coat hanging on the wall. Stephen was right-handed; the papers would be in that pocket. I put my fingers in, drew them out, and looked only long enough to be sure they were the ones from Jack's book.

"Jack's handwriting," I said as I jammed them into my pocket.

We hurried through the properties room, and while the sound of pounding at the back door echoed along the corridors, I led the way up the stairs to the second story. The door to the instrument room stood wide open. The Octavian kept a large collection. Cellos, violas, trumpets, flutes, oboes, clarinets—and four violins. I opened two of the cases. Mr. Bertault was opening the others—

"*Voila*!" he hissed. In his hand was a red book, perhaps six inches by nine. He flipped it open. Over his shoulder, I could see columns of numbers and lists, in style and order almost exactly like the pages in my pocket.

"*Merde*. His initials are on every page. And here's his name."

"At least we found it."

He stuffed it into his coat. "Hurry."

We ran down the stairs and across the back hallway, but our luck had run out. There was a commotion outdoors and banging on the back door, alternating with the low, solid slams of something being wielded against the front door. They would be inside in minutes.

"We're too late," I whispered. "They'll search us."

He whirled toward me, his face determined. "There must be somewhere to hide it."

I shook my head. "We can burn it. There's a stove in Drummond's office. It's only natural that he'd burn it himself, if he was worried about it being discovered."

Wordlessly, he thrust the book toward me. "I'll hold them off as long as I can. Make sure there's nothing left."

I was already running toward the back hallway. My brother might consider arresting me himself if he knew what I was doing—

For the third time that night, I entered Drummond's office. I went straight for the potbellied stove and thrust the book in, its binding spread flat, the pages fanned open. Then I drew out the pages from my pocket and pushed them in on top. There were still some coals burning, but they couldn't burn fast enough to suit me. For a moment I thought I'd smothered the flame. I stood up, frantically searching for matches. I remembered seeing a box on the desk, snatched it up, and scraped a match. I was too rough with it, and it broke. But somehow, at last, the pages were burning. I crouched before the stove, watching as the edges blackened and gave way to orange and bright yellow flames.

The door slammed open behind me. "What are you doing there?" came a man's angry voice.

I whirled. The man started toward me. Reddish hair and a star-shaped scar. Barrow, with a gun in his hand.

By rights, I should have been terrified. But instead, I felt a sort of cool resignation, as if my mind simply refused to take in any more terror tonight. I stood, slowly, as the door began to close behind him and the matches and box fell from my hands onto the floor.

His eyes darted toward the stove, and he gestured with the gun. "Get it out!"

I began to back away. The ledger was burning brightly but still salvageable. "It's no use, it's gone," I lied.

"It's not gone, damn it." He strode across the room and dragged me toward the stove, a hand on my forearm as if to force my hand inside, into the flames. I let out a scream that seared my throat. The door slammed open once more, and Matthew came in like a bear, a revolving pistol in his hand, raised.

"Barrow! Let her go!"

The death grip on my arm lessened, and I wrenched away and fell to the floor, pain shooting hot from my wrist all the way to my shoulder.

Barrow straightened. His chin came up. "Well, you want me dead. Now you have an excuse. You can say you did it saving her." He jerked his head toward me.

"I want you dead, but I want you to hang in front of everybody." Matthew's voice was wooden. "You'll stand trial for William Crewe's murder, as well as for this." His gaze shifted to me, for no longer than it takes to blink.

I should have anticipated it, of course. In the split second that Matthew had looked at me, Barrow's gun had come up, time slowed, and with a scream of warning, I turned away, my hands over my ears.

The shot seemed to explode the entire hall. I heard a body slump to the floor, and sure that it was Matthew's, certain that I was next, I shut my eyes and held my breath.

Suddenly, I felt arms around me and heard Matthew's voice saying my name. He was holding me so tightly that I couldn't speak and uttering curses that I'd never heard before, not even here at the Octavian.

At last, he drew back, his blue eyes wet. "What in God's name are you doing here?"

I couldn't answer.

His gaze darted over my shoulder. "And what's burning?"

Mutely I shook my head. But he had already started toward the stove, turning his truncheon so he could use the handle as a rake.

"Matthew, wait!" I choked out. "Please. You don't need it. You'll find plenty of proof about Drummond's affairs. And there are crates of stolen valuables in a secret room. I can show you where."

He turned toward me, his expression astonished.

"I'm protecting a friend. A good friend. Someone worth saving." I was begging now, and the tears were coming fast. "*Please.*"

He studied me for what felt like a long time, and I don't know what he saw, but slowly he straightened up, put his truncheon away, and closed the stove door. "All right, then."

"Inspector! Mr. Hallam!" came shouts from the corridor.

"Come along," he said gently, and drew me out of the room, leaving the fire to go to ashes.

Chapter 32

*I*n the corridor, we found Mr. Bertault braced against the wall, his forehead and palms against the crumbling plaster. One police constable held him firmly at the collar, while another searched him for a weapon.

Mr. Bertault caught sight of me, and an expression of profound relief came over his face. "*Dieu merci. Tu vas bien.*"

I laid my hand on Matthew's arm. "Matthew, this is François Bertault. He's Drummond's brother-in-law—but he's not part of the Fleet. He's only here because he was helping me." I glanced down the hallway that led to the properties room. "There's no one else here right now except . . ."

My voice trailed off as I saw vividly in my mind the figure of Stephen looming over me, his mouth in a horrible rictus. And although I knew that Stephen had been treacherous and selfish and brutal, I felt a stab of grief in the center of my chest. That first night at the Octavian, when he had come out, violin in hand, doing his best to please the audience, I had not only felt a sympathy and affinity for him; I had admired him.

"Nell." Matthew had me by the shoulders, not roughly but firmly, and his eyes were staring into mine. "No one here except whom?"

I swallowed down the tightness in my throat. "Stephen Gagnon."

"Who's that?"

"One of Drummond's men. He played violin here. You'll find him in the secret room under the stage—it's where the Fleet boys stay during the day." I took a deep breath. "I . . . I had to shoot him. Or he'd have killed me."

Matthew dropped his hands and stared, completely dumbfounded. And then I remembered what else had happened in that room, and I clutched at his arm: "Matthew, Tierney was here last night."

He stiffened. "You're sure?"

"A large man, dark hair, three ruined fingers."

"Yes," he said, rather hollowly. "That's Tierney."

"He met with Drummond—"

"What time was this?"

"Between eight and nine o'clock. They were with a constable for the River Police. There's a shipment leaving from Greenland Dock this morning. There will be barrels of gin on top, for which they'll have some sort of proper bill—I can't remember what they called it—"

"A bill of lading."

"That was it. And the guns are hidden underneath."

"He said so?"

I nodded. "They were going to Calais first and then going to be transferred to a steamer heading for Montenegro."

His eyes were glittering as though he'd had three glasses of whiskey. "Greenland Dock? You're absolutely certain?"

"That's what they said. Tierney was going to be there himself."

"We heard rumors about a shipment of guns, but we thought it was next week—and we heard it was leaving out of St. Katharine's," Matthew said, more to himself than to me. Then he turned and shouted, "McFarr!"

I heard quick footsteps, and a lanky plainclothesman came around the corner. "No one upstairs."

"The shipment left from Greenland Dock early this morning," Matthew said tersely. "Crates of guns underneath gin barrels. Take three men with you. Keep your eye out for Tierney; he'll be there somewhere. And hurry. I'll be right behind you."

"Yes, sir." Without a word, McFarr went back up the passageway. A minute later, he and three uniformed policemen were running out the back door.

"Inspector!" Another young man in uniform came hurrying along the passage. "We've found a man in the cellar. 'E's been shot."

There was something familiar about the man—but I didn't recall him at first. Then I realized it was Hodges, the young constable who'd brought us news of Kendrick's being found by the docks. But today Hodges looked as if he filled out his uniform a bit more.

Matthew nodded. "We'll take him to the morgue later." He gave me a quick, hard embrace, which I returned just as fiercely. Then he strode up the ramp and out the back door. Mr. Bertault and I followed at a much slower pace.

As we left the Octavian, the dawn was dropping its pale, pearly light over the houses. The city noises were still distinguishable as separate sounds; in another hour they would become a steady, grinding hum. Just outside the back yard, two hansom cabs stood in Hawley Mews. One of the drivers, a middle-aged man with a black beard going to silver and a hat that had seen too many London storms, sat on his box, his eyes closed and the reins loose between his fingers. The other, a thin young man with pinkish cheeks, was standing by his horse's head, adjusting a feed bag.

Mr. Bertault and I walked past them, heading west toward Mr. Tindale's house. And as we turned off Hawley Mews onto Wickley Street, a shaft of sunlight came from behind us and cast our two long shadows toward a new day.

Epilogue

"Did you see this?" Matthew turned the paper toward us. "The sewer system is finally going to be finished. Honestly, the more I read about it, the more I think that Bazalgette is a genius for his foresight."

The three of us were together at the breakfast table looking over the papers and talking, as had become our wont in the months since the night of the raids.

"Do you mean his insistence on the doubled diameter of the pipes?" Jack asked. "I think you're right. Although I read an article yesterday that claimed that his predictions about London's population were only to justify the added expense. Did you see that?"

"Yes, but I think that was politically motivated," Matthew said. "Dr. Everett knows some of the scientists who helped with the study, and he says that by nineteen hundred, London might very well have another three hundred thousand people . . ."

I went back to my reading, hiding my smile. When Jack had first come to us to recuperate, Matthew had been civil but uncharacteristically reserved for several weeks; it pleased me to no end to see how well they got on now.

Finally, when the tea and toast were gone, Matthew pushed back his chair and laid his napkin by his plate. "What are you planning for the day?"

"We're going to see my uncle this morning," Jack replied. It was the anniversary of his mother's death, and Mr. Bertault had asked us to come to the shop.

Matthew's expression changed. "Dash it, I'm sorry. Of course. I'd forgotten. When are you going?"

Jack and I both glanced up at the clock. "Shortly, I expect," Jack replied. "He said he had some appointments this afternoon."

"I'll leave with you, then."

The three of us departed together, opening the front door to find a fine morning, with a brilliant blue sky and a breeze that was warm for September. Contentedly, I walked between the two of them to Regent Street, where Matthew climbed into a cab, and Jack and I continued on toward the piano shop. A sideways glance told me that he was in a reflective state of mind, so I tucked my hand into his elbow, and we walked in companionable silence.

It had taken all of us some months to recover from that night in June. At first, when the other detective inspectors learned what had happened, there had been a good deal of ill feeling toward Matthew over Barrow's death. But as the truth about the man's corruption emerged and the results of that night's work became clear, Matthew's standing at the Yard had recovered. The raid had captured seventeen of the ship captains, all of whom were compelled to confess because of the stolen goods, counterfeiting equipment, and pages of records in their possession; and the two thousand guns only made it as far as Blackwall Reach before the River Police found the ship riding low in the water. The only unfortunate outcome was that Tierney had managed to evade their grasp. This didn't rest easily with Matthew. He knew a man like Tierney wouldn't slip gently into ordinary life; he'd resurface eventually.

Jack had suffered the worst of us, for Dr. Everett's premonition had been correct: he had become ill with an infection that brought with it a high fever and delirium. There were four days when the doctor's face was very grave, and I barely left Jack's side. But at last his fever came down, and he opened his eyes and knew me. He was installed in our spare room downstairs, and for nearly a month afterward, Dr. Everett continued to come every evening, and Peggy fixed all of her best custards and jellies to tempt Jack's appetite. Eventually, he was declared out of danger.

Still, his physical injuries healed more rapidly than his spirits. He sometimes wore his old shuttered look, and I gradually learned the signs for when it was a kindness to leave him alone with his thoughts. It helped him greatly to know that many of the younger boys from the Fleet had been gathered up and sent out of London to several new orphanages run by Anglican nuns, rather than left to an uncertain fate. Rob and Gus, however, had stayed; Mr. Bertault had found them light work with some friends of his, and they attended school and slept in the small second bedroom above the shop.

I had sprained my wrist badly in my struggle with Barrow, and the injury had been compounded by an infection where my skin had been abraded by the rope, for which Dr. Everett prescribed a series of poultices and a sling. It had taken several weeks to heal, and during that time, I had received an unexpected letter. The envelope had borne a French stamp with the Ceres head and contained a single sheet of paper.

Chère Nell,

You have been a true friend to me, and it pained me to leave without saying goodbye. I am better each day and safe. Please believe that I appreciate everything you've done for us. I hope someday to return, to see you performing on a stage yourself. Until then, try not to worry. I see signs of greatness in you, not illness, and a kind and loving heart.

Votre M (et S)

The writing was faint and shaky, which only made me treasure the note all the more. It told me that Marceline knew how much I'd be worrying and had written a letter as quickly as her injuries would allow. Gratefully, I'd refolded it and slipped it into my armoire drawer, and as my eye caught my own bandaged arm, I'd smiled to think of how we were alike in this. We'd both been injured, but we would also both recover and return to our work.

When eventually Dr. Everett said I was healed enough that I might try the piano again, it was a profound pleasure to me, although my hands were stiff, and my wrist ached after only a few minutes. After another fortnight, I even took out my sheet music for the Mozart and the Chopin.

And yet, as I returned to my daily practice, I came to realize my feelings about playing had altered. Several times Jack had broached the idea of my applying to one of the smaller conservatories in

London or of looking for another teacher. But I found myself putting him off, even becoming cross when he pressed me. At first, I couldn't put into words the reason for my opposition, but recently I'd begun to realize that the object of my ambition had changed, and I could trace it to the moment in Drummond's office, when I thought that either Matthew or I might die. In my mind, it had become a test that I'd passed. For if that terrifying moment hadn't precipitated me into my mother's disease—well, perhaps I could trust my mind not to betray me. I longed to become better acquainted with this less fearful, more susceptible version of myself. But it was a nascent, tender thing, like one of Mr. Bertault's fragile rose cuttings, and I wanted to protect it, to allow it to develop sturdiness and resilience in its own time. Perhaps if we visited the garden this morning, that might be the right place to explain this to Jack.

As we turned onto Samson Lane, he finally spoke, his tone somewhat hesitant. "Nell, I've got something to tell you."

"What is it?"

"My uncle may ask you to play for him today."

"You mean to see if I'm ready for an audition?" I grimaced. "You're steering me, the pair of you, as if I'm a wheelbarrow."

"Please, Nell." Jack looked at me entreatingly as we neared the door. "He feels sorry that I kept you from it. As do I."

We'd gone around about this matter several times. I insisted that it hadn't been his fault Matthew had chosen that night for a raid, but Jack believed that if it weren't for him, I'd be in the Academy by now.

"He also told me it would do him more good than a bottle of fine wine to hear you play," Jack added as he put his hand to the door.

I felt something in me soften. "Well, that's different. Of course I will. I don't think I could refuse your uncle anything. Certainly not today."

His smile was relieved as he turned the handle. The bell tinkled, and Mr. Bertault emerged from the back, with outstretched arms.

"*Bonjour.* I'm so glad to see you both. And look at you, Jacques, with barely even a limp." We sat together at the table in his little office drinking coffee, and Mr. Bertault discussed his plan to visit friends in Edinburgh, once Jack was able to work a full week.

When we'd finished, Mr. Bertault turned to me. "Well, my dear, I've a favor to ask. I just finished repairing a piano that I'd like you to try."

I smiled and rose. "I'd be happy to."

"Here it is," he said, leading me to an instrument in the front room. "I think it will suit you." It was a Stingl, made of wood the color of ripe chestnuts. I brushed my fingers over the frame and peeked inside at a pale soundboard with metal pins and wire that looked beautifully straight and with hammers at the ready.

I sat down and looked up at Jack and his uncle. They looked back at me expectantly, like children waiting for sweets, and I swallowed down a laugh. "What would you like me to play, Mr. Bertault?"

"Whatever *you* would like to play."

I didn't want anything sad or tender. Today it needed to be lighter of heart.

The Mozart Sonata I had prepared for my audition would do. After the first twenty measures, I glanced up at Mr. Bertault. His expression was full of excitement, but when I finished, he merely said, "And now the Chopin."

The command might have sounded rude to anyone else, but I

understood. Just as I wanted to be certain in myself, he wanted to be sure of what he was hearing.

Before I began, I paused to allow the feeling of gratitude to work upon me—gratitude for the kindness of these two men; gratitude also for my brother, for Dr. Everett, for Marceline, for Peggy. Then I let my fingertips touch the keys, and somewhere in the first dozen measures the music took me over, and I let it, finding in the range and depth of the piece a profound reassurance that every moment of the past months—indeed, every minute of delight and sorrow and fear and longing that I would ever have—had been felt and written into melody by someone else. I'd never be alone in it. By the final notes, I had played myself out. And when I took my hands away, they were tingling.

When I looked at Mr. Bertault, his cheeks were wet.

"I'm sorry," I whispered, filled with remorse. "I didn't mean to make you cry."

"I'm not crying," he said.

"Yes, Uncle," Jack said softly. "You are."

Mr. Bertault put his hand up to his cheek and looked at his palm wonderingly. *"Oui, je pleure."*

"Goodness, my dear," came a voice from behind me.

I turned. In the arch that led to the back room stood a tall man beside a woman of medium height, with light curly hair pinned up under a modish hat.

"You play beautifully," she said.

"Thank you," I replied. She looked vaguely familiar, but I couldn't place her.

And then she smiled, and I recognized her from images I'd seen in the newspapers. Clara Schumann. Composer, pianist, performer. Wife of Robert Schumann.

I couldn't say a word. Dumbly, I let her take my right hand in both of hers.

"François told me you played well, but of course I had to hear for myself. I hope you don't mind the subterfuge."

Mr. Bertault spread his hands in a gesture that suggested both innocence and an apology.

I turned back to her. "It was probably for the best I didn't know you were here. I haven't played for an audience in months."

"I understand," she said. "Plenty of us take time away."

"You're very kind, saying 'us.' I'm hardly in your category."

"No," she conceded frankly. "Not yet. But with training, you could be."

I had to swallow hard before I could answer. "Thank you," I said again. "It's generous of you to say so."

She let go of my hand then, beckoned to the man who had been standing a few feet behind her, and settled one hand on his arm. "This is Mr. Edwin Spencer, from the Royal Academy. I believe you were supposed to audition several months ago."

"Yes." I flushed. "I'm so sorry, Mr. Spencer, for missing it."

A smile appeared under his heavy mustache, and his brown eyes twinkled. "Well, Miss Hallam, I understand there were circumstances."

"Yes." A rueful laugh escaped me. "There were."

"I would like to offer you a place nonetheless."

"A place?" I repeated.

"A place in our incoming class," he clarified. "Unless you've accepted elsewhere, of course."

I turned to Jack and Mr. Bertault. Jack was smiling broadly, and Mr. Bertault's delight was writ large on his face. They wanted this so desperately for me.

Mr. Spencer's face was expectant as well, and the room fell silent, with everyone waiting for me to thank him and accept.

How on earth was I going to explain? How could I say that for now, I wanted to be alone with my piano, to hear what it had to say to me, and to play without anyone judging or correcting me?

Haltingly, I began. "Mr. Spencer, you're very kind, and . . . and please believe that I understand just what you're offering—not only a place, but you're overlooking that I didn't audition properly, which . . . well, it's very understanding of you." I bit my lip. "But I'm not certain I'm ready yet."

Mr. Spencer frowned and glanced at Mr. Bertault before he replied. "Are you concerned about your wrist injury?"

"It was a—a difficult summer, and it changed things for me. I—I suppose I'm still getting used to myself at the piano again." I hesitated. "I'm sorry. I think I may just need some time."

He looked rather puzzled but nodded. "Very well. You can take it. We've no plans to close down."

My smile was genuine and full of relief. "No, I'm sure not."

Mrs. Schumann inclined her head, her smile still warm and gentle. "It was a pleasure to hear you. I do hope we see you soon."

"I hope so, too," I said gratefully.

And after a few additional pleasantries, Mr. Bertault walked them to the door. He had barely closed it behind them before I burst out, "I'm so sorry, you went to such trouble—"

"*Pas du tout.*" He shook his head as he came toward me and settled a hand on my shoulder. "Not at all. You are right to wait, if you feel it best. But you have a place. Now you can choose. That is all I wanted."

And then he melted away, leaving Jack to sit down next to me on the bench with a sigh. He looked pale, and I realized the walk here had tired him. For my sake, he'd pushed himself harder than he should have. But I knew he wouldn't want me to point it out, so instead I said, "You hoodwinked me."

He nodded unapologetically. "I did."

"Do you have any other tricks up your sleeve?" I asked.

"No." He smiled and turned his two palms up. "See?"

The very openness of the gesture made something in my heart ache, mostly in joy, but there was pain there, too.

I was still no good at speaking at such times, when the currents of feeling ran so deep and fast; it was as if three pieces of music were playing at once. I couldn't sort them out, much less convey them.

So I didn't try. Instead, I put my hands up and drew him close for a kiss.

Acknowledgments

Nell's piano at the Octavian, with most of its eighty-eight keys desperately in need of tuning, is perhaps an apt metaphor for what was the first draft of this book. It began life as *The Phrenologist's Daughter* and was worked on for years before reaching a stage of being suitable for use. Also, I am sure there are at least eighty-eight people who have helped bring it into being, whose books I've read for research or who have taken a personal interest and encouraged me along the way.

My gratitude to all my friends and family members who have not only supported me through the years but read sections (sometimes two or three times) of this manuscript at various stages, especially Jeanne Arnold, Kate Fink Cheeseman, Kristin Griffin, Dottie Lootens, Jennifer Lootens, Anne Morgan, Stefanie Pintoff, and Anita Weiss. A special thanks to Masie Cochran, who worked with me on a very early draft; also to friends who have over the years talked me out of giving up on writing, including Jules Catania, Wendy Claus, Mame Cudd, Jody Hallam, Christie Maroulis, and Nancy Odden. I am grateful to all those who supported me so generously when *A Lady in the Smoke* was published, by inviting me as a guest to their blog, hosting me at their book clubs, and helping me discover the lovely collaborative world of fellow writers and readers of historical fiction, especially Ann Marie Ackermann, Jessica Bohl, Donna Cleinman, Denise Kantner, Ruth Lebed, Susan Elia MacNeal, and Marshal Zeringue.

Thanks to Heather Chaney and Roger Ruggeri, for advice on music; to Dr. Amelia Gallitano-Mendel, for talking me through mental illness and the specifics of bipolar disorder; to Kathryn Adamson, Librarian at the Royal Academy of Music, and to the Royal Academy itself, whose exhibit on their nineteenth-century students and Victorian music helped me to realize my story; to Jon Freeman, the building manager at Wilton's Music Hall in Graces Alley, who allowed me to prowl around and patiently answered all my questions about this music hall, established in the 1840s and still in existence; to Nikasha Patel, for the Latin translations; and to the authors whose books I read in search of accurate histories and information. (For a partial list, see the Further Reading section. All factual errors in my novel are my own.)

Thanks to my extraordinary editor Priyanka Krishnan, who believed in both this book and *A Lady in the Smoke;* to my wonderful agent, Josh Getzler, and the entire crew at HSG; to the entire William Morrow editing, marketing, and publicity team, including Jen Hart, Elle Keck, Amelia Wood, Caro Perny, Dale Rohrbaugh, and Diahann Sturge; to my copy editor, Brenda Woodward; and a special thanks to Elsie Lyons for a lovely cover.

Finally, as always, my deepest gratitude to George, Julia, and Kyle; and Rosy Bea, my faithful furry friend.

Insights,
Interviews
& More . . .

About the author

About the book

Read on

Meet Karen Odden

Tina Celle

KAREN ODDEN received her Ph.D. in
English literature from New York
University and has taught at the University
of Wisconsin–Milwaukee and the
University of Michigan–Ann Arbor. She
formerly served as an assistant editor for
the academic journal *Victorian Literature
and Culture.* Her debut novel, *A Lady in
the Smoke,* was a *USA Today* bestseller.

Behind
A Dangerous Duet

I can trace the beginnings of this novel, about a young woman pianist in Victorian London, to two experiences I had in 2012—one that struck me painfully and close to home, and one that I encountered fortuitously thousands of miles away on the other side of the Atlantic. Together, they led me toward certain themes and to my heroine, Nell Hallam.

The first was that my father, a pianist, died suddenly, in a car accident, in May. We had never been close, but after his death, I came to understand him better and to see that for him, music was, at times, a language more instinctive and satisfying than speech. His piano, a baby grand, stood in our 1970s living room, its three wheeled feet resting on a goldenrod shag carpet. As a child, I took lessons from him, though I really didn't have the ear or the talent. But my son has my father's gift, and over the years, the very tilt of his head when he plays, so like my father's, has raised questions for me about just what we inherit from our ancestors.

This question, about what is "bred in the bone" (that is, genetic) was widely debated by medical men and laymen alike in the 1800s. A group of pseudoscientific endeavors in vogue at midcentury—including phrenology, which claimed that the bumps on the skull indicated proclivities for everything from music to licentiousness—poked at questions about inherited characteristics and the ▶

role of the brain in determining character. Serious scientists and medical men were also tackling these enigmas. For example, in the 1850s, two Frenchmen, Jean-Pierre Falret and Jules Baillarger, each wrote about what we would now call bipolar disorder; and during the 1800s, a range of hospitals came into being, including specialty hospitals, to develop treatments for those with mental illnesses, incurable diseases, and other ailments.

Fueled by my research into pianos and Victorian medicine, ideas for the novel began to coalesce: a mother who is a brilliant pianist but whose brain is at odds with her well-being; music as a language and a passion; Nell's fear that she might be prone to mental illness herself. But I still needed to learn more about Nell's character and what she wanted, and to find a setting that was perfect for her story line.

The second thing that happened in 2012 was that my husband went to London for work, and I could tag along. (It's always fun to go on an expense account. London is so pricey!) While he was in meetings, I visited the Royal Academy of Music on Marylebone Road. The Academy, which is the oldest conservatory in London, opened in 1822, and from the beginning it enrolled young women. There, with the best luck ever, I found a special exhibit about students in the nineteenth century—and Fanny Dickens's name, written "Dickens, Frances Elizabeth," next to the name of her sponsor, Thomas Tomkison, a piano maker from Soho. I just stood there, staring at the faded ink on a foxed page.

Charles Dickens's older sister, Fanny (born Frances, in 1810), attended the Academy to study piano with Ignaz Moscheles, who had studied with Beethoven himself. Her tuition was costly— thirty-eight guineas a year—which the Dickens family could ill afford, as their father was a spendthrift. A rising star in 1824, Fanny's early musical success was cut short in 1829 because her tuition had gone unpaid, and she had to leave, though she was later awarded an honorary membership. All this got me thinking: What would Fanny have done if her parents had refused to pay her tuition initially? Given that she was a talented musician, what could she have done to earn her way?

I knew that in the 1860s, London's music halls were centers for the kind of countercultural humor that celebrates bawdiness and sexuality and makes a joke of religion and politics. (Think *Saturday Night Live* skits, not a beautifully staged Broadway show.) But I wondered if that sort of place hired pianists. So my next stop was Wilton's Music Hall, one of the few Victorian music halls still standing (https://www.wiltons.org.uk). I remember finding it, in Graces Alley in Whitechapel, and walking through the narrow pair of doors into the bar. I prowled all over the place, upstairs and down, and asked questions of the building manager. When I peered through a small window to see the U-shaped hall and the stage, Wilton's morphed into the (fictional) Octavian in Soho. I could imagine Nell taking her place in the piano alcove beside the stage, and I sensed that the piano itself was becoming an important symbol for my book. My father once explained that the piano is both a percussion instrument and a string instrument, in that the key hits the hammer, which strikes the strings. And because I am attracted to things that are both/and, the piano became an emblem of the many dualities and literal and figurative duets throughout. At the music hall, acts are both art and artifice; the audience members are both spectators and participants; Nell is both pretending to be a man and a woman in pursuit of her goals.

I had some elements for Nell's character and plot, but what about a mystery? And how could they intertwine?

Having read my Dickens, I knew about the infamous "lads-men," the nineteenth-century version of criminal bosses, who trained boys to steal and then fenced or pawned the goods they brought back. (Remember Fagin and Oliver Twist?) I started combing through my Victorian history books for more stories of thieving by children: of thief trainers such as Thomas Duggin, who worked in the St. Giles slum, and Charles King, who ran a gang of pickpocket boys; and of "flash houses," where gangs of young thieves lived and were supervised by a "captain." The crimes I describe in this book are merely updated versions of those. As a counterpoint to those stories, I also read Haia Shpayer-Makov's excellent book *The Ascent of the Detective*, about the rise of Scotland Yard. The accounts I found there became the basis for Nell's brother, Matthew.

Like my first book, *A Lady in the Smoke, A Dangerous Duet* is set in the 1870s, partly because it was a time of extraordinary political, social, and economic flux. The Second Reform Bill of ▸

Behind *A Dangerous Duet* (continued)

1867 had extended the vote to roughly 40 percent of men, and suffragists were beginning to petition Parliament. The 1870-71 Franco-Prussian War had tipped the balance of power in Europe toward Germany. In 1874, Disraeli and the Conservatives were voted in after years of Gladstone and the Liberals. Ideas about class and gender were evolving unevenly, partly as a result of significant laws passed in the late 1860s and 1870s—laws that concerned education, divorce, the rights of married women to hold property, the rights of infants and children to protection, and the hours of factory work. I feel that a complex historical context always adds depth to a story.

The process of writing a book isn't unidirectional—and by that, I mean that the book writes back to me as well. It was only during final revisions that my manuscript showed me that I was really trying to write a book about truth and value.

In the 1990s, I worked at Christie's auction house in New York. There, I learned how the value of objects could fluctuate wildly depending on various factors. For example, a footrest could be sold for many times its ordinary value if Barbra Streisand had owned it. A book with its original endpapers brought more than one without. And if a Picasso sold for a high price at Sotheby's, a Picasso at Christie's might receive a price boost. This held true in Victorian England as well. For example, let's consider a pair of silver candlesticks. Did their value reside in their craftsmanship, confirmed by the maker's mark on the bottom? Or in their provenance? Or in the weight of the raw silver? Or in the number of sixpence that could be made from the silver? The more philosophical question is: what anchors or guarantees or determines an object's value?

And by extension, what anchors or determines a person's character? For Nell, the music hall brings into sharp relief how character doesn't reside in the clothes we wear, or our names, or even the stories we tell others about ourselves, on any stage, literal or figurative. Where does our character reside? In our brains? Our hearts? Our patterns of interacting with others? Is our character determined by the consistency with which we act, day in and day out? I'm not sure there are incontrovertible or fixed answers to these questions, but I like the conversations that happen when we ask them. ∾

Further Reading

ON MUSIC HALLS

....

The Victorian Music Hall: Culture, Class and Conflict by Dagmar Kift
Murder, Mayhem and Music Hall: The Dark Side of Victorian London
    by Barry Anthony

ON VICTORIAN HOSPITALS AND MEDICINE

....

The Victorian Hospital by Lavinia Mitton
The Medical Profession in Mid-Victorian London by M. Jeanne Peterson

ON PIANOS AND MUSIC

....

*The Piano Shop on the West Bank: Discovering a Forgotten Passion in
    a Paris Atelier* by Thad Carhart
Piano Man, BBC podcast with Ulrich Gerhartz
"The Virtuoso" by James B. Stewart in *The New Yorker* (January 1, 2018)

ON SCOTLAND YARD

....

*The Ascent of the Detective: Police Sleuths in Victorian and Edwardian
    England* by Haia Shpayer-Makov

ON VICTORIAN CRIME AND CONTEMPORARY EVENTS

....

The Victorian Underworld by Donald Thomas
Gangs of London by Brian McDonald
The Good Old Days: Crime, Murder and Mayhem in Victorian London
    by Gilda O'Neill
London Labour and the London Poor by Henry Mayhew
The Blackest Streets: The Life and Death of a Victorian Slum by Sarah
    Wise

For further historical context, please visit Karen Odden's website,
www.karenodden.com, where she has blog entries on a variety
of subjects, including Victorian music halls, Scotland Yard and
the police, Victorian crime, and Victorian pianos and female
pianists. ❧

Reading Group Guide

1. Mental illness was poorly understood in the 1870s in England, though some medical men and scientists were working in the emerging field. What do you make of the different explanations that Dr. Everett and Peggy give for Nell's mother's illness? What would twenty-first-century knowledge of psychology suggest?

2. Music halls were places where the lower classes came to be entertained and celebrate their own brand of bawdy, raucous humor. This flew in the face of the rigid and righteous middle-class morality epitomized by the Society for the Suppression of Vice (founded in 1787), which deplored profanity, gaming, and brothels, among other things. Do you see any similarity between the music halls and any venues or entertainment genres today?

3. Do you believe that character is something that can change over time? Do you find Jack's account of his father's change believable? When do you first feel you understand Stephen's true character?

4. Although many characters have experienced the pain of loss, numerous acts of kindness reverberate throughout the story. Do you see good and evil behaviors having a ripple effect?

5. Were you surprised by the revelation about Dr. Everett and Charles Tindale? In England, homosexual acts were made a felony by the Buggery Act in 1533 under Henry VIII. The punishment was death by hanging until 1861 in England and Wales. Did you find the representation of a same-sex relationship realistic for the period? Why or why not?

6. Dr. Everett says that the piano is a "dangerous partner" for Nell. To what extent do you think Nell's love of her piano may derive from her longing for danger? Or for her mother? Or another kind of longing altogether? In what ways is her dilemma about playing the piano related to the question of how she should live her life?

7. Clearly the boys in the Fleet are being exploited, but given Jack's comments about where many of them came from, do you find his comment that they might be better off in the Fleet compelling? Do you see places where this sort of ambiguity exists in our society today?

8. Amalie and Nell are to some extent similar: each is talented; each comes to the Octavian with dreams. As you learned more about Amalie, were you surprised by her past and the way she had managed her life? Were there any other characters that surprised you?

9. Nell and Matthew's relationship mirrors Marceline and Sebastian's in some ways. Nell understands Marceline's desire to protect her brother, and Nell's desire to reunite Marceline with Sebastian drives the first half of the book. But how is Sebastian alike or different from Matthew? Do you think Sebastian behaves with his sister's best interests at heart?

10. In the 1870s, Scotland Yard was not the respected division it is today, and the public didn't necessarily trust plainclothes detectives—a distrust that wasn't unfounded. In fact, in 1877, two years after this novel is set, the Yard came under fire for a huge corruption scandal, and four senior detectives were put on trial, with three sentenced to prison. In investigating men in his own division, Matthew is like some other courageous police figures in pop culture. What do you think of this archetype? Do you feel it resonates for particular time periods? ∽

An Excerpt from
A Lady in the Smoke

LIVERPOOL STREET STATION, LONDON,
MAY 1874

My mother's nerves were brittle as a
porcelain teacup worn thin around the
edge, which is why she took an extra dose
of laudanum before we boarded the train
home that day. I doubt anyone around
us on the crowded platform could have
guessed that she had a tincture of opium
and alcohol running through her veins
at half past eleven o'clock in the morning.
Looking at her, they'd see only a well-
dressed gentlewoman, her face tranquil,
and her fair hair beautifully arranged
under an expensive hat.

But I knew. In the ten years since
my father had died, I'd learned how to
recognize when she'd taken an extra sip
from the brown bottle she kept in her
reticule: by her dreamy silence, by the
faint smile that came and went without
cause, and a certain softness to her chin,
like a blur in an unfinished portrait.

I glanced sideways. Yes, she was very
different now from what she'd been a
mere ten hours ago, when we were alone
in our rooms—her voice hard, her face
contorted with fury—

A shriek cut through the dull roar
inside the station, and our train rounded
the corner, the racket of the wheels driving
the pigeons off the rafters and into a
whirl of feathers. The engine came to a
halt, belching steam and filling the air

with the smells of coal dust and burned oil. "Up train to York," bellowed the stationmaster, "running express to Hertford and stopping at all points north!"

Railway servants in red uniforms rushed to the first-class carriages with sets of wooden steps, and passengers started to disembark. In a few minutes, we'd be on our way out of this godforsaken city.

"Lady Fraser! Lady Elizabeth! Oh, my dears!" shrilled a woman's voice. I kept my face averted. I didn't want to see anyone I knew. *Please, please just let us get on this train and be gone.*

"Lady Elizabeth! I say, Lady Elizabeth!"

I sighed and turned to see a plump woman trying to shift her way through the crowd. What was her name? Miss Rush. She was one of my distant relations who had been at Lady Lorry's ball last night. Her round face was splotched pink with the effort she was making to reach us, and I felt a pang of pity. She must exist on the furthest fringe of society, for apparently no one at the ball had felt there was any social currency to be gained by telling her the rumors about us. Otherwise, Miss Rush would have been watching us slyly and leaving us quite alone.

"Are you taking this train home, then?" she asked breathlessly as she drew near.

I forced a smile. "Yes, we are. And you?"

"Oh, yes." Miss Rush gave a quick, curious glance at my mother, who was staring into midair. Then she gazed wistfully at the train. "But of course *you* are riding in a first-class carriage! Alas, when one is retrenching, every farthing matters, as you know—but, then"— a little, tentative laugh, and a wave toward the second-class carriages, close behind the smoking engines—"you *wouldn't* know, my dear— but no matter! I'd have endured any sort of travel for such a ball! I didn't see *you* dancing very often; but when you're married, I'm sure you'll have a ball *just* as beautiful."

I winced and looked away. The first passengers were being helped aboard, and people around us were beginning to push forward. I took my mother's arm and said apologetically, "I'm afraid my mother is very fatigued. We should go to our—"

"And your cousin looked *just* as a bride should with her new husband!" She leaned forward as if she were about to confide a ▶

secret. "I've heard that Americans are brash and uncouth, but he wasn't dreadful at all! In fact, he was—"

I let the crowd draw us apart, raised my hands helplessly, and called over my shoulder, "I'm sorry we must go. I wish you a pleasant trip home."

"Oh! Of course! Goodbye, dear." She smiled brightly, like a child pretending not to be hurt, and gave a little wave as we turned away.

Something inside me shriveled at my selfishness, for not taking her hint and inviting her to share our compartment. But if I had to listen to her prattle on about that wretched ball for hours, I'd throw myself off the train like one of those mad people I'd read about in the papers.

"Miss?" One of the railway servants for the first-class carriages had his gloved hand out, waiting to help me aboard.

Mama was already inside, and as I stepped up, I could feel the vibration of the train under my feet. I followed Mama down a corridor so narrow that it was a good thing birdcage crinoline skirts were no longer in fashion. Our compartment was the middle one of three and quite spacious, but the windows were small, and the green velvet cushions lumpy and frayed. On the backward-facing wall was a painted advertisement for Hudson's Dry Soap that featured a busy harbor at sunset. Mama took the forward-facing seat near the door; I sat down between her and the window and closed my eyes. Even at rest, the train trembled with a fierce energy. Something near my ear rattled, and I opened my eyes to see one of the windowpanes jiggling against the frame. I put up my gloved hand to still it.

Through the dirt on the glass, I saw a figure on the platform that looked familiar, and my heart jumped.

Could that be Anne?

But my friend was supposed to be with her brother Francis at Venwell, their family estate in Scotland, for another fortnight.

I found the least grimy part of the window and peered out. The woman had Anne's dark hair, coiled in the same style Anne always wore and the same slim shoulders wrapped in a blue coat. As she turned her head to look at the train, my hand was already up to wave—

But it wasn't Anne. Of course not.

The disappointment pushed like a weight at my chest. I leaned back against the velvet, watching the young woman disappear into the crowd of people, all shoving and bumping against one another, like sheep in a shearing corral.

If I'd had Anne with me last night, I could have borne it. When that first pair of ladies darted looks at me and raised their fans to hide their mouths, Anne would have raised her own fan and whispered things that would've helped me swallow down my growing discomfort. But the entire Reynolds family was avoiding the Season because of an awful article about Anne's brother that had appeared in the *Courier* a few months ago. So I'd stood alone, half hidden by a marble pillar, and tried to keep the color from mounting to my cheeks while I wondered what on earth people could be saying. I was an heiress with a respectable dowry of ten thousand pounds per annum. I was twenty years old, not unattractive (though I lacked the fair beauty of my mother), with a name and title that stood well up on the list of landed gentry, and no scandal attached to me. As such, I was considered a fine catch in the marriage market—as Anne and I joked dryly, much like tenderloin at the butcher. And it was only my third Season, so it's not as though my goods were rotting.

I had opened my dance card and noticed that it was oddly empty. And then, as I stood with my gloved hand pressed against the pillar, I heard Lady Nestor say that she had it on good authority that my family's fortunes were slipping, and my ten thousand pounds per annum was soon to be a thing of the past.

I felt a sick churning in my stomach, and the ballroom suddenly seemed unbearably hot. I slid farther behind the pillar, resisting the urge to find my mother then and there, to ask whether what Lady Nestor said was true. I forced myself to compose my face, remain where I was, and wait the two agonizing hours until we were finally back in our rooms. And then there were two more agonizing hours listening to her rage at me that, yes, it was true—and wasn't I sorry because now I would pay for my stupidity—I, who was selfish— selfish—*selfish*—always—

Our carriage rattled as heavy cargo doors slammed closed; the stationmaster blew his whistle again and made the last call for people to board. I turned to look at my mother. She gazed ▶

vaguely at the soap advertisement, her gloved hands resting on her reticule, the laudanum smile hovering around her lips. I didn't know if I preferred her screaming at me or completely absent like this.

Over the years, I'd learned that when there was a raw edge to her rage, it was often because she had missed her laudanum, or because she'd drunk more than a glass or two of champagne. But her accusations from last night still hurt me, and frightened me, too. I wasn't such a fool as to believe that my personal charms were enough to preserve my place in the marriage market. Without a dowry, I would no longer be one of the choicer cuts of beef. I wondered bitterly what I'd be now. The skirt steak, perhaps, in need of a hearty sauce to conceal its indifferent quality.

I swallowed the lump in my throat and looked back out the window, wishing desperately that the train would pull out of the station. What on earth was taking so long?

The handle to our compartment turned with a sharp click, and the door swung in. A heavyset, well-dressed gentleman entered our carriage and stowed his briefcase on the rack overhead.

How strange! We'd reserved a private compartment—at least, I thought we had. But perhaps this was part of our change of fortune, a small way that my mother chose to retrench, as Miss Rush put it. My mother merely smiled distractedly at him, and I didn't want the fuss of calling a porter, or whomever one called in such cases. Without taking a bit of notice of us, he sat down opposite, facing the rear of the train, placed his hat on the seat beside him, folded his hands across his chest, and closed his eyes.

He would've caught Anne's painterly eye. His bald head was egg-shaped, narrow at the top, and fuller at the bottom; he had eyebrows as bristly as Mr. Jaggers's in *Great Expectations,* and his thin lips turned down sourly. He remained utterly still, except for his jowls, which shuddered as the train began to move.

Rain knifed against the windows as we pulled out of the station. Finally, after several weeks away, we were going home. I'd never liked London, with its rotten yellow air; its hordes of people and cabs and carriages that fought for space on the streets; the working men who walked with their shoulders hunched, as if merely getting through the day was a burden on their backs. And the gossip that filled the air like mosquitoes over a swampland.

I'd never come here again if I could help it.

As the train sped up, the silver telegraph lines above dipped and curved faster than my eyes could follow, and the wooden poles blurred together. The rhythm of the wheels lulled me into a sort of stupor, and eventually I slept.

Then came a high-pitched screech of metal wheels on the iron track, and I was flung across the compartment before I could put up my hands. ᴄᴡ